THE PEOPLE VS. ALEX CROSS

THE PEOPLE VS.
ALEX CROSS

JAMES
PATTERSON

LITTLE, BROWN AND COMPANY

NEW YORK   BOSTON   LONDON

Little, Brown and Company
Hachette Book Group
1290 Avenue of the Americas, New York, NY 10104
littlebrown.com

First Edition: November 2017

Little, Brown and Company is a division of Hachette Book Group, Inc. The Little, Brown name and logo are trademarks of Hachette Book Group, Inc.

ALEX CROSS is a trademark of JBP Business, LLC.

The publisher is not responsible for websites (or their content) that are not owned by the publisher.

The Hachette Speakers Bureau provides a wide range of authors for speaking events. To find out more, go to hachettespeakersbureau.com or call (866) 376-6591.

ISBN 978-0-316-27390-9 (hc) / 978-0-316-50881-0 (large print) / 978-0-316-41674-0 (Barnes & Noble edition)
LCCN 2017932695

10 9 8 7 6 5 4 3 2 1

LSC-C

Printed in the United States of America

*For Carole—my baby sister, absolutely one of my
three favorites, definitely the smartest Patterson*

Prologue

A HOT SUMMER'S EVE

ONE

FROM INSIDE A RAMBLING WHITE Colonial home on a shaded street that smelled of blooming wildflowers, a woman called in a pleasant Southern accent: "TW-Two? Where are you? Mama needs you to go to the store now."

There was a pause before she called again. "TW-Two? Deuce?"

Timmy Walker Jr., TW-Two, also known as Deuce, was twelve and standing just inside the woods that adjoined his backyard.

Go to the store? Deuce thought. He had better things to do than ride his bike all the way there and back for his mom. As a matter of fact, he had much better things to do.

The back porch door opened with a creak.

"Deuce," his mother called. "C'mon, now. I'll take you out for an ice cream sundae later?"

That was tempting, but Deuce stuck to his plan and eased off on a familiar path that led downhill to an old logging road and a creek that meandered through the woods. It was late in the day. The light was slanted, coppery, and the air was still sticky and hot.

Holding a beat-up old pair of binoculars his granddad had given him, Deuce thought: *Hot and sticky. That's good. Seems there's way more activity when it's all hot and sticky this time of day, getting on into night.*

Deuce looked down at his camouflage T-shirt and shorts and thought, *I'm dressed perfect. Should be able to get real close, and I've got the right gear.*

Mosquitoes whined. He slapped at one that bit his ear, hearing the building thrum of cicadas in the trees and smelling smoke from a distant fire. He dug in his pocket and got out a cigarette he'd taken from his mom's secret pack.

He lit it, took a drag, and blew smoke at the mosquitoes. That helped.

Still smoking, Deuce crossed the creek and kept on the logging trail, which paralleled the waterway for almost a mile before splitting off. He went left, then started uphill, pausing every few moments to listen. Nothing.

Even so, the boy remained certain he'd see something good tonight. It was late Friday afternoon. Prime time. Late summer. Primer time. And you didn't always have to hear them first. He'd learned that, hadn't he?

When Deuce neared the top of the rise, he put on a camouflage head net that almost matched the T-shirt and shorts. He eased slowly up onto the crest of the hill, peering through the tangle of vines and leaves in the last golden rays of day. Nothing.

He took a step. Nothing. Another step.

There!

Deuce smiled, hunched over, and snuck forward and down-hill toward a clearing at the end of a rutted dirt road. There were beer cans and wrappers strewn about, a brush pile, and, on the far side of the clearing, a lone blue Toyota Camry.

The engine was off. The windows were down. No music was on. Deuce was sure he knew why the car was there. He lifted the binoculars and peered across the clearing into the Camry's backseat, where a couple was writhing.

Deuce saw the naked back of one of them. The girl!

Perfect.

And blond! More perfect.

She sat up suddenly; she was seventeen, eighteen—beautiful! Then another topless blonde, younger, very pretty, rose up beside the first one. They began to kiss and caress.

TWO

THE TWELVE-YEAR-OLD THOUGHT he was going to have a heart attack, the scene made him so breathless. Shakily, Deuce lowered the binoculars, dug in his pocket, and came up with an iPhone 4 he'd bought used online. He found the camera icon and pressed it.

This is going to be epic, Deuce thought. *No one will ever forget this one.*

He took a soft step, and then another, which brought him right up to the clearing. He focused a moment on the passionate girls in the backseat of the car but did not raise his binoculars for a closer look.

He was on a mission now. Deuce thumbed the camera mode to video and pressed Record.

He stayed just inside the trees, in the shadows, and circled the clearing, going past the brush pile toward the Camry and coming up on it from behind and to its right. He imagined himself a panther and moved slow and careful until the car and the girls were down a bank and slightly below him, not twenty yards away.

From that angle, he could see the girls were both completely naked. He was flustered, fascinated; part of him wanted to go even closer, right in the backseat if he could. But that wouldn't get him anywhere, now would it?

He had them framed perfectly. And the light wasn't bad at all. He was sure this would be his best effort yet. *Two blondes? I'll be a hero!*

Deuce almost laughed out loud but became transfixed when one girl's hand left the other one's breasts and slid south toward —

The boy heard the grumble of an engine and looked around. It sounded like a vehicle was coming fast and heading toward the clearing. The girls heard it too and scrambled for their clothes.

Are you kidding me? Deuce groaned.

He heard a shriek. He looked back at their car. One of the girls was staring out the window at him.

"There's some pervo kid in camo out there!" she yelled. "He's filming us!"

Deuce freaked and ran. He bolted deeper into the woods and then arced back the way he'd come, jumping logs, dodging trees, and smiling like he'd just escaped some tower with a king's jewel in his pocket.

And in a way, he had, hadn't he? He glanced at the phone gripped tightly in his hand as he continued to sprint back toward the trail. It wasn't the epic video he'd hoped for, but it was still —

Deuce heard a vehicle roar into the clearing and skid to a halt. One of the girls screamed.

Deuce stopped and looked back. Sweat dripped down his face, and he strained to see the clearing through the thick foliage.

The boy told himself to go, get home fast, upload the video to his computer, and spend the night reliving his victory before trying to figure out which website to sell it to. But his natural curiosity overwhelmed him, propelled him back toward the clearing's edge.

The sun was setting. Shadows were taking the opening in the woods. A white Ford utility van with a souped-up motor was idling next to the Camry, blocking Deuce's view of the girls.

He lifted his binoculars, saw the van's windows were darkly tinted. A magnetic sign on the near side said DISH NETWORK.

Dish? Out here? Wasn't that like a—

"No!" one of the girls shouted from the other side of the van. "Please! Don't do this! Help! Kid! Help us, kid!"

Deuce realized she was screaming for him and didn't know what to do.

Another scream followed, louder, terror-stricken. One of the girls was sobbing, blubbering, begging for mercy.

Deuce began to tremble with fear. A voice in his head yelled, *Run!*

A car door slammed. The van door slid shut, muffling the girls' cries.

I'm probably wrong for taking the video, Deuce thought, *but this is seriously messed up. I've got to do something.*

He dug furiously in his pocket, came up with a little magnetic doubling lens that he fitted to his phone's camera lens. He slid the mode to photo for better resolution and zoomed in on the van's rear license plate, lit by its parking lights, some sixty yards away.

The van's headlights went on. The engine revved. They were leaving.

Deuce squeezed the upper volume button of the iPhone to shoot without flash or autofocus. *Click, click, click.* He got five shots in all before the van rolled forward, picked up speed, and left the clearing.

The boy watched the van go, then raised his binoculars to look at the Camry. It was empty in the last fading light. No movement. Both girls were gone.

The boy began to tremble; he felt sick. Those girls had been screaming.

Deuce decided he had to do something. He needed to erase the porn part, make up some story about why he'd seen all this, and then tell it to the police. They'd go find the Camry, figure out who the girls were, and find whoever was driving that Dish van.

And he had to do it sooner rather than later.

He looked at his phone. He punched 911 but got no connection. *No Service,* the screen read. He'd have to go back to the other side of the creek before reception turned solid.

Deuce looked around, got his bearings, and set off toward the logging trail. It would be dark before he knew it, but he'd been walking around in these woods since he was four.

When the boy hit the logging road, a three-quarter moon was rising behind him. He broke into a jog and went up and over the rise.

Right where the trail got steep again, Deuce caught a glimpse of something dark, heavy, and long coming right at him.

He tried to duck, but it was too late.

A forearm smashed into the boy's neck and clotheslined him. Deuce's feet went out from beneath him, and his upper body, arms, and head whipsawed violently before crashing onto the logging road.

The boy felt bones break on impact, and he took a nasty crack to the head. He saw stars, and his limp fingers and arms flung wide. His iPhone sailed off into the woods, along with all the wind in his lungs.

For a second, maybe two, Deuce was dazed and saw only shadows and darkness. He heard nothing but the sound of his own choking and felt nothing but pain that seemed everywhere.

Then the boy heard a man's voice right beside him. "There, now," he said. "Where did you think you were going, young man?"

Part One

PLATINUM DAMAGES THE BRAIN

CHAPTER

1

I LOOKED IN MY BEDROOM mirror and tried to tie the perfect necktie knot.

It was such a simple thing, a ritual I performed every day before work, and yet I couldn't get it right.

"Here, Alex, let me help," Bree said, sliding in beside me.

I let the tie hang and said, "Nerves."

"Understandable," Bree said, coming around in front of me and adjusting the lengths of the tie.

I have a good six inches on my wife, and I gazed down in wonder at how easily she tied the knot.

"Men can't do that," I said. "We have to stand behind a guy to do it."

"Just a difference in perspective," Bree said, snugging the knot up against my Adam's apple and tugging down the starched collar. She hesitated, then looked up at me with wide, fearful eyes and said, "You're ready now."

I felt queasy. "You think?"

"I believe in you," Bree said, getting up on her tiptoes and tilting her head back. "We all believe in you."

I kissed her then, and hugged her tight.

"Love you," I said.

"Forever and ever," Bree said.

When we separated, she had shiny eyes.

"Game face, now," I said, touching her chin. "Remember what Marley and Naomi told us."

She got out a Kleenex and dabbed at her tears while I put on my jacket.

"Better?" Bree asked.

"Perfect," I said, and opened our bedroom door.

The three other bedrooms off the second-floor landing were open and dark. We went downstairs. My family was gathered in the kitchen. Nana Mama, my ninety-something-year-old grandmother. Damon, my oldest child, down from Johns Hopkins. Jannie, my high-school junior and running star. And Ali, my precocious nine-year-old. They were all dressed as if for a funeral.

Ali saw me and broke into tears. He ran over and hugged my legs.

"Hey, hey," I said, stroking his head.

"It's not fair." Ali sobbed. "It's not true, what they're saying."

"Course it's not," Nana Mama said. "We've just got to ignore them. Sticks and stones."

"Words can hurt, Nana," Jannie said. "I know what he's feeling. You should see the stuff on social media."

"Ignore it," Bree said. "We're standing by your father. Family first."

She squeezed my hand.

"Let's do it, then," I said. "Heads high. Don't engage."

Nana Mama picked up her pocketbook, said, "I'd like to engage. I'd like to put a frying pan in my purse here and then clobber one of them with it."

Ali stopped sniffling and started to laugh. "Want me to get you one, Nana?"

"Next time. And I'd only use it if I was provoked."

"God help them if you are, Nana," Damon said, and we all laughed.

Feeling a little better, I checked my watch. Quarter to eight.

"Here we go," I said, and I went through the house to the front door.

I stopped there, listening to my family lining up behind me.

I took a deep breath, rolled my shoulders back like a Marine at attention, then twisted the knob, swung open the door, and stepped out onto my porch.

"It's him!" a woman cried.

Klieg lights blazed to life as a roar of shouts erupted from the small mob of media vultures and haters packing the sidewalk in front of our house on Fifth Street in Southeast Washington, DC.

There were fifteen, twenty of them, some carrying cameras and mikes, others carrying signs condemning me, all hurling questions or curses my way. It was such a madhouse I couldn't hear any of them clearly. Then one guy with a baritone voice bellowed loudly enough to be heard over the din:

"Are you guilty, Dr. Cross?" he shouted. "Did you shoot those people down in cold blood?"

2

A BLACK SUBURBAN WITH TINTED windows rolled up in front of my house.

"Stay close," I said, ignoring the shouted questions. I pointed to Damon. "Help Nana Mama, please."

My oldest came to my grandmother's side and we all moved as one tight unit down the stairs and onto the sidewalk.

A reporter shoved a microphone in my face, shouted, "Dr. Cross, how many times have you drawn your weapon in the course of duty?"

I had no idea, so I ignored him, but Nana Mama snapped, "How many times have you asked a stupid question in the pursuit of idiocy?"

After that, it took everything in me to tune it all out as we crossed the sidewalk to the Suburban. I saw the rest of my family inside the SUV, climbed up front, and shut the door.

Nana Mama let out a long breath.

"I hate them," Jannie said as we pulled away.

"It's like they're feeding on Dad," Ali said.

"Bloodsuckers," the driver said.

All too soon we arrived in front of the District of Columbia Courthouse at 500 Indiana Avenue. The building is a two-wing, smooth limestone structure with a steel-and-glass atrium over the lobby and a large plaza flanked by raised gardens out front. There'd been twenty vultures at my house, but there were sixty jackals there for my rendezvous with cold justice.

Anita Marley, my attorney, was also there, waiting at the curb.

Tall and athletically built, with auburn hair, freckled skin, and sharp emerald eyes, Marley had once played volleyball for and studied acting at the University of Texas; she later graduated near the top of her law-school class at Rice. She was classy, brassy, and hilarious, as well as certifiably badass in the courtroom, which was why we'd hired her.

Marley opened my door.

"I do the talking from here on out, Alex," she said in a commanding drawl just as the roar of accusation and ridicule hit me, far worse than what I'd been subjected to at home.

I'd seen this kind of thing in the past, a big-time trial mob with local and national reporters preparing to feed raw meat to the twenty-four-hour cable-news monster. I'd just never been the raw meat before.

"Talk to us, Cross!" they shouted. "Are *you* the problem? Are *you* and your cowboy ways what the police have become in America? Above the law?"

I couldn't take it and responded, "No one is above the law."

"Don't say anything," Marley hissed, and she took me by the elbow and moved me across the plaza toward the front doors of the courthouse.

The swarm went with us, still buzzing, still stinging.

From the crowd beyond the reporters, a man shouted in a terrified voice, "Don't shoot me, Cross! Don't shoot!"

Others started to chant with him in that same tone. "Don't shoot me, Cross! Don't shoot!"

Despite my best efforts, I could not help turning my head to look at them. Some carried placards that featured a red *X* over my face with a caption below it, one reading END POLICE VIOLENCE and another GUILTY AS CHARGED!

In front of the bulletproof courthouse doors, Marley stopped to turn me toward the lights, microphones, and cameras. I threw my shoulders back and lifted my chin.

My attorney held up her hand and said in a loud, firm voice, "Dr. Cross is an innocent man and an innocent police officer. We are very happy that at long last he'll have the opportunity to clear his good name."

3

THE POLICE OFFICERS MANNING THE security checkpoint watched me as I entered the courthouse, the media still boiling behind me.

Sergeant Doug Kenny, chief of court security and an old friend, said, "We're with you, Alex. Good shoot, from what I hear. Damn good shoot."

The other three all nodded and smiled at me as I went through the metal detectors. Outside, the horde descended on my family as they fought their way toward the court entrance.

Nana Mama, Damon, and Jannie made it inside first, looking shaken. Ali and Bree entered a few moments later. As the door swung shut, Ali faced the reporters peering in. Then he raised his middle finger in a universally understood gesture.

"Ali!" Nana Mama cried, grabbing him by the collar. "That is unacceptable behavior!"

But with the security team chuckling at him and me smiling, Ali didn't show a bit of remorse.

"Tough kid," Anita said, steering me to the elevators.

"Smart kid," said the young African American woman who'd just appeared beside me. "Always has been."

I put my arm around her shoulders, hugged her, and kissed her head.

"Thank you for being here, Naomi," I said.

"You've always had my back, Uncle Alex," she said.

Naomi Cross, my late brother Aaron's daughter, is a respected criminal defense attorney in her own right, and she'd jumped at the chance to help me and work with the renowned Anita Marley on my case.

"What are my odds, Anita?" I said as the elevator doors shut.

"I don't play that game," she said crisply, adjusting the cuffs of her white blouse. "We'll inform the jury of the facts and then let them decide."

"But you've seen the prosecution's evidence."

"And I have a rough idea of their theory. I think our story's more compelling, and I intend to tell it well."

I believed her. In just the past six years, Marley had won eight high-profile murder cases. After I was charged with double homicide, I reached out to her, expecting to get a refusal or a "too busy." Instead, she flew from Dallas to DC the next day, and she'd been standing by me in legal proceedings ever since.

I liked Anita. There was no BS about her. She had a lightning-fast mind, and she was not above using her charm, good looks, or acting skills to help a client. I'd seen her use all of them on the judge who oversaw pretrial motions, motions that, with a few disturbing exceptions, she'd won handily.

But mine was as complex a trial case as she'd ever seen, she said, with threads that extended deep into my past.

About fifteen years ago, a psychopath named Gary Soneji went on a kidnapping and murder spree. I'd put him in prison, but he escaped several years later and turned to bomb-building.

Soneji had detonated several, killing multiple people before we cornered him in a vast abandoned tunnel system below Manhattan. He'd almost killed me, but I was able to shoot him first. He staggered away and was swallowed by the darkness before the bomb he wore exploded.

Flash-forward ten years. My partner at the DC Metro Police, John Sampson, and I were helping out in a church kitchen. A dead ringer for Soneji broke in and shot the cook and a nun, and then he shot Sampson in the head.

Miraculously, all three survived, but the Soneji look-alike wasn't found.

It turned out there was a cult dedicated to Soneji that thrived on the dark web. The investigation into that cult led me, in a roundabout way, to an abandoned factory in Southeast DC, where three armed people wearing Soneji masks confronted me. I shot three, killing two.

But when police responded to my call for backup, they found no weapons on any of the victims, and I was charged with two counts of murder and one count of attempted murder.

The elevator doors opened on the third floor of the courthouse. We headed straight to courtroom 9B, cut in front of the line of people trying to get seats, and, ignoring the furious whispers behind us, went in.

The public gallery was almost full. The media occupied four rows on the far left of the gallery. The front row behind the prosecution desk, which was reserved for victims and victims' families, was empty. So was the row reserved for my family, on the right.

"Stay standing," Marley murmured after we'd passed through the bar and reached the defense table. "I want everyone watching you. Show your confidence and your pride at being a cop."

"I'm trying," I whispered back.

"Here comes the prosecution," Naomi said.

"Don't look at them," Marley said. "They're mine."

I didn't look their way, but in my peripheral vision I picked up the two assistant U.S. attorneys stowing their briefcases under the prosecution table. Nathan Wills, the lead prosecutor, looked like he'd never met a doughnut he didn't eat. In his mid-thirties, pasty-faced, and ninety pounds overweight, Wills had a tendency to sweat. A lot.

But Anita and Naomi had cautioned me not to underestimate the man. He'd graduated first in his class from Boalt Hall at UC Berkeley and clerked at the Ninth Circuit Court of Appeals before joining the Justice Department.

His assistant, Athena Carlisle, had a no less formidable background. A descendant of sharecroppers, Carlisle came from abject poverty in Mississippi and was the first person in her family to graduate from high school. She'd won a full scholarship to Morehouse College, graduated at the top of her class, and then attended law school at Georgetown, where she'd edited the *Law Review*.

According to profiles of the prosecutors that had appeared the week before in the *Washington Post*, both Wills and Carlisle were ambitious in the extreme and eager to prosecute the federal government's case against me.

Why the U.S. government? Why the high-powered U.S. Attorney's Office? That's how it's worked in Washington, DC, since the 1970s. If you're charged with a homicide in the nation's capital, the nation is going to see you punished.

I heard shuffling and voices behind me, turned, and saw my family taking their seats. Bree smiled at me bravely, mouthed, *I love you.*

I started to say it back to her but then stopped when I saw a sullen teenage boy in khakis and a blue dress shirt with too-short sleeves enter the courtroom. His name was Dylan Winslow. His father was Gary Soneji. His mother had been one of the shooting victims. Dylan came up to the bar, not ten feet away from where I stood, pushed back his oily dark hair, and glared at me.

"Frickin' hell's in session for you, Cross," Winslow said, his smile smug and malicious. "Honestly, I can't wait to see you go down in flames."

Ali jumped up and said, "Like your dad did?"

I thought Winslow was going to go ballistic and attack my younger son. Damon did too, and he stood up behind Ali.

Instead of taking a swing at Ali, the teen smiled even more malevolently.

"That's right, kid," he said coldly. "Exactly like my dad did."

"All rise!" the bailiff cried. "Superior Court of the District of Columbia is in session. Judge Priscilla Larch presiding."

A woman in her mid-fifties, with thick glasses and dyed-black hair pulled back in a severe hairdo, Judge Larch stood four foot ten. She was so short she looked almost comical climbing up behind the bench.

But I was not laughing. Larch had a richly deserved reputation for being a hanging judge.

After striking her gavel twice, Judge Larch peered out through those glasses and in a smoker's voice growled, "The People versus Alex Cross. This court will come to order."

4

Six weeks earlier…

JOHN SAMPSON TRIED TO REMAIN calm, tried to tell himself that he would be okay with whatever decision awaited him on the other side of wooden double doors on the fifth floor of the Daly Building in downtown DC.

But Sampson couldn't remain calm. He smelled his own sweat and was almost consumed by anxiety.

His stomach did a flip-flop when the secretary at last nodded to him around five p.m. and said, "He'll see you now, Mr. Sampson."

"Thank you," Sampson said. He got to his feet and, like the therapists had taught him, widened his stance to counter the occasional bouts of vertigo he'd suffered since the gunshot wound to his head.

Sampson walked to the door, trying to exude confidence. He opened it, stepped in, and spotted Bryan Michaels sitting behind his desk, signing documents. Silver-haired and in amazing physical condition for a man in his mid-fifties, DC's chief of police looked up, smiled perfunctorily, and waved Sampson to a seat.

"If it's okay, sir, I'd rather stand," Sampson said.

Chief Michaels's smile disappeared, and he set his pen down as Sampson approached and stood at ease. The chief leaned back in his chair and studied the big man for several long, disquieting moments, glancing more than once at the scar on the left side of the detective's forehead.

"You shot well in qualifying, I see," the chief said at last.

"Not a stellar performance, but I passed, sir."

"You did," Michaels said. "And you almost matched your personal best in the physical tests."

"I've worked very hard to be here, Chief."

Sampson caught Michaels glancing again at the scar on his forehead.

"You *have* worked hard, John," Michaels said in a tone that instantly troubled Sampson, made him feel lost and, well, about to be discarded.

The chief went on. "But I also have to use my best judgment in deciding whether or not to return an officer to the field after the kind of trauma you sustained. And I have to ask myself if you will be a liability to other officers in times of crisis."

Sampson had wondered the same thing, but he said nothing, just gazed at the chief without expression. A beat went by, then two.

Chief Michaels broke into a smile, stood, and offered his hand. "Welcome back, Detective Sampson. You've been greatly missed."

Sampson grinned, grabbed the chief's hand, and pumped it wildly. "Thank you, Chief. You won't regret this."

"I know I won't," Michaels said. "You're an inspiration to many of your fellow officers. I want you to know that."

"Yes, sir. Thank you, sir."

"You'll be needing a new partner," the chief said, his face falling a bit.

There was an awkward moment before Sampson said, "I'm ready for that."

Chief Michaels studied him a moment and then said, "I hate that there's a gorilla in the room."

"Yes, sir. But I believe the gorilla will win out eventually."

Michaels softened. "I hope so. How is he?"

"Hung out his shingle to pass time until the trial," Sampson said.

"Give Alex my best. I mean that."

There was a sharp knock at the door, and in stepped an angular and highly agitated redheaded woman with a detective's badge on a chain around her neck.

"Fox?" Michaels said, irritated. "I hadn't asked you in here yet."

Fox glanced at Sampson, then back at the chief. "I apologize, sir, but Detective Sampson and I, we just pulled a bad one. Kidnapping and shooting at Washington Latin."

"Latin?" Sampson said. "Ali Cross goes to that school."

CHAPTER

5

ALI WAS BADLY SHAKEN BUT physically okay when Sampson found him on the steps of the Washington Latin Public Charter School, his backpack between his knees, wiping away his tears. A patrolman said Ali had seen the entire brutal incident. So had five other students involved in an after-school debate program.

"You okay, buddy?" Sampson said, folding his huge frame down beside Ali and putting an arm around the boy's shoulders. It was mid-October, chilly with night falling, and he was shaking.

"My dad's coming," Ali said in a flat tone. "So is Bree."

"Tell me what happened."

Before he could, Detective Ainsley Fox said, "Detective Sampson? Could I have a word?"

She was standing at the bottom of the steps, frowning at him.

"Hang tight," Sampson said. He patted Ali on the back, got up, and climbed down the steps to her.

In a low, scolding voice, Fox said, "You may have forgotten during your leave that we have rules against physical contact with minors."

Sampson squinted at her. "The kid's like my own, Fox."

"But he's not your own, and the rules are the rules. Shot in the head or not, you've got to play by them or suffer the same kind of consequences your old partner now faces."

Sampson gritted his teeth, said, "Fox, there are five other kids to interview *by the rules.* They're right over there."

Fox hesitated, put off, but then lifted her chin and strode toward the cluster of other upset children. Sampson returned to Ali in time to see Alex Cross and Bree Stone running past the crime scene tape. Alex grabbed up Ali and hugged him fiercely. Ali hugged his dad back just as intensely and started to cry.

When they'd both calmed down, Sampson again asked Ali to describe what he'd seen.

Ali said it was dark out when he exited the charter school behind a group of his friends on the debate team. He was the youngest and shortest by far, so his view was blocked when the screaming started. Then they all started running in different directions. Ali didn't follow them. He stood his ground and got out his cell phone.

"You called 911?" Bree asked.

"No, I videoed them."

"You videoed them?" Sampson said, impressed.

"I wasn't going to fight them," Ali said, pulling out his phone and starting the video.

The footage was shaky at first, but then steadied, showing three men in dark coveralls and masks dragging a screaming blond teenage girl across the terrace in front of the charter school toward Second Street.

"That's Gretchen Lindel, Dad," Ali said. "She's, like, a junior."

On the screen, the kidnappers almost had Gretchen Lindel to the sidewalk. A woman came barreling into view from the left. She was spitting mad and went straight at the masked men.

"Ms. Petracek," Ali said softly. "Our debate coach."

On-screen, one of the men let Gretchen Lindel go, pivoted, and, with zero pause, shot Ms. Petracek in the face at point-blank range. Sampson pulled back at the coldness of it.

The courageous teacher of English and public speaking at Washington Latin died in a heartbeat. Her body fell hard. The gunman turned to Gretchen, who was being forcibly held between two parked cars.

Ali said, "Here's the worst of it."

Siren wailing, blue lights flashing, a Metro DC patrol car came screeching up in front of the kidnappers. The men yanked open the cruiser's doors, threw Gretchen in the back, and jumped in themselves, and then the patrol car, tires squealing and siren still wailing, sped out of sight.

CHAPTER

6

SHORTLY AFTER SHE TOOK ME in following the death of my mother down south, Nana Mama caught me sad and lazing around on her front porch, doing just about nothing.

I was ten. Nana asked me what I was doing, and I told her the truth.

"Breathing," I said.

"Not hard enough," Nana Mama said. "I know you don't like it here, Alex, but give it time. You will. Between now and then, I want you busy. You up to nothing but breathing? You come see me. I'll give you something to do."

"What if I don't feel like doing anything?"

My grandmother, eyebrows raised and hands on hips, said, "In my house, you don't get that option. And you know what? When you're all grown up and gone from here, you won't get that option either, 'less you marry some rich girl or win the lottery."

Ironically, almost four decades later, my grandmother, in her nineties, did win the lottery—the Powerball, in fact. She took the single-payout option, paid a whopping tax bill, and immediately formed a foundation to promote literacy, aid the poor, and provide hot-breakfast programs at local churches.

She also made sure my kids could have whatever education they aspired to. Even then, Nana Mama had enough money left over that the entire Cross family could have sat on the front porch doing just about nothing until we were all pushing up daisies.

But that wouldn't fly with my grandmother. She was all about having a purpose in life that bettered and benefited others. After months on suspension pending my murder trial, and even though I'd been helping Anita and Naomi with my defense, Nana Mama felt I needed to do more than figure out ways to keep myself out of jail. She was right. I'd caught myself "just breathing" too often for my own comfort.

I'd decided that if I couldn't be a cop for the time being, I had to have a reason to get out of bed, a way to be useful to someone besides myself. So I returned to my first profession, psychological counseling.

I fixed up an office in the basement that had its own separate entrance, put up my framed master's and doctorate diplomas from Johns Hopkins, and hung out my shingle after nearly two decades in law enforcement.

I called every social services agency in the metro area, offering my skills and asking for referrals. Luckily I'd gotten a handful, and then a few more, and my practice slowly built.

Two days after Ali witnessed a kidnapping and a murder at Washington Latin, I was down in my office and heard a soft knock at the outer door.

I glanced at my scheduling book: *Paul Fiore. First visit.* Right on time.

I went to the door and opened it, saying, "Welcome, Mr. Fio—"

The stocky man who stood before me was five ten, maybe two hundred pounds, with curly dark hair, brown eyes, olive skin, and a baby face. I couldn't have guessed his age. But by his clothes, I certainly knew his calling.

"I'm sorry, *Father* Fiore," I said. "Please, come in."

7

THE CATHOLIC PRIEST LOOKED CHAGRINED as he came into my office. "I should have told you on the phone, Dr. Cross. I just didn't know what you'd think."

"I'd think I'd be glad to meet you," I said, shutting the door behind him. "And how can I help?"

Father Fiore smiled, but it was strained.

"Please, Father," I said, gesturing toward an overstuffed chair in my office.

"This *is* odd," the priest said, sitting down and looking around.

"How so?"

"I'm usually the one hearing confessions."

I smiled and took my chair. "If you don't mind my asking, doesn't the church provide counselors?"

"It does." Father Fiore sighed. "But I'm afraid this is a delicate subject, Dr. Cross, one they frankly might not understand even in the enlightened age of His Eminence Pope Francis."

"Fair enough," I said, picking up a yellow legal pad. "Why don't you start at the beginning?"

Fiore told me he got the calling to the priesthood when he was fourteen. He was ordained at twenty-two and worked in some of Chicago's poorest neighborhoods. He made such an impression there that the church transferred him to Washington, DC, where he split his time between the parish of St. Anthony of Padua and the cardinal's office, working to fund programs for the poor.

"My grandmother's foundation makes grants to similar programs," I said.

Fiore's smile was genuine. "How do you think I got your name?"

I had to laugh. Leave it to Nana Mama to get me a priest for a client.

"She's quite a lady, your grandmother," Fiore said. "Won't take no for an answer, and yet extraordinarily generous in spirit."

"That describes her to a tee. But let's get back to why you're here."

The priest's face fell a bit as he continued his story. He explained that earlier in the year, he'd attended a fund-raiser with the cardinal at a hotel in Georgetown. He'd found a young woman named Penny Maxwell alone and weeping in a back hallway. He stopped to console her.

Mrs. Maxwell was a widow. It was the second anniversary of her husband's death in Afghanistan, and try as she might, she couldn't keep her emotions bottled up.

"She was suffering, grieving," Fiore said. "So I did what a priest does. I listened and talked and prayed with her."

After the party, he walked with her along the Georgetown

Canal and spent three hours listening to her describe the challenges of her life as the widow of a gifted army surgeon and the mother of two wonderful boys.

Fiore was amazed and inspired by how courageous Penny was, by how determined she was to raise her sons right, and by how much she wanted to honor her late husband's memory in their lives. To his surprise, Fiore learned Penny went to St. Anthony's for services from time to time.

"Penny started bringing the boys to Mass, and I got to know them," he said. "We did things together, hikes, a trip to the beach, and it was like I experienced a dimension of life that I'd thought I understood, but didn't."

"And what dimension was that?" I asked.

"Love," Fiore said, sitting forward, hanging his head, and rubbing his hands. "I didn't just fall for her, Dr. Cross. Penny became my best friend, and I became hers. And those boys are just...every time I leave them, Dr. Cross, I feel as if my heart has a new hole in it."

"Does Penny know how you feel?" I asked.

He nodded. "We both feel this way."

"Have you slept together?"

"No," he said firmly. "We both believe in the sanctity of marriage."

"But the church does not believe in married priests," I said.

He nodded miserably, said, "So what do I do, Dr. Cross? Leave the only calling I've ever had or leave the only woman I've ever loved?"

8

AN ASHEN-FACED AND DISTRAUGHT woman walked to a bank of micro-phones.

"Please," Eliza Lindel said in a tremulous voice. "I beg you, from a mother's broken heart, if you know anything about my daughter's kidnapping, come forward, call the police or the FBI, and give me hope. Gretchen is a sweet, innocent young woman. Please help us find her before it's too late."

The feed cut away to a local station's news desk and an an-chor who began prattling on about the kidnapping.

In her office downtown, Bree hit the mute button on her re-mote. She didn't want to hear the talking heads sum up the case. She knew the situation cold.

The critical first forty-eight hours of the investigation had elapsed with little progress. Part of that was due to the fact that the FBI had stepped in to take over the case because it was a kidnapping and Gretchen had likely been taken across state lines. Bree and DC Metro had been largely cut out at that point, especially after the FBI reviewed the tape of the snatching and saw the police car. As far as she knew, there'd been no ransom note, no attempts by the kidnappers to contact anyone.

"Chief?" Sampson said, knocking at her door. "We've got something."

Before Bree could reply, Detective Fox barged in front of Sampson and said, "I think we should be reporting this to the FBI. They're the higher authority now."

Bree's expression hardened. Ainsley Fox had never met a regulation or rule she didn't worship as gospel.

"Detective Fox," Bree said. "Last time I looked, your badge said DCMP, and you report to me. Anything you have, I want to hear."

"For Christ's sake, Fox," Sampson said when the detective hesitated. "I'll tell her if you won't."

Sampson took a seat, opened a file, and began by noting that all DC Metro patrol cars carried GPS trackers that transmitted their locations to databanks. A check of those banks showed no Metro cruisers in the vicinity of Washington Latin at the time of the kidnapping and murder.

"But Ali Cross's video clearly shows a patrol car with all the right markings and decals of a Metro rig," Sampson said. "Someone detailed that car to perfection, even configured the sirens and blues exactly the way we do."

"Where does that take us?" Bree asked. "To body shops? Places that rent stunt vehicles to the movies?"

Sampson glanced at his new partner and said in a grudging tone, "At some point, maybe, but Detective Fox *has* turned up a more promising lead."

Fox almost smiled. She pushed back her lank hair, got out her laptop, typed something, then spun the screen around.

Bree saw a picture of a blond woman, late twenties or early thirties, earth-mama sort, no makeup but very attractive in a wholesome way. She was vaguely familiar.

"Cathy Dupris," Fox said. "She disappeared from her home in small-town southern Pennsylvania ten weeks ago."

Bree remembered, then said, "The neighbors claimed an ambulance came, and men dressed in EMT uniforms rushed into her house and took her out on a stretcher. But there was no record of a 911 call or a private ambulance request."

"And no ransom note," Fox said, nodding.

"What's the connection?" Bree asked.

Fox called up another photograph of another pretty blonde, Delilah Franks, a bank teller in Richmond, Virginia, who'd vanished six months before.

Bree said, "Don't they think the boyfriend's responsible?"

"She was having an affair behind his back," Fox said. "But maybe that's just a coincidence. Maybe Delilah was taken for some other reason."

"You think you know that reason?" Bree said.

"Show her the pair first," Sampson said.

Fox typed a third time and showed Bree a split screen featuring school portraits of two teenage girls, both blond, both very cute.

"That's seventeen-year-old Ginny Krauss on the left," Fox said. "Alison Dane, sixteen, is on the right. Both girls disappeared nearly seven months ago from rural Hillsgrove, Pennsylvania."

Bree frowned. "I haven't heard anything about this."

"Because the families and police up there have kept it mostly quiet," Fox said. "The parents of both girls are devout Christians. They and the sheriff's investigators believe the girls ran away because of their parents' extreme views about the evils of lesbianism."

"The girls are gay?" Bree said.

"And in love, evidently," Fox said, and she typed again.

She pulled up a photograph of a blue Toyota Camry in a muddy clearing in the woods. The rear and front windows were blown out, and the driver's door was ajar, revealing shattered glass on the seats.

"The day after the girls failed to come home, sheriff's investigators found Alison's car at a popular party and make-out spot in a clearing way out in the state forest," Fox said, typing some more. "Now here's the change in pattern."

Bree sat forward when she saw a handsome little boy.

"Timmy 'Deuce' Walker," Fox said. "Twelve years old. The same day the girls go missing, Deuce vanishes from his neighborhood, which is less than a mile from where the car was found. A month later, a hiker discovers Deuce's remains in the woods roughly six miles from where the girls' car was."

"You think they're all related?"

"I don't believe in coincidences," Fox said, typing.

The screen jumped to a web page that displayed the photos of the missing women against a backdrop of chalk outlines of bodies on a pavement. Across the top of the page there was a platinum wig that looked like Marilyn Monroe's hairdo the night she sang "Happy Birthday" to President Kennedy.

Below the wig, letters that looked like melting red wax spelled out the site's name: www.Killingblondechicks4fun.org.co.

CHAPTER

9

I STUDIED FATHER FIORE AND saw the priest's anguish. I took a deep breath, let it out, and said, in sincere sympathy, "That is a doozy of a dilemma, Father."

"It's torn me apart," Fiore said, tears welling. "I want what I can't have."

I didn't know what to say; not at first, anyway.

But then I asked, "Do you think God lays out a path for all of us?"

"I do," he said without hesitation.

"So you think you were meant to meet Penny and her sons?"

"I believe that's true. But why? As a test of my faith?"

"I don't think anyone could ever question your faith, Father. And I don't think this is a lesser-of-two-evils situation. More like the greater of two goods."

"I don't follow," Fiore said.

I set my notepad aside. "If you stay a priest, you'll sacrifice personal happiness to continue to help the poor and the members of your congregation. But if you leave, you could find similar, rewarding work, marry Penny, and raise her sons with as much love as possible, which is a noble thing too."

He thought about that. A sharp knock came at my outer door.

"I should go," Fiore said, looking at the time.

"They can wait."

"No," the priest said, standing. "You've given me much to pray about, Dr. Cross. I appreciate it. I really do."

I shook his hand. "You'll let me know what you decide, Father?"

"I will," he said. "And say hello to your grandmother for me."

I followed him into the hallway and to the door. When I opened it, John Sampson was standing there. The two men nodded to each other, then Father Fiore climbed the stairs and left, and John came in.

"You here for counseling?" I asked Sampson, shutting the door behind him.

"Got that covered," he said, going into the office and taking my chair. "I'm here off the record—*way* off the record. Not supposed to be talking to you about cases at all, per order of your wife and Chief Michaels. But my new, uh, temporary partner is driving me up the wall, and I needed your perspective."

"Honored to give it," I said, glancing at the scar on Sampson's forehead, remembering how he'd looked in the moments after he was shot by a follower of the late Gary Soneji. It was a miracle I was even talking to him.

John brought me up to speed on the crimes that appeared related to the disappearance of Gretchen Lindel. Then he logged on to my Wi-Fi and said, "My partner, Ainsley Fox, was in a chat room where people were discussing the kidnappings and murders, and she found this hyperlink."

He showed me the screen and a link that read XRAYBLOND.BIZ.

He clicked it, and it took him to a site called Killingblonde-chicks4fun.org.co. I studied it several moments before asking, "Is this for real? I read that fake sites often use a double thing like that, dot org and then dot co."

"Hold that thought," Sampson said.

He showed me several pages on the website dedicated to kidnappings and killings. The writing was atrocious and, according to John, had many of the facts wrong. But each page did contain links to legitimate news articles about the cases, as well as clips from local TV broadcasts.

"Why does the original link not match the name of the website?" I asked.

Sampson smiled. "You noticed. There's more. When you Google either site, or use any other search engine, you get nothing. No results."

I thought about that. "So it's part of, what, the dark web?"

The dark web was a secret part of the Internet accessible only via encrypted software.

"Hold that thought too," Sampson said, clicking on Reenactments. The screen jumped to a page of MPEG thumbnails.

He clicked on one titled "Delilah Goes Down." A picture of Delilah Franks, the Richmond bank teller, came up, a photo I'd seen on the web page dedicated to her disappearance.

The image dissolved into a poorly lit, shakily shot video of a blonde being chased through the woods; it was taken from a camera mounted on her pursuer's chest or head. You could hear footsteps that matched the jerking motion of the camera, which quickly got close enough to the woman to show the back of her filthy, tattered dress and reveal that she was barefoot and bleeding.

She seemed to sense how close her pursuer was; she looked over her shoulder and screamed hysterically before jumping down the side of a steep embankment. She slipped, tumbled, and sprawled in the mud at the bottom.

"Don't," she wept, pushing herself up on all fours in the muck, shaking her head back and forth. "Please, not that. Haven't I been through enough?"

The camera focused down on her, and a computer-altered voice said, "It's never enough, Delilah. Once is never enough."

CHAPTER

10

A KNIFE BLADE APPEARED IN the camera frame, obsidian black and curved tightly back toward an ornate knuckle guard and the fingers of the cameraman's gloved right hand. The wicked-looking blade began a slow, sinewy dance in the air. The chest-mounted camera jiggled as it moved even closer to the shaking woman.

The woman looked up, saw the knife, shrieked in terror, and tried to scramble away. The camera swung crazily after her and blurred the action for several moments.

When it stilled, a gloved left hand had the hysterical woman by her blond hair, and the right hand held the knife so the curve of the blade's cutting edge was poised just above the crown of her head.

"Do blondes have more fun, Delilah?" the computer-altered voice said.

Before she could respond, the screen froze on the image of the two hands, the knife, and the back of her blond head. Superimposed over the image, an icon of a lock appeared.

"Dark web," Sampson said. "Encrypted. Completely out of our league."

"Are all the videos like this?" I asked. "Blocked at the moment of crisis?"

"Yup," Sampson said.

"Think he killed her?"

"That's the point. You've got someone with a high-def GoPro camera mounted on a chest harness, wearing gloves, and carrying that knife. He turns loose the screaming woman, chases her down, and takes her right to the point of complete terror before the screen locks. You're left hanging, wanting to see the ending."

"And how do you do that?"

"I don't know. There's no promo offer anywhere on the site that I can see, but Fox found references to the site and comments about it on an open bulletin board for hackers and coders. They're extensive, and disturbing."

Sampson called up the hackers' website, and it was quickly apparent there was a significant cheering section for Killingblondechicks4fun.

I want in to that site, read one comment from Lone Star Blondes Must Die. *I can contribute. Help. Break some skulls, even.*

Death to all blondes, read a post by Brunette Lover. *Platinum damages the brain.*

Scalp every one of them bitches, read another by 1889B1.

There were, according to Sampson, more than two hundred posts on the hackers' board in that vein from ninety unique posters, all callous, merciless, and hateful. Why? Because of a woman's hair color? What the hell was that all about?

I said, "Any idea who built it? Owns it?"

"None," Sampson said. "But don't you know a cyberwizard at the FBI?"

"I know a cyber*witch* at the FBI," I said. "I can call her if you—"

I heard the door at the top of the basement stairs open.

"Alex?" Bree called. "Are you down there?"

Sampson shut his laptop. I got up fast and called out, "Still with a client, hon. I'll be up soon."

"Oh God, I'm sorry," she said. "I thought you'd be done by now."

The door shut and clicked. I didn't like deceiving Bree, but I didn't want to get John in trouble on his third day back on the job, and it felt so good to be on a case with him again.

"I'm sliding out of here," Sampson whispered, getting up.

"It's dark out, and I'll turn off the outside light over the stairwell."

"It'll be like I was never here," he said. He stopped at the door to gaze at me. "That felt good in there—you know, natural, me and you."

I smiled. "It did feel good. It does."

"You're gonna beat this, Alex. We'll get back to the routine again."

"Natural you and natural me," I said, and we bumped fists. Then I opened the door and the best friend I've ever had slipped off into the night.

Part Two

A KILLER'S SON

CHAPTER

11

THE NEXT AFTERNOON, I STOOD in the stands inside the field house at the University of Maryland, watching Jannie, my sixteen-year-old, jog and loosen up on the track. I clapped as she came by. She gave me the thumbs-up and smiled, but I could see something troubled in her expression, as well as something that I'd never seen on her face before a race: the fear of the unknown.

That wasn't good. I supposed it was understandable for the first race back after a long layoff due to an injury, but it wasn't good. In the past Jannie had always gone to the starting line confident, loose, and ready for battle.

But she'd broken one of the two sesamoid bones in the ball of her right foot during a race, and it had healed excruciatingly slowly. The sesamoids act like the kneecap of the foot, only much smaller; they protect the major tendons and ligaments coming off the big toe. Without the sesamoids, the only way you can run is in burning pain.

Jannie's coaches and doctors had cautioned her not to run

until it healed. That was like asking a cheetah to sit still, and it had depressed and frustrated her no end. But she'd endured and built her strength, and now the X-rays showed the sesamoid had solidly fused.

That was ten weeks ago. Since then her coaches had been taking her workouts up slowly, trying to get her in shape before—

"Alex?"

I turned to my right and saw a fit man in his fifties with graying hair coming at me in silver warm-up pants, a blue hoodie, and white Asics running shoes. A small pair of binoculars and a stopwatch dangled around his neck.

"Nice of you to come, Coach," I said, shaking Ted McDonald's hand.

"Couldn't miss wonder girl's return," McDonald said. "How's she looking?"

"A little stiff and a little scared, frankly," I said.

The coach's face fell. "That's not good."

"I know," I said. "But let's see how it plays out."

"Only thing we can do. In the end, it's up to her."

McDonald was a private coach from Texas who'd started working with Jannie the year before the injury. At the time, he'd been talking about her track-and-field potential in Olympic-level terms. I wondered if that would be the case an hour from now, or ever again.

"This is a good test for her," McDonald said, as if he could read my mind. "Good surface. Short track. And tight curves. No matter how Jannie runs, her sesamoid will be stressed."

"How's that a good thing?"

McDonald had always been straight with me, so I expected candor, and I got it.

"We'll know quick if we're beyond this setback," the coach said. "And if we are, we can turn our attention to something other than the bottom of her foot."

No wonder Jannie was feeling uncertain, I thought. No wonder she was afraid. This was like a verdict coming down.

I tried not to let my mind wander to my own upcoming trial, and I kept up an easy conversation with McDonald before the four-hundred-meter competitors were called to the line. Jannie stepped up in lane three of the stagger, as ready as she'd ever be for two laps around the indoor track.

She'd gained ten pounds of muscle since she'd last raced, but she was still built like a gazelle, with long springy legs and arms, and still fairly thin compared to the other, older competitors moving to their starting blocks.

McDonald pointed at the young lady in lane five. "That's Claire Mason, Maryland high-school indoor record holder in this event. She just signed a national letter of intent to run at Stanford."

"Our girl know that?"

"Nope," McDonald said. "She's just down there to work her plan."

The starter called the runners to their marks. My stomach was doing flip-flops. In her last race, Jannie fell coming out of the blocks, which may have contributed to the fracture.

"Set," the starter said, his pistol raised in the air.

Jannie coiled.

At the crack, she broke clean and I heaved a sigh of relief at the way she came out attacking, her legs churning, her torso fighting to get upright, and her arms pumping toward the first curve and the first real test of the injured bone.

She blazed through the tight turn with relative ease in no

evident pain and accelerated down the backstretch. The staggering of the runners began to evaporate as they came through the second turn, Jannie in fourth.

"Be disciplined, now," McDonald said, glancing at his stopwatch.

Jannie raced down the front stretch, picked off the girl in third, then passed the one in second. That left only Claire Mason in the lead with one lap to go.

"Damn it, Jannie," McDonald said. "That's not what we—"

My daughter thundered after the Maryland high-school champion, but Mason held her off through the third turn. From my daughter's past performances, I figured that the second time down the backstretch would be Jannie's surge, that she'd find some reserve no one had predicted and blow past the girl in the lead.

Instead, Mason pulled away from Jannie. The girl in third overtook Jannie in the fourth turn. Jannie was gritting her teeth, giving it everything she had. But forty meters from the finish, the girl in fourth passed her. The girl in fifth got by her two feet before the wire.

Jannie slowed to a stop, glanced around in bewilderment, then looked up at Coach McDonald and me.

She threw up her hands in despair and exploded into tears.

CHAPTER

12

I JOGGED ALONG THE REFLECTING pool between the Washington and Lincoln Memorials. The dawn was cool, almost crisp, and it felt good to be moving and breathing fresh air.

During my morning runs, I usually tried not to think about anything besides putting one foot in front of the other. But that day I couldn't get my mind off Jannie.

Coach McDonald had told her before the race that she wasn't there to attack the leaders and win; he wanted her to get a clean start, stay close to the leaders, and kick at the end. A training session and a test of her foot.

Instead, Jannie got full of herself and went after what she wanted instead of staying with McDonald's program. It had caused a rift between them. The coach told me he was rethinking how much time he had to dedicate to her.

Nonetheless, her foot had held up. No pain. No discomfort.

I checked my watch and picked up the pace until I was nearly sprinting up the marble stairs toward the imposing statue of the sixteenth and greatest president our country has ever known. I'd been inside the rotunda where the figure of Lincoln presided and read his quotes dozens of times, but they always gave me a chill.

I didn't have a chance to glance at them today because a petite, intense, Indian American woman in a blue business suit and a trench coat stepped out from behind one of the columns. She carried a briefcase and a large Starbucks coffee cup, and she tilted her head, indicating we should leave.

"I should not even be here," FBI special agent Henna Batra said in a low voice. "I should be talking to Sampson or your wife."

"But you're here," I said as we climbed down the memorial steps. "Did you look at the website link I sent you?"

Batra did not reply, just cocked her head in a way that said I was a fool to have even asked.

Men and women far smarter than me will tell you that we are on the verge of the singularity, a moment in time beyond which all human brains will be able to access all possible information through the power of the Internet. As far as I was concerned, Batra was *already* at one with the Internet. Plugged in, she could reach across vast digital landscapes, unlock almost any door, and peek into some of the web's dimmest hiding places.

She was also one of the smartest people I'd ever known. Before Batra had even graduated from the Massachusetts Institute of Technology, she had eight high-paying job offers with the search-engine-and-social-networking crowd. Instead of accepting any of them, she'd joined the FBI and its growing cybercrimes unit. I'd met her during the course of the investigation that led to the murder charges pending against me.

That alone explained Batra's reluctance to meet me in a public place. She was proud of being FBI, and she was a woman of great personal integrity who cared deeply about her reputation. But she'd come, which meant she thought it was worth the risk, which meant she had looked at Killingblondechicks4-fun.org.co.

"C'mon, Batra," I said. "Any luck unlocking those videos?"

"Can a pickpocket pick?" Batra said, heading toward the Vietnam Memorial.

"What did you find?"

"Nothing," she said. "The videos all end a second or two past the locking point. I suspect if a user has the correct passcode, the two extra seconds are revealed and a secret onion router message is sent to the webmaster. At that point, the webmaster would send back an onion router message with the complete encrypted film attached."

"Hold up," I said. "Most of that went right over my head. Start with onion."

The cybercrimes specialist took a sip of her coffee and said an onion was a digital message or order that left a computer surrounded by layers and layers of encryption and code, almost like an onion. "When you send out an e-mail or look at a website," she said, "you're leaving digital tracks all over the so-called clear web. But when an onion message or order is sent, the surrounding codes direct it through dozens of routers on the deep, or unorganized, web. Each router peels away layers of encryption and metadata that would identify the original sender.

"Onions guarantee anonymity," Batra said. "We can't look at them. The NSA can't even look at them. Why? Because we won't even know they exist. Done right, they leave virtually zero trace."

"You're kidding," I said, disappointed.

"I'm not kidding," Batra said, her face clouding as we entered the Vietnam Memorial. "This is serious black-net stuff you've gotten yourself into, Cross. Almost everything having to do with that website was done through onions, so I have no idea who built it or who maintains it."

"Can't you hack it?"

"What's to hack?" Batra said. "The website is anonymously built and self-sustaining. I can shut down whatever the hosting URL is, but I'd imagine there are dozens of mirroring sites with the content on them already."

I thought about that. "You said *almost* everything having to do with the website was done through onion routers."

Batra arched an eyebrow and said, "You're smarter than you look, Cross."

"One of my redeeming qualities. What was *not* done through an onion?"

"Those posts on the hackers' bulletin board. *Those* I could track. And I did."

"All of the posters?" I said, impressed.

"Just the high-volume ones so far," Batra said.

"What do we know about them?"

"Creeps," the FBI agent said, taking another sip of coffee.

I was getting chilled, so I untied the hoodie around my waist and put it on as she continued.

"On the clear net, they troll porn," Batra said. "In the darknet areas where I can track them, they're into lots of the sicker stuff. I wrote it all down."

"Where are they?"

"You mean physical location? All over the world, though one of the regular creeps posting is definitely local."

"How local?" I said, stopping.

"Right here," she said, waving her coffee cup. "DC."

"You have a name? Address?"

Batra studied me several beats, calculating what to tell me, no doubt, and then said, "Close enough."

13

LEAVING THE BROOKLAND-CUA METRO stop later in the day, I knew damn well I shouldn't have been walking up John McCormack Drive. I could hear Bree in my head saying I had no authority here and that my time would be better spent working on my defense for trial.

But I was back in the game, and who was going to tell Bree or anyone?

The creep?

Not a chance. The creep would want to avoid any contact with legitimate law enforcement. And I just might learn something useful about Gretchen Lindel and the other missing blondes, which would more than justify my actions as a concerned citizen.

With that firmly in mind, I went to the security guard at the main entrance to the Catholic University of America and asked how to find the alumni office. The guard gave me a map. I thanked him and started in that direction until I was around a corner and out of sight.

Then I made my way to Flather Hall, a brick-faced dormitory for male freshmen. Classes were over that Friday. Rap and heavy-metal music pulsed and dueled from inside open dorm rooms. I spotted a few underage drinkers and smelled hemp burning as I made my way to the second floor and down a long hallway that reeked of too many young men living on their own for the first time.

The door I sought, number 278, was ajar. I stood there, listening, hearing nothing, and then knocked. No response.

I pushed open the door, saw bunk beds to my right and a single twin bed across the room. Two white males in their late teens sat on a love seat between the single bed and me, wearing Beats headphones and holding video-game controllers. They were absorbed in a violent game playing on a screen on the wall, oblivious to my presence.

Beyond them, at a desk tucked in the corner, there was a third white male, small, scrawny, oily brown hair, lots of acne. Three computer screens dominated the small desk where he sat, and he had headphones on as well, engrossed in the screens.

I reached over and flicked the dorm room light off and on twice.

As if a hypnotist had snapped his fingers, all three of them came up out of their virtual trances and looked around groggily. The closest kid, a chubby towhead named Fred Vertze, spotted me first. His double chin retreated, and he tugged off his headphones.

"Who are you?" he said. "What are you doing in here?"

I waited until the other two removed their headphones before making a show of shutting the door behind me and locking it. They were alarmed when my cold attention swept over them.

"Who are you?" Vertze demanded again.

"Who I am is irrelevant," I said.

"Hell it is," said Juan Cyr, the other young man who'd been playing the video game. Cyr was built like a fullback and stood up to show me he was no one to be trifled with.

Brian Stetson, the kid with the acne and the three computer screens, said, "Don't do anything *el stupid-o,* Juan. I'm calling campus security."

"Do that and I'll have to tell campus security what I know about what goes on in this dorm room," I said.

They glanced at one another uncertainly.

Vertze, who could have used a shower or two, said, "We don't know what you're talking about, man."

"Okay, let's cut right to it, then, before I alert the NSA, the FBI, and six other law enforcement agencies. Gentlemen, which one of you is Lone Star Blondes Must Die?"

14

VERTZE'S EYELIDS DRIFTED ALMOST SHUT. Stetson frowned, as if he'd heard a foreign phrase spoken at a distance. Cyr acted like I'd punched him in the gut.

Then the burly teen's expression shifted from shock to anger. He twisted his shoulders and hissed at Stetson, "I told you messing around with that kind of crap was mind poison."

"Shut up, Juan," Stetson said, studying me calmly. "Who *are* you?"

"The worst kind of poison, unless you come clean," I said, feeling like I'd identified the leader of this crew. "How old are you, Brian?"

"Eighteen," he said. "How do you know my name?"

"I know all your names. I know you get your kicks exploring the dark web. Pushing the boundaries. Looking into nasty places."

"Free world," Stetson said.

"Dogfights?" I said. "Explicit war clips? Hardcore S-and-M fantasy sites?"

"There some law against watching I don't know about?" Stetson said.

"No, but there are several against abetting the kidnap and advocating the murder of five women."

That seemed to rock the kid, who looked less certain as he said, "I know what that means, *abetting*, and no one in this room abetted anything."

"Didn't you post a comment on a bulletin board about the Killingblondechicks website? Quote: 'I want in to that site. I can contribute. Help. Break some skulls, even.'"

He looked at me dumbly, then at his computer. "You hacked me?"

"FBI hacked you, Stetson. You screwed up. Forgot to use onion routers. Which means that I should go to the dean's office and tell him what you've been up to, which means you most certainly will be expelled, which means your parents will be called, which means you'll be escorted out of here in complete disgrace and humiliation."

I let that sink in before saying, "Or you can talk to me."

After several tense beats, Vertze said, "I'll talk."

"Fred," Stetson said. "Don't."

"Brian, my old man will skin me alive if I get expelled," Vertze said sharply.

"I'll talk too," Cyr said.

Stetson's face flushed. He glared at me, caught in a fierce internal argument, and then finally said sullenly, "What do you want to know?"

Over the next twenty minutes or so, the story came out.

Stetson was a math and computer genius who should have gone to Caltech, but his father was a trustee and fervent supporter of Catholic University. His first night at the school,

Stetson had introduced Cyr and Vertze to the dark web. They'd found the Killingblondechicks website and started posting about it for fun.

"Fun?" I said.

"C'mon," Stetson said. "No one thinks those videos are real."

"Have you unlocked the videos?"

"You can't. I tried. The locked world, the unknown, it's just part of the fantasy of virtual reality, man, a place to safely experience and vent frustrations without consequences."

I reappraised the eighteen-year-old, thinking that he was entirely too smart for his own good. "You boys experience frustration with blondes?"

"Hasn't every guy on the face of the earth?" Vertze said.

Cyr and Stetson both started laughing. I had to admit it was a funny line, and I fought not to smile.

Finally, I said, "If I look around in your pasts, am I going to find a blonde one of you disliked so much that she ended up kidnapped? Or dead?"

Cyr said, "My first girlfriend was a blonde. Caught her messing around with my best friend's older brother. They're married now. Not kidnapped. Not dead. Just miserable."

Vertze said, "My anti-blondeness stems from a severe German teacher junior year who had zero sense of humor. I thought about sticking a pin in her ass but refrained—at least, long enough to get an A."

Stetson and Cyr laughed again. I couldn't help it and smiled.

"What about you, Brian?" I said, looking at Stetson.

Stetson sobered and said, "My blonde story is like all blonde stories. They're all about the princess complex that's sold to them each and every day."

CHAPTER

15

AFTER DINNER, ONCE JANNIE HAD gone upstairs to do homework and Ali had settled in to watch *Meru,* an excellent documentary about extreme mountain climbers, I told Bree and Nana Mama about Brian Stetson, disguising him as a client and not revealing his name.

"The princess complex?" Bree said. "And how exactly did he define that?"

"He said it starts at birth with blond girls," I said. "They're dressed as princesses in the crib. Then they're sold the princess story in movies, in advertising, all around them, until they believe that if they can just be beautiful enough, they'll attract Prince Charming and live happily ever after."

Nana Mama said, "An eighteen-year-old told you all that?"

"A sharp one. He had the root theory of blonde stories figured out."

Bree said, "I knew a blonde who was just like that, treated

like a princess her whole childhood. Leanne Long. She was an honest-to-God nice person, and she became a nurse and married a really nice guy, so it doesn't always work according to that kid's theory."

"This old lady needs her sleep," my grandmother said, taking her cane and getting up.

"We're right behind you," I promised. "We'll make sure the place is spotless for you in the morning."

"Bless you, dear," she said, and she kissed my forehead.

When Nana Mama was out of earshot, Bree turned serious and said, "Alex, how long did you think you could be involved in the Gretchen Lindel investigation without me knowing?"

"The client story didn't work?"

"Uh, no."

I told her the truth, the whole truth, and nothing but the truth.

When I was done, Bree was spitting mad.

"What were you thinking, going onto campus like that?" she demanded. "Entering a dorm room without a warrant? Threatening possible witnesses without authority and while on suspension due to pending homicide charges?"

I'd known most of that was coming, but it still hurt. I'd let her down.

"I wanted to be useful, Bree," I said. "It felt like I was back in the game."

"Your clients and practice are your game now. Have nothing to do? Work on your defense. Help Anita and Naomi make your case ironclad. And the next time you feel the need to lie or hide things from me, Alex? Please don't."

I had a hollow feeling in my stomach and said, "You're right. I just... you're right. It will never happen again."

I hoped she'd forgive me. I hated going to sleep when one of us was mad at the other.

After several moments, Bree sighed and said, "So you don't think those college boys are involved?"

My shoulders relaxed. I felt like we were getting back to level ground.

"Beyond the posts, no, not as far as I could tell."

"You don't think we should get a warrant for their computers?"

"And get them all expelled for being smart, nosy, teenage male nerds with blonde chips on their shoulders?"

"Well, when you put it like that," Bree said, getting up and extending her hand to me.

I took it, kissed the back of her hand, and said, "Princess?"

She started laughing, said, "Charming?"

I got up, grinning. "That's me."

CHAPTER

16

JOHN SAMPSON HAD NEVER HEARD a collective grief quite like this. The crying, wailing, and whimpering seemed to come from every room he passed.

Innocence destroyed, Sampson thought. *Up until now, their lives have been one shooting star after another, and that's gone.*

Looking shell-shocked, Wally Christian, Georgetown University's security chief, walked beside Sampson and Detective Ainsley Fox down a hall on the first floor of Village C West, a residential building for freshmen. A DCMP patrol officer stood aside so they could go through the double doors into the common area.

Sampson paused just beyond the doors and took in the carnage with one long, sweeping glance.

A young brunette in a Hoyas sweatshirt was sprawled on a couch, dead, a gunshot to her neck. A second young woman with short brown hair lay facedown and dead on the carpet. EMTs rushed out of the room with a gurney carrying a very large Samoan American male with two chest wounds.

"How many saw it?" Sampson asked.

"Seven," Wally Christian said. "We've moved them to the common room upstairs. The chaplains are with them."

"Who's the missing girl?" Fox asked. "The blonde?"

"Patsy Mansfield," Christian said. "A sophomore. Real star."

"As in, people knew who she was?" Sampson said.

"On campus, you bet. She plays lacrosse, all-American as a freshman, and, well, you've seen the picture of her I put out with the Amber Alert. She's quite the looker."

As all of them took the stairs to the second floor of the dorm, Sampson thought of what Alex had told him over the phone about the three freshmen at Catholic University with bad attitudes about blondes. He wondered if they were involved here and made a note to check on their whereabouts at the time of the incident.

The seven witnesses to the homicides of the brunettes and the kidnapping of Patsy Mansfield all told much the same story. Eleven students were hanging out in the lounge around seven that Saturday evening when two men came in from outside. They wore black balaclavas and olive-green workman's coveralls with *Georgetown University* written on the back. They drew pistols with silencers and ordered everyone to the floor except Patsy Mansfield.

"Wait," Detective Fox said. "They used her name?"

"Definitely," said Tina Hall, a freshman. "They knew who she was."

Hall and the others said the two men told Mansfield that things would go easier if she just went with them. But then Keoni Latupa, a linebacker on the football team and a good friend of Patsy's, grabbed one of the men and threw him to the ground so hard that his gun clattered away. Latupa scrambled for it, but the other man shot and wounded him before he could get to it.

The loose gun came to a stop at the feet of Macy Jones, the brunette in the Hoyas sweatshirt. She went for it and was shot too. At that point, Denise O'Toole, Jones's roommate, went to help her friend. She was shot in the leg.

"Then the first guy got up and retrieved his pistol," said Tina Hall. "He went over to Keoni and shot him again. Then he went to Denise, who pleaded with him not to shoot her, just to take her but not shoot her."

Hall paused, tears welling in her eyes and then dripping down her cheeks. She went on, "Know what he said before he killed Denise? He said, 'Why would we take you? Nobody pays for brunettes anymore.'"

CHAPTER

17

THE DC POLICE UNION HAD referred my latest client to me. She knocked on my basement door shortly after nine Monday morning.

I opened the door and found a dark-haired woman in her mid-thirties standing there, her shoulders slumped. I knew her, but she was so haggard I almost didn't recognize her.

"Tess?" I said, holding out my hand. "It's good to see you."

Detective Tess Aaliyah lifted her head, tears streaming down her cheeks. "I'm embarrassed and uncomfortable to be here, Dr. Cross, but my union rep said you were the only counselor available on short notice."

"Come inside, and please don't be embarrassed or uncomfortable. I'm not a detective now and not here to judge you in any way. You need to talk. I'm available to listen. And, of course, nothing said ever leaves the room."

The detective hesitated and then came inside. I followed her into my office, remembering the confident, smart, and attractive woman who'd helped save my family after they were taken by a madman named Marcus Sunday.

Aaliyah was from a police family. Her father, Bernie, had been a top detective in Baltimore, and she'd lived and breathed the job when we'd worked together. I knew some of the trauma she'd been through lately, and as I shut the office door, I prayed that I was up to the task of counseling her.

I got coffee for her and gestured to a chair. She sat down, her head tilted low and her upper torso and shoulders rolled forward, as if in surrender.

"How are you feeling?" I asked.

"You've seen the news? How should I feel?"

"Forget the news," I said. "Lift your chin, straighten your shoulders, and give me your side of it."

Conflicting emotions flickered on the detective's face as she made a slight alteration in her slouch before telling me the story.

She and her partner, Chris Cox, had gone to a high-rent apartment complex off Judiciary Square to serve a warrant on and arrest one Drago Kovac. Kovac had immigrated to the U.S. from Serbia when he was nine, become an American citizen at fifteen, and become a car thief shortly thereafter. He wasn't very good at his chosen field at first. Kovac was caught and convicted of grand theft auto twice before his eighteenth birthday. After that, he wised up and got sophisticated. He formed an auto-theft ring that worked the Miami-to-Boston corridor, boosting in-demand cars, chopping them up for parts, and then selling the parts over the Internet.

Kovac was now twenty-seven and operating his illegal enterprise from his luxury flat on Third Street in DC. Aaliyah, looking for spare parts for her Ford Explorer, had happened on one of his websites, which offered "gently used" parts for a third of what other sites and stores were asking. When she learned the company and Kovac were based in DC, one thing led to another, and then to a year of additional investigative work.

"We had him," Aaliyah said. "I mean, this was a major criminal operation. Millions of dollars, and we had him dead to rights."

"So you go to Kovac's apartment building to serve the warrant," I said, pushing her toward the awful truth.

"Yes." Aaliyah sighed. "We went in at the exact same time arrests in this case were supposed to go down all over the East Coast. Synchronized, you know?"

But unbeknownst to Aaliyah and her partner, several warrants had been served early. When police in New Jersey went through the front door of a Kovac chop shop, one of his men got off a text warning of the raid.

"Seconds before we reached the tenth floor of his apartment building, Kovac and his men left his flat," Aaliyah said. "Cox saw them at the far end of the hallway and ordered them to the ground. They ran, and when we pursued, they shot."

"They definitely shot first?"

"No question," Aaliyah said, a smolder of the old fire in her eyes. "Surveillance cameras back us up."

"Okay. Kovac and his men shoot first. Then what?"

That glowing ember died in Aaliyah's eyes. Her neck muscles went taut as piano wires before she said, "Then it all became a nightmare."

Provoked into a gun battle, Aaliyah and her partner followed protocol and returned fire. Her first shot hit the meat of Kovac's thigh. Her second and third shots missed the car thief, who, howling in pain, lunged into the stairwell.

"I was in pursuit when the wailing started behind the door at the end of the hall," Aaliyah said, and she broke down sobbing.

I knew the rest. She and Cox caught and arrested Kovac and two accomplices, but at an unfathomable cost. The bullets that went wide of the car thief had gone through the door of the apartment belonging to the Phelps family—Oliver, a young, successful attorney; Patricia, a young, successful physician; and their twins, four-year-old Meagan and Alice.

Alice had been playing in the front hallway. The nanny had rushed to get her at the first shot.

"What are the odds, Dr. Cross?" Aaliyah asked, still weeping bitterly. "What are the odds of wounding the nanny and killing the girl?"

18

AFTER AALIYAH POURED OUT HER anguish, her grief, her guilt and despair, she pulled her feet up under her on the chair, wrapped her arms around her knees, and stared off into the distance.

"In the end, I'll always be the cop who killed a child," she said hollowly. "No matter who I was before or who I become after, that's who I will be."

"To who? You?"

"I pulled the trigger, Alex. That's what they'll write after I die."

"I empathize with the pain and regret you must be feeling, but you don't know what the future holds for you. None of us do."

She blinked slowly, said, "There is a way to know your future for certain."

That got my attention and concern. "Have you thought about that, Tess?"

Aaliyah took a big breath and then shook her head. "No. Not really."

"Not really?"

"Not at all. I'm just trying to find a way to process this, you know?"

There was little conviction in the detective's voice, and she appeared preoccupied.

"Are you sleeping?" I asked.

"Some days it's all I do."

"Self-medicating? Alcohol? Drugs?"

"Honestly, I wish they'd work, but they don't, so I don't."

"When does the civil suit go to trial?"

Aaliyah continued to avoid eye contact. "I don't know what they expect to get from me. This has already cost me everything."

I continued to watch her, thinking about the flat affect in her voice and expression, the defeated way the detective was holding herself, and some of the statements she'd made, especially talking about herself in the past tense.

"Tess, I think I'd feel more comfortable if, for your own safety, we take you somewhere to get a proper, in-depth evaluation of your current condition."

Aaliyah raised her head for the first time in many minutes, gazed dully at me, and said, "I'm nowhere near the padded room."

"Given what you've been through, suicidal ideations are cause for serious concern, Tess. This could be a medical issue that—"

"No one's putting me in a psych ward," Aaliyah said, getting to her feet angrily. "Least of all me."

"Tess—"

"Sorry," she said, heading for the door. "I thought I could trust you and I was wrong. Good-bye, Dr. Cross."

After a long look at the situation I came to a decision, grabbed my jacket, went outside, and hailed a cab.

CHAPTER

19

WE PULLED UP IN FRONT of the DC Police Union building twenty minutes later. I paid the cabbie, went inside, and asked to see William Roth.

Did I have a meeting set up with Mr. Roth? the receptionist asked. No. Had I tried to call him? I'd thought it was a dire enough situation to come down to talk with Mr. Roth in person. It wasn't until I told him it might be a matter of life and death that he called upstairs.

Mr. Roth was in an important meeting, the receptionist told me after hanging up the phone.

"You didn't explain the gravity of the situation. Call back."

The receptionist rolled his eyes, snatched up the phone again, and dialed. "He says break into the meeting. It's that important," he told someone.

The receptionist waited, waited, and then hung up and said, "Go on up, third floor, second door on the right. Roth's not happy."

"I don't care," I said, and I took the stairs up.

I knocked on the door and then entered an anteroom with a very irritated secretary at her desk. "Mr. Roth has been working for this meeting for six months," she said.

"Would it matter if someone you cared about was in danger?"

"Well," she said, flustered. "I suppose so."

"Where's Roth?"

"Roth's right here," said a flushed, bald man who appeared in the open doorway behind the secretary. "This better be good. I've got people at the table I never expected to—"

"It's Tess Aaliyah," I said, walking past the secretary into Roth's office. "You're her rep, correct?"

"Aaliyah?" Roth said with mild disdain. "Dear God, what's she done now?"

"You sent her to me this morning for an evaluation. I believe she's depressed and possibly suicidal."

"No," Roth said, taking a seat at his desk. "I saw her last week. She was bummed but knew it wasn't her fault that the little girl was playing in the front hall before the shooting started."

"I don't think Aaliyah cares. About anything. Which can be chemical, and which is why I need your help getting her into a psych ward for three days so she can be evaluated by medical professionals."

"You want me to commit Aaliyah?" Roth said incredulously. "No, absolutely not. Even if I had that authority, and I don't, absolutely not."

"Aren't you supposed to look after her, represent her?"

"In the shooting, yes, but this? No."

"The depression and suicidal thoughts followed from the

shooting," I said firmly. "She needs help. More than I can give her."

"You tell her that?"

"I did."

"What did she say?"

"That she was upset but fine and nowhere near the padded room."

"There you go, then," Roth said, getting up. "I have a meeting to run."

I blocked the door and said, "You don't care about Aaliyah's well-being?"

"I care," Roth said. "But if you want her in a psych ward, convince her doctor or someone in her family to recommend it. Or get the department to make it a stipulation of her suspension revocation. Any way you try to do it, though?"

"Yes?"

"Expect her to fight."

20

AFTER SEVERAL UNSUCCESSFUL ATTEMPTS TO reach her, I spoke with Esther Dodd, an attorney for the police department. It was obvious by her curtness that Ms. Dodd was none too happy to take my call, probably due to the murder charges pending against me. She listened impatiently and dismissed out of hand my request to have Aaliyah undergo psychiatric evaluation as soon as possible as a stipulation of her rejoining the force.

"She's on suspension with a lawsuit pending," the attorney said. "That puts Detective Aaliyah in limbo and gives us very few options, especially since your evaluation was done on behalf of the police union. With all due respect, it holds no weight from a legal perspective. Good-bye, Dr. Cross."

I tried to find Aaliyah's doctor next and lucked out when a friend in the human resources department checked some old records and gave me a name, Dr. Timothy Cantrell. I looked Cantrell up and found he was not only an internist but affiliated with GW Medical Center and its famous tropical medicine division. I called Cantrell's office but found that the physician, a member of Doctors Without Borders, was currently out of the country, working in Brazil to stem a yellow fever outbreak.

I was frustrated but refused to give up without making every effort.

At 2:12 p.m., after making the long drive, I turned down Francis Street in the small town of Arbutus, a suburb of Baltimore, and soon found a small blue-and-white bungalow with a neatly tended yard.

A raw northeast wind had picked up and caused me to shiver as I ran up the walk and knocked at the door. A tall and very put-together redheaded woman in her late fifties answered the door.

I introduced myself, and her features softened.

"I've seen you on the news," she said. "Tess and Bernie say you're innocent, wrongfully charged."

Her name was Christine Prince. She was Aaliyah's father's girlfriend and was happy to tell me that Bernie had gone off surf-fishing, his passion in retirement. I asked when he'd return, and she said that he'd gone to one of his favorite spots out on Assateague Island, so he probably wouldn't be back until around midnight.

After a few moments' hesitation, I asked if she knew where on Assateague he went to fish.

"You're going all the way out there?" she said after showing me on a map.

"I need his advice, and I think he'd want to give it to me sooner rather than later."

"Tess?" she said softly.

"You're a mind reader, Christine," I said. "Thank you for the help."

Two hours later, I pulled into Assateague Island State Park. The ranger station was closed, and I found Bernie Aaliyah's Jeep Wagoneer parked right where his girlfriend said it would be.

When I got out, the wind clipped me, and the sky spat rain. I dug in the trunk of my car and came up with an old rain jacket and a pair of calf-high rubber boots I kept around for crime scene work. I put them on, and with my hood up to block the wind, I walked up the trail, through the dunes, and onto the beach.

The Atlantic was gray and roiling. But to my left, there were surfers out on the swells, clad head to toe in black neoprene, and to my right, there were six or seven anglers. I stood there, looking at the anglers one at a time, until I saw an older man limp fast toward the crashing surf and then use his powerful shoulders to whip out a heavy fishing rod with a big pink lure.

I thought the lure's arc would die quickly in the wind, but it had just the right angle, and it punched through, landing in the water far offshore. As I started toward him, he pumped the rod tip up and down several times, paused, then did it again. When I passed his chair, his cooler, his tackle box, and two Coleman lanterns yet to be lit, he twitched it a third time.

"Bernie Aaliyah?" I said.

The old man startled and looked over his shoulder at me, huddled in my rain jacket and hood. "I know you?" he said.

I pushed back the hood. "Alex Cross, sir."

Tess's father's face broke into a toothy smile. "So you are. Been a long time, Dr. Cross. I've been following your career from way back."

"I followed yours when I was at Johns Hopkins, sir," I said.

"Hold on, let's do this proper," Bernie said, sticking the butt end of his fishing rod into a piece of white PVC pipe buried in the sand. "There, now."

He turned awkwardly, due to a gunshot wound to his pelvis that had ended his remarkable career in Baltimore Homicide, but he shook my hand with the vigor of a man half his age.

"To what do I owe the honor of you driving all the way to hell and gone to see me?" Bernie asked.

"It's about Tess," I said. "It's serious."

21

AFTER I DESCRIBED MY CONCERNS and the evidence to support them, Bernie Aaliyah was quiet for several moments, standing there, looking off toward the waves crashing in the falling light.

"I saw my daughter three days ago," he said at last. "Tess was still grief-stricken, still remorseful, but I didn't see suicidal, Dr. Cross. And I certainly will not go to court over her wishes."

"I don't discount your observations, Mr. Aaliyah," I said. "And maybe you don't want to legally compel Tess to undergo a full psych evaluation. But you could convince her to commit herself. If I'm wrong, I'm wrong, but I'd rather stand here with my tail between my legs than stand next to you at a grave."

Before Aaliyah's father could reply to that, there was a sharp popping noise. We both turned to see his surfcasting rod bending hard, the line straight and quivering.

"That's a good one!" he cried, scrambling over to the fishing rod and grabbing it before it could come free of the PVC pipe.

Bernie held the rod tight about two feet from the bottom,

the butt still in the pipe. He leaned back, testing the weight of the fish and its strength.

"Oh, Jaysus," Bernie said. "He's gonna go forty minimum, maybe fifty!"

The reel started to whine. Aaliyah's father reached down and adjusted the drag to let the unseen fish run. He let it tear out a hundred yards and saw the line slacken before he snatched up the pole from the PVC pipe and reset the drag.

"Bernie," I began.

He barked, "I've been waiting on this quality of fish for two years running, Cross. So you can either leave or wait until I'm done here."

I held up my hands. "Don't let me get in your way."

So I stood back and watched the retired homicide detective engage in an epic battle on the beach. Every time Bernie was able to pull and crank the fish closer to shore, it would make another run that left him gasping.

"He could go sixty," Aaliyah's father said with a grunt twenty minutes into the struggle. "Big, big striper."

Thirty-five minutes into the fight, he said, "Maybe seventy pounds. My God, what a pig of a fish!"

Fifty-two minutes into the battle, Bernie had the striper in the surf thirty yards right in front of him. We saw the leader and a flash of a big fin before the pig of a fish rolled over and started to shake its head against the pressure of the line and the hook.

Then the fish ran, leaped up out of the water, head still shaking, and crashed sideways into the surf. I was shocked at the size of it. So was Bernie.

"Jaysus H," he said in awe. "He has to be pushing the world rec—"

The striper thrashed once more. There was a twanging noise as the line snapped in two. Bernie staggered and fell back into the sand.

I felt bad and expected him to be mad, curse his luck, or at least cry out in dismay. But Aaliyah's father just sat there in the sand, holding his fishing rod, staring at the surf and what could have been.

After several minutes, he said, "You get a chance at some things only once in this life, and sometimes they slip right through your hands. I'll support you, Dr. Cross. One way or the other, I'll see to it that Tess gets the help you say she needs."

22

JOHN SAMPSON KNOCKED ON THE door frame of Bree Stone's office.

"Chief, we've got her in interrogation," he said.

Bree looked up from a stack of papers, put her pen down, and got up.

She and Sampson went to a booth with a one-way mirror overlooking an interrogation room. A young woman with elaborate parrot tattoos on both arms, multiple face piercings, and half her jet-black hair shaved off sat at the table, staring at the mirror.

In an accent that sounded straight out of Appalachia, she said, "Sally Sweet doesn't have all day. You either want to know or you don't."

Detective Ainsley Fox was also in the observation booth. She said, "Let me talk to her alone, Chief. Get her to relate to me."

Sampson wondered whether that was possible, given that Fox was one of the most abrasive, obnoxious people he'd ever worked with.

Bree was skeptical too, and shook her head. "Detective Sampson will take the lead. He has years of experience at this kind of thing."

Fox scowled but offered no argument as she trailed Sampson out into the hallway. Sampson stopped and said, "You listen. You study. You learn."

His partner did not like that, but she nodded. She and Sampson entered the interrogation room and sat down in front of the woman.

"Sally Sweet?" he said after introducing himself.

"It's what my driver's license says," she said, smiling. "For real. Approved by the court, even."

"Taken in on charges of soliciting prostitution," Fox said. "And possession of a controlled narcotic."

Sampson had to fight not to ask Fox to leave right then.

Sweet shrugged. "Like I told the vice cop, the Oxy I got legit, cause of a herniated disk in my lumbar, and anyway, I got a get-out-of-jail-free card, and I want to use it."

"Describe the card," Sampson said.

"It's a big one."

Fox leaned across the table as if to speak. Sampson put his hand on his partner's thigh and squeezed it hard. Fox sat back and looked at his hand and then at him in outrage.

Sampson squeezed harder, and then let go. He looked at Fox, then turned his head to Sweet, who couldn't figure out what was going on.

"I can't promise you a thing until I hear what you have," Sampson said, ignoring the fact that Fox's normally pale skin had gone beet red. "If it's strong evidence, we'll inform the prosecutor who draws your case. In return for testimony, you'll get some kind of deal."

Sweet's lips curled as if she'd sniffed something foul. "I didn't say nothing 'bout testifying. This is a tip. I give the tip to you. You let me go."

Fox was about to open her mouth, but Sampson pushed back from the table, stood up, and said, "I guess we're done, then. You'll be taken back to central holding. Detective Fox?"

Fox didn't move for a beat but then stood up stiffly.

"Wait, what?" the hooker said. "Shit, okay, then. I'll talk, but Sweet Sal's got to get some good out of this."

Still ignoring Fox, Sampson sat back down and said, "So talk."

Sweet told him to check with the Kansas State Police for a missing-persons report on a seventeen-year-old blonde, Emily McCabe of Wichita, who'd run away and came east after her uncle allegedly abused her.

McCabe lived on the streets until she met a man named Neal Parks; he introduced her to coke, meth, and heroin and turned her into a call girl. Sally Sweet also worked for Parks, who set up meets with his girls and johns via smartphone, like a cyberpimp.

"Emily was good people," Sweet said. "I liked her, even when she became Neal's favorite for a while."

Parks evidently lavished attention on the new girls so they'd do anything he asked. Sweet had once been favored like that. In fact, she still had a key to the pimp's apartment.

"Neal was holding cash back on me, and I knew where he kept it," Sweet said. "Lemme back up a second. Right around then? I hadn't been seeing Emily regular like I used to, and Neal said she'd gone up to New York to work for a friend of his for a few weeks. I waited until Neal went out to eat one night with another of the girls, and I got into his place."

Sweet said she retrieved a lockbox hidden in the ductwork above Parks's computer desk, got the key for it from his dresser, opened it, and took out fifteen hundred in cash.

"Just what he owed me," she said. "I put the rest back."

"What does this have to do with Emily?" Fox said impatiently.

Smug, the hooker said, "When I climbed up there to put the box back, I accidentally kicked Neal's computer mouse. The screen lit up on his desktop. There was a picture of Emily on the monitor."

Sweet realized the image was part of a video, so she played the clip.

"It looked like Neal shot it with his GoPro," she said. "From his—what do you call it—point of view?"

Sampson remembered the GoPro videos on the Killingblondechicks4fun website, and he nodded, thinking that Sweet's story might have legs after all.

"What did you see?" Fox said.

"Neal in full dominance mode," Sweet said, sounding shaken. "He was hitting Emily, saying and doing nasty things to her. And she's all submissive. And then, like, he's got a rope in his hand, and he flips it around Emily's neck."

She stopped, her lip quivering at the memory.

"Neal started to strangle her," Sweet said at last. "He put the camera in her face. You could see how terrified she was before the screen went black."

CHAPTER

23

AT HOME AROUND TEN THIRTY that evening, Bree said she was exhausted and going to bed.

"You coming?"

I said, "I'm going to type up some notes downstairs, catch the eleven o'clock news, and then I'll be up."

"Don't fall asleep in front of the TV again," she said, and she kissed me.

"I'll try not to," I said, and I kissed her back.

"You promised Jannie and Ali you'd go for an early run with them."

"I remember. Love you."

"Love you too," she said and waved her hand wearily as she left the room.

I waited until Bree had climbed the stairs and shut our bedroom door before going to my basement office and putting on a dark jacket and baseball cap. Then I hit Send on a text I'd written an hour before.

I opened the outside door as quietly as I could, slipped out into the night, and went along the side of my house, creeping under our bedroom window. The light went out up there, and I trotted down the sidewalk to a waiting car.

I climbed into the passenger seat. John Sampson was at the wheel.

"Glad you could make it," he said, and then he smiled and put the car in gear.

"You going to explain why we have to sneak around?" I said.

"I am," Sampson said, and he told me about Emily McCabe, Sally Sweet, the video Sweet saw on Neal Parks's computer, and how the clip had ended before the strangulation was complete.

"You believe her?" I said.

"We're here, aren't we?"

"Warrant?"

"We got blowback on the ask," Sampson said. "Can't get a search authorization based solely on the hearsay of a prostitute eager to avoid jail time. But I figure blonde lives matter, and think we should have a chat with old Neal Parks sooner rather than later."

"Why me?" I asked. "What about Fox?"

Sampson shook his head wearily. "She's threatening to file a complaint against me for squeezing her leg hard when she refused to follow my lead during my interrogation. She has total disregard for rank. Even dissed Bree on the deal."

"So things are going well between you?"

"Oh, yeah, just peachy," he said. "Which is why you're here."

"For a talk?"

"I figure we rattle Parks's cage a little. See if we can shake anything loose."

I knew I should ask him to pull over and get a taxi home. Bree would have a fit if she found out I was out with one of her detectives and both of us were defying her direct orders. But still, it felt so good and achingly familiar to be rolling with Sampson late at night that I blocked out my promise to Bree.

We cruised through the city, heading for a saloon Neal Parks liked to frequent after eleven o'clock at night. The Parrot was a serious dive bar by DC standards; it occupied the first floor of a shabby six-story building near the Maryland state line. Parks lived on the fourth floor.

"Convenient if you're an alcoholic," Sampson said.

"Is he?" I said.

"No idea," he said, parking down the street. "Sally says he sits in a booth and handles business there until the Parrot shuts down. Runs the whole thing off his phone. Cyberpimp."

"How are we going to see the video clip of Emily McCabe?"

"I thought about just going up there to watch it for ourselves," Sampson admitted, climbing out of the squad car. "But we risk fruit of the poisonous tree. If we can get a warrant, we don't want that clip excluded at trial."

Trial, I thought, getting out the other side. My own day in court was fast approaching, and yet I seemed to be doing everything I could to avoid facing the issue head-on. What was that about?

"There's an alley exit, and the front door," Sampson said, gesturing down the block at the neon-blue macaw flickering above the bar's entrance.

"I'd take the back," I said, "but I'm unarmed."

John stopped, stooped into the car, and retrieved a small Ruger nine-millimeter, which he handed to me. "I'm coming in the back," he said. "You go in, make him, and wait."

I looked down at the pistol a moment, knowing this was the worst idea I'd had in weeks, but I stuck it in my waistband at the small of the back and pulled my shirt down over it.

We split up. I strolled up the street and entered the Parrot. The place was a pleasant dive doing a healthy business, considering the hour. On the jukebox beyond the two pool tables, Lenny Kravitz was singing "Are You Gonna Go My Way?" The bar itself was to my left; a row of booths lined the opposite wall.

Photos, paintings, and posters featuring parrots were everywhere, and two live African gray parrots croaked and fluttered in a large wire cage near the center of the saloon. One of the parrots climbed the cage wall using its talons and beak. As I passed it on the way to the bar, the parrot cocked its head and goggle-eyed me a moment before squawking, "Five-O! Five-O!"

How the bird knew baffles me to this day, but it just kept squawking, "Five-O!" Many eyes were on me as I stepped up to the bar. The bartender ignored me, so I looked over my shoulder. On the other side of the parrot cage, a lanky guy with short orange hair was slipping out of the third booth from the front door.

Neal Parks glanced my way.

Our eyes met.

Parks bolted.

24

FOR A SPLIT SECOND I thought he was headed straight for the back door, the alley, and Sampson. Instead, the pimp dodged right in front of me and vaulted over the bar before I could grab him.

John stormed into the room with his gun drawn and his badge up.

"Parks!" he yelled. "Stop! Police!"

Parks disappeared through the curtains to the back. Patrons began to scream and yell, and pool players dived for safety. I jumped onto and over the bar, then barreled at the bartender who'd ignored me. He looked like he was thinking of blocking my way, but I yelled, "Five-O!" and he stood aside.

Sampson came around the bar and reached the curtains first. Remembering the day he was shot, I said, "Be cool now, brother."

He hesitated and then tore back the curtains, revealing a room with empty kegs, a walk-in freezer, and a staircase that climbed up into darkness. We went to the stairs and heard Parks running above us.

Sampson charged after him, and I charged after Sampson. We ran up a utility stairwell with cleated steel treads and steel fire doors on every floor. As we passed the third floor, a door above us opened and then slammed shut.

"Stop," Sampson whispered.

We did. Nothing.

"He's going for his apartment, for the computer and that video clip," Sampson said softly, and he started to climb again.

We reached the fourth floor and opened the stairwell door. Several quick looks revealed no one in the hallway. I grabbed the sleeve of Sampson's coat and said loudly, "His place."

Then I let the door shut and held my finger to my lips. Sampson nodded. We stood there in the stairwell, listening. Ten seconds went by. Then twenty. I was about to concede that Parks had indeed gone to his apartment when I heard a squeak above me, and then another.

"Neal Parks?" Sampson yelled. "This is DC Metro. We've got you surrounded."

We could hear him pounding up the stairs again, and we chased him and saw him climb up a ladder bolted into the wall. It gave access to a hatch, which was open. John went first, climbing up and onto the gravel roof. The bluish light cast by the Parrot's neon sign made the shadows strange.

Sampson gestured to me to take the left flank while he went right. We flipped on Maglites and cast the beams about. There were air-conditioner compressors on the roof, eight of them. Parks was either hiding behind one of them or going for a fire escape.

We crept forward, staying parallel to each other, about

eighty feet apart, using the flashlights to pierce the shadows and the darkness. We'd gone by the fifth and sixth compressors when Sampson flushed him out.

Parks exploded from behind one of the two remaining compressors and ran at a diagonal across the roof. I flipped off my light and tried to cut him off.

He was running out of roof and I was running out of time when I realized he meant to jump to the roof of the next building.

The pimp was three steps from doing just that when I managed to snag him by the collar of his jacket and shirt. I meant to haul him back and down. Instead, his momentum yanked me forward two steps.

My lower legs hit the raised roof edge hard, so hard I started to topple over, along with Parks, into the seventy feet of air that separated us from the pavement in the alleyway below.

25

MY HEAD WHIPPED FORWARD AND smashed into Parks's head as my body jerked backward. Sampson had somehow gotten two handfuls of my shirt, and he pulled both me and Parks to safety.

My heart was racing, my stomach had turned sour, and I gasped for air. I'd almost fallen six stories to certain death. The pimp was equally shaken and offered no resistance when Sampson cuffed and searched him.

Parks was unarmed and without his cell phone, which was suspicious, given that Sally Sweet told Sampson that Parks operated his entire cyber-prostitution ring with it.

"Where's your phone?" I asked, shining my flashlight in his face.

"Lost it the other day," Parks said, blinking and lowering his head. "I was going to get a new one tomorrow."

"Uh-huh," Sampson said. "Why'd you run?"

"I like to run," Parks said.

"You mean you like to run prostitutes," I said.

"No, like, for fitness," he said, calm and collected now.

"No, like, for hookers," Sampson said. "You've got a whole stable of them."

"Not true," Parks said, and he laughed. "Now, who says that?"

"Vice."

He looked up then, squinting, and said, "You're not vice?"

"We're homicide," Sampson said. "You know Emily McCabe?"

Parks acted puzzled. "No, I don't know an Emily McCabe."

"Don't be cute," I said. "We can prove you know her."

The pimp said nothing.

"We're investigating her murder," Sampson said.

"Her murder?" he said, seeming genuinely surprised. "She's dead?"

"She's dead, and you killed her," I said. "Strangled her on-camera."

Parks seemed thrown. His mouth hung slightly open, and he stared down at the ground, his mind whirling with questions, no doubt. How had we gotten hold of the video? How should he respond?

Sampson said, "We know you made a snuff film, Neal. We're gonna see you fry for it."

"No way," he said. "I didn't kill no one."

"You put a rope around Emily's neck while you were having S-and-M sex with her," I said. "And then you strangled her to death."

"No," he said. "I—"

"Killed her," Sampson said.

"No," Parks said, struggling, and then he apparently resigned himself to the situation. "Look, okay, I know Emily, but I did not kill her, because she is not dead. That video was just a fantasy. She made it for me as a kind of going-away present."

"Give us a break," I said.

"It's true," Parks said. He went on to claim that Emily McCabe had told him she'd saved enough money to quit the business and was going to school in Florida somewhere.

"Florida somewhere?" Sampson said. "That's the best you can do?"

Parks lost his cool then and snapped, "It's the only thing I have. Look, I liked Emily. A lot. I would never kill her."

"So tell us how to reach her," I said.

"I don't know how to reach her," he said. "She didn't want me to know. She wanted a clean break and an entirely new life. I respected that."

"No phone number?" I asked.

"Lost my phone, remember?"

"I'm not buying it," Sampson said, marching him back toward the roof hatch. "We're taking you in, and we'll be searching your apartment. That snuff film you made is going to send you to prison for the rest of your life."

"No, wait," Parks said. "I'm not lying. Emily's alive. Somewhere."

"Hell of a defense," I said.

He said nothing this time. After I'd climbed down through the hatch, Sampson removed Parks's handcuffs and ordered him at gunpoint onto the ladder. The pimp dropped down and offered no resistance when Sampson put the cuffs back on.

When we led him down the staircase, Parks said, "How about I help you and you help me here?"

Sampson grunted. "How can you help us, Neal?"

Parks licked his lips and said, "I want you to know that I could be killed for saying this, but I can tell you about real snuff films and the crazy, sick bastards that make them."

"Uh-huh, and what good does that do us?" I asked.

Parks hesitated again but then said, "Maybe you'll figure out what happened to those blondes that have been disappearing."

"Like Emily McCabe?" Sampson said.

"No," Parks said. "Like two blond lesbian bitches from Pennsylvania."

26

TWO GIRLS CRYING.

Those were the last clear sounds Gretchen Lindel had heard, and that had been hours ago.

Two girls crying, Gretchen thought, and she strained to hear more.

But through the plywood walls, the seventeen-year-old heard nothing. No voices. No floorboards creaking. Not even a jangle of chain. Or a desperate sob.

The silence made Gretchen mad beyond reason. She kicked and shook the chain that ran from her left ankle to the wall, and she glared at the little camera mounted high in the far corner, where she couldn't reach.

"Who are you?" she screamed. "Why am I here? What do you want?"

Gretchen collapsed into sobs as she had too many times since she'd woken up in a plywood box about the size of a prison cell dressed in a cheap white flannel nightgown, lying on a new mattress still in its wrapper, and covered with thick wool army blankets.

There'd been food. A big tub of Kentucky Fried Chicken and bottles of Gatorade. A metal bucket to relieve herself in the corner where her chain would reach. And the single LED light overhead that never went off.

The constant light had made Gretchen lose track of time. As her crying subsided and she pulled the blankets up around her, she realized she had no idea how long she'd been in the box. Three days? Five? A week? Longer?

The kidnapping itself had felt like a nightmare, like something that she'd wake up from. But no matter how many times she slept in the box or how hard she tried to forget, she kept seeing the men grabbing her, kept seeing Ms. Petracek murdered.

They shot her like she was nothing.

What will they do to me?

Gretchen felt panic surge and tried to turn her thoughts to something else. She'd heard her father talk about doing that many times as a way out of pain.

She breathed deep into her stomach, held it, then exhaled slowly, seeing her father and mother in her mind, so in love and yet so apart now.

What is this doing to Dad? To Mom?

Gretchen felt sick at these questions and wanted to cry again.

He doesn't deserve this. Neither does she. Haven't they suffered enough, God? Haven't they suffered enough?

She thought of her best friend forever, Susan, and her sometime boyfriend Nick. *What are they thinking? Are they trying to find me? Is anyone?*

Curling up into a fetal position, Gretchen tried to find strength in prayer and in her belief in the good. But the questions kept circling and elbowing their way back into her thoughts.

Why am I here? Why is this being done to me? What did I do, God, to deserve this? What if I never see Dad or Mom again?

The soft squeal of metal on metal stopped her thoughts, made her sit up and stare in fear at the crude door with the two dead bolts. It had never opened before.

The door swung inward.

The teenager's hand flew to her mouth, and she stifled a scream.

He was football-player big and dressed in black, from his motorcycle boots to his wool cap and tinted paintball visor. There was a blinking GoPro camera mounted in a harness on his chest. But she was focused in terror on his right gloved hand, which held an ornate knife with a curved and wicked-looking blade.

"Hello, Gretchen," he said in a strange electronic voice. "Are you ready to play a game for us?"

CHAPTER

27

I SLIPPED INTO BED SHORTLY after one thirty in the morning, unsure of how much of Neal Parks's story I believed and too tired to think about it anymore.

It felt like only minutes passed between my head hitting the pillow and someone shaking my shoulder.

I came to consciousness thickly and cracked open a groggy eye to see Jannie and Ali standing by my bed, dressed for the morning jog I'd promised them. I could feel the heat of Bree's body behind me, and not wanting to wake her, I held a finger to my lips.

They nodded and crept out of the room. I got up, feeling a little dizzy and wanting three, maybe four more hours of sleep. But these days a promise to my kids was a promise I tried to keep.

I got dressed in the closet and eased out of the room, smelling coffee brewing downstairs. I went to the kitchen, where Nana Mama, in her navy-blue nightgown and robe, was already pouring me a small cup of coffee. Jannie and Ali were tying their shoelaces.

"Bless you," I said when she handed the cup to me.

"You fall asleep in front of the TV again?" Nana Mama asked.

I nodded and took several reviving sips of the coffee.

"I think that TV should have an automatic shutoff," my grandmother said.

"It does," Ali said. "Or the cable box does."

"Let's go," I said, wanting to end the conversation. I set the empty cup down. "I have a new client coming this morning, and I don't want to be late."

We went outside. The first light of day showed in the sky, and the air was cool when we started to run. We took a route that led to Lincoln Park and back, about four miles round trip.

When I ran alone, I rarely thought, and yet I often got home to find I'd figured out one problem or another. The subconscious at work and all that. But a mindless run was impossible with Ali, especially once Jannie picked up her pace after a mile and left us in the dust.

"Dad?" Ali said, jogging beside me. "Did you know that running for more than thirty minutes promotes brain-cell regeneration?"

I glanced down at him, in wonder again that a nine-year-old, my nine-year-old, could know about brain-cell regeneration.

"Can't say that I did," I said, puffing along. "I mean, I know it's good for your heart."

"And good for your brain," he said. "I saw a thing about it online. That's why I told Jannie I wanted to start running with her."

"So you could regenerate your brain cells?" I said. "C'mon,

bud, you're nine. You're still growing brain cells and will be for a long time."

Ali looked at me with mild indignation. "I'll grow more by running."

I raised my hands in surrender. "I'll trust you on this."

He smiled and said, "But not too much running, otherwise my brain will get too big, and my head will explode, won't it, Dad?"

There was my nine-year-old boy.

"Dad?"

"No, your brain won't explode from running too much."

"You're sure?"

"You think Jannie's head's going to explode?"

I glanced over and saw he was alarmed by that idea.

"No one's head is exploding from being fit," I said as we neared the arboretum. "Next subject."

Ali didn't say anything until we'd reached the park, reversed direction toward home, and were jogging down South Carolina Avenue.

Then he said, "Dad, do some police in our country hate some people so much they'll just shoot them for no reason?"

CHAPTER

28

THAT ONE SHOCKED ME, AND I slowed to a stop, hands on my hips and sweat dripping down my nose. "Why would you say that, son?"

Ali heard the tone of my voice, looked uncertain, and said, "I saw some people on TV say that black kids get shot just 'cause they're black and that you shot those Soneji people just because you hated that dead guy they worship."

My stomach felt hollow. A caustic taste came up my throat and made the back of my tongue burn.

At last, I said, "Let's start with the first part. Are *you* scared a police officer might shoot *you* because of the color of *your* skin?"

"Should I be scared?" Ali asked, crossing his arms. "They said it happens all the time."

"First off, being a police officer is a very difficult job. You understand that, right?"

"I guess. Yes."

"Second, too many black men *are* getting shot," I said. "And some of them by racists. But, on the whole, I think it's more a question of police officers who aren't trained correctly, who don't follow the rules and the most up-to-date methods of law enforcement."

Rather than getting calmer, Ali became more upset and started to run away. I ran after him, stopped him, and saw he was in tears.

Before I could ask him what the matter was, he blubbered, "You don't follow the rules, Dad. That's what the people on TV said. They said you were out of control and represented everything wrong with the police in America today."

That felt like a kick to the head. "Do you think that?"

Wiping at his tears, Ali sniffled. "But that's what people are saying, Dad. Even at school."

I put one knee down on the sidewalk and looked up at my son, who was searching my face for answers.

"I wasn't out of control that night, Ali," I said. "I shot those people because they were trying to shoot me."

"But they said—"

"I know what they've said," I said, trying to keep my voice from breaking. "All I can say is it's not true, son. Your dad is not a cold-blooded killer. It was self-defense. You have to believe me. You do believe me, don't you?"

Ali studied my face for so long I thought I'd lost him, but then he nodded and hugged me so tight that tears welled up in my eyes and love choked my throat.

"Thank you, little buddy," I said hoarsely. "I don't think I can do this without you watching my back."

29

TWO HOURS LATER AND SITTING in my basement office, I was feeling depressed by my conversation with Ali. I suppose it's always a blue day when your nine-year-old questions your personal and professional integrity.

I tried to get my mind off it by thinking about the things Neal Parks had told us the night before. The pimp said he'd seen a fully downloaded video from—

There was a sharp knock at the outer door to the basement. I glanced at my watch. My new client was five minutes early.

When I opened the outer door, I found a wrung-out, sandy-haired man with sad, sunken blue eyes and weathered looks that made it hard to judge his age. He was dressed in pressed jeans, a starched white shirt, and polished boat moccasins with no socks, and he wore a hammered-gold wedding ring, a Rolex watch, and a tiny gold crucifix on a chain around his neck.

"Mr. Lindel?" I said, holding out my hand.

"Alden Lindel," he said, shaking my hand and training those

sunken eyes on me. "So glad you could make time to see me, Dr. Cross."

"Glad I could find an opening," I said, even though he was my only appointment for the day.

I steered him toward my office. "Lindel. That's an unusual name."

"Not in Norway," Lindel said.

"No, it's just that I've heard it twice recently and—"

"Gretchen is my daughter, Dr. Cross," Lindel choked out. "She goes to the same school as your son, yes?"

"Yes," I said, seeing him new all over again. "Yes, of course she does. Ali and I and my entire family, we've all been praying for her safe return."

"Thank you, Dr. Cross," he said as his eyes reddened and he gazed toward the ground. "We need…I need…"

I've always found that if you ask a direct question, you get a direct answer, so I said, "How can I help, Mr. Lindel? Why are you here?"

Lindel hesitated and then looked at me while turning his palms upward. "To be honest, I'm here to see Dr. Cross the shrink because of my guilt and anxiety, and Dr. Cross the detective because of my dwindling faith in my daughter's survival."

I took a seat. "You do know that I'm suspended pending trial?"

"I read that," Lindel said. "I also read that before your recent troubles, you were one of the best detectives in the country."

"Whoever wrote that was being too kind," I said. "And I know the FBI agents in charge of your daughter's case. They're top-notch."

"When my mom bakes a cake, she says you can always use

more frosting," Lindel said. "Please say you'll help me find Gretchen before it's too late and…"

Tears dripped down his cheeks. "She, our daughter, our Gretchen, she's everything to us, and now they're torturing us with these unspeakable images."

"I'm confused," I said. "Who's torturing you?"

Lindel took a tissue and wiped away his tears before reaching into his jeans pocket and coming up with a small blue flash drive in a plastic baggie.

"This was in the mailbox when I checked this morning before breakfast," he said. "Go on, plug it in."

30

I TOOK THE BAGGIE AND looked at the flash drive, a Toshiba with 128 GB printed on the face.

"You didn't give this to the FBI?" I asked, putting the baggie down and finding latex gloves.

"I was on my way here and wanted you to see it first. I...I don't think the FBI can get to the bottom of this without you. Can you make a copy and give the original to them for me? I have to catch a plane to New York right after I leave here. On top of everything else, my mother's in the hospital."

Reluctantly, but curious to see what was on the drive, I nodded. With latex gloves on, I took out the drive and plugged it into my laptop. The screen flashed brightly before a video came up that I found sickeningly familiar.

A blond girl in a white nightgown ran through a dim, leafless forest with the camera operator in full pursuit. It was dusk, and when he caught her and knocked her down, you could not make out the girl's features for the graininess.

"Please don't," she begged when the gloved cameraman pulled her up to her knees by her hair.

"No?" the computer-altered voice said. "Then you want it to be the last time? No more cat-and-mouse? No more fun?"

"I just want this to be over," she whimpered, a vague shadow now in the gathering darkness on my screen.

"Okay, then," the voice said. "You'll get your wish."

I saw a dark slashing motion across her neck. I heard a slick, slicing sound and a disturbing *pah* noise before the screen froze and that icon of the lock appeared above a link that read www.Itsoverblondie.org.co. "Tell me if it's a fake or not," Lindel said, crying again. "That's all I want you to do. Stop this torture before it drives my wife and me mad."

I didn't have a private investigator's license. I was suspended pending trial. I should have expressed my sympathy and turned him down flat.

But I was a father too, and I could see the turmoil the kidnapping and now this possible snuff film were churning up in him.

"You're sure that's Gretchen?" I asked.

"I'd know her voice anywhere," he said, looking at me like I was his last best chance.

"I'll do what I can," I said.

His fists clenched, Lindel smiled through his tears and said, "Bless you, Dr. Cross. From the bottom of my heart, bless you."

CHAPTER

31

FBI AGENT HENNA BATRA CROSSED her arms and stared furiously at me from behind the main security station at Quantico.

When I cleared security, I said, "I'm sorry, but you weren't picking up your phone, and I needed to talk to you."

Agent Batra didn't answer, just pivoted on her black high-heeled pumps and marched down the hallway. I hurried to keep up. When I was abreast of her, she hissed, "Coming here like this? Are you trying to get me fired, Cross?"

"I said it was critical. And I'm obviously not on a watch list. Sidney let me right through the front gate."

"Sidney's known you eighteen years."

"Well, exactly. We're on the same team."

"You don't get it, Cross. You're being tried for murder in DC. That puts your case within the Bureau's purview."

"Believe me, I get it. But what if analyzing this video can save Gretchen Lindel's life? Or at least put her parents' fears to rest?"

She squinted at me. "I'm confused. Why didn't Lindel give this drive to the agents investigating his daughter's disappearance?"

"He was in rough shape, hadn't slept in days when I saw him, and he was on his way to New York. His mother's been hospitalized."

Batra walked a few more steps without comment and then stopped. She bit her lip, looked at the ceiling for a moment.

"Video analysis isn't exactly my thing," she said at last. "For that we have to go to the basement. And Dr. Cross?"

"Agent Batra?"

She studied me with cold eyes and said, "Before we go downstairs, you need to swear, in writing and in the presence of two witnesses, that you'll never tell a soul what you see down there."

Ten minutes later, I got in a secure elevator outside the cybercrimes unit feeling like I'd just signed a little bit of my life away. Agent Batra stepped in beside me, put a digital keycard in the lock, and hit SB2.

"That made me feel quite the criminal," I said as the doors closed.

"Close enough these days," Batra said.

"Want to clue me in to the reason for all the secrecy?"

"You're a bright guy, you'll figure it out," Batra said as the elevator passed the first subbasement and began to slow.

I noticed a throbbing and thumping sound that got louder and more distinct when we reached the second subbasement. The elevator doors opened and we were blasted with electronic techno-pop music. It was loud. It was pulsating. It oddly made me want to dance.

The music obviously had the same effect on the guy with

the flaming-red Mohawk twerking and gyrating inside the glass-walled lab directly in front of us. He wore denim shorts, a denim vest over a sleeveless black tee, and nothing else. Barefoot, and in time with the beat, he was shaking his booty, pumping both fists, and slashing the air with his Mohawk.

I broke into a smile. Batra didn't.

She exited the elevator and crossed the hall to the lab door. I followed her, saying, "Okay, who the hell is that?"

"Keith Karl Rawlins," she said, sounding pained. "He calls himself KK or Krazy Kat, depending on the occasion."

CHAPTER

32

SPECIAL AGENT BATRA STOPPED AT the lab door and looked back at me in real discomfort.

I said, "He works for the Bureau? That's why the no-disclosure?"

Batra glared at me. "Rawlins is as brilliant as they come if you want to analyze anything digital. Far better than me, as a matter of fact."

That surprised me. I'd always thought Batra was one with the Internet. Then I realized the reason for Rawlins's banishment to subbasement two.

"He doesn't fit the conservative J. Edgar G-man image, does he?"

"No," Batra said, twisting the doorknob. "KK definitely does not."

The music was even louder inside the lab. Past benches clogged with electronic test equipment, on the far side of the room, Rawlins danced before an arced array of eight large computer screens. The screens all showed the same video: people dancing in urban streets, shaking their rear ends to the addictive beat of the music.

Batra got around in front of Rawlins and waved wildly at him.

Rawlins made his hands into pretend guns that he pointed at Batra, and then he punched a key on a control board that looked like it belonged in a recording studio. The lab went quiet. Rawlins stopped dancing.

He waved his fingers playfully at Batra and in a soft voice that reeked of New Orleans, he said, "I'll forgive you this time for interrupting my daily Diplo fix. I was just about done regenerating my brain cells anyway."

"My son told me about that," I said before Batra could reply. "Exercising for brain regeneration."

Rawlins saw me, studied me, and then smiled. He picked up a hand towel from the chair and came over to us, still smiling and patting his sweating skull on either side of the Mohawk. He had a gold hoop through his left nostril, and his earlobes featured stretched piercings. In shiny sequins across the chest of his T-shirt were the words GODDESS DANCES.

"You're bigger in person, I must say," Rawlins said coyly. "And your son must have read the same article. What are the odds of that, Dr. Cross?"

"I don't know."

"I do," Rawlins said. "Two in one-point-six-four billion, unless you look at it from a string-theory perspective, in which case the chance of brain waves vibrating out and crossing others rises exponentially with every person who reads that article."

"I have no idea what you're talking about," I said.

"That's a pity," Rawlins said with a pout. "I so enjoy fiery brains and rippling brawn in a single package."

33

I CHUCKLED. "YOU'RE OUT OF luck on both counts, Special Agent Rawlins, which is why I came to see you."

Rawlins glanced at Batra and laughed. "No *special* this or *agent* that, Dr. Cross. It's just KK or Krazy Kat. I'm a contractor. The Federal Bureau of Investigation could never make me a sworn agent. Am I right, Big Baby B.?"

Batra rolled her eyes, said, "We're here to work, Kat, not wallow."

"I think I'd be quite a badass crime fighter." Rawlins sniffed. "Despite appearances, I'm honest to a fault and expect the same from those with whom I work. Tell me, Dr. Cross, did you murder those Soneji followers for sport?"

"No."

"Or to right some wrong?"

"It was self-defense."

He studied me for tics and tells but saw none. "How can I help you?"

"First, a little context."

I gave him a synopsis of the story the cyberpimp Neal Parks had told Sampson and me. Parks claimed he had been in Newport News, Virginia, several weeks before, scoping out the military town for an expansion of his business. Partying in a strip club there, the pimp met two men in their early thirties who went by Billy Ray and Carver.

The three men hit it off and drank and snorted too much late into the night. Billy Ray, who was more a talker than Carver, told Neal Parks they were trolling for blondes to use in movies they produced for several profitable sites on the dark web. One of the most recent, and most successful, Billy Ray said, featured two young blond lesbians from Pennsylvania. He gave Parks the URL of one of the websites: www.Itsoverblondie.org.co. I dug in my pocket and came up with the Ziploc containing the Toshiba flash drive. "The same URL is featured on the video on this drive. I want to know if the video's real or not."

Rawlins became all business at that point. He took the bag and asked where I'd gotten the drive, and I told him about Gretchen Lindel's father.

"He should have brought this directly to the agents on his daughter's case," Rawlins said, moving toward one of his workbenches.

"It's complicated," I said.

"You've watched what's on the drive?"

"If it's real, it's the first actual snuff film I've ever seen."

"You just want to know if it's fake?"

"He wants to know everything and anything," Batra said. "So do I."

Rawlins said, "You make a copy?"

"On my laptop at home," I said.

"No crashes?"

"Worked fine."

"I'll check it anyway," he said, sitting down at a computer. He donned latex gloves, got out the drive, and inserted it into a USB port.

A few moments later, I watched a scanning icon count down the minute and forty-five seconds it took to do a full inspection of the flash drive. At the end of the scan, a message appeared: *No known anomaly detected.*

"Well, all righty, then," Rawlins said.

He disconnected the flash, took it to the larger control board below the eight big screens, and plugged it into a server linked to the internal FBI network.

A digital index of the drive popped up on the large center screen; it showed the icon of the single MPEG movie file. Rawlins clicked on it. There was a brilliant flash, and then the clip played—the grainy video of the hysterical blonde running through the forest with the cameraman in hot pursuit.

"What was that?" Batra asked. "That flash at the beginning there?"

"I don't know," Rawlins said, freezing the video.

I said, "You know, come to think of it, when I hit the icon on my laptop, it did the same thing, only my screen's much smaller and older, so it wasn't as bright as that."

Rawlins grunted and gave his computer orders to list all running processes and applications. The directory opened and showed them in a stack sorted by the time each was launched, beginning with the most recent app.

"That's what just flashed there?" Batra said with an arched eyebrow. "Porngrinder?"

34

RAWLINS LAUGHED AND SAID BLITHELY, "Oh, no, Porngrinder is on me. What can I say? It's a lonely life in the basement at times."

"My God," Batra said, disgusted. "The Bureau frowns on that kind of thing."

"Have them sue me, won't you?" Rawlins said.

"What was the flash?" Batra said.

"I don't know. A blip, a screen hiccup. They happen, you know."

"Or a bug in the plug-in that drives the video player?" Batra said.

Rawlins held up a finger. "A momentous occasion. Special Agent Henna B. and I might agree."

Batra rolled her eyes. "Tell us about the video."

I won't bore anyone with the details of Rawlins's technological savvy and instincts, but they were shrewd and his results conclusive. At first, he used ordinary software to try to access the video file's so-called dark data. No luck. The video had been run through an onion system similar to the one used to create the Killingblondechicks4fun website. The dark data had been stripped away.

"Not surprising." Rawlins sniffed. "But I've still got the dust rag."

The "dust rag" was software Rawlins had designed and coded himself to raise the faintest trace of old dark and metadata. He compared the software to the Hubble Space Telescope looking for cosmic debris a thousand miles behind a comet's long tail.

Sure enough, his screen was soon filled with fragments of code that played out in sync with the video. By focusing on the moments where the lighting was dimmest and the noise of the alleged killing most pronounced, Rawlins found evidence in the data dust that suggested an audio splice in the sound track roughly six seconds long. Those six seconds included the knife-across-the-throat slitting noise and the *pah* that sounded like air bursting out of a frightened and dying chest.

"She's alive," Rawlins said barely fifteen minutes after starting his examination. "Or at least, those weren't the sounds of *her* murder."

I sighed with relief. I wouldn't have to give Alden Lindel or his wife more heartbreaking news. "Explain how you know. The parents will ask."

Rawlins said, "The sound patch itself is fairly sophisticated CGA. Computer-generated audio. So someone's had advanced training in sound effects. You're looking for a film-school grad or someone who worked in a special-effects company out in Hollywood, not a coder."

"Why's that?" Batra asked.

Rawlins gave his computer a command, and the video on

the center screen rewound to the beginning of the six-second splice. A second screen showed the remnants of the dark data. He pointed out a jagged line of data that almost connected top to bottom.

"That's your digital splice," Rawlins said. "A more adept coder would have hidden it better, sewn it up as clean as a plastic surgeon. There wouldn't have been even a hint of a scar."

"So this is basic sound-editing work?" I said.

Rawlins touched his Mohawk as if it were a high-fashion hairdo and said, "Three steps above butchery. And that's all I can manage now. I have a lot to do before Goddess opens."

I was puzzled.

"His favorite dance club," Batra explained.

"Do you dance, Dr. Cross?" Rawlins said.

Before I could reply, my cell phone buzzed in my pocket. I pulled it out, saw the number.

"My son's school," I said. "I have to take this."

CHAPTER

35

ALI CROSS BELIEVED HE WAS smarter than the average kid at Washington Latin but not brilliant, not a genius. The kids he considered supersmart were also the shyest and the most awkward. He decided within a month of starting at the charter school that brilliance was overrated. He'd take very bright, very hardworking, and very curious any day of the week.

Ali was the youngest kid in fifth grade at Latin by at least a year. With his attitude and sense of humor, he fit in with most of his older classmates. But, as his father always said, there were jerks in every crowd.

Ali met two of them shortly after the school bell rang to announce the end of classes. He had fifteen minutes before debate practice and decided to go sit outside. It was a nice sunny afternoon, not too cold.

Ali stopped on the front steps and looked toward the plaza, remembering the hooded men who'd grabbed Gretchen Lindel and shot Ms. Petracek. Rather than dwell on those violent events, he sat up on the wall at the top of the stairs and started playing a game on his phone.

He was aware of knots of kids walking past him, and he caught snatches of their conversation. Suddenly, someone grabbed him by the collar, right below his chin, and pushed as if to shove him backward off the wall. Then whoever it was yanked him forward again.

Shocked, surprised, Ali felt his stomach go sick with adrenaline and fear before he'd fully realized what had happened. George Putnam, a burly sixth-grader, still held Ali so tight by the collar, he was having trouble getting his breath. The older boy laughed at his reaction.

"Saved your life," Putnam said. "You little turd, Cross."

"Let go!" Ali said. "You're choking me!"

Putnam's buddy Coulter Tate was taller and already fighting acne. Tate leaned over, got right in Ali's face, and gave him a crazed, zitty look.

"How's it feel to be a killer's son, Cross?" Tate said. "How's it feel to have murder in the genes?"

Putnam tightened his hold, making Ali's eyes feel like they were swelling. There was no thought, no consideration on Ali's part after that. He just pulled back his head and then slammed it forward. His forehead connected with Tate's nose, and he heard a distinct crunching noise.

Tate screamed and stumbled back, holding his hand to his nose, which was gushing blood.

"He broke it!" He sobbed in disbelief. "He broke my nose!"

Putnam was still holding on, looking shocked as he stared at his bleeding buddy, and Ali punched him in the throat. Putnam let go of Ali's collar and went down on the stairs, bug-eyed and coughing, his hands to his neck.

Ali was still in a fighting stance and trembling head to toe when Mrs. Dalton, the headmistress at Washington Latin, came running out of the school.

"My God, what's happening?" she cried.

Ali didn't reply or move. He kept his attention on the two sixth-graders, as if daring them to get up.

"He broke my nose, Mrs. D.!" Tate said, the blood dripping between his fingers. "And the little frickin' insane-o hit George in the throat!"

"Ali?" Mrs. Dalton said. "Why did you—"

"I'm not talking until my dad's here," Ali said, trying to stay calm.

"You will tell me now, young man," she said, sounding angry and full of authority. "Right now."

"Sorry, Mrs. Dalton," Ali said, feeling weak as he dropped his fists and turned to face her. "Please get my dad here, or a lawyer, and then I'll tell you exactly what happened."

36

TRAFFIC WAS SNARLED AS I crossed back into the district, and I wondered what Ali had gotten himself into that was so bad it deserved an immediate meeting. The headmistress wouldn't tell me a thing.

Inching over the Theodore Roosevelt Bridge, I decided to call Alden Lindel. He answered on the third ring.

"This is Alex Cross, Mr. Lindel. I'm happy to tell you that Gretchen did *not* die in that video. It was a fake."

Her father made a noise partway between a cough and a cry.

"Oh, good!" He gasped. "Oh, thank God! Are you sure? How do you know?"

"Because a very talented FBI computer wizard said that the video's audio was altered. The sounds weren't real."

"But it was Gretchen's voice," he said. "I'd swear it."

"I believe you, Mr. Lindel. But that wasn't the sound of her dying. I wanted you to know. Please tell your wife."

"Yes. Yes, right away."

"I'll be in touch if I hear more."

"Well, I could still use someone to talk to, Dr. Cross," he said. "Eliza, Gretchen's mother, and I…we were separated before Gretchen was taken, and this has been even more of a strain. And my mother's not well, and we're thinking about endings."

"I'm sorry to hear all that, Mr. Lindel. Give my office a call tomorrow. We'll make an appointment."

"Thank you, Dr. Cross."

"You're welcome," I said, and I clicked the phone off.

Traffic was moving, finally. Fifteen minutes later I parked close to Washington Latin and hurried inside toward the waiting area outside the offices of the headmistress and the other school administrators.

From well down the hallway I could see Coulter Tate sitting on the right side of the waiting room. He held an ice pack to his face. A woman I took to be his mother had her arm around his shoulders and was whispering in his ear.

Two or three chairs away, George Putnam pressed a bag of ice to his throat. Sitting beside him was a man I figured was his father, a big dude with a wrestler's build stuffed into a five-thousand-dollar suit. He was staring bullets across the room at Ali, who sat with his eyes closed.

"Dr. Cross?"

I looked behind me and spotted Mrs. Dalton hurrying over.

"Dr. Cross," the headmistress said with an exasperated sigh. "Before we get to the fight, I must speak to you first about your son's insubordinate behavior. A school like Latin—"

"Please, I'd like to speak to my son in private, right now."

"Dr. Cross," she said, raising her chin. "I don't think you—"

"As far as I'm concerned, and with all due respect, I think Ali did the right thing by not talking, Mrs. Dalton. He's a minor, but he has certain rights. Among those is his right to have a parent present during questioning."

"That's with the police," she said. "I run a school, and I wish to be present when he first tells his side of things."

"You really want to fight me on parental rights? Because you'll waste a bunch of money on lawyers and you'll lose."

Mrs. Dalton was a smart woman used to getting her way, a woman who hated losing. I could see it in her eyes.

But she said, "Very well, Dr. Cross. You can use my office. Ten minutes. There are other parents and students to consider."

"Thank you, Mrs. Dalton. I know you're in a difficult situation, and I appreciate your handling it with such grace."

She hesitated, but then tilted her head and gestured toward the waiting room. I walked in. When I did, Coulter Tate, the kid with the broken nose, shrank away, curled up, and whined fearfully.

"What's gotten into you, honey?" his mother said, craning her head over her shoulder to look at me.

"He kills people, Mom," Tate said. "He teaches his kid to kill too."

"Shut up, Coulter," Ali said, opening his eyes. "You are such an ass."

"Language," I said.

Ali looked relieved, got up, and hugged me. I looked at Mrs. Dalton and ignored the others. She led us down a hall to her office and closed the door after we went inside.

"You okay, bud?"

"My forehead hurts," he said, and he hugged me again.

"Mrs. Dalton's not happy," I said. "So give me the truth, everything."

37

I OPENED THE DOOR TEN minutes later and found Mrs. Dalton standing there looking flustered.

"I was about to knock," she said.

Or you were trying to listen in, I thought, but I said, "Call in the others. They'll want to hear Ali's side of things."

"Why?"

"Because those boys are lying to you. And Ali can prove it."

Five minutes later, three kids and three parents were crammed into Mrs. Dalton's office. None of us looked happy.

"Expect a suit for damages, bucko," George Putnam's father said, shaking a big finger at me. "I'm a lawyer."

"You're kidding," I said. "I never would have guessed."

"Let's be respectful, shall we?" Mrs. Dalton said. "Hear Ali's version?"

"He's a liar," George Putnam said in a hoarse voice.

Ali shook his head. "You dolt, Putnam, I haven't said anything yet."

I put my hand on Ali's shoulder and squeezed.

"Stick to the facts," I said. "No name-calling. Address Mrs. Dalton."

Ali wasn't happy, but he nodded and told Mrs. Dalton that Putnam had grabbed him while he sat on the wall and pushed him back, hard. If he'd let go, Ali would have dropped close to six feet to the concrete and probably would have been gravely injured.

"But I didn't let go," Putnam said. "I pulled you back. It was a joke. Saved your life. Jeez."

Ali said, "He did pull me back, and he did say, 'Saved your life.' But then Coulter stuck his face in mine and started talking trash about my dad."

"So you head-butted him?" Tate's mom said bitterly. "You can't do that. They were fooling around, but you took it as a chance to really hurt someone."

"Like father, like son," Tate said.

"It's true," Putnam's father said. "Ali didn't have to punch George in the throat. The game was over, and he suckered my boy."

"George was still choking me after I head-butted Coulter," Ali said, looking Mrs. Dalton right in the eye. "I feared for my life. I swung for his face, but I hit him in the throat."

"Feared for your life?" Putnam rasped. "Are you kidding?"

"Did you have hold of my collar when I hit you, George?" Ali said. "All the other kids have gone home, but I know someone must have seen it. They'll back me up eventually, so tell the truth now."

Putnam opened his mouth angrily, painfully. He hesitated, swallowed hard, and said, "I might have been holding your collar, but I never choked you."

"Never?"

"No."

Ali unbuttoned several buttons on his shirt and then spread the lapels. There were raised welts around his neck.

"Clear sign of attempted strangulation," I said.

"What?" Putnam's father cried. "That's BS. You could have done that when you were in talking to him!"

Ali held out his phone, said, "I may be nine, but I'm not stupid. I took pictures in the bathroom an hour ago. A bunch, all time-stamped. So case closed. This was self-defense, or should we take you all to court and sue for batteries?"

I hid my smile and said, "That's multiple counts of battery."

"Oh," Ali said, grinning. "Right."

There was a long silence in the room. Finally Mrs. Dalton said, "George? Coulter? A five-day suspension."

"Are you serious?" Coulter's mother whined.

"No," Putnam's father said.

"Yes," Mrs. Dalton said. "And if they're ever involved with something like this again, they will be expelled from Washington Latin."

"I'm writing the board of overseers about this," Putnam's father said. "Five days for them and nothing for the kid who did the damage? I don't think so."

"I didn't say that," Mrs. Dalton said, and she looked at me and then my son. "Ali, a three-day suspension."

"What?" he cried. "It was self-defense."

The headmistress was unmoved. "You signed a code of conduct when you enrolled in Washington Latin. That code says, among other things, 'No fighting will be tolerated under any circumstances. None.' Remember?"

"Yes, but—"

"No buts," she said, looking at me. "He signed the contract. So did you, Dr. Cross, and your wife."

"Yes, we did," I said. "And we will abide by it."

"Dad?"

"Case closed," I said.

38

THE NEXT MORNING, AFTER A long jog with Jannie and an excellent shower, I went down to the kitchen with Nana Mama and poured a mug of coffee for Bree. She shuffled to the table, yawning and running on fumes. There'd been a gang fight the evening before, three dead on top of a homicide caseload that was already bulging with backlog. She hadn't gotten home until two and now she had to turn around and go back in for a meeting with the chief at nine.

I put the coffee in front of her.

"Bless you, baby," Bree said, smiling weakly. She sipped the coffee.

"I'll be your barista anytime," I said.

"So tell me about Ali."

"Humph," Nana Mama said, and she went back to stirring eggs for a scramble.

I took a seat across from my wife. "Well, he was like a little pro arguing his defense in there. Very logical. And it was his idea to lay a trap for them by not mentioning the neck welts to Mrs. Dalton before then."

"A regular Perry Mason," Nana Mama said, and she didn't mean it in a good way. "Fighting on the school steps. That would not have happened back when I was a vice principal. Never."

My grandmother, dressed in her quilted blue robe, still had her back to us and was whipping the eggs furiously. Bree shaped an O with her lips and tried not to smile.

"Nana," I said, "what was Ali supposed to do? Let himself be choked to death?"

"I didn't say that," she said sharply, and she turned to face me. "I'm just concerned for your son's reputation, which takes a long time to build."

Hearing echoes of similar things she'd said to me over the years, I said, "Yes, ma'am. That's a fact."

"Long as it takes to build, a reputation can die in two seconds, Alex," she said, and she made a *shh* sound of disgust.

"I know that, and honestly, Nana, I think Ali did the right thing, considering the circumstances, and he's getting punished for it, so he's learning the world can be unfair sometimes."

"I agree," Bree said. "In a lot of ways, Ali's reputation will only be stronger after this. I mean, he's nine years old, and he stood up to bullies who were twelve. Be proud of him, Nana. He did good even if it meant getting suspended."

My grandmother looked perplexed. I got up and hugged her. "Sometimes you have to break the rules. Sometimes you have to protect yourself."

Nana Mama held herself rigid at first, but then she melted and hugged me back. "You know I don't like fighting."

"I do."

"Where'd he learn to fight like that?"

"He says from YouTube videos on Krav Maga, the Israeli fighting system."

"Maybe his time on the Internet should be limited?"

"I agree," I said and kissed her sweet old head.

My cell phone rang. I let go of my grandmother and answered. "Alex Cross."

"Bernie Aaliyah, Dr. Cross," he said gruffly. "It's Tess. She's barricaded herself in her bedroom. She's got a gun, and I'm afraid she's going to kill herself if you don't come talk to her."

39

SUSPENDED DC METRO DETECTIVE TESS AALIYAH lived in a duplex row-house walk-up near downtown on a street heading from renovation toward gentrification. Dumpsters squatted in front of three or four other row houses on the block; hammers and saws popped and whined inside them.

A circular saw squealed nearby, masking the sound of me climbing up to Tess's front porch. Her father opened the door before I could ring the bell, and he limped out to shake my hand. Bernie Aaliyah was pale, and his face was scratched and bruised. I could see everything from fright to anger in his eyes.

"I told you I'd get Tess the help she needed, Dr. Cross," Bernie said in a low, agitated voice. "And I tried in the best way I knew how. But she got real defensive when I suggested the evaluation. When I told her it was for her own good, just to know what's what, she went out of her mind. She attacked me, scratched me, and hit me with something that knocked me on my ass."

He shook his head in disbelief and sorrow. "Tess was always like her mother, always levelheaded, even as a little girl."

"She's still your little girl," I said. "But she's been wounded."

"Talk to her. Make her see it wasn't her fault."

Feeling his desperation, I took a deep breath and said, "I can try. Where's her bedroom?"

"Top of the stairs, to the right."

"The gun?"

"Her backup. She surrendered her service pistol."

"You know what prescriptions she's taking?"

"What isn't she taking? The kitchen counter's covered with them."

"Then I want to take a look there first."

He led me inside, past a steep staircase and into a small modern kitchen. The counter held a blooming array of prescription drugs.

I picked up the canisters one by one and studied them. Some names I recognized. I got out my smartphone and typed names of the medicines I didn't know into Drugs.com. I scanned all the drugs' therapeutic effects, scribbled a few notes, and then used the site to look for possible interactions.

When I finished, I was upset, and I whispered, "Bernie? Is Tess taking all of these? Or just some?"

"She won't tell me, and I can't get her damn doctors on the phone."

I grabbed the bottles and looked for the prescribers' names. In all, five physicians had prescribed twelve different meds for Tess Aaliyah in the past six weeks.

Her father said, "What do you think?"

"If she's taking half these drugs at the same time, it's a wonder she hasn't been committed for psychotic behavior already."

"Jesus H. Christ." Bernie moaned. "I knew it. I told my girlfriend something was wrong. But, Jesus, I…I just didn't push it."

"Tess is a grown woman," I said, and I patted him on the arm. "You coming? She'll want you at some point, but please don't say anything unless I give you the nod. Okay?"

He didn't like that. "I've done my share of talking people off ledges."

"I bet you have, Bernie. But it's like a surgeon operating on a close relative or a man acting as his own lawyer in court. Never a good move."

Tess's dad gave me a sour expression but said, "I won't speak unless you give me the green light."

"Let's go upstairs, then."

40

THE CARPETED STAIRS MADE NO noise as I climbed to a narrow landing. I turned right and went around the banister to Tess Aaliyah's bedroom door. Before I could knock, I heard her in there talking.

"Rats," Tess said in a soft voice that sounded bewildered. "I saw rats. Here? Believe it. I saw…I heard…them scratching in the walls…and her screaming. Mom screaming. Mom's always screaming." Tess cried quietly. "Always screaming."

She sounded so close, I squatted down and saw a shadow that suggested she was sitting on the floor with her back to the door.

I got up, took a deep breath, knocked, and said softly, "Tess?"

"Go 'way," she said in a whisper that I had to strain to hear.

"It's Alex Cross," I said, a little louder. "I wanted to see if we could talk."

"Quiet!" she snarled. "I know my…my rights. I'm not seeing another shrink. No more rats chattering in my closets, no way."

Before I could reply, Tess said, "Alex, you're the big rat. One chitchat, and you start all this drama…put nasty thoughts in my dad's head. 'Poor Tess. She's crazy enough now. Stick her in a hole.'"

"I'm not here to stick you in a hole."

Tess sniggered. "Course you are."

"I'm not. I just want to talk things over."

For several seconds, there was no reply. The door creaked as she leaned against it. I heard her shift position on the floor.

I glanced over at her father, who stood at the head of the stairs looking like he was listening to someone drown.

"Tess?" I said. "Can I just talk, then? Would that be okay?"

"Whatever you want," she said, returning to that bewildered voice. "Just do it nice and quiet. I hear you fine."

I paused, trying to think ahead, trying to figure out the best way to get her to come out and turn over the—

Saa-chunk.

CHAPTER

41

THE SOUND FROZE MY THOUGHTS. I'd heard it a thousand times in my life, maybe more, the particular noise a double-action revolver makes when a thumb cocks the hammer into firing position.

"Tess," I said, stepping quietly to the side of the door and out of the potential line of fire. "Do you have a gun in there?"

In that off voice, she said, "Hate rats in my closets."

I glanced at her father, motioned for him to be patient, and said, "A lot of people care about you, Tess. They'd like to help you. I'd like to come in and help you. Your dad would too."

"No need," Tess said wearily, sounding as if she might be falling asleep. "Ask my dad. Tessie's an impatient girl, can't wait for pest control to do its thing."

"Will you do me a favor? Will you put the gun down beside you, at least?"

"No, Alex," she whispered. "What would be the point of that?"

I decided to shake her a bit. "I asked you before if you were self-medicating. You said no. But your dad just showed me twelve different meds in your kitchen."

After a pause, she said, "Legitimate prescriptions from licensed docs."

"Except I don't think the other doctors knew everything you'd been prescribed, Tess," I said. "There are several drugs down there—antidepressants and antipsychotics—that pose a significant risk when combined. You could have a very serious drug interaction, one that could stop your heart, trigger a stroke, potentially damage your brain, wipe out your long-term memory."

In a slow, modulated whisper, Tess said, "Hasn't. Worked. Yet."

The gun barked.

It startled me so badly I jumped back before feeling the horror and disbelief well in me. Tess had shot herself. She was dead, right there on the other side of that door. My knees went to rubber and I grabbed at the banister, feeling like I was going to be sick. Bernie Aaliyah roared in panic and despair, "No!"

He limped fast to her door and pounded on it. "Tess! Answer me! Tess, you answer me right now!"

In the short silence that followed, I said, "Bernie?"

Tess's father twisted his head to look at me, enraged. "Shut up, you. I never should have called you, Cross. You've killed her, that's what you've done!"

Part Three

THE PROSECUTION OF ALEX CROSS

CHAPTER

42

Four weeks later…

STRIKING HER GAVEL TWICE, Judge Priscilla Larch peered out through thick-lensed glasses and in a gravelly voice said, "The People versus Alex Cross. This court will come to order. Sergeant Holm, you may seat the jury."

"Yes, Your Honor," the bailiff said, and he went out.

"I'm praying we chose right," my niece Naomi said.

Anita Marley nodded stiffly and looked to her opening arguments, not bothering to watch the five men and seven women who held my fate in their hands now filing into the courtroom and taking their places in the jury box. I understood why. Anita was still upset with me about jury selection.

During voir dire—the questioning of potential jurors by the prosecution and defense prior to jury selection—we'd disagreed over two picks: juror five and juror eleven. Five was a man in his seventies who had something wrong with his spine. His upper back was twisted and hunched. He walked slowly with a cane and had to turn his shoulders and rib cage to look up at you.

Juror five had also been sharp in his answers, especially when it came to describing his general skepticism about nearly everything in life. An electrical engineer before retiring, he said he took his time making decisions, tried to get to the truth before he acted, and was firm in his convictions.

Anita had wanted to dismiss juror five because he had a friend whose son had been shot by the Baltimore police. But he also said that he had "nothing against cops. They have a tough job. I can apply the law fairly, given that."

I overruled Anita's objection to juror five, telling her we wanted people skeptical enough to hear the facts and honest enough to deal with them fairly.

Juror eleven was a big, stylish, and beautiful woman in a gray Chanel suit. A brassy redhead, she had a beaming smile, an infectious laugh, and an accent as smooth as West Texas honey. She worked for a big PR firm in DC and was friends with several U.S. Capitol Police officers. Anita wanted her off the jury because a police officer had hit her brother with a baton during a riot at a music festival in Austin.

But juror eleven had also said that her brother "deserved to be hit because he was drunk, crazy, and took a swing at two cops." I reminded Anita of that and overruled her.

The others we agreed on. On the whole, my jury seemed a cross-section of the capital. In addition to jurors five and eleven, there was a thin, hyper woman who worked as a U.S. Senate aide and was furious she hadn't been excused from serving, a beefy guy who wrote a tax newsletter, a lobbyist for agribusiness, and a young mother from Adams Morgan who seemed delighted to serve, apparently seeing it as an extended break from her kids. There was also a male nurse who worked at GW Medical Center, a retired teacher, and a bartender at the Four Seasons Hotel. Two grandmothers and an ex–merchant mariner completed the dozen people who would decide whether I would go on with my life or take a very long detour into a federal penitentiary.

When they were seated, Judge Larch said, "The floor is yours, Mr. Wills."

43

"**THANK YOU, JUDGE,**" the assistant U.S. attorney said, and he got up. Wills tucked his shirt in over his big old belly, smiled sheepishly, ambled midway to the bench, and stopped.

The federal prosecutor took a breath, played the silence a moment, and then said, "Some police officers in America believe the judicial system is in ruins. They get so frustrated, they begin to see themselves as judge and jury, and then executioner. They do. I am with the U.S. Justice Department, and I'm telling you that in every major police force in this country, there is one or a pair or even a handful of cops who believe they are above the law."

Wills paused and then directed his attention at me. "The defendant, Alex Cross, is a prime example of a police officer who thinks he is above the law, a cop who believes that he alone can identify evil and that he alone has the ability to stop it, even if it means his killing someone in the process."

The prosecutor nodded to Athena Carlisle, his co-counsel,

and she hit a button on her computer, bringing up two pictures, a man and a woman, on a screen opposite the jury.

Wells said, "Virginia Winslow was a mom, a welder, and a survivor of terrible abuse during her years married to Gary Soneji—"

"Virginia's a martyr!" someone in the courtroom yelled.

I pivoted in my chair to see a bearded man with wild eyes standing in the aisle and pumping his fist. He shouted, "So's Lenny Diggs!"

Judge Larch banged her gavel. "Bailiff, have this man removed from my court. I said I would not tolerate any outbursts and I meant it."

"Both were persecuted!" the man shouted. "Both were killed by the chief persecutor, Alex Cross!"

Two U.S. marshals grabbed the guy, who offered no resistance and said nothing more as he was taken out. I guess he figured he'd made his point.

"The jury will ignore the outburst," Judge Larch said. "Mr. Wills, make it snappy. We've got a lot of ground to cover."

"Yes, Judge," the prosecutor said, and he walked to the jury box. "Ladies and gentlemen, it is critical for you to know one thing about Virginia Winslow. She was sick and tired of being targeted by law enforcement simply because she'd unknowingly been married to a vicious criminal.

"Virginia changed her last name after divorcing Gary Soneji. The cops still came for her. She moved. They found her. She tried to hide her teenage son, Dylan, from his father's legacy. But in this case, the defendant, Cross, acted to cruelly change that, seeking out and telling the boy in lurid detail what his father had done and making the young man feel as if he were also to blame."

Wills turned to look at me. "Alex Cross made him feel that way because Alex Cross did indeed hold Gary Soneji's son, his ex-wife, and everyone else who had ever been associated with the deceased killer partially responsible for the man's crimes. Alex Cross was obsessed with Gary Soneji. He hated all things Soneji with such a passion that he decided he had to go above the law. He decided these Soneji people had to die, be wiped off the face of the earth. He'd kill every one of them."

Wills paused and looked around. I heard Ali whisper, "He's lying, isn't he, Damon? That man is standing there and lying 'bout Dad. How come no one's saying a thing?"

"Shh," Damon said. "We'll get our chance."

The assistant U.S. attorney went on. "The evidence will show that Detective Cross used intimidation tactics to get an admirer of the late Gary Soneji to take him to meet the leader of a group of people interested in the dead killer. Alex Cross defied well-established police protocol. He went alone, without backup. He marched into what turned out to be a trap, a trap that featured people wearing masks and clothes that made them look like Gary Soneji, all part of a performance designed to evoke a reaction from Detective Cross.

"They got more of a reaction than they expected," Wills said somberly. "Alex Cross shot three of them down in cold blood. Virginia Winslow died first. Cross shot and killed a cameraman, Leonard Diggs, next. Then he tried to kill Claude Watkins. Watkins lived, but he's paralyzed and confined to a wheelchair. Now, you will hear the defense assert that all three victims were armed and threatening the detective when he shot them. That is a false statement, and the evidence will prove it."

The prosecutor put both his hands on the jury-box rail and looked at each of the jurors in turn.

"Dr. Cross and other rogue cops across the country have gone above the law and gotten away with murder over and over again. Isn't it time that we, as a nation, as a people, say, 'Stop. That's enough. No more killings by cop'?"

Wills paused for dramatic effect, and then with anger laced through his voice he said, "I'm asking you, ladies and gentlemen of the jury, to look at the evidence. And I'm asking you to say, 'No more.' I am asking you to say, 'That's enough, Alex Cross. You might be a great detective. You might have solved many cases. But you will not kill with callous disregard for our judicial system ever again. You will be judged on the facts in a court of law. And you *will* be found guilty and you will be punished for your cold-blooded actions.'"

44

WHEN WILLS SAT DOWN, JUDGE LARCH rapped her gavel, called for a ten-minute recess, and hurried off the bench.

I glanced at the jury and saw jurors five and eleven looking at me as if I were some lower order of species.

"That went well," Anita Marley said.

"If that went well, I'd like to see your version of getting crucified," I said.

"Take a breath, Uncle Alex," Naomi said. "It's not that bad."

"Pretty damning."

"No, Naomi's right," Anita said. "Did you notice there weren't a whole lot of bombproof facts mentioned? They've got a few, but not enough. If they had enough, they'd have said so. That's why prosecutors try to tie in some national trend to their cases. All spin aside, it means they haven't got enough to try the case on the merits."

Before I could reply, I heard, "Alex?"

I looked over and saw Bree at the bar. She waved her cell phone at me. "I've got to go."

I walked over and hugged her. "Thanks for being here."

"I want to be here every minute," she said, and she kissed my cheek.

"I know. But go to work. I've got good people fighting for me."

Bree wiped at a tear when we broke apart, nodded, and left with a little wiggle of her fingers at Nana Mama, Damon, and Ali. I winked at my sons and my grandmother. Ali winked back. Damon smiled weakly. Nana nodded without conviction and worried the small string of rosary beads she'd brought along.

"All rise," the bailiff called.

Judge Larch strode back into the court.

I was too far away to smell it, but I knew she'd have the odor of Marlboro cigarettes about her. Larch was forever trying to quit and never succeeding, which contributed to her general surliness on the bench. At least, that's what her clerk had told me once.

"Ms. Marley, you may proceed," Judge Larch said, and she popped a mint in her mouth.

My defense attorney looked at me and smiled. Then she put her hand on my shoulder. She stood up and kept her hand there, gazing at the jury, sweeping her eyes over each one of them.

"*Not* this man," Anita said, and she paused for several moments.

"This man is not the creature that Mr. Wills just described. This good man is Alex Cross, and let me tell you a few hard facts about Dr. Cross, facts that cannot be denied or molded like mud into something other than the truth."

She left my side. "Alex Cross won a scholarship to Johns Hopkins University, where he graduated with high honors. He took a PhD there in criminal psychology as well. He worked seven years as a member of the FBI's Behavioral Science Unit, the people who hunt serial killers by profiling them. Cumulatively, he has been a homicide detective with the Washington DC Metropolitan Police Department for more than fifteen years.

"During all that time with the FBI and DC Metro, Dr. Cross has been repeatedly cited for, among other things, bravery in defense of fellow police officers, arresting bombers, rescuing kidnap victims, capturing mass murderers, and defeating a terrorist plot to blow up Union Station. Did I mention that the last citation was signed by the president of the United States? It was."

CHAPTER

45

JUROR FIVE WAS CRANING HIS neck and shoulders to look at me, and juror eleven seemed impressed enough to jot something down on her notepad.

"Sadly, that is why the U.S. Attorney's Office is pressing this case," Anita Marley said, returning to my side. "You see, with the rash of police shootings across the country, the Justice Department needs a prominent individual to prosecute as a way of demonstrating to the outraged masses that the government is actually doing something about police violence."

She put her hand back on my shoulder and said, "But, ladies and gentlemen of the jury, I ask you not to be swayed by the government's tactics because the facts of this case are on this good man's side, and they demonstrate far, far beyond a reasonable doubt that he is innocent. Let me lay them out for you."

Anita took the jurors through a straightforward summary of the events that led me to shoot three followers of Gary Soneji in self-defense, starting with telling them about the Soneji, a violent cult that had risen up around the myth of the late kidnapper and bomber.

"The cult targeted the investigators who had hunted Gary Soneji," Anita said. "They targeted Detective John Sampson, and they targeted Alex Cross. They made death threats to Dr. Cross and to his family."

Then she explained how the FBI Cyber Division identified a woman named Kimiko Binx as the secretive builder of a website dedicated to the cult. Records showed that Binx had a partner in the website named Claude Watkins. When he was sixteen, Watkins was tried as an adult and convicted of carving the skin off a little girl's fingers.

"Ms. Binx told Dr. Cross she could take him to see Watkins, who had served his time and was now a successful artist," Anita said. "Ms. Binx led Dr. Cross to an abandoned factory where Watkins and a group of his followers were waiting, all dressed up as Soneji, using Hollywood-quality masks."

She nodded to Naomi, who hit a button on her laptop. An old mug shot of Gary Soneji popped up on the courtroom screen along with a crime scene photograph of one of the masks.

"Three of the cult members wearing masks like this one were armed," Anita said. "They carried nickel-plated pistols that they used to threaten Detective Cross, an officer in the course of his duties. Dr. Cross gave them fair warning, and then he defended himself.

"When he left the crime scene to meet police and ambulances he'd called to the factory, someone took the three pistols. The defense believes a member of the cult did this in order to frame Dr. Cross, to portray him as yet another policeman gone over the edge."

Anita paused, and then showed outrage. "The U.S. Attorney's Office should be ashamed for buying into what is obviously a fabricated story. The Justice Department and the attorney general should be ashamed as well. They don't care about Alex Cross's exemplary record with the FBI. They don't care about the great good he's done repeatedly in the course of his career. They just want a high-profile scapegoat, and Dr. Cross fits the bill."

She crossed back to me, put her hand on my shoulder, and said in an even, forceful tone, "But, ladies and gentlemen of the jury, I say to you: Not Alex Cross. Not this good man. This good man will not be made a scapegoat. This good man's reputation as one of the country's finest detectives will not be dragged through the mud. Dr. Cross's remarkable career will not be ruined, and he will never see the inside of a prison cell, because this good man is completely innocent of these charges."

46

PRISCILLA LARCH CALLED FOR A lunch recess at the end of Anita Marley's opening argument, and judging from the body language of jurors five and eleven as they left for the jury room, it seemed that my lawyer's remarks had evened the score.

Nana Mama thought Anita's speech was strong as well. But my grandmother was tired after the stressful morning and said she was going home for a nap.

I encouraged the kids to go with her. Both boys refused. Jannie decided to accompany Nana, do some studying, then go to practice.

Damon and Ali went out for lunch. Anita, Naomi, and I ate takeout Chinese in a conference room down the hall from the courtroom as we went over the testimony of several witnesses who might be particularly hostile to my case.

Assistant U.S. Attorney Wills had a reputation for not holding back at trial. He liked to attack with his strongest evidence right off the bat to make a deep impression on the jury. We were preparing for a rough afternoon.

We had no idea how rough it would be.

The prosecution started the after-lunch proceedings by calling DC Metro detective Harry Chan, the first investigator to arrive at the factory after the shootings. Two patrolmen had driven into the lot five minutes before Chan, but I'd kept them outside pending arrival of detectives and criminologists.

"He wanted to keep the scene as uncontaminated as possible," Chan said.

"Can you describe the defendant when you first encountered him that day?" Wills asked.

"He was excited, talking fast," the detective said. "He was sweating and pacing. He complained of being dizzy and having a headache."

"What happened then?"

"The ambulances and Chief Stone arrived," he said. "She wanted him—Dr. Cross, her husband—kept away from the scene, and she took him home without giving me much time to interview him. I entered the factory with the EMTs and my partner, Detective Lorraine Magee. When we got to victim one, Virginia Winslow, she was dead of a gunshot wound. Victim two, Leonard Diggs, was barely clinging to life. Victim three, Claude Watkins, was more alert but badly wounded. Diggs died en route to hospital."

The prosecutor paused as if to think about that and then said, "Did you see a nickel-plated pistol in the hands of or around any of the three victims?"

"We did not."

"And did crime scene techs find pistols hidden in the factory?"

"No," Chan said.

"Any footprints near the victims?"

"Lots of them," he said. "Watkins and some of his followers had been living there for some time."

"Nothing conclusive?"

"Not in my book."

"Any gunpowder residue on the hands of any of the victims?"

"No."

"Your witness," the prosecutor said to Anita Marley.

Anita smiled and stood. "Tell me, Detective Chan, have you ever been in a gunfight with three assailants?"

"No."

"But, given your years of experience, would it be reasonable to say that having survived such an ordeal, Dr. Cross would be excited, sweating, talking fast, pacing out of nervous energy, and even dizzy or suffering a headache from the gunshots?"

Chan said, "I suppose it's as reasonable as saying Dr. Cross had just shot three people for his own ends and was acting that way because he was trying to figure out if he'd done it well enough to fool me."

Anita looked annoyed. "Objection, Judge. Will the Court instruct the witness to answer my question?"

"Asked and answered, Counselor," Larch said. "Motion denied."

"Defense reserves the right to recall Detective Chan at a later time," my attorney said, and she sat down.

"The United States calls Norman Nixon to the stand," Wills said.

"Jesus, they're not fooling around," Naomi muttered under her breath.

CHAPTER

47

NORMAN NIXON WAS A HEARTY-LOOKING man in his fifties, neatly groomed with scrubbed skin, slick iron-gray hair, and a competent, earnest expression. He wore a khaki suit and a blue-striped tie, and he carried a file folder to the witness stand.

After Nixon was sworn in, Wills quickly established the witness's bona fides as an expert on police shootings. Nixon had been a decorated cop in Chicago before joining the FBI, where he had worked as an investigator in the civil rights division. He was involved in the U.S. government's investigation into police killings. After his retirement from the Bureau, Nixon continued to study the forces that contributed to citizens' death by cop.

"Sometimes the officer's a racist," Nixon said. "Sometimes the officer's just burned out from the day-to-day pressure of the job and is feeling inordinately threatened. And sometimes, more often than you'd think, the police officer shoots because he believes he's above the law."

Wills looked at the jury. "In your opinion, Mr. Nixon, does Alex Cross fit the profile of a police officer who believes he's above the law?"

"Objection—argumentative," Anita said.

"Overruled," Judge Larch said. "Answer the question, Mr. Nixon."

"He does fit the profile," Nixon said. "In fact, he's a prime example of the phenomenon."

"A prime example," Wills said. "What does that mean?"

"It means I've studied him at length," Nixon said, looking earnestly in my direction. "It means I've researched every shooting Dr. Cross has ever been involved in."

"Wait," the prosecutor said. "Dr. Cross has been involved in shootings other than the three in question today?"

Anita sprang to her feet. "Objection! Relevance?"

Wills said, "We're trying to give the jury the context in which these three shootings took place."

"Overruled," Larch said.

"Judge!"

"Overruled!"

Wills said, "Was Alex Cross involved in other shootings before the three in question?"

"Yes," Nixon said.

"How many times does the average police officer in America discharge his weapon in the course of a career?"

"Zero," Nixon said. "The vast majority of police officers never fire their weapon in the line of duty."

"Zero," Wills said. "And how many times has Dr. Cross discharged a weapon in the course of his careers at the FBI and DC Metro Police?"

The witness shifted in his chair, said, "I don't have *all* the records. Some are sealed. But just from the public documents I've looked at, Alex Cross has fired his weapon at least thirty-one times."

I blinked and felt my stomach go sour. There was a louder reaction in the audience, which caused Judge Larch to pound her gavel. "Order."

By their expressions, jurors five and eleven had turned against me again. And no wonder. I was as shocked as they were to hear the number.

Thirty-one times. Is that true? And have I shot more than that? He said at least, *didn't he?*

Wills said, "Can you break down the shots for us in a meaningful way?"

Nixon nodded. "The records I've seen indicate that Dr. Cross missed fourteen times and wounded someone eight times."

"And the other nine times Dr. Cross pulled his trigger in the line of duty?"

"His shots were perfect," Nixon said. "All of his victims died."

48

BY THE END OF THE first day of the trial, I felt like that side of beef Rocky Balboa used as a punching bag.

For three solid hours, Wills and Nixon had kept up a relentless barrage of facts about the nine deadly shooting incidents that they said collectively cast me as a cop who believed he was above the law.

"They've almost got me believing it," I said after court was adjourned for the evening. We'd gone to a conference room to reassess before heading home.

Anita said, "You must absolutely not believe it."

Naomi nodded. "She's right. Your belief in your innocence has to shine through your body language. The jury will pick up on the slightest doubt you feel."

My lead attorney put her hand on my forearm. "This is classic Nathan Wills, from what I understand, and we still have more than a few cards up our sleeves. Go home, Alex. Be with your family. Don't watch the news. We'll see you in the morning."

I nodded. "Sampson's picking me up in the garage."

"Perfect," Naomi said. "And have you thought about that interview request from Gayle King?"

"I don't see an upside."

My niece said, "The upside is you get to tell your story to a national audience and counter all the horrible things people have been saying about you."

"I'll think about it," I said, and left.

Sampson was waiting for me in the garage in his Jeep Grand Cherokee.

"How'd it go?" he asked after I'd shut the door.

"Slightly better than the Spanish Inquisition."

"Shit. And here I was, hoping the iron maiden and the rack were making a comeback in our legal system."

I glanced at him, saw him grinning, and laughed. "Yeah, I get it. I suppose it could have been worse. I just don't know how."

We left the courthouse garage, skirted around the media mob waiting for me to exit the building, and headed home.

"Anything I can do?" Sampson said.

"Not unless you can speed up lab work faster than Bree can."

He looked over at me, puzzled.

"Some saliva tests Anita wanted done. They might help."

"With what?"

"I can't talk about it."

"I understand," he said, but his tone said he didn't, and there was a strained silence between us the rest of the ride.

Sampson pulled over well down the street from the small

crowd of journalists camped outside my house. "You best take the alley home."

"It'd be easier," I said. "Thanks for being a standup guy, John."

He paused, and then nodded and said, "I have a great role model."

He drove away. Knowing Sampson still had my back, I felt okay as I walked down the alley that ran behind my block. Even better, the air smelled like garlic and basil when I went through the back gate and stole through the side door.

Ali and Jannie were on the couch in the great room, watching the NBC evening news with Lester Holt, when I came in.

"Dad!" Ali said, running over and hugging me.

Jannie's eyes avoided mine. She was barefoot but still in her warm-ups, watching the screen. Holt wrapped up a piece on the latest budget impasse in Congress and then turned grim and said, "Thirty-one times."

Behind him, a dark silhouette of a man appeared. He held a pistol. Beneath the image, a caption read POLICE GONE BAD?

Holt said, "The trial of noted detective Alex Cross opened today in Washington, DC, amid what prosecutors are saying is a long-needed discussion in America about police gone bad and gone violent, above the law."

The screen jumped to footage of me and Anita entering the courthouse that morning, with Holt talking in a voice-over. "After opening statements, the prosecution brought in star witness Norman Nixon and almost immediately there were fireworks and harsh accusations, including the stunning news that Detective Cross has fired his weapon at least thirty-one times in the course of duty when the average police officer never fires his gun at all. Before the two killings he's on trial for, Cross's shots have proven fatal nine times."

The screen jumped to a frizzy-haired woman identified as a sociology professor sitting in front of a wall of books. "Thirty-one times?" she said. "He kills nine before these two? I'm sorry, but this is a cop who shoots first and asks questions later."

49

"TURN IT OFF," I SAID.

Jannie didn't move.

"Jannie," Ali said, going over and grabbing the remote.

"Don't," she said. "I want to know how bad it really is."

Ali hit the power button and the screen went dark. Jannie glared at him and then at me before jumping up and leaving the room.

"What's with her?" Ali said.

I gazed after Jannie as she stormed through the kitchen. My grandmother popped up from behind the counter.

"I'll ask later," I said, and then I went into the kitchen, where Nana Mama was finishing dinner preparations.

She patted me on the back. "Hang in there. The truth will out, son. It always does."

"I know," I said, but there was little conviction in it.

Nana Mama motioned me into her arms. It was still a miracle to me how such a tiny old woman could radiate so much positive energy.

"Don't let them get you down," she said, rubbing my back. "When they hear your side of what happened, old Lester Dolt and Chuck Fraud will be singing a different song."

I laughed and looked down at her. "Lester Dolt and Chuck Fraud?"

"That's what I call him and the political reporter guy."

"But Lester Holt is not a dolt."

"And Chuck Todd's not a fraud," Nana Mama said. "But calling them that when all the news is depressing gives me a reason to smile."

I gazed into my grandmother's eyes and saw both confidence and fear.

"You are one complicated old lady," I said, touching her cheek.

"I should hope so," she said, pulling away. "Dinner in fifteen minutes?"

"What's cooking?"

"Chicken roasted in Nana's special herb rub. Go on, wash up. Bree texted she'll be home any minute."

I was about to head up the stairs when Bree came through the front door. There was strain everywhere about her, and she dropped her gaze and hesitated before coming into my arms.

"I'm sorry I wasn't there," Bree said. "It must have been awful."

"Sobering," I said. "Thirty-one times. I had no idea."

Bree lifted her head to look me in the eyes with cold curiosity. "And the nine dead and the eight wounded?"

"I remember each and every one of them," I said. "You can't

forget things like that. Ever. Even when they were righteous shoots."

She studied me, her eyes welling with tears, then hugged me tight.

"Jesus," she said hoarsely. "They want to tear you apart."

"They better pull hard," I said, and I kissed her head.

CHAPTER

50

GRETCHEN LINDEL LAY CURLED UP on her filthy mattress, scratching her head, staring at the plywood walls that imprisoned her, and wondering if her torture would ever end.

Coated in grime, her nightgown in tatters, Gretchen reeked, and her feet were cut and swollen. Her hair was tangled with burrs, leaves, and twigs. She couldn't pick them out, no matter how hard she tried, and she hadn't tried in days, at least since the last time they'd come for her.

How long had that been? Five days ago? Six?

She couldn't tell, and in the end it didn't matter.

I'm here until I'm not, Gretchen thought. *It's like I'm not even me already.*

How bad can the last step be?

The big man in black, the one wearing the tinted paintball visor and carrying the knife, had come for her four times since her kidnapping. Each time it had been dusk when he'd untied her blindfold and she'd found herself in the woods.

There were two or three others there, all dressed similarly, all laughing at her when the big one said, "Run, now. Give yourself a chance, and give the boys a show."

Gretchen played competitive volleyball, and she ran hard the first time, took off, not caring about the stones and sticks that jabbed her bare feet. She'd gotten ahead of them and thought she'd lost them.

Before it turned dark.

Then they were all suddenly around her, yelling in the woods, taunting and calling, "Where are you, blondie? Where are you, uptown girl?"

They had to have been wearing night-vision goggles or something like that, because they'd caught her every time, and every time they'd taken her right to the point where she believed with every cell that they were going to kill her, slit her throat and watch her bleed out, all on-camera, all to their delight.

The first three times they'd hunted her, Gretchen had survived by focusing on her friends and her parents and on how desperately she wanted to see them all again, especially her dad. She shared a special relationship with him, a real friendship as well as respect and love.

It would kill him, she'd thought when she'd wanted to give up and ask them to end it. *It would kill him, and I can't do that to him. To either of them.*

The fourth time they'd hunted Gretchen, the last time they'd hunted her, had been different. They'd barely let her run before catching her. They'd dragged her to a building in the woods. The big one had torn off her panties while the others held her down. They'd—

She'd gone to a far-off place in her mind then, where there

was no hurt, no feelings at all, as if she'd already found death. That feeling of passing, of being already gone from her body, had stayed with her even after they were done, even after they'd thrown her back in her plywood box, even after days without eating.

Someone threw the door's dead bolts.

Gretchen cringed and tried to keep staring at the plywood wall.

"You don't eat, you don't deserve to play the game," the strange electronic voice said. "You don't eat, drink, keep your strength up, you don't deserve to live."

"I don't want to live like this."

"We kind of thought that."

She looked at the big guy in black wearing the GoPro camera and the paintball visor and saw something that cut through her feelings of nothingness, made her retreat.

He wasn't carrying that knife he'd brought the first four times they'd played the game.

This time he carried a coil of rope tied at one end into a hangman's noose.

CHAPTER

51

JUDGE LARCH GAVELED THE COURT to order at precisely eight a.m. She took care of several administrative issues before reminding Norman Nixon he was still under oath when he returned to the witness stand.

"Ms. Marley," Larch said. "Your cross-examination, please."

Anita patted me on the thigh, got up, and said, "Mr. Nixon, of the nine fatal shooting incidents you looked at involving my client, how many were judged wrongful police conduct?"

He shifted uncomfortably. "None. It's a—"

"So you're saying that in each of these cases, Alex Cross was investigated and found to have taken prudent action in accord with police and FBI protocol?"

"I don't know about prudent when you end up with a dead suspect."

"Objection," Anita said.

"Sustained," Judge Larch said. "But rephrase, Ms. Marley."

Anita seemed taken aback for a moment. Then she said,

"Was Dr. Cross found to be in compliance with police and FBI protocols in each of those nine shootings?"

Nixon acted like he had something stuck in his teeth but eventually said, "He was."

"All nine?"

"All nine."

"And in the cases of wounding?"

"Yes, but——"

"A simple yes will do, Mr. Nixon. Since you have had a chance to look at Dr. Cross's record in such detail, would it be fair to say that the criminals involved were dangerous people? Violent people?"

"Doesn't mean they had to die by a police bullet," Nixon said.

"It's a yes-or-no question."

"Yes, they were dangerous."

"Killers?"

"Often."

"Bombers?"

"Their crimes are not the issue here."

"They most certainly are the issue," Anita said. "Dr. Cross has a reputation for going after the worst criminals, taking on the biggest cases, isn't that so?"

"He's well regarded as an investigator."

"Did Dr. Cross put himself in personal danger to solve the cases you looked at?"

"Every cop in America is in danger every day."

"Point taken," Anita said. "But in light of the *kinds* of cases Dr. Cross worked for the FBI and DC Metro, wasn't he bound to come into contact with more violent suspects than the average cop?"

Nixon paused and then said, "Probably a higher incidence of contact with that sort of criminal, but I can't tell you what that is statistically."

"A higher incidence of contact will do," Anita said, and she smiled at the jury as she went back to the defense table. She put on reading glasses and scanned her notes for a moment.

When she was done, she pivoted and looked at the witness. "Just to summarize, Mr. Nixon, in each of the nine fatal cases you looked at, Dr. Cross, because of his job, came into close contact with a hardened criminal, correct?"

He thought about that and then said, "Correct."

"And violence ensued," she said.

"Violence ensued and someone died by Cross's hand."

Anita removed her glasses and cocked her head at him. "In those nine fatal incidents, Mr. Nixon, how many times did Alex Cross shoot first?"

He cleared his throat. "It's more telling to look at escalation, Ms. Marley."

"How many times did Dr. Cross shoot first?"

Nixon looked ready to argue but then said, "Zero."

"Zero?" she said, looking at the jury. "And how many times did Alex Cross shoot first in any of the wounding incidents?"

"Zero."

"Zero," Anita said, looking right at jurors five and eleven. "Not once in Dr. Cross's career has he fired his weapon in anything but self-defense. He deals with the worst of the worst. He tries to avoid conflict, but these people are violent, and he has the right to defend himself, isn't that right, Mr. Nixon?"

"No," Nixon said. "That's not right. Cross seeks conflict. He charges in."

"Sounds to me like a brave cop doing his job."

"Objection," Wills said.

"Sustained," Judge Larch said. "The jury will ignore that."

But of course they couldn't. I could see in jurors five and eleven that Anita's line of questioning had been effective and revealing. To those two, at least, maybe I wasn't the out-of-control cop the prosecution described earlier.

"I have nothing further for this witness, Your Honor," Anita said.

Wills stood and said, "The prosecution calls Kimiko Binx."

CHAPTER

52

KIMIKO BINX RAISED HER RIGHT arm and took the oath. A fit Asian American woman in her late twenties, Binx wore a chic gray pantsuit. Since I'd seen her last, she had grown out her hair and gotten it cut in a geometric style.

She perched in the witness chair and slowly swept her gaze around the courtroom, looking at everyone, it seemed, but me.

"You may proceed, Mr. Wills," Judge Larch said, and she coughed.

The assistant U.S. attorney adjusted his pants, grinned sheepishly at the jury again, and then said, "Ms. Binx, what is it you do exactly?"

"Web design and coding," she said.

"Good at it?"

"Very."

"Well," Wills said, and he smiled at the jury once more. "Do you remember the afternoon and early evening of March the twenty-ninth?"

"Like it was yesterday."

The prosecutor led Binx through her version of events. She reported that she'd found me waiting for her outside her apartment door when she came in from a run, that I'd tracked her through a website dedicated to Gary Soneji that she'd designed, and that I asked her to take me to see her partner in the website, Claude Watkins.

"What's your big interest in Gary Soneji?" Wills asked.

Binx shrugged. "It was a phase, like that woman who wrote the book where she visits all the graves of assassinated presidents? Kind of ghoulish, but interesting at the moment, you know?"

"So you're not obsessed with Gary Soneji?"

"Not anymore. Seeing friends of mine killed for their intellectual interests soured me on it."

"Objection!" Anita said.

"Sustained," Judge Larch said. "The jury will ignore the last statement."

Wills bowed his head, crossed to the jury box. "So you led Dr. Cross to an abandoned factory to see Mr. Watkins, isn't that correct?"

Binx nodded and said that Claude Watkins and some of his friends had been using the old factory as an art studio and living space.

"Did you coerce Dr. Cross in any way to go find Watkins?"

She leaned forward to the mike. "I didn't have to. He wanted to go."

"But you wanted him there as well, correct?"

"Well, Claude did, that's right."

"Why's that?"

"Claude's an artist—visual and performance. He thought it

would be interesting and telling to see what Cross would do if he were confronted with one Soneji after another."

Under further questioning, Binx continued her tale in mostly accurate fashion until she had us moving deeper into the factory and reaching a large rectangular room. At that point, she began to lie through her teeth.

Wills said, "When you went inside, was Claude Watkins at the far end of that long room wearing the Soneji disguise?"

"Yes," Binx said.

"Was Mr. Watkins armed?"

"No."

"No nickel-plated revolver in his hand?"

"No. Claude had his hands open, and he turned his palms to show Cross."

53

I LEANED OVER TO NAOMI, whispered, "That is categorically false."

My niece patted me on the arm. "Don't worry. We'll get our chance."

Wills said, "What happened next?"

"Cross aimed his gun at Claude and told him to drop the gun and get down on the floor."

"Did he?"

"He didn't have a gun, but Cross didn't seem to care. I knew he was going to shoot Claude, so I hit Cross's gun hand. Claude took off and tried to hide."

"What was Dr. Cross's state before you hit him?"

"He was acting weird, creepy."

"In what way?"

"Sweating, looking like he was loving the fact he was aiming down on Claude, you know, like he dug it."

Wills crossed to a blown-up diagram of the factory floor and pointed at the far left end of the rectangle. "Watkins was here before he ran?"

"Yes, in front of that alcove."

"What happened then?"

For the first time, Binx looked over at me. "Cross went crazy."

"Objection!" Anita cried.

"Overruled," Judge Larch said. "Continue."

Binx testified that Virginia Winslow stepped out of the shadows of an alcove in the middle of the far long side of the factory room and that I then shot Soneji's widow without provocation.

"Was Mrs. Winslow armed?" Wills asked.

"No way," Binx said. "She hated guns."

"Tell us why she was part of this performance in the first place."

"Virginia told me that she couldn't get away from Soneji's legacy, so she'd decided to try to make art out of it, a bitter commentary, you know?"

"And Dr. Cross shot her?"

"Right in the chest. I couldn't believe it. I started screaming, but he didn't care. He just kept shooting, Claude, and then Lenny Diggs."

"All of them unarmed?"

"Yes. And after he shot Lenny, he was swinging his pistol around and yelling for more."

"What exactly was Dr. Cross yelling?"

"Like 'Who's next? C'mon, you bastards! I'll kill every single Soneji before I'm done.'"

Wills looked at the jury. "'I'll kill every single Soneji before I'm done.'"

Juror five was shaking his head. Juror eleven was shaking hers.

Wills rubbed his hands together as if he were washing them and said, "Thank you, Ms. Binx, that must have been difficult. Your witness, Ms. Marley."

54

ANITA HAD BEEN SCRIBBLING NOTES on her legal pad. She looked up and said, "Your Honor, the defense asks the Court's leave to delay our cross-examination of Ms. Binx pending an ongoing line of inquiry we are following."

"An ongoing line of inquiry?" Wills asked.

"Right," Anita said.

Judge Larch didn't like that. "How much of a delay are you asking for?"

"I would think tomorrow afternoon would work, Your Honor."

Larch got a sour look on her face, but then seemed to think of something that brightened her mood. She said, "Ms. Binx, you are excused for the day. Ten minutes' recess before Mr. Wills calls his next witness."

The judge banged her gavel, got up fast, and hurried for the door, no doubt dreaming of that first puff.

Larch came back in a much better mood exactly ten minutes

later. She returned to the bench, popped a mint, and said, "Mr. Wills?"

"The prosecution calls Claude Watkins to the stand."

I heard a creak as the double doors to the courtroom swung open. I turned to see a man in a wheelchair being pushed by Gary Soneji's son, Dylan. Claude Watkins was in his late forties with salt-and-pepper hair, a stubble beard, and a buff upper body. A blanket hid his withered legs.

Dylan left him at the bar, and Claude Watkins rolled the chair over in front of the witness stand.

The prosecutor looked at Judge Larch and said, "I'd like to treat the witness as hostile. He has been highly uncooperative."

Larch glanced at the man in the wheelchair, who looked fuming mad.

"You going to answer questions under oath?" she asked.

"Depends on what's asked," Watkins said, not looking at her.

She ordered the bailiff to administer the oath, which he did without enthusiasm.

"How are you, Mr. Watkins?" Wills asked.

Watkins sneered at him. "About as good as you can be when you're confined to a wheelchair and have to use a catheter to take a piss."

"How did you wind up in that chair?"

Watkins's face bunched up in loathing before he pointed at me and said, "He put me in it. Cross. Shot me for no good reason."

"Objection," Anita said.

"Overruled," Judge Larch said. She popped another mint into her mouth.

Wills said, "Can you take us through the events of March twenty-ninth?"

Watkins grudgingly said he'd gotten interested in Soneji and then me by accident. But the more he read about me, the more he was convinced I was "borderline out of control" when it came to the mass murderer.

He testified that he decided to entice me into a situation that could result in an "interesting and revealing piece of performance art." He would lure me to an abandoned factory where he'd confront me with one Soneji after another.

"So *you* could see his reaction?" Wills asked.

"Oh, hell no. I wanted *everyone* in the world to see Cross's reaction."

Beside me, Anita cocked her head to one side.

Wills squinted as if he'd heard something new from the witness and said, "How were you going to do that?"

"By filming it, of course," Watkins said.

"What?" Wills said.

"What?" Naomi whispered.

Anita said, "What the hell is—"

"You had to have found them," Watkins said. "I mean, you had to have searched the factory and found the smartphones with the add-on lenses, right?"

Anita and the prosecutor's assistant both shot to their feet.

Anita said, "Judge, there has been no mention of any such cameras or phones in discovery."

"Because we found no cameras or phones," Wills said.

Watkins looked like he wanted to spit in disgust. "I put them there myself. What is this? A cover-up? I was wondering why you weren't badgering me about them from the get-go. I'm telling you, we got the whole thing from three different angles!"

55

THE COURTROOM ERUPTED. JUDGE LARCH banged her gavel, demanding order. She told the jury to ignore Mr. Watkins's testimony for the time being and ordered both prosecution and defense into chambers along with the U.S. marshals who worked in her courtroom.

"Judge, the government asks that it be given time to find the phones Mr. Watkins claims are in that factory," Wills said when they were all in chambers.

"Judge, there is no way to know if these phones, if there are any, have been put there after the fact as a ploy by Mr. Watkins," Anita said. "Whatever is on them should be excluded."

"That factory has been sealed for months," Wills said.

"But not guarded."

"We don't even know if the phones exist, Ms. Marley," Judge Larch said. She looked at one of her marshals. "Collins, you and Avery, please go talk to Mr. Watkins. Find out where he says he hid these phones, call a forensics team, and go look. If you find them, establish a perfect chain of custody and bring them here."

"Judge, that's the rightful role of the government," Wills said.

"We're seeking swift truth and justice here, Mr. Wills," Larch said. "If the cameras are there and they do show what happened that day, we'll all see it together. At the same time. Here. In my chambers."

The marshals left. The judge ordered that the jury be sequestered and given lunch. We ate down the hall, all of us wondering how the cameras could have been missed, and me worrying about the confidence with which Watkins had revealed them. What would they show?

An hour later, word came that three smartphones with extender lenses had been discovered where Watkins said they'd be: in recesses cut into the factory's support beams, hidden with thin pieces of sheet metal.

An hour after that, Larch's marshal entered her chambers with three evidence bags, each holding an iPhone 6s. They were dusty and their batteries were dead. Between the group of us, we had enough cords to recharge the devices.

One by one, they blinked on. Claude Watkins was asked to provide the security codes for the phones, which he did. They all used his birthday.

U.S. Marshal Avery, a thin woman with an intense bearing, wore gloves to enter the codes. Then she attached the first phone to a laptop computer, and the laptop to a screen on the wall of Judge Larch's chambers.

Fifteen minutes later, as the last of the three videos played, there was dead silence in Judge Larch's chambers. I felt steamrolled and had no doubt I was heading to a federal pen for a long, long time.

"Compelling, Judge," Wills said, triumphantly. "The government wishes to introduce these into evidence immediately."

Anita said, "Your Honor, you cannot allow these videos to be introduced until we've had time to analyze them."

"I'd say the videos speak for themselves," Wills said. "The important parts, anyway. To ignore them would be a travesty of justice, Your Honor."

"Allowing them into evidence without giving us the chance to examine them would be a gross miscarriage of justice, Your Honor," Naomi said.

Judge Larch sat back in her chair, closed her eyes, and puffed on an electronic cigarette.

"Your Honor?" Wills said.

"I'm thinking," Larch said. "You've heard of that, right, Counselor?"

The prosecutor was taken aback but said, "Of course, Your Honor. I've been known to think myself every once in a while."

The judge opened one eye and fixed it on Wills. "I'll allow the videos to be introduced."

"What?" Anita cried. "Judge—"

"Ms. Marley," Larch said curtly. "The prosecution wants the videos introduced. If you can impeach their value and credibility, you'll be free to do so at the appropriate time."

"With all due respect, Your Honor," Anita began, "these will bias the—"

"For a few days, perhaps," Larch said, putting her e-cig on her desk. "If they're fake, you'll know soon enough, won't you? And maybe you'll make Mr. Wills look like a fool for being so impetuous."

"Your Honor?" the prosecutor said, looking as if he'd sniffed something unpleasant.

"I've given you lots of rope, Mr. Wills," she said. "Try not to hang yourself with it."

Wills blinked and said, "Yes, Your Honor."

CHAPTER

56

NANA MAMA SAW THE DEVASTATED look on my face when we returned to the courtroom. She came to the rail.

"You okay, son?"

"It's bad, Nana."

"The truth will out. Just stay fixed on that."

I nodded but felt like the weight of the world was on me when Judge Larch gaveled the court back into session and announced to the jury that she was admitting the videos. She also cautioned them that the government had decided not to analyze the videos before they were shown to the jury.

"In that light, keep an open and skeptical mind," she said. "The defense will have its say about these videos, I'm sure."

As Marshal Avery called up the videos on a screen facing the jury, Nathan Wills was so pleased he jigged a little as he crossed to the witness box. Claude Watkins was again sitting there in his wheelchair.

"Mr. Watkins," Wills said. "Have you seen this footage?"

"No."

"They're all black-and-white, three or four minutes long. We'll watch them simultaneously. You'll see the scene from three angles at once."

The deputy marshal hit a key on her computer. The screen, divided into three frozen feeds, lit up.

On the left, there was an elevated, look-down perspective on the dimly lit rear of the factory where the shooting had occurred. It was a long and largely empty assembly-line space with dark storage alcoves off it on all four sides.

From the perspective, I figured the smartphone had been placed atop an alcove in the middle of the long south wall of the room. On the opposite wall, a mural was lit by soft spotlights.

The middle of the screen showed the feed from a smartphone camera that had been hidden almost directly across the room, above the opposite northern alcove, and aimed back at the floor area, though you could see the bottoms of the three spotlights.

On the far right of the screen, we were afforded a view from above the west alcoves. That angle showed the full length of the factory floor and the spotlight beams bisecting it right to left.

The deputy hit Play and all three feeds started. The people in the courtroom saw me enter the space at the east end of the factory floor, carrying my service weapon and leading Binx along by her handcuffs. Exactly the way I remembered it.

At the west end of the room, Claude Watkins stepped out. He was dressed as Gary Soneji, and in a cracking, hoarse voice he said, "Dr. Cross. I thought you'd never catch up."

"Freeze them," Wills said. "Show feed three only."

A moment later, the screen was filled with Watkins in disguise standing there, palms turned out.

"No gun," Wills said. "Absolutely no gun."

It was the second time I'd seen the image and the second time I got furious thinking that, if I wasn't guilty, I was being railroaded by pros.

"That's fake," I whispered to Naomi. "I don't know how they did it, but that is wrong."

Before my niece could answer, the screen unfroze. The three videos showed me raising my service pistol, aiming at Soneji, and moving toward him, shouting, "Drop your weapon now or I'll shoot!"

Watkins's right hand moved, but there was nothing there, and nothing like the clatter of a gun dropping that I remembered.

"Facedown on the floor!" I shouted. "Hands behind your back!"

Soneji started to follow my orders but then Binx came up from behind and hit my gun hand with both her fists. The blow knocked me off balance, and my gun discharged before a fourth spotlight went on, blinding me.

Then the lights died. I threw myself to the factory floor. I stayed there several moments, peering around, before I lurched to my feet. Gun up, I ran hard to the nearest alcove on the north wall.

I shouted, "I've got backup, Gary. They're surrounding the place!"

Leaving the alcove, I moved west along the north wall of the factory to the next anteroom, the one directly beneath the mural. The camera on the opposite roof caught me from behind and gave the viewer a decent look inside the north alcove, where large rolls of canvas were stacked on tables made of plywood and sawhorses.

From deep in that alcove, Virginia Winslow, disguised as her late husband, stumbled out of the darkness. Stooped and far forward on the balls of her feet, she took two sharp, halting steps before straightening up. The camera zoomed in on us. Her right hand started to rise.

"Stop," Wills said.

The screen froze on Gary Soneji's widow with her palms almost turned up.

"No gun," Wills said.

The videos started again.

Mrs. Winslow opened her mouth and raised her hand. I shot her. She fell and Binx screamed.

It went on like that for several more minutes, with Wills stopping the videos to show Watkins dressed as Soneji and me shooting him, then taking cover behind two old oil drums. The prosecutor froze the video one last time to show Leonard Diggs unarmed and up on the roof above the north alcove just before I shot him. Before the videos mercifully ended, you could hear Binx sobbing.

I blew out some air and looked over at the jury. Juror five had recoiled in his chair and was studying me like I was a war criminal. Juror eleven covered her mouth with a well-manicured hand and shook her head in horror.

CHAPTER

57

THE NEXT AFTERNOON, I COULD see outright suspicion on the normally guarded face of Gayle King, co-anchor of the CBS morning news.

As a sound tech hitched me up to a microphone in our house, King came over and said, "Five minutes, Dr. Cross?"

"I look forward to it, Ms. King."

"Call me Gayle. And we're agreed? No ground rules?"

"Ask away," I said. "I've got nothing to hide."

"Your grandmother?" King said. "She's something."

"She is that."

She smiled, but I saw some pity in it. She walked away.

Bree came over and handed me water. "You're sure about this?"

"Anita and Naomi seem to think it will humanize me. And there's nothing else we can do until Anita's experts have a go at those videos."

At the close of court proceedings, Judge Larch had granted

Anita's motion to adjourn through the following Monday morning to do just that.

"Your FBI friends?" Bree asked, adjusting my tie.

"Mum," I said. "Not surprising. I would think the U.S. Attorney's Office got Rawlins analyzing the videos for the prosecution."

"Well, that would be good, right? He'll find the flaws."

Before I could answer, King said, "Dr. Cross?"

"Good luck," Bree said and kissed me on the cheek.

The journalist gestured to a chair across from her. I mirrored her posture, sitting on the first third of the chair, back straight, chin up, and facing her with my hands relaxed, open, and resting on my thighs. Two small spotlights lit us. King put on reading glasses.

"You're on," one of the camera operators said.

The morning news anchor got right to it and pulled no punches, noting that the introduction of the video in court the day before had to have been a devastating blow.

"Understandably, we weren't happy about it, Gayle," I said. "But we're confident the video's been doctored and we intend to prove it."

"How many times have you drawn and fired your service pistol in the course of your career, Dr. Cross?"

"Norman Nixon says at least thirty-four times, counting this case," I said.

"And killed eleven now in the line of duty?"

"In all those cases, I acted in accord with proper police protocol. Until the shootings I'm on trial for, I had never pulled the trigger first. But I was at close quarters in that situation. When I saw the guns, I gave them one chance to drop them and then fired to save my own life."

"You still maintain the three victims were armed?"

"I do."

King said, "The prosecution paints you as an 'out-of-control' cop."

I controlled my temper, said, "Every time an officer fires his weapon in the course of duty, there's a diligent investigation. I've gone through the process more than most officers, but in every instance I have been cleared."

"What do you say to those who characterize those earlier cleared cases as having been whitewashed?"

58

I LOOKED DIRECTLY IN THE camera with the red light glowing and said, "Read the investigative documents yourself, Gayle. I'll give them to you, and you can post them on the CBS website where anyone can read them. I'm confident that you'll agree with the shooting boards' assessments."

"I like that," King said, and she paused. "Are you above the law, Dr. Cross?"

I had to fight not to let my hands curl into fists and said, "No, Gayle, I am not above the law, and I'm frankly insulted at the characterization. I have spent my life in service to the law as a homicide cop and an FBI agent. I have more than twenty meritorious citations for my actions with both agencies and not one reprimand for excessive violence or any other disciplinary action. Not one."

King's eyes locked on mine. She said, "Did Gary Soneji deserve to die ten years ago?"

I thought about that and said, "Personal opinion?"

"Is there any other kind?"

"Then my opinion is yes."

King's eyes went wide. "Yes?"

"Soneji bombed people with impunity. He kidnapped and tortured others. He used a baby as a human shield while trying to bomb Times Square. I chased him into the New York subway system when he was wearing an explosives vest. He tried to kill me. I did everything I could to make sure the vest did not go off, including killing him. So, yes, if I've ever met someone who deserved to die, it was Gary Soneji."

"Are you obsessed with him?"

"No more than you'll be obsessed with me when you move on to your next story. Look, being a detective is my job, not a crusade or a vendetta. I do my best. I move on."

"'I do my best. I move on.' I like that," she said, and she smiled and took off her glasses. "Virginia Winslow and Leonard Diggs. Did they deserve to die?"

"No," I said. "But they made decisions that led me to make decisions as a police officer that ended their lives. I still don't have a crystal-clear rationale for their actions other than their wanting to frame me."

"In the video, none of your victims are seen carrying guns."

"In person, they were all holding nickel-plated revolvers," I said.

She chewed on one arm of her reading glasses. "And you, what, believe that Claude Watkins's followers somehow erased the images of them?"

"Something like that, yes."

"If you watch that video, you look like the coldest of killers, Dr. Cross."

"Or the biggest of patsies."

King put her glasses back on, referred to her notes. "With all the shootings across the country involving white cops killing black kids, isn't it ironic that there was no real federal involvement in this issue until the U.S. Justice Department put a black cop on trial?"

I felt my expression harden as I said, "I've never really wanted to play that card, but it sure makes you think, doesn't it?"

It went on for another twenty minutes before King finished. When the cameras were off, I stood and let the tech remove the microphone while King spoke with her producer.

She came over afterward, shook my hand a second time, and said, "I apologize for some of the tougher questions. Like you said, it's the job."

"I don't mind tough questions as long as they're unbiased."

"How'd I do?"

"I thought you were fair. How'd I do?"

King held my gaze before saying, "You're either a pathological liar and a killer or you're being framed by real smart folks."

"That how you're going to spin it?"

"No spin, Dr. Cross," King said. "We'll lay out both sides as we go and let the viewers decide."

59

BREE, ANITA, AND NAOMI WERE convinced I'd done myself a great deal of good with the interview. And Nana Mama was still buzzing with the excitement of meeting Oprah's best friend forever, which I thought was kind of sweet and funny.

But as the hours ticked by I grew more anxious. What if Anita's analysts weren't good enough? What if we couldn't prove the video had been doctored?

Around nine that evening, I was feeling claustrophobic. Ali found me pacing around in the kitchen.

"Dad?" he asked. "Can I see those videos everyone's talking about?"

"Why would you want to see things like that?"

He shrugged. "Your attorney Ms. Marley thinks something's wrong with them. I wanted to see if I could see it."

I thought about that for several moments and then said, "I don't think I'd be the best father if I let a nine-year-old see a recording of people dying needlessly."

"Oh," my son said, sounding taken aback. "I just wanted to help."

"I know you did, bud," I said, and I hugged him.

Ali left me looking disappointed, which made me feel even more claustrophobic. I went upstairs and got changed into sweatpants, an old FBI hoodie, and running shoes. I found Bree in the front room watching *The Voice* and said I was going out for a jog.

"You want company?"

"Not this time," I said. "I need to get some things straight or I won't sleep."

Bree gave me an even gaze. "Just for the record, Alex, I think it sucks you're going through this. It guts me."

"It does suck," I said. "But like Nana Mama said, the truth will out."

"I don't want you spending a day in prison before that happens."

"Me neither," I said.

"Don't forget Jannie's racing in the morning."

"I won't be longer than I have to be," I said, then kissed her and went out the door. I ran down the block well out of sight before slowing and hailing a cab.

I got in the back and gave the driver an address. Twenty minutes later I was climbing out into a crowded parking lot in a light industrial area off I-95 not far from Dumfries, Virginia. I'd probably driven by the steel building there several thousand times while I was based at Quantico and never noticed it.

Then again, ten years before there had been no big glittering sign on the side facing the road that said GODDESS!

Throbbing electronic music pulsed from the building. For a moment I thought the two shaved-head bouncers weren't going to let me in because of what I was wearing, but the manager happened by and said, "The FBI is always welcome. More and more of you brave ones every day."

I paid the twenty-five-dollar cover fee and went inside the club, an homage to 1970s disco, with black walls, lots of mirrors, and flashing balls spinning and flickering above the dance floor, which was packed with gyrating gay men in all manner of dress, from tuxes to leather bondage outfits.

As I moved around, I turned down two offers to dance myself before spotting the man I'd come to see. Krazy Kat Rawlins was right in the middle of the mob of sweating dancers, shaking his booty, tossing his red Mohawk around, and waving his tattooed arms overhead as if he were at a revival for some of that old-time religion.

When the song changed, Rawlins came off the dance floor sweating, gasping, grinning, and flirting with several pals before he spotted me. Suddenly, the FBI's top digital analyst wasn't so exhilarated anymore.

"Unless you drive on my side of the highway, what are you doing here?"

"You haven't been returning my calls."

Rawlins patted his Mohawk, gauging its stiffness, before saying, "I don't believe you deserve to talk to me or to Batra anymore."

"Excuse me?"

He squared off, crossing his arms. "I've looked at the videos, Dr. Cross. Metadata's all there and I don't see any evidence that the sections that show the victims' hands have been altered in any way."

The words took a moment to sink in, and then I felt detached from my body. I looked around the dance club as if it were part of some weird dream.

"I saw guns, pistols," I said.

"The data doesn't lie," Rawlins said.

"No, that's not right. I'm telling you, Krazy Kat, that—"

"I can't help you."

I put my hands to my head. "I feel like I'm in some alternate universe, like I'm losing my mind."

He knit his brow. "Then you should go talk to someone, like a therapist, someone who can help you understand what you've done."

"But I didn't—"

"The videos say you did," Rawlins said. "The videos say Winslow and Diggs were unarmed. You killed them in cold blood, not self-defense."

"I saw guns!"

"Then your brain invented the guns so you could deal with what you'd done. You'd gotten off before. You'd do it again."

The FBI tech guru walked away and disappeared into the mass of writhing bodies on the dance floor with me staring dumbly after him.

CHAPTER

60

I HAVE NEVER BEEN A quitter in my entire life, never tried to do anything but face my responsibilities and duties head-on. But sitting in another cab twenty minutes after Rawlins vanished back onto the dance floor at the club, I felt like telling the driver to take me to National Airport or Union Station instead of home.

I wanted to flee, get a new identity, and hide out on a South Sea island, do anything except go home to tell Bree, Nana Mama, and the kids what Rawlins had said. There'd been no guns. I'd been deluded at best, downright evil at worst. In either case, I was going to federal prison, probably for life.

I shut my eyes, trying to remember the entire incident, clearly seeing the gun in Watkins's hand, and in Virginia Winslow's, and Leonard Diggs's. It made me sick to my stomach when I thought of the videos, clearly showing no guns before I shot.

How in God's name was that possible?

I thought back again, trying to remember every instant, and recalled that I'd felt odd, light-headed when Kimiko Binx and I arrived at the factory. Inside the factory, I'd felt…giddy? Why would I have been giddy? There were people with guns trying to kill me and I'd been…elated?

Maybe Rawlins was right. Maybe I did need to see a shrink, or at least someone who might understand what I was going through, someone like…

"Driver," I said. "Change of plans. Take me downtown."

He dropped me on a corner not far from the courthouse. I walked north several blocks to a familiar street with lights blazing in some of the town houses and big dumpsters out in front of the ones that were dark.

There were a few lights on in one of the duplexes, which did and didn't surprise me. Bernie Aaliyah had been fixing up the place.

As I climbed the stairs to the porch and the front door, my mind fled back to the last time I'd been here. I remembered being outside Tess Aaliyah's bedroom door, hearing the gunshot, and jumping back in shock and despair. And poor Bernie Aaliyah pounding on the door, begging the silence for an answer, some hope.

I shook off the memory, hesitated, and then knocked. A few moments later, the dead bolts were thrown and the door opened.

"Dr. Cross?"

"I wonder if I could talk to you."

"I'm doing good since we last spoke," Tess said, and she smiled. "We have another meeting set, don't we?"

"This time it's not about you," I said.

"Oh," she said, and frowned. "Well, then, of course, please come in."

61

I FOLLOWED HER INSIDE, REMARKING to myself how good she looked after only a month off the various interacting drugs that had helped put her behind a locked door with her backup pistol talking about rats, and her father and I outside thinking suicide.

It turned out that the construction projects up and down the street had disturbed the neighborhood's urban rat population and caused a migration. Tess had seen rats twice in her closet upstairs earlier that day. After her fight with her dad, and in a semidelusional state due to the drugs, she decided she'd clean out the closet, put crackers and birdseed in a pile, and then sit back and wait for a shot. It was why she'd insisted on talking quietly. She'd been hunting.

After Tess shot the rat, the ringing in her ears was so loud that for several long, agonizing moments, she didn't hear her father pounding on the door. Then she'd opened the door and looked at us with bloodshot, drug-puzzled eyes, as if she couldn't imagine what we were so upset about.

It had taken several hours to convince Tess to enter a psychiatric facility in Virginia so she could be properly evaluated. But she eventually agreed and spent a week there getting clean and undergoing tests. She'd gone into the psych ward taking a multi-pill cocktail and left on a single drug for depression. The doctors said that in her effort to forget, she was lucky she hadn't done permanent brain damage.

"You want a beer?" Tess said. "Dad left some."

"Water if you've got it," I said.

"Coming up," she said and got me some chilled from the fridge.

I sat in Bernie Aaliyah's favorite chair. Tess gave me my water, curled her feet under her on the couch, and said, "Thank you again for helping me, Alex. You were the only one who saw I was a danger to myself."

"I'm glad you agreed to get help," I said. "Which is why I came to see you."

"Okay?"

"Have you been following my trial?"

She shook her head. "My therapist advised me to go on a no-media diet for a few months."

"That's not a bad idea," I said, but then I brought her up to speed on the latest trial developments, including the video and Rawlins's contention that it had not been doctored.

"But you saw those pistols?"

"Every time I close my eyes, I see them," I said.

"Any chance you imagined them?"

I started to tell her absolutely not but then said, "Part of me doesn't know anymore, Tess, and it's got me scared that I did something heinous and that my mind has somehow erased it and put something else in its place to justify my actions. Does that make sense? Has that ever happened to you?"

Pain flickered on her cheeks before she shook her head. "I remember every detail, the first shots, me returning fire, and then hearing the Phelps's nanny wailing beyond that apartment door. I can't forget a second of it."

"That's how the other part of me feels."

"Then those pistols were there and removed from the videos. You just have to prove it."

My cell phone dinged, alerting me to a text. I pulled it out, saw it was from Bree: Where are you, Alex? I'm worried.

I texted back, Talking to an old friend. On my way.

I looked at Tess and said, "I have to go. Thanks for talking."

"One good deed deserves another."

We both stood and headed toward the door. I opened it and looked back at her before leaving.

"I forgot to ask. How are you keeping busy?"

Tess smiled wistfully and said, "Running twice a day, reading, and trying to learn how to forgive myself without a bunch of drugs in my brain."

CHAPTER

62

AT TEN THE FOLLOWING MORNING, I was in the stands inside the Johns Hopkins University field house with Damon, a sophomore now. We were watching Jannie take her last warm-ups. She'd been quiet on the ride up for the meet, so quiet that I had finally asked her what was going on.

Jannie didn't want to talk at first, but she eventually admitted that she was upset because someone had uploaded the shooting videos to YouTube. Social media was incensed. Terrible comments had been directed at her and at the boys.

That only made the day worse. When I'd told Bree the night before that Rawlins said the videos had not been doctored, I'd seen something in her eyes that I swore I'd never see there. Doubt. Not open suspicion, not a lack of faith, but doubt about the facts of the shootings as I'd described them.

"How are *you* doing, Dad?" Damon asked.

"Let's focus on Jannie," I said. "I'm sick of thinking about everything else."

"How's our girl looking?" Ted McDonald asked, breaking into my thoughts.

I was surprised to see him. "Thought you couldn't make it, Coach."

"My plans changed last night."

"Does Jannie know?" Damon asked.

"She will after the race."

"You mean after you see if she executes your race plan," I said.

"That too," McDonald said. "The field's pretty much the same as last time, including Claire Mason, so we can kind of hit reset today."

"Same tactics you recommended before?"

"A few tweaks based on her recent practice times," he said, and he dug in his pocket for a stopwatch.

Jannie had pulled the inside third lane. Claire Mason, the Maryland state champion and future Stanford athlete, was two wide in the fifth slot.

Whatever frustration and hurt Jannie might have been feeling on the ride to Baltimore appeared to be bottled and corked when the race starter called the young women to their marks. Our girl went to the blocks bouncing, shaking her arms, and rolling her head, all the while staring into the middle distance.

McDonald lowered his binoculars, said, "She's good."

I thought so too. She looked like the old Jannie out there, especially when she smiled after the starter said, "Set."

At the pistol crack, my daughter came out of the blocks well, more smooth power than explosive. Her stride lengthened, her legs found a relaxed cadence, and her arms were driving fluidly by the end of the first straight. She ran the curve cleanly and confidently, no sign of foot pain.

Exiting onto the backstretch, Jannie was exactly where she'd been in the previous race, in fourth, just off the shoulder of the girl in third, with Claire Mason leading by two body widths. But there was no move for the front. Jannie stayed right in her groove through the second curve and back up the near straightaway.

"Nice," her coach said, clicking his stopwatch as she flashed by. "I like that number a whole lot."

Claire Mason tried to run away with it coming out of the third turn, but the three athletes chasing her, including Jannie, reeled the state champion in down the backstretch. They were running in a tight bunch entering the final, far turn.

"Well done," McDonald said, watching through his binoculars. "Now gallop for home, girlie-girl."

Jannie seemed to hear her coach's words in her head because he'd no sooner said them than she found another gear. She passed the girl in third and was right off the shoulder of the athlete in second coming out of the last curve.

I couldn't help it; I started yelling, "C'mon, Jannie!"

Damon shouted, "Show them who's boss, sis!"

My daughter did something then that I hadn't seen since the foot injury. Her gait became more like bounding, and she blew by the girl in second place and bore down on Claire Mason with thirty yards to go. Mason gave a backward glance, saw Jannie coming, and ran in fear. But even sheer terror wouldn't have helped the state champ's cause that day.

With fifteen yards remaining, Jannie caught Mason. She was a full body width ahead at the wire.

63

JANNIE SLOWED, LAUGHED, AND THREW her arms up to the sky. Damon cheered. I whooped and hollered and felt better than I had in days. Poor Claire Mason looked shell-shocked; she was a senior heading to a top track program, and she'd been bested by a junior just back from a long time off for a foot injury.

McDonald clapped when Jannie came up a few moments later.

"That is *exactly* how you do it," he said, giving her a high five. "The win's nice. So is beating Mason. But I'm prouder of you for being a disciplined and smart athlete."

Beaming, Jannie said, "It worked staying just off them. I felt like I had a lot in the tank when it counted."

"Sometimes I do know what I'm talking about," McDonald said, and he winked at her. "Enjoy the moment. I'll talk to you Monday."

"Leaving already?" Damon asked.

"Noon flight to Dallas," he said, and he looked to Jannie. "Ice bath ASAP."

Jannie groaned. "I hate ice baths."

"But she'll do it," I said.

After we'd left Damon to his studies, Jannie was bubbling with excitement as she got into the car and for half the way home. Then she checked her cell phone and got quiet again.

"They giving you a hard time?"

For several moments Jannie did not reply, but then she said, "They're idiots, Dad. They don't know you like I know you, so I think it's time I do some serious de-friending and maybe take a week or two vacation from all social media, even Snapchat and Instagram."

"Two weeks? I read somewhere that it's virtually impossible for teenage girls to get off their smartphones."

"Alert Mark Zuckerberg. I'm going to be the first."

I laughed. "Good for you."

"I'm sorry for the way I've been acting. I guess I could only see what the trial was doing to *my* life."

"And I'm sorry you've had to suffer for my actions. It's not fair to you or to your brothers."

We drove on in silence for a while. "Dad?"

I looked over and saw tears dripping down her cheeks.

"What's the matter, sweetie?"

"I love you, Dad, and I believe in you, but I'm also really scared for you."

A big ball of emotion surged in my throat. "I love you too, Jannie, and don't be scared for me. We're going to be all right."

But the closer we got to DC and home, the less I believed it.

ALI CROSS HEARD JANNIE COME through the front door, and the excitement in her voice and then in Nana Mama's, but it wasn't enough to get him up from the desk in his father's attic office or make him take his eyes off the computer screen showing a YouTube video of his father shooting three people.

Ali had heard about the videos on Facebook and had watched them nearly twenty times by then. The first playing had been the most difficult. He'd jerked back and shut them off when his dad pulled the trigger, killing Virginia Winslow. It reminded him so much of seeing his debate teacher shot during the kidnapping of Gretchen Lindel that he almost got sick.

Deciding not to finish the tape, he almost shut down the browser. But then he remembered Ms. Marley, his dad's attorney, quoted in the *Washington Post* the day before, saying that there was something wrong with the videos, that they had been altered somehow. And he saw the comments people had posted on YouTube, most of them saying that Alex Cross was guilty as hell and deserved to spend life in prison or worse.

Ali had fought off the urge to cry reading the posts and forced himself to play the videos to the end, and then again and again, freezing the screen whenever one of the victims' hands was visible.

No gun. No gun. No gun.

But his dad said they'd all had guns, so he'd watched the videos over and over and over again. It wasn't until the fifteenth or sixteenth time that Ali noticed that the lighting seemed to change in the moments before each of the victims appeared, going dimmer but not dark enough that you couldn't see them and then brightening so you could see their empty hands just before the shot.

Ali had looked at those parts of the videos in detail at least three times and could not figure out what the change in lighting meant. He reached for the computer mouse and was about to play the videos yet again when he heard someone climbing the stairs.

Heart pounding, Ali clicked off the browser, revealing a Microsoft Word file that he pretended to be scanning when his dad came in.

"Nana Mama says you've been up here all morning," he said.

"I have a paper due on Monday," Ali said, still not looking up.

"Really? What's your topic?"

"Magic," he said, lifting his head. "Like Harry Houdini magic."

"The best there ever was," his dad said. "How's it going?"

The truth was Ali had finished writing the paper two days before, but he said, "Pretty good. I should be done on time if I work hard."

"Good for you," his dad said, looking around at the stacks of boxes that crowded the little office. "I've got to do something about this. I can't move in here half the time."

"Bree said it's evidence stuff and not to touch it."

"Too much evidence stuff," his dad said, distracted. "Don't stay up here all day. Go ride your bike at some point, or maybe we can go shoot a few hoops."

"That'd be good," Ali said, and he smiled. "Why was Jannie so happy?"

"She won her race, beat the strongest girl in Maryland."

"Wow," Ali said. "And no foot pain?"

"None," his dad said and turned to leave.

"Dad?" Ali called after him. "Do you think real magic exists? That there are people who can make things appear and disappear for real?"

"No," he said. "It's all deception, sleight of hand, smoke, light, and mirrors."

Ali nodded. "I think so too."

"You want lunch?"

"I'll come down in a bit," Ali promised. He watched his dad duck his head going out the door and listened to him drop to the second floor, then the first.

Ali felt a moment of guilt before launching the Internet browser again. He didn't like lying to his father or directly disobeying him, but someone had to figure out what was wrong with the videos.

He hit Play again and decided not to fast-forward, to watch them all from the beginning. He focused on the middle camera, the north one, looking back across the width of the factory floor with the bottoms of the three spotlights on the roof of the southern alcoves visible. Ali froze the screen and zoomed in.

He'd hoped to see some shadow there behind the spotlights, the suggestion of a silhouette, but he saw none. He hit Play again and noticed a tiny blue pinpoint light flash. And then it was gone.

It took Ali three attempts to freeze the middle video feed on that tiny blue light. He zoomed in on it but couldn't tell what the light was attached to. Frustrated, he hit Play again. He focused on the third feed, the one showing the length of the factory room, with the spotlights aimed toward the mural.

He zoomed in on the spotlights, but saw no one behind them.

Who was running the lights? And where was that blue pinpoint? Try as he might, he couldn't spot it.

"Ali!" Nana Mama yelled up the stairs. "I've got your bacon, lettuce, and tomato down here waiting."

"Coming, Nana," he cried. He cleared the browser's history to cover his tracks, then shut down the web page.

Ali got up and headed toward the stairs, only vaguely aware of the stacks of evidence boxes he passed. Indeed, he was thinking so intently about that pinpoint blue light that he barely noticed that the box on the filing cabinet closest to the door was labeled AUTOPSIES.

CHAPTER

65

WE WERE FINISHING UP LUNCH when I heard a knock at our side door.

"Who's that now?" Nana Mama grumbled. "A damn reporter again?"

"If it is, I'm calling a real cop," I said, grinning and tousling Ali's hair because he seemed lost in thought.

I put my dishes on the counter, crossed to the side door, and opened it. A distressed Alden Lindel stood there.

"Mr. Lindel?" I said, stepping out and closing the door.

"I'm sorry, Dr. Cross," the father of the kidnapped girl from Ali's school said. "I know you've got your own issues, but I didn't know where else to turn."

I took a deep breath and then gestured to the basement door.

In my office, Lindel reached into his jacket pocket and came out with another flash drive in a baggie. "This time they hanged Gretchen."

He dropped into the chair, hid his face in his hands, and sobbed. "God damn it, they hung my daughter, or made it look that way, and they're selling tickets to the show on the Internet."

I flashed on Jannie and felt sick to my stomach. I walked over, put my hand on Lindel's shoulder, and said, "I can't imagine what you're going through."

He looked up at me with bloodshot eyes. "My wife and I barely talk. I can't work. My boss has threatened to fire me. Some days Gretchen's all I think about. And then, just for a while, she slips my mind. I get a little rest, and then something like this shows up in the mailbox. What do they want, Dr. Cross? Why are they doing this?"

"I don't know," I said. "But you need to take the drive straight to the FBI. I've been cut out of the loop because of my trial."

He continued to look at me, his face wretched. "You can't help me?"

"I want to," I said, sitting down across from him and leaning forward, my elbows on my knees, hands clasped. "Mr. Lindel, I want to help find your daughter and the other missing women in the worst way. I really do. But the ugly truth is, given my situation, I'm afraid I'd be more of a hindrance than a help to you. I hope you understand, sir. I'm not much good to you at the moment."

He didn't understand, not really. He got up, looking abandoned.

"You were our last chance," Lindel said, defeated. "But I wish you luck in your trial."

Feeling helpless, I shook his hand. "Don't give up. They're keeping Gretchen alive, which means there is hope you'll see her again. But the FBI can't find her if you're not turning over things like this flash drive."

He nodded. "I'll take it straight to their office."

When Lindel left, I went back into my office and collapsed on the couch. I felt bad, but what choice did I have? I couldn't have gotten Rawlins or Batra to expedite an analysis of the flash. They thought I was a killer.

My cell phone rang. It was Anita Marley.

"Alex," she said. "I've got bad news. Judge Larch is in the hospital. Possible stroke."

"What?" I said, shocked. "When?"

"She was taken to GW last night," Marley said. "They got drugs into her fast, so they're hopeful, and they're running more tests."

I shook my head, seeing little Judge Larch striding up onto the bench in a way that made her seem ten feet tall, larger than life. A stroke?

I said, "What if she can't go on?"

Anita sighed. "It will be a mistrial."

I shut my eyes. "And months before any kind of verdict."

"Let's wait to hear the diagnosis."

"I've got some bad news too," I said. "The videos weren't monkeyed with. At least, according to the metadata."

There was a pause. "And how do you know that?"

"A well-placed source in the FBI told me last night."

When Anita spoke again, she was irritated. "And you didn't think it smart to alert me or Naomi? We've lost twelve, maybe fifteen hours of—"

"The news was pretty devastating. I guess I wasn't thinking straight."

She sighed and said, "Well, I'm trying. My people are still working on those videos despite what the FBI tells you. And I do have a bit of good news. The saliva tests are done. I've put in a call to an old chemist friend in San Francisco just to make sure I'm interpreting the results correctly, but let's just say they're interesting."

"Can they clear me?"

"Given our inability to impeach the videos, no, it's not enough. But if I'm right, with luck, we'll be able to muddy the prosecution's waters a bit, show there were mitigating circumstances."

I started kneading my forehead and said, "Mitigating circumstances? Sounds to me as if I should be getting my affairs in order."

There was a long pause before Anita said, "Always better to be prepared."

CHAPTER

66

THE FOLLOWING TWENTY-FOUR HOURS were some of the lowest of my life. When Bree came home, I took her for a walk and told her what Anita had said. We held each other for the longest time.

"I can't believe this is happening," Bree said.

"Makes me wonder what I did to deserve this."

"No self-pity. What do we do?"

"No self-pity, and we move to protect you, Nana, and the kids," I said. "I can't have you all being punished for something you didn't do."

The next morning, after church, we went down to my basement office, shut the door, and made a list of things that would have to be done if I was convicted. Transfer my personal bank account to Bree. Find a trustee to step in to oversee my grandmother's philanthropic foundation. Transfer sole medical authority for Jannie and Ali to Bree. Transfer authority on the kids' college funds to her. Ask Nana Mama if she still wanted me as the executor of her living will. Make Bree my executor should I die in prison.

"I feel like we're getting ready for a funeral," Bree said.

There was a knock on my office door.

"Dad?" Jannie said.

"We're busy, sweetheart," I said.

"There's someone here to see you."

I closed my eyes. *When did people stop believing in Sundays?*

"Tell them to come back tomorrow."

Nana Mama said, "I think you'll want to come out."

Throwing up my hands in surrender, I went over, opened the door, and found Sampson and my father, Peter Drummond, a big, robust black man in his late sixties, standing there in the hall. Drummond had a face almost devoid of expression due to nerve damage associated with a large burn scar that began beneath his right eye and spread down much of his cheek to his jaw.

"Dad?" I said.

"I came to provide some moral support," Drummond said and he gave me a hug and a clap on the back. "John picked me up at National."

"It was supposed to be a surprise," Nana Mama said.

"It is a surprise," I said. "It's…good. Is Alicia here too?"

"Indisposed, but sends her prayers," Drummond said.

"Let's go upstairs," Nana Mama said. "I'll make a big breakfast."

Afterward, my dad, Bree, Sampson, and I took a walk. My father asked a lot of questions. Drummond knew as much about murder as we did and more about enduring tough times than we could imagine. He'd worked sheriff's homicide in Palm Beach County, Florida, for thirty-two years. Before that he'd served in the first Gulf War, where he was caught in an oil-well explosion that burned his face.

After we'd walked several miles and I'd brought him up to speed on everything, he said, "I know your case looks bleak, son, but you can't lose hope. I'm living proof of that. I lost hope of ever seeing you or Nana or your children, and then there you were down in my neck of the woods, looking for Reverend Maya. Miracles happen every day."

"From your lips to God's ears," Sampson said, and he checked the time. "I've got to go. Promised Billie I'd watch the Redskins game with her."

"Any progress with the blondes?" I asked. "Anything from that latest video of Gretchen Lindel? The one showing her hanged?"

Sampson glanced at Bree and then shook his head. "I haven't heard about that one. But on my end, it feels like I'm banging my head against a brick wall."

"And the new partner?"

"She's the brick wall."

"John," Bree said, but she couldn't hide a smile. "It's not that bad."

"If you say so, Chief," he said. Then he gave us a salute and walked away.

CHAPTER

67

AT FOUR THIRTY THE NEXT afternoon, a Monday, there was a knock at the basement door. Closing my laptop, I got up, happy for the new client and grateful to have something beyond my own fate to think about.

I opened the door to find a tall and very attractive woman in her early thirties. Her hair was long, luxurious, and black, her skin mocha and flawless, and her exotic chocolate eyes were wide and turned up at the outer corners. She wore a tight black skirt, stiletto heels, a chic white blouse, and a simple strand of pearls beneath a black leather jacket. Lots of other jewelry. No wedding ring.

"Ms. Cassidy?"

Annie Cassidy smiled weakly, adjusted the cuff of her jacket, and said, "It's so good of you to see me on such short notice, Dr. Cross."

"Any friend of Father Fiore is always welcome," I said. "Please come in."

I stood aside, and she looked at me uncertainly before coming down the stairs. As she passed, she glanced up shyly before continuing on into my office, leaving the faintest smell of her perfume.

After I closed the door, I found her on my couch, fiddling with her iPhone.

"Just making sure no bells," Cassidy said.

"I appreciate it," I said, taking a seat across from her.

She set the phone facedown on the table beside her and then took a big breath and blew it out. "I'm sorry. I've never done anything like this before."

"Just so you know: There are no judgments here. Ever. And nothing you say will ever leave this room."

"Okay. Don't I have to fill out forms or whatever?"

"You'll do it electronically. I'll give you the information after we decide if we can work together."

Cassidy thought about that, said, "Fair enough."

"So," I said, picking up a notepad and a pen. "How can I help?"

She hesitated, squinted, said, "Are you a sleepwalker, Dr. Cross?"

"Is that what you're having trouble with? If so, I can refer you to an excellent sleep specialist."

Cassidy made a show of crossing her legs. "I'm not a sleepwalker myself, but I'm wondering if you are so I can understand you before I try to explain."

It seemed like an odd and convoluted reason for the request, but I said, "I don't think I have sleepwalked since I was a child."

"Or since you were married," she said, her head tilted in deference.

"I'm afraid I'm not following."

"Of course not," Cassidy said, and she smiled. "Sleepwalker."

As I readjusted my position in my chair, I was thinking that I might have someone mentally unstable on my hands.

She straightened her legs and then crossed them the other way. "To be plain: I'm an addict, Dr. Cross, and I need your help."

"Opioids?" I said with a sigh. "If so, there are better—"

"No, not opioids."

"What then?"

"How does that old Robert Palmer song go?" Cassidy asked, smiled, and then sang quietly, "'Might as well face it, you're addicted to love.'"

Her happiness vanished. "That's the long and short of what's wrong with me, Dr. Cross. I'm a straight-up, strung-out, love junkie if ever there was one."

CHAPTER

68

I'D HEARD AND ENCOUNTERED PATHOLOGICAL love stories before, especially when unrequited desire and obsession were motives for murder. But in the hour that followed, Annie Cassidy gave me a crash course in the little-studied, rarely discussed world of love junkies and so-called sleepwalkers like me.

Cassidy told me she was like most of the love junkies she knew in that, as a little girl, she'd bought hook, line, and tiara into the myth of the fairy-tale princess. Cassidy's mother dressed her up as a princess when she was young. She entered Cassidy in beauty pageants. And every night before bed, she read her daughter fairy tales where Prince Charming always appeared to scoop the princess out of her poor Cinderella life and ride her into the happily ever after on the back of his valiant white steed.

As I listened, I realized this story was a variation of the princess story the computer geek at Catholic University had told me as a way of explaining the minds of blond women, but I kept my mouth shut and kept an open mind.

"All my life, I dreamed of happily ever after," Cassidy said wistfully as she sat back on the couch. "When Kevin appeared in my life, senior year at NYU, I was sure he was my Prince Charming. I'd never felt like that with anyone before. Breathless. Sick when we were apart. And when we were together, I could hold his hand, feel his love coursing through me, and tell him every dark secret in my heart. Is that what falling in love was like for you, Dr. Cross?"

I thought of Bree and me in our early days, how smitten I'd been by her, breathless and tongue-tied after our first kiss, and how euphoric we were to be together after we'd been apart.

"Yes," I said. "We couldn't get enough of each other."

"Roughly two years of that, right? Like there's no one else in the world who matters?"

I smiled. "Yes."

"That's because when you fall in love, there's a chemical cocktail mixing in your brain. First it's norepinephrine, and then the serotonins kick in, give you wild energy. It's like bathing your brain in cocaine."

"I think that's right," I said.

"You would do almost anything for that feeling once you have it. You might do crazy things that no sane person would do. Like abdicate a throne. Or walk away from your family, your life, just to be with your new love."

Cassidy said she and Kevin fell into that kind of passionate love. They married after college and were still living the romance two years later.

Their third year together, however, Kevin began working longer hours, and when he was home, he was too tired to do much beyond sit in front of the television with his computer in his lap. He gained weight. He lost interest in her.

She grew more frustrated, in part because, while the chemicals of falling in love carry with them the rush of amphetamines, the chemicals of long-term love are more like a gentle opioid calming the brain, sedating it, in a sense.

"In retrospect, there was that, for sure," Cassidy said. "I felt groggy all the time, like a sleepwalker. Even through the haze, I could see that I'd screwed up. I realized I hadn't married the Prince Charming in my fairy tale. I'd married the frog."

That crushed Cassidy. She felt like she'd settled for less than the perfect love and the beautiful life she'd been promised. Shortly afterward, she met Chet, a man who came to work at her real estate firm. Chet was handsome and funny. They flirted. He listened to her. The chemicals of new love trickled in her brain.

"I came awake, alive again," Cassidy said. "But I did the right thing."

She said that many women raised in the traditions of the princess myth will ask for a separation from the frog, hinting that they might be willing to recommit at a later date. They string the frog out for years, punishing him with hopes of reconciliation dashed, unwarranted restraining orders, and false charges of abuse and neglect.

"It's all done out of spite," she said. "They feel cheated. The fairy tale is not true, so they take their rage out on the husband while getting some love chemicals on the side.

"But I absolutely did not do that. I did not play torture-the-frog just because Kevin was not Prince C. He could have easily turned out to be an ogre, am I right? The point is that as soon as I had a commitment from Chet, I told Kevin to his face that I had to be free to love and that I wanted a divorce."

Cassidy moved in with Chet until the chemical attraction

wore off, about two years later. Chet's place in her heart was soon occupied by Steven. Twenty-six months later, she met Carlos, a deep sleepwalker, who was ten years into his marriage.

"I woke Carlos up," Cassidy said, and she chuckled. "In a big way."

I glanced at the clock. "Our hour's almost up, but I have a quick question."

Cassidy said, "Okay."

"What do you want out of our sessions? If we go on, I mean."

She sighed, studied the ceiling, and said, "I've been eighteen months with Carlos. He's a stand-up guy. He divorced his wife for me, and I really do love him. Not only that, I genuinely like him. He's my best friend ever. But I know what's coming in six months, a year at the outside, and I...I guess I want to learn how to be a sleepwalker and stay with someone forever."

I smiled. "That's a good goal."

"Something we can talk about next time?"

"Sounds like a plan."

Cassidy took her iPhone off the table and got up. "Thank you, Dr. Cross."

"You're more than welcome. I'll need an e-mail address to send my forms."

"Oh," she said, her brow knitting. "I had a computer virus over the weekend and I'm between e-mails at the moment. I'm opening a new account on Gmail tonight. Can I ping you with it?"

"That works."

"Thank you for understanding all this."

"It's what I do."

"And you do it well," she said. She smiled uncertainly and left.

I stood there a few moments, wondering if Bree and I were sleepwalkers, then deciding that if we were, I was more than happy in my semiconscious state of marital bliss.

Remembering I had to take some leaves I'd raked and bagged out front for pickup, I went outside. The light was fading. Drizzle fell. I got the leaf bags, carried them around the house, and put them on the sidewalk.

I happened to look down the block and saw Cassidy getting into a black Nissan Pathfinder. Wondering if her Carlos might be driving, I walked a few yards that way and was in deep shadow near a retaining wall when the Pathfinder came closer, headlights off.

I could see the silhouette of Cassidy sitting sideways, facing the driver, who was just a dark shape until the Pathfinder crossed beneath a street lamp. For a second his face was clearly visible through the windshield.

Recognition stopped me cold. I was confused.

What was Annie Cassidy doing with Alden Lindel?

69

GRETCHEN LINDEL'S FATHER USED TO tell her that the brain could be the strongest part of the body, or the most fragile.

"It's your choice, Gretch," he'd said not long before she'd been taken captive in the twisted world of sickos.

Lying on her filthy mattress in her plywood cell, holding her left leg so it wouldn't be irritated any further by the manacle around her ankle, the seventeen-year-old was doing everything she could to keep her mind strong.

I am going to get out of here, Gretchen kept telling herself. *I just have to survive long enough to get the chance. I'm going to be like Dad. Nothing they've done hurts me in any way. It makes me stronger. This only makes me stronger.*

But it had been several days since they'd come for her. Hour upon hour of silence created all sorts of dark voices in her mind.

Doubt crept up on Gretchen and whispered that she'd die there in the box. Fear wormed its way into her stomach and said they'd take her again before that happened. Self-pity wrapped her head and heart, told her she was defeated.

But time and time again, whenever Gretchen realized the voices of despair were taking control of her thoughts, she'd think of her father and everything he'd endured, and she'd take heart.

I will survive. They can't hurt me. This will only make me—

The dead bolts turned. She closed her eyes, not knowing if this was a meal or another of their twisted games. If it was a game, she was done crying. She was done being scared. They seemed to feed on her fright, and as the door swung open she vowed to give them none.

The big one in black came in carrying a semiautomatic AR rifle. Her father had one just like it.

"It's time, Gretchen," he said from behind the paintball mask. "We're all but done here. Cleanup time now."

Gretchen said nothing, just stared through him as if he didn't matter anymore, as if nothing mattered anymore.

Be like Dad, she thought as he went to work on her ankle manacle.

For God's sake, be like Dad.

70

HAD THAT BEEN GRETCHEN LINDEL'S father driving the Pathfinder?

I kept trying to convince myself I was wrong, but each time I closed my eyes, I saw Alden Lindel clearly. But why? And how?

When Annie Cassidy called to set up the appointment, she'd said that Father Fiore had referred her, hadn't she? Well, now that I thought about it, she hadn't actually used his name. She'd said she'd gotten my number from "a mutual friend, a priest with challenging problems."

And Lindel? He'd contacted me directly. No reference that I remembered.

What were the odds of two people who knew each other coming to my office and never mentioning it to me?

I thought about Gretchen Lindel's mother, Eliza, and how distraught she'd been in the days after her daughter's kidnapping. Was Annie Cassidy the reason she and her husband separated? Had she used fake names for her lovers? Was Alden Lindel actually Carlos?

I went inside, told my grandmother I was going out, and got the car keys.

By the time I drove into a residential neighborhood west of the Cabin John Parkway, it was pitch-dark and the rain had stopped. I found the address I was looking for and parked the car across the street from a brick-faced Colonial with a big flower bed gone dormant, a crushed-gravel driveway, and a bronze Volvo station wagon. Lights gleamed in the narrow windows that flanked the front door.

I climbed out, smelled wet leaves, and started toward the house, wondering about the reception I'd get, a lone man at night unannounced. My cell phone buzzed. I ignored it, climbed the stoop, and rang the bell.

A dog started barking. A small Jack Russell terrier was soon bouncing and barking an alarm on the other side of the lower right window.

"Tinker!" a woman said. "Get back, girl!"

The dog kept barking and then yelped in protest when the woman grabbed her and held her in her arms. She peered blearily out the window at me. Despite the exhaustion and despair that seemed to hang off her like rags, I recognized her.

"Mrs. Lindel?" I said. "Eliza?"

The terrier in her arms showed her teeth.

She said, "If you're a reporter, please go away, you're not helping the situation. No one's helping the situation here."

"I'm not a reporter," I said. "My name is Alex Cross. I'm a…my son Ali goes to school at Latin with Gretchen."

Eliza studied me a long moment before opening the door. The dog growled like a little demon.

"Hush, now," Eliza said, and the dog stilled but kept a close eye on me.

The missing girl's mother was in her mid-thirties but looked older in baggy sweatpants, Birkenstock sandals, and a George Mason University tee. Her hair was in disarray and graying at the roots. Her eyes were bloodshot, rheumy.

"Alex Cross," she said. "You're that cop on trial for murder."

"Innocent as charged."

"I read you've killed eleven people."

"In the course of duty I have, that's true."

"I also read you've found kidnapped girls before."

"That's also true. Including my niece, who today is part of my defense team. Life *can* go on after an abduction, Mrs. Lindel."

"That why you're here?"

"In part. Can I come in?"

She hesitated, then stuck her face in her dog's face. "You be good now, Tinker, hear?"

Tinker licked her cheek. Eliza set the dog down. The Jack Russell eyed me when Eliza stood aside and I entered. I smelled gin and cigarettes as I walked past her into a center hall lined with hooks where pictures had once hung.

"Is there somewhere we can sit and talk?" I asked.

"The kitchen. Straight ahead."

She followed me down the hallway through an open doorway into a dingy white kitchen where dirty dishes were piled high in the sink, newspapers and unopened mail covered the table, and prescription bottles took up two entire shelves of a bookcase. I caught a whiff of something antiseptic and thought I heard muffled voices.

"How are you holding up?" I said.

Eliza pushed back a strand of hair. "How does it look like I'm holding up?"

"I can't help asking—the pictures in the hall?"

She stared at me. Her lower lip quivered. "I couldn't take looking at Gretchen anymore. She was ripping me up every time I walked through there."

"The stress must feel unbearable."

"You don't know the half of it."

"Your husband?"

She stiffened. "Alden? Alden's Alden. A trouper. Never gives up hope. Never says die."

"I'm a clinical psychologist by training. I don't know if he's told you, but he's been seeing me for therapy."

She crossed her arms and studied me skeptically. "No, he didn't say anything."

"Two sessions."

"Really? You'd think he would have told me. Why don't we go ask him why he didn't?"

My pulse quickened. "He's here? I just saw him heading toward Capitol Hill. He looked like he was out for a night on the town. With another woman."

"Another woman?" She laughed sarcastically. "I bet he smelled of cheap perfume, didn't he?"

"I didn't get close enough."

"Well, you can now," she said, gesturing at a door at the far end of the kitchen. "Alden's right through there, watching *Game of Thrones.* Let's go talk to him. Get things out in the open."

"Let's do that," I said. I crossed the kitchen and went through the door.

71

A WAVE OF ANTISEPTIC SMELLS hit me as I stepped down into a space set up as a hospital room.

To my right, shelves bulged with medical equipment, supplies, and clean linens. To my immediate left there was a tall green oxygen tank with a hose that ran over to a hospital bed with its back raised.

Beyond the tank, an array of electronic monitors cheeped and beeped over the sounds coming from a speaker system linked to the big screen mounted on the opposite wall. According to a tag in the lower right corner of the screen, season 3, episode 4, of *Game of Thrones* was showing.

I took a few more steps into the room and saw a man in the bed. He reminded me of the physicist Stephen Hawking, gaunt, bent, and curled up by disease. Breathing oxygen through a nasal cannula, he lay on his right side, wore glasses, and watched the screen intently, seeming to have no idea we were there.

"That's not the Alden Lindel who came to see me," I said.

"I didn't think so," Eliza said.

"I don't know why I didn't check."

"Why would you? We're private about Al's challenges because that's the way he wants it. How could you have known he has end-stage ALS?"

"I suppose," I said, and I felt baffled until I realized that the man who'd posed as Alden Lindel brought me the flash drives that showed the mock executions of Gretchen Lindel.

No one had sent those drives to him. He was part of Killing-blondechicks4fun. And so was the love junkie.

Tinker darted by us and jumped up on the bed, wagging her tail.

"E-liza," an electronic voice said.

She smiled at me before going to his side. "Right here, Al."

"N-ext?"

"You're not even through that one yet, and the next is in the queue," she said with a glance at me. "He loves this show."

"S-mart dwarf," he said. "B-oobs."

"Yes, Tyrion and lots of boobs," she said matter-of-factly. "I'd like you to meet someone, Al. He's trying to find Gretchen for us."

I came over to her husband's bedside. Laboring for breath, the real father of the missing blond girl rolled his eyes up to me.

"I'm Alex Cross, sir," I said.

He had a digital tablet next to him on the mattress. He rolled his eyes down and blinked eleven or twelve times, maybe more.

"I know you," the tablet said a few seconds later.

"Wow," I said. "How does that work?"

Eliza said, "The tablet's built with three camera lenses that triangulate to pick up where he's looking on the screen, which shows a keyboard layout. He looks at a letter on the keyboard and blinks. When he blinks twice, he's done with the word. Blinks three times and the voice comes on."

"That's amazing."

"I think so."

The tablet voice said, "B-lows, you ask me."

Lindel was peering at me again, and I nodded in sympathy.

He looked at the tablet. A few seconds later, the voice said, "Where's my Gretch?"

Thinking about the fake Alden Lindel and Annie Cassidy coming to my office, I said, "She could be closer than we think. Within driving distance."

The missing girl's father looked down at the tablet. His synthesized voice said, "Can't even cry for her."

Eliza's hand shot to her lips. "It's true. His tear ducts are shutting down. We have to put drops in every two hours."

Her husband rolled his attention to the tablet for the longest time yet before the voice said, "My time is near, Cross. My last wish is to see my Gretch again. One last time."

He peered up at me. Even though his body and face were virtually frozen, I could see the desperate hope in his eyes.

"I'll do my best, Al," I said. "Just hang on."

I gave Eliza Lindel my cell phone number, said good-bye to her and her husband, and left the house feeling humbled.

The day before, with the weight of the evidence in my murder trial so stacked against me, I'd been thinking that life was treating me pretty damn unfairly. But here the real Alden Lindel's life was being squeezed from him by a disease that was killing him one paralyzed muscle at a time. And there was his courageous wife, caring for him and worried sick about their missing daughter.

All in all, I had nothing to bitch about.

I got in the car thanking God and the universe for the blessings in my life: my wife, my family, my home, my health, my friends, my—

My cell phone rang. It was Anita Marley.

"Judge Larch had a transient ischemic attack," she said. "No stroke."

"Hey, that's good news."

"It is," she said. "I like Judge Larch. A lot. Her clerk's saying we're back in session the day after tomorrow."

"Even better."

"You still sticking with your story about the guns?"

"Yes. I'm telling you I saw them."

"My analysts agree with the FBI. There's no evidence of doctoring. But we'll try to raise some reasonable doubt based on the fact that the phones were supposedly in the factory for months."

I wasn't convinced it would do any good. Later, as I was turning onto Fifth, my phone rang again.

Sampson said, "Are you busy tomorrow?"

"No trial until Wednesday."

"Tell Bree I'm taking you fishing in Pennsylvania to get your mind off things. I'll pick you up at five."

72

IN THE CHILL GRAY LIGHT of an autumn dawn, I watched fog swirling around the trunks and through the branches of leafless oak trees. Clusters of acorns still clung to some, but many more littered the forest floor. It was quiet but for the distant sound of a creek and the irregular patter of oak mast falling.

"Alex?" Sampson said behind me. "I got it to work finally."

I turned to find him looking at an iPad on the hood of his Grand Cherokee. Still clutching my second big cup of fast-food coffee, I walked over and looked at the iPad, which had a satellite connection.

Sampson had the Google Earth app launched. It gave us a bird's-eye view of a rural area forty miles northwest of Williamsport, Pennsylvania, where several creeks met and formed a trout stream roughly three miles from where we were standing. The stream ran by a fifty-acre property adjoining an unpaved country road. A long two-track driveway wound from the road past meadows to a line of mature pines that shielded a large hollow between two ridges.

A modest ranch house sat in a clearing in the bottom of the hollow. There was a barn larger than the house and five other sheds and smaller structures. A substantial garden flanked the back of the barn. Beside the garden stood a big satellite dish.

I tapped on the dish. "That what they're keying on?"

Sampson nodded. "Big bandwidth coming and going. Lots of electricity being used on the property. And many of the recent uploads to Killingblondechicks have evidently come through that satellite dish. We've got the IP address."

"Seems strange," I said. "When Krazy Kat Rawlins looked at that website, he couldn't tell where most of the videos of blondes were coming from because they used onion routers. And our guys were able to track them?"

"Maybe the guys making them got lazy," Sampson said. "It happens."

"The woods around here do look like the woods in the videos of Gretchen Lindel and Delilah Franks," I said. "The blondes running in the trees?"

"I remember," Sampson said. "And the lesbian girls disappeared less than sixty miles east of here. They could all be in that house or in any of those outbuildings."

"Wish you'd gotten the search warrant."

"Not enough evidence yet, the judge said. Which is why you're here and Fox isn't. Like I said, we're going fishing."

We got back in the car. It felt good to be riding shotgun with Sampson again. My world seemed even better than it had leaving the Lindels the evening before.

I switched the iPad app to Google Maps and used it to navigate the labyrinth of dirt roads around the property. Somewhere on it, there was a computer belonging to a twenty-seven-year-old named Carter Flint. In the satellite image, there were six or seven vehicles in Flint's yard.

But driving past that line of pines into the hollow, we spotted only two: a faded red Ford Ranger pickup and an old Toyota Corolla that looked in need of springs, both with their noses toward an embankment below the ranch house.

Sampson parked sideways behind them, blocking anyone trying for a quick exit. We got out. The fog was lifting from the ridges above the hollow. A dog barked in the distance beyond the pole barn. Closer, I heard the blatting of a sheep and the squeal of a pig or two.

We went up a crumbling brick walkway and knocked on the front door. No answer. No sounds inside. Sampson knocked again, and I thought I caught a flutter of movement in a window to my right. But again there was no answer.

"Let's take a look around," I said. "Maybe he's in the barn."

As we crossed the yard and got closer to the barn, the animal sounds got louder, more frantic, the dog barking, the sheep blatting, and the pig squealing. I knocked at a side door, then tried the knob. It turned. I pushed the door open. Bells hanging on the inner knob jangled.

The pig started squealing in an even higher pitch. The sheep blatted in terror. So did the dog; it sounded desperate, crying and yelping.

We stepped inside and took in the cavernous space in one long, sweeping, and horrified glance.

"Jesus Christ," Sampson said. "This isn't right."

73

THE PIG WAS FORTY POUNDS or so. It was in a low wire pen and was missing a two-inch-wide strip of skin along the length of its spine; it was clearly in terrible pain.

A lamb was in a pen beside the pig. Three of its legs were broken and it was struggling piteously.

The dog, a beagle, had been beaten with a blunt object. It tried over and over to get to its feet, but it kept falling and yelping for help.

Three GoPro cameras on tripods were aimed at the cages. Beyond the pens, a long workbench stretched the length of the side wall. On it were dozens of pieces of grotesque taxidermy, animals stuffed in their tortured state.

Behind the bench, the rear sliding door of the pole barn was open to the big garden. Thirty, maybe forty more creatures—small dogs and cats, wild things like skunks and opossums, even an owl—were stuffed in positions that preserved their agony and set in the garden in neat little rows. A few were dressed in doll clothes, which only made the situation more disturbing.

"We need to call in the locals," Sampson said.

Before I could reply, a man wearing headphones appeared in the open doorway to the garden. Bone thin and dressed in painter's pants and a green wife-beater, he had skin as pale as a fish belly, pinkish eyes, and wispy hair the color of snow.

Two steps into the barn, as he was smiling at the wounded animals in their pens, he spotted us over by the door. He ripped off his headphones.

"Who the hell are you?" he demanded.

"Police," Sampson said, holding up his badge. "You Carter Flint?"

Shock locked Flint in his tracks for a second as he looked from John's badge to the suffering animals. Then he whirled and flew out the barn door.

I tore after him. I had no jurisdiction. I wasn't even a cop, technically, but after what I'd seen, I wasn't letting the sadist who'd done it get away.

Neither was Sampson; he was off my left shoulder, exiting the barn into the garden. Flint was surprisingly fast and nimble. He was already beyond the garden's borders and racing behind two other outbuildings toward the north tree line at the base of a ridge a hundred and fifty yards away.

"If he makes those woods, we'll lose him," Sampson growled.

I gritted my teeth and danced through the stuffed animals until I hit the grass, then I told myself to be like Jannie—relax and run. For thirty yards I was convinced I'd catch him, but Flint was younger and, judging from the way he was gaining ground, much fitter than me.

But not fitter than Sampson, who blew by me.

When Flint was forty yards from the woods, he hit tall, tangled grass. It slowed him. But it didn't slow John, whose long legs had him leaping after the sadist. Flint looked back in desperation and then lunged for the woods.

Sampson ran up a hummock in the weeds and dived after him.

74

SAMPSON'S SHOULDER AND HIS two hundred and twenty pounds drove into the back of Flint's legs, flattening him in the deep wet grass. I ran up, gasping, as John straddled the sadist and kept his shoulders pinned.

"My knee." Flint moaned. "Something snapped. And I got broken ribs."

Sampson dug out zip cuffs and wrenched Flint's arms up behind him, which provoked another round of howling.

"My ribs!"

"Screw your ribs," Sampson said. "And screw your knee. You're lucky I don't kick out your front teeth."

I helped Sampson up and then pulled Flint to his feet. His left leg buckled, and he began to whimper.

"I can't help it, man. I got a mental sickness. I tried to stop. I did, but—"

"Save it for a judge," Sampson said.

"Where are the blond women?" I said. "Which building?"

He didn't react at first. Then he looked confused. "What blond women?"

"The ones you made those movies of," Sampson said. "Fake executions. Uploaded them to the Killingblondechicks site."

"No," he said. "I watched some free videos on that site, but that's not me."

"All the recent uploads have been coming from your IP," Sampson said.

Flint shook his head. "I've never submitted to that site. Never. I do animals for animal sites. Not humans. I'd never do humans."

"Try telling that to a jury after they've seen your barn," I said.

"I'm telling the truth," he said. "Maybe I deserve punishment for what I've done, who I am. But if those blonde videos came through my IP, man, someone frickin' hacked and hijacked my computer! I'm being framed!"

Part Four

IN DEFENSE OF ALEX CROSS

CHAPTER

75

SHORTLY BEFORE DARK, SAMPSON DROPPED me off at the entrance to
the alley that runs behind my house. With my trial starting up
again in the morning, there were bound to be more journalists
in front of my house.

There'd been other journalists gathered at the bottom of
Carter Flint's road when we left. After Sampson called the local sheriff to tell them we'd made a citizen's arrest, we'd waited
until Flint was in custody and the three animals mercifully
euthanized before we helped in the search for the girls. We'd
found enough disturbing evidence to put Flint behind bars or
in a psychiatric institution for years but no trace of Gretchen
Lindel or Delilah Franks or the four other missing women.

I used the back gate to our yard, happy for the darkness,
and went in the side door. My dad and Jannie were watching a
tape of her race at Hopkins. Bree was in the kitchen with Nana
Mama.

"How was fishing?" my dad said.

Before I could answer, Bree called archly, "Yes, how *was* fishing?"

I gave my dad a chagrined look and walked to the kitchen. "You know?"

She crossed her arms. "I know everything. What were you thinking, going up there and just barging in like that?"

"That was John's call on his own time. I just tagged along."

She really wasn't happy. "You said you'd be straight with me."

I lowered my voice, said, "Straight with you? Okay, it was bad. The worst animal cruelty I've ever seen. I feel like I've been dipped in a jar of creepiness, but we stopped more animals from being tortured by that piece of shit."

Bree struggled, her eyes searching mine, and then threw up her hands. "Go take a shower."

Turning from the stove, Nana Mama said, "Dinner in half an hour."

"Smells good. What is it?"

"It's a secret."

"I'll be right back down," I said. I leaned over Bree's cold shoulder and kissed her on the cheek.

"There's something on the table in the hall for you, Alex," my grandmother called after me as I left the room.

In the front hall I spotted a small U.S. Postal Service mailer addressed to Dr. Cross. No return address. I opened it to find the same kind of flash drive that the fake Alden Lindel had shown me. It was inside a plastic sleeve.

"You might want to see this," I said, waving the envelope at Bree.

We went down to my basement office. Bree put on latex gloves and plugged the drive in. A few moments later, a

QuickTime App launched and showed a low-light video of a handcuffed, barefoot woman in a tattered white nightgown. She had a white hood over her head and was being led to a mossy stone wall by two guys dressed in black from shoes to hoods.

When they reached the wall, one of the men spun her around. The other yanked off the hood, revealing a gagged blond teen.

I felt sick, said, "Gretchen Lindel."

They took off the gag. The camera pulled back to show three men about fifty feet from Gretchen. They were all hooded, all dressed in black, and all carrying AR rifles.

"Ready," the cameraman said.

The three men shouldered their rifles.

I expected Gretchen to go to her knees and beg for mercy.

But instead, she stood tall against the stone wall and stuck her chin out at the firing squad.

"Go ahead!" she yelled at them. "I'm not afraid. You can do anything you want and I am not afraid of any of you!"

"Aim," the cameraman said.

"You won't do it!" Gretchen screamed. "You kill me, you don't get to play your games anymore. You kill me—"

"Fire!"

The guns went off. In the low light, orange flames shot out of their muzzles. By the sparks the ricochets threw, the bullets hit stone inches around her head.

It broke Gretchen, who went to her knees, shaking in terror. "Don't," she wept. "Don't."

Then the screen froze, and I heard the voice of the fake Alden Lindel say, "Next time, it's for real, Dr. Cross. Next time every blond bitch, including little Gretchen, dies. And forget about finding me before then. I exist in the digital void, invisible, ten steps ahead of you and the FBI."

The video ended with that same brilliant flash I'd seen the first time I'd plugged in one of his thumb drives.

"He's definitely part of the Killingblondechicks conspiracy," I said, thinking about Flint's insistence that someone had hijacked his computer.

Then I thought about the fact that the fake Alden Lindel had mailed the flash drive to me rather than bringing it in person.

"He knew I'd figured him out," I said.

How? That flash at the end of the videos kept playing in my mind until I formed a very strong suspicion.

"I think there's a good chance he's bugged my computer somehow," I told Bree. "And maybe the FBI's. That would keep him ten steps ahead of us, wouldn't it?"

CHAPTER

76

WHEN I FINALLY GOT IN the shower, I was no longer merely suspicious but convinced my computer had been compromised by the fake Alden Lindel. I'd called Rawlins and Batra at the FBI to alert them, but neither of them picked up the phone. I left them messages saying that I believed their system was at risk as well, and I hoped they'd call sooner rather than later.

Under the hot water, I felt sickened again at what Flint had done to those animals and at the fact that he claimed there were tens of thousands of subscribers to the websites he sold his footage to. Was that true? What possible pleasure could someone find in innocent animals suffering?

It was so beyond me that I got angry. That anger only deepened when I considered my inability to make headway in the hunt for the missing blondes, especially Gretchen Lindel. What a brave thing she'd done, standing up to those men like that, defying them.

When at last I turned my thoughts to the trial, I got angrier still, and then depressed.

Two eyewitnesses had testified that I'd shot three people without just cause. There were videos of the shootings and no sign of computer-generated imaging or anything to suggest I was being framed.

The weight of those cold, hard facts kept growing as I showered myself into a darker mood. A conspiracy had been hatched and directed at me. The conspiracy was working. The gears of justice were grinding, and I could see no path out.

I got dressed and went downstairs in a black cloud.

"Doesn't it's-a-secret smell incredible?" Bree said when I came back into the kitchen.

Distracted, I nodded.

Out in the great room, my dad chuckled. "I think I love it's-a-secret."

"You will," Nana Mama said. "Where's that Ali?"

"Where he's been the past four days," Jannie said with a roll of her eyes. "Up in Dad's old office in the attic with the door shut."

"He's still working on his Houdini paper?" I said. "I'll go get him."

"Let me," my dad said, coming into the kitchen. "Give me some time to bond with my grandkiddo."

Drummond disappeared. I helped Bree set the table, wondering how many more times we'd get to do this simple chore together. I opened a bottle of white wine and poured myself a generous glass.

Bree was watching me.

"One healthy one," I said.

"You deserve two healthy ones."

"Dinner's on," Nana Mama said, bringing a big iron skillet with a lid to the table. She set it on a lazy Susan. "Rice is coming. Where's that Ali, now?"

Before I could reply, she left the kitchen and went to the bottom of the stairs. "Dinner, Ali! You don't want dinner cold, you better come on down."

"Two minutes," my dad called. "He's showing me something."

My grandmother came back, muttering under her breath. She'd always been a stickler for us being at the table when she was ready to serve, and she had a sour expression on her face when she brought a big bowl of steaming jasmine rice in and sat down.

"Let's say grace," she said. "We don't have to wait."

When we were done thanking God for the meal, Nana Mama lifted the lid on the skillet. The smells that wafted up made me close my eyes and smile.

My grandmother said, "Tiger shrimp in fresh tomatoes, onions, garlic, and it's-a-secret."

"Mmm, Nana," Jannie said after taking her first bite. "What is that?"

"That's the secret," she said, smiling. "Good, isn't it, Alex?"

"Amazing," I said, but my mind was elsewhere.

"You don't sound very amazed," Nana Mama said.

I set my fork down. "It's delicious, Nana, really, but I think we all need to talk about what life will look like if I'm sent to prison."

Nana Mama's face fell. Bree grew distant. Jannie's eyes welled with tears, and she said, "I don't want to think about that, Dad. I—"

Ali came running into the kitchen. "Dad, you won't believe it!"

My grandmother said, "Now is not a good time, Ali."

My son stopped short. "But I—"

"Not now, Ali!" Jannie shouted, and she broke down in tears.

My father came in behind Ali and said to me, "You better listen to him, son."

77

LOOKING WEAK BUT DETERMINED, JUDGE LARCH rapped her gavel and called the court to order at nine the next morning. Bree and my dad sat behind me. I'd been up until three a.m., had slept fitfully, and was feeling fuzzy and on edge from two cups of high-test Brazilian coffee.

Larch stared down through her thick lenses and said in a restrained voice, "Ms. Marley, have your analysts examined the videos?"

Looking chagrined, Anita said, "They agreed that they have not been tampered with digitally. The defense has no further objection to the videos."

The judge seemed disappointed. Assistant U.S. attorney Nathan Wills was stone-faced but nodding his head and jiggling his knee, probably already working on his closing arguments in his mind.

"Mr. Wills?" Larch said.

"A moment, Your Honor," the prosecutor said, then he

leaned over to his assistant, Athena Carlisle, and whispered something in her ear.

Carlisle drew back with a startled expression and shook her head emphatically. Their conversation got heated, and then Wills stood up.

He glanced at his scowling assistant and threw back his shoulders, which thrust his belly forward against his starched white shirt.

"The People rest, Your Honor."

That surprised me and it didn't. According to the witness list Wills and Carlisle had provided, there were six or seven more people slated to appear, mostly to testify about ballistics and other basic crime scene evidence. But why bother when the videos were legitimate?

"Ms. Marley," the judge said. "You're up."

Anita had evidently been half expecting the prosecution to rest as well, because without hesitation, she said, "Defense calls Kimiko Binx for cross."

Binx came forward wearing black slacks, black pumps, a black blouse with a high collar, and costume pearls. I got the distinct feeling she was more concerned about her appearance than about facing the formidable Anita Marley.

"You're still under oath, Ms. Binx," Judge Larch said.

The web designer nodded and sat down with composure and poise.

Anita said, "Ms. Binx, did you alert Claude Watkins that you were on your way the day of the shootings? Call to tell him you were coming to the factory with my client?"

"No," she said. "I don't think so."

Naomi handed Anita a plastic evidence bag. Anita took it over to Binx.

"Recognize this?" Anita said.

Binx frowned and took the bag, saw what it was. "It's a SPOT."

Anita looked to the jury. "A SPOT is a satellite personal tracker, a GPS device that tracks the wearer. Runners like Ms. Binx use them to plot their workout routes, isn't that correct?"

Binx nodded. "And in cases of emergency, you can send an SOS signal."

"There's also a button that allows you to send a prepared text to people you list on the SPOT website, correct?"

"Um, I guess."

"Actually, we looked at your account with SPOT, Ms. Binx," Anita said. "On the day of the shootings, from your apartment and twenty minutes before you arrived at the factory, you pressed that button and sent a text to Claude Watkins that read 'Game on.'"

"I don't remember that," Binx said, pushing back her hair. "And what does it matter?"

Anita smiled and said, "It shows premeditation, Ms. Binx."

CHAPTER

78

BINX'S FACE FELL, BUT SHE said, "Premeditation of what? Performance art?"

Anita did not answer. Instead, she said, "As I understand it, you were taken into custody after the shootings. Is that correct?"

"They let me go after they figured out the truth."

"But you were booked, yes? Fingerprints. Cheek swabs. Photographed for your mug shot."

"It was humiliating," the witness said coldly. "I'd done nothing wrong."

Anita returned to the defense table. Naomi handed her several thin files and a large sealed plastic bag. Anita handed one of the files to Wills and then went to the bench.

"The defense would like to introduce exhibits A, B, C, and D," she said, handing Judge Larch a file. "Exhibit A includes chain-of-evidence documentation for cheek swabs taken from Ms. Binx by DC Metro Police shortly after the shootings. Exhibit B documents the FBI's chain of evidence following cheek swabs taken two days later from my client upon his arrest. Exhibits C and D include the results of tests of those swab samples that the defense requested from the FBI lab."

"Genetic analysis?" Judge Larch said.

"Your Honor," Wills said, rising. "This is the first we've heard of any swabs or lab analysis."

"Not true," Anita said. "My assistant found reference to the swabs in the materials you sent us during discovery, Mr. Wills. And no, Your Honor, we did not do genetic analysis. We had tests done on the saliva, not the cheek cells used for DNA testing."

"I'll admit the files," Larch said.

"Your Honor," Wills said.

The judge fixed the prosecutor with a withering stare, and I realized it was well past her usual time to recess for a puff or two. Wills was swimming in very dangerous waters.

"The reports are in, Mr. Wills," Larch said. "Ms. Marley?"

Anita brought a copy over to Binx, handed it to the witness. "Can you look at page four of Dr. Cross's saliva-test results, third line of the summary?"

Carlisle and Wills were frantically turning the pages of the report. Judge Larch was already studying her copy. Binx glanced up sharply at Anita.

"Can you read it out loud, please?" my attorney said.

Binx twisted uncomfortably, looking as if a lasso had been looped over her head and cinched snug beneath her rib cage.

In a dull monotone, she read, "'Saliva tests detected the presence of methylenedioxymethamphetamine, MDMA, a hallucinatory drug also known as molly or ecstasy.'"

79

ECSTASY. MOLLY.

I flashed back to that weird giddy state I was in when I entered the factory and how I'd screamed in an uncontrollable rage that I was going to kill every Soneji in sight. No wonder my emotions had been on a roller-coaster ride that entire day. No wonder I'd felt like hell for days afterward.

Anita pivoted from Binx to the jury and said, "MDMA. A euphoric, mind-altering drug. A drug that doctors say leaves the body at a fairly predictable rate based on dosage. Ms. Binx, what does line four of the summary say?"

Binx was clearly uncomfortable now but read, "'Further tests indicate dosage of one hundred and forty milligrams or more of MDMA introduced to subject forty-two to forty-eight hours prior to the gathering of samples.'"

Anita said, "One hundred and forty milligrams of ecstasy taken forty-two to forty-eight hours before the saliva samples were taken. That is a six-hour time span that, if I'm not mistaken, includes the two hours prior to the shootings when you were with Dr. Cross, Ms. Binx."

I expected Wills to object. His assistant, Athena Carlisle, obviously expected the same thing because she glanced at her boss. When she saw he wasn't moving, she stood up.

Carlisle said, "Your Honor, is Ms. Marley honestly laying the foundation for an insanity plea? Saying Dr. Cross was out of his mind at the time of the shooting because of ecstasy?"

"We are not, Your Honor," Anita said hotly. "Dr. Cross is one of the sanest people I've ever known. I'm just setting the context for what Dr. Cross did or did not see that day."

"Objection," Wills said, standing beside his assistant. "Who's testifying here, Ms. Marley or Ms. Binx?"

"Ms. Binx," Anita said, and she returned to the witness box. "Can you look to page five of the report, the results of tests done on saliva samples taken from *you* several hours after the shootings? Lines three and four?"

Binx lowered her head and then shook it. "That's not true."

"The FBI says it is indeed true," Anita said, and she looked to her own copy of the files. "Line four, quote, 'Further tests indicate a dosage of a hundred and nineteen milligrams introduced to bloodstream four to six hours prior to the gathering of sample.'"

Binx said nothing.

"Did you ingest ecstasy earlier on the day of the shootings?" Anita asked.

Binx looked around warily. "That would be illegal, wouldn't it?"

"Answer the question."

Binx hesitated for several moments before straightening up in her chair and saying, "I refuse to answer on the grounds that it may incriminate me."

That set off a hubbub in the courtroom. Larch gaveled for quiet.

Amused, Anita said, "You're invoking the Fifth Amendment for taking ecstasy?"

"I didn't say that," Binx said.

"You kind of did."

"Objection!" Carlisle cried.

"Sustained," Larch said. "The jury will ignore that."

Anita showed no reaction. "Ms. Binx, the morning of the shootings, after you came back from your run, do you remember tripping in your apartment and Dr. Cross catching you before you could fall?"

She hesitated, frowned. "No."

"Yes, you tripped over an electrical cord. When Dr. Cross caught you, you put a piece of clear adhesive tape on the underside of his forearm, didn't you?"

"Objection," Wills said wearily. "Where is the foundation for this?"

Anita said, "Your Honor, Dr. Cross and his wife, DC chief of detectives Bree Stone, will testify that they found a piece of tape on the underside of Dr. Cross's right forearm in the hours after the shootings. We believe that the ecstasy was on that tape in a gel or powdered form and that it was absorbed into Dr. Cross's bloodstream transdermally, through the skin."

"Where is this tainted tape?" the prosecutor said. "Render the body, Counselor."

Anita ignored him, said to the judge, "Neither Dr. Cross nor Chief Stone thought much of it at the time, and they threw the tape out at GW Medical Center."

Wills shook his head even more wearily. "Move to strike

everything Ms. Marley has said about this phantom piece of tape, Your Honor."

"So moved," Larch said.

"Your Honor—" Anita started.

"No tape, no talk about tape," the judge said sharply.

Anita sighed, said, "Ms. Binx, did you dose Dr. Cross with ecstasy?"

Binx blinked, chewed on her lip, glanced at Wills, and then said again, "I refuse to answer on the grounds that it may incriminate me."

80

WHEN JUDGE LARCH CALLED FOR lunch recess and left the courtroom slowly, the prosecutors weren't looking quite as confident as they had earlier.

Anita had asked Binx several more questions about the ecstasy, including how it was that she had been given the perfect dose of MDMA for her weight and how it was that I was given the perfect dose for mine.

Binx had replied to every question about the drug by taking the Fifth.

"Tripping on ecstasy doesn't get your client off," Wills said to Anita as she packed away some files.

"No?" she said. "Fortunately, a jury gets to make that decision."

"No tainted tape, no causality. Even you can see that."

Anita gave him a blank expression. "Save it for your close."

Athena Carlisle said, "Given the videos, are you open to talking plea bargain? Dr. Cross might get out in time to meet his great-grandkids."

Anita glanced at me. I shook my head.

Carlisle puffed her cheeks, then blew out air. "We tried."

"Suit yourself," Wills said, and he chuckled as he left. "But I hear it's hell for an ex-cop in prison."

Naomi, Bree, my dad, and I ate takeout pulled-pork sandwiches in a conference room. Even though Anita had scored big points with her cross-examination, we were a somber, focused bunch.

For the first time in a week I felt jurors five and eleven leaning a bit my way, or at least developing some skepticism regarding the prosecution's case. But Wills had been right. The ecstasy might be a mitigating factor, but it wouldn't be enough to acquit me of two murders and an attempted murder.

We were back in court with two minutes to spare. Anita was already there.

"We good?" I asked.

She leaned over to me, murmured, "Pray for a knockout."

"And David slew Goliath," I said before the bailiff called, "All rise."

Judge Larch looked considerably less agitated when she retook the bench and called the court to order.

"Ms. Marley," Larch said, "do you wish to cross-examine Mr. Watkins now, or does the defense have its own witnesses in mind?"

"Defense witness, Your Honor," Anita said. "We call Ali Cross to the stand."

I twisted in my seat in time to see Ali enter the courtroom holding my dad's hand with Jannie and Nana Mama behind them. My boy was in his Sunday best: gray pants, an ironed white shirt, and a paisley bow tie. Juror eleven smiled seeing him.

At the bar, Nana Mama whispered something in her great-grandson's ear, and he nodded. Ali did not look at me or Anita before pushing open the gate and walking confidently to the witness stand.

Wills said, "Your Honor, the defense gave us no notice of this witness."

"Ali is Dr. Cross's son, Your Honor," Anita said.

Judge Larch looked skeptical. "And he has business before this court?"

"Yes, Your Honor, he has a few things to say."

The judge peered over at Ali, who was standing in the witness box now.

"How old are you, Ali?"

"Nine, but I'm in fifth grade already."

"Where do you go to school?"

"Washington Latin."

Larch smiled. "Good for you. Swear him in."

Afterward, the bailiff had to get pads for the witness chair so Ali could sit higher and be seen easier by the jury.

Once he'd settled in, Anita said, "Ali, do you normally do what your father tells you to do? By that I mean, when he gives you a direct order, do you obey it?"

"Yes, ma'am. I try."

"But you defied one of his direct orders recently, didn't you?"

"Yes, ma'am, I did."

"Objection," Wills said. "Your Honor, where is the relevance of this?"

Anita looked at him, said, "The Court is about to find out."

"Get to it, Ms. Marley," Larch said.

"What did you do that your father didn't want you to do?" Anita said.

Ali said, "My dad told me not to look at the videos of the shootings in that factory, but I secretly looked at them on YouTube."

"Once?"

"No, like a hundred and seventy times."

That provoked some nervous laughter, and I could tell juror five, the retired engineer with the hunched back, did not like the idea of a nine-year-old boy looking at those videos even once, let alone one hundred and seventy times.

"Why did you watch it so many times?" Anita said.

"To figure out where the guns went so Dad wouldn't go to prison."

Anita glanced over at Wills and then at the jury. "Did you figure out where the guns went?"

"I think so."

"Objection," Athena Carlisle said. "Your Honor, we've been through this. Real experts have looked at the videos and found nothing wrong with them. We're expected to believe a nine-year-old discovered something that they didn't?"

"Ms. Marley?" Judge Larch said.

"Let the boy speak, Your Honor," Anita said in a reasonable tone. "Echoing what you said when you allowed the videos to be introduced, the prosecution is free to rebut if Ali is wrong."

The judge adjusted her glasses and then looked over at Ali. "Did you really figure it out?"

"I think so," he said.

"Let's hear it."

Naomi put the videos up on the screen and gave Ali a remote control. Stopping the three videos in strategic places in much the same way the prosecution had made its case against me, Ali was able to show the jury how the lighting changed in the videos, how it grew slightly dimmer before each victim appeared and then brightened considerably just before I shot.

"What do you think is happening there with the lighting?" Anita said.

Ali said, "Whoever was controlling the spotlights dimmed them just before Mrs. Winslow, Mr. Watkins, and Mr. Diggs stepped into view. It's hard to see them in that weaker light, but they're there, and then the spotlights are boosted and you see the empty hands just as my father shoots."

"Okay," Anita said. "So what?"

"That's what I kept thinking," Ali said. "So what?"

"Until?"

"Oh, until I read the autopsy reports."

81

JUDGE LARCH WHIRLED HER CHAIR around and glared at me through those Coke-bottle lenses.

"You let a nine-year-old read autopsy reports, Dr. Cross?"

"I wasn't supposed to, Judge," Ali said, twisting in his chair to address her. "But I did it anyway."

Larch looked away from me, squinted at my boy, and said, "You on the road to criminality, son?"

Ali smiled nervously. "No, ma'am. Uh, Your Honor."

"No, I know you're not," Larch said, softer, and her expression eased toward amused resignation. "Go ahead."

Ali testified that he'd defied Bree and me and dug out the autopsy reports on Virginia Winslow and Leonard Diggs, looking for something odd about the gun hands of the three victims.

"Did you find something odd?" Anita asked.

"Yes," Ali said.

"Gunpowder residue?"

He shook his head. "They had sticky stuff on their palms."

"Adhesive glue?"

"Yes, like from tape. And there was also, like, some silicone."

"Is there an explanation for the glue or silicone in the report?"

"No."

"Can you explain why it was there?"

My son sat up straighter. "I think I can explain why, but not exactly how. That's like physics, and I haven't studied that yet. Maybe next year."

The jury members started laughing. Anita smiled, letting the moment last, then said, "Why was the glue and silicone there?"

"Well, if you think about it, because of this," he said, running the videos back and stopping them. "See the three spotlights in the middle feed? And to the right at the bottom of the right spotlight there's a pinpoint blue light? That's where I almost had it figured out. But like I said, the rest is physics that I don't get."

Anita smiled. "Thank you, Ali. Your Honor, if it please the Court, I'd like to call a second witness who can explain more clearly than Ali can what the pinpoint blue light, the glue, the silicone, and the dimming and brightening mean. Mr. Wills can cross-examine them both afterwards."

"Any objection, Mr. Wills?"

Wills and Carlisle conferred. Wills looked irritated when he turned from his assistant and said, "Be my guest, Counselor. Take us on a wild-goose chase."

"The defense calls Keith Karl Rawlins," Anita said.

Krazy Kat came in wearing a fine blue Italian suit, black loafers buffed to a high shine, and a coral-pink shirt open at the collar. His Mohawk was down, dyed black, slicked over to the left side of his head, and tucked behind his ear.

As he walked past Ali, who was leaving the stand, Rawlins nodded and winked at him. Wills and Carlisle acted like someone had brought a jester into court, but they didn't know what to do about it yet.

After he was sworn in, Anita said, "Dr. Rawlins, can you describe your academic training and current position?"

Rawlins said, "I have dual PhDs from Stanford, one in physics, the other in electrical engineering. I'm working on my doctorate in computer science at MIT, and I am currently employed as an independent contractor by the Cyber Division of the Federal Bureau of Investigation."

Wills and Carlisle jumped to their feet.

"Objection," Wills said. "No one at the Bureau informed the prosecution this witness was testifying."

Carlisle said, "Your Honor, agents are required to notify the U.S. Attorney's Office that—"

"I am not a special agent, and I'm not even an employee," Rawlins said. "As such, I am not obligated to notify the FBI or the U.S. Attorney's Office. I came at the request of a very bright young man who sought me out at my home during my free time and presented his rather brilliant theory of the videos. I do not speak for the government, only for myself, as a citizen compelled to tell the truth."

"Your Honor, we still object to—"

"Asked and answered, Mr. Wills," Judge Larch said.

Both prosecutors looked like they'd swallowed worms, but they sat.

Anita said, "What kind of work do you do for the FBI, Dr. Rawlins?"

"It's classified, so I can't give you specifics. But you could say I help the Bureau on the techno side of things."

"Physics involved?"

"Sometimes."

"Is physics involved here—with the video, I mean?"

"Yes," he said. "Basic physics. Wave theory."

82

ANITA GLANCED AT THE JURY. A few, including juror five, were attentive. The eyes of the rest, including juror eleven's, the PR executive, appeared glazed over by this turn in the trial. Physics? Wave theory?

But Anita had foreseen this response. She looked to Naomi and nodded.

As my niece got up and left the courtroom, my attorney said, "Dr. Rawlins, let's keep it very basic, shall we?"

Rawlins shrugged and looked to the jury. "All you really need to know is that light travels in waves, just like in the ocean. When the waves from different light sources collide, they're both changed, just like waves on the ocean coming from different directions and crashing into one another."

Naomi came back into the courtroom pushing a cart loaded with several cardboard boxes and a small spotlight.

"Keep that in mind," Rawlins said, getting up from the witness stand. "Waves colliding on the ocean. With the Court's permission?"

"Granted," Larch said. "I always liked show-and-tell."

"I was a big fan too," Rawlins said.

He went to Naomi, took the spotlight, and set it up on a tripod.

"Judge, can I use an assistant?" Rawlins said.

Larch waved her hand, and the FBI contractor called Ali from the audience.

Rawlins got a manila envelope from the cart, drew out something he kept hidden, and put it in Ali's palm. When my son opened his hand, you had to look closely to see what seemed to be one of those protective films people put on cell phone screens. Thin, translucent, and rectangular, it was affixed to Ali's palm and went up to the first joints of his fingers.

"What is that, exactly?" Judge Larch asked, peering over the bench.

"A piece of medium," Rawlins said. "A polymer that includes silicone. On the medium itself, there is an encoding of a light field captured in the form of an interference pattern. Remember the waves crashing? If you can imagine looking down at the sea crashing around rocks and then taking a three-dimensional picture of it and freezing that moment, you're on the right track."

"Okay?" Judge Larch said.

Rawlins had Ali stand with his left shoulder to the bench, facing the jury box. Then he positioned the spotlight at an angle to Ali.

Anita said, "Can we have the courtroom lights dimmed?"

Larch nodded, and the bailiff dimmed the lights until Rawlins, who was holding a small light meter in his hand, said, "Stop."

You could still see Rawlins and Ali and everyone else in

the windowless courtroom, but it was like looking at them in a grainy photograph. Then Naomi hit a switch. The spotlight beam found Ali, who put on sunglasses.

Every one of the jurors was sitting forward, watching intently. Juror five rested his chin on his hands, which were folded on the curve of his cane handle.

Rawlins said, "The coding on the medium, that snapshot of light waves crashing, is done with lasers, tiny intense light beams that are of a specific high-wave frequency."

He came over in front of the jury, brushed back his strip of lank black hair, and said, "The interesting thing about this three-dimensional coding is that we can see the snapshot of the waves crashing around the rock only if it's lit by lasers tuned to the same exact wave frequency as the ones used to encode the image in the first place."

"That went right over my head," Judge Larch said.

"It's one of those things better seen anyway," Anita said.

She moved in front of the bench and faced Ali's left side. Rawlins stood over by the bailiff's desk facing Ali's left side at a forty-five-degree angle.

Naomi killed the spotlight. We were all cast back into that dim, grainy vision of the courtroom. Three hair-thin, gray-blue laser beams flipped on, one held by Anita, one by Rawlins, and the last by Naomi. The beams were easy to see at their sources, but the farther the streams got from the lasers, the harder it was to make out the beam as it passed through the gloom.

But not so the dull blue dots at the end of each laser beam. The three dots danced over Ali's side and arm before finding his outstretched palm.

"Get it bull's-eye, now," Rawlins said. "Exact spot."

The blue dots quivered and squiggled to a meeting dead center of the encoded medium affixed to Ali's empty hand.

Gasps went up in the courtroom.

"Son of a bitch!" Wills said, standing in disbelief.

Even I couldn't believe it. But there it was.

My nine-year-old son's hand looked like it was wrapped around the pale blue holographic image of a nickel-plated .357 Colt Python revolver.

83

NAOMI SWITCHED ON THE SPOTLIGHT. The gun vanished from Ali's hand. He was grinning wildly.

Rawlins said, "The gun disappeared because the waves of the spotlight came crashing down and drowned the waves of the laser beam so they could no longer reach the code in Ali's hand."

Naomi killed the spotlight. The hologram of the gun reappeared in Ali's hand, provoking another round of murmurs, and many in the jury box shook their heads in wonder. Even juror five seemed impressed.

Rawlins then showed the court what the hologram looked like through a video camera set to black-and-white and adjusted to take in a specific amount of light. In the dimmed courtroom, you could see the hologram of the pistol clearly, but through the camera lens and on the screen, there was only a gray wash in Ali's palm. The spotlight beam came on, and even the gray wash was gone from the image on the courtroom screen.

"Your Honor," Anita said.

"One second, Counselor," Judge Larch said. She stood up behind the bench and gazed down at Ali. "How did you figure this out, young man?"

Ali took off the sunglasses and said, "Um, when I couldn't see anything from just looking at the videos, I figured I had to think about it in another way."

Ali explained that he'd stopped watching the videos and started thinking how a gun could be there and yet not be there. He thought for almost a day before he remembered the holograms he'd seen on some of the rides in Disney World, and he started reading about holograms on the Internet.

"There was stuff about the photographic medium being clear and silicone-based, and the wave frequency of the lasers being the key. And I remembered the glue and silicone on the victims' hands from the autopsy report and thought maybe the glue could have been to hold the film in place. But Dr. Rawlins figured it all out for real."

"Just the details, no more," Rawlins said with a bow toward Ali. "The kid had it nailed before he rang my bell."

"Where did the film go?" Larch said.

Ali said, "I think after the shootings, after my dad went out to call for backup, someone stripped the holographic film from the victims' hands and left with the cameraman who shot the video."

"Objection," Wills said. "This entire exercise is a clever and, I must admit, very creative stunt, but there's nothing here that's concrete. No holographic film has been introduced into evidence, so no testimony about holographic film should be allowed. Move to strike this entire line of questioning."

"There's evidence," Ali said hotly. "That tiny blue light I

showed you. Someone had the laser on by mistake for four point seven seconds. And the silicone? And the glue? Were you even listening?"

Wills shot my son a contemptuous glance but didn't answer.

Anita said, "Your Honor, the defense has given a plausible explanation for the apparent absence of the guns in the videos and for the glue residue and silicone found on the victims' palms. Let the jury decide."

For several long moments, the judge showed no reaction and made no response. She studied the top of the bench so long, I figured she was having some kind of fit. At last she said, "Overruled, Mr. Wills."

"Judge Larch—"

"I said overruled, Mr. Wills. We'll let the ladies and gentlemen of the jury decide which explanation they believe. Ms. Marley?"

"Move to dismiss."

"Denied."

"Move to suppress the testimony of Kimiko Binx and Claude Watkins."

"Denied."

Anita called Watkins back to the stand for his cross-examination, and he steadfastly maintained he'd had no holographic film on his hands at any time in his entire life.

"And yet glue and silicone were found on your hands after you were shot."

Watkins snorted. "I'm a sculptor, and who knows what was on that factory floor to begin with."

"But you wanted your encounter with Dr. Cross to be recorded. Were you trying to provoke him into shooting with the holograms?"

"I repeat, no holograms," Watkins said firmly. "And, sure, I wanted to film him. I wanted to see how he'd handle himself, whether he'd revert to the mean of police behavior and go violent. But no one expected to get shot. Least of all me."

"Do you hate Dr. Cross?"

"I hate the violence he stands for."

"Enough to frame him?"

"Not enough to take a bullet in the guts and through the spine," Watkins said. "That's a fact. No one would wish this on themselves no matter how much they hated someone."

"No further questions," Anita said.

When Watkins had wheeled through the gate, Judge Larch said, "Ms. Marley?"

Anita glanced at me. I nodded.

She said, "The defense rests, Your Honor."

CHAPTER

84

ANY COURT BUFF WILL TELL you that a quick verdict favors the prosecution. So after the jury heard closing arguments, received instructions, and were sequestered for deliberations, we treated every minute without word as a minor miracle. Hours passed. Then a day.

I tried not to think about the verdict but found that impossible. My case had dominated local news and was featured on national and cable news coverage. The talking heads babbled about Ali's holographic demonstration, the presence of ecstasy in my blood the day of the shootings, and whether together they were enough to create reasonable doubt in the jurors' minds.

A few were confident it would. But more sided with the prosecution, noting as Wills had in his closing argument that for the hologram theory to be true, the three victims had to have knowingly put themselves in harm's way in order to frame me. He'd argued that it ran counter to self-preservation, pointed at Claude Watkins in his wheelchair, and asked if anyone could believe he'd risk paralysis to see me in prison. Other commentators continued to hammer the fact that I'd been at the center of nine other officer-involved shootings in the course of my career, and they championed the idea that I should go to jail to set an example for police conduct across the nation.

At noon on Friday, I couldn't take it anymore. I snuck out of the house and down the alley with my laptop. Sampson picked me up on Pennsylvania Avenue and we went to Quantico. Special Agent Batra met us at the gate, and before long we were in Rawlins's underground lab.

"I don't know if we are bugged or not," Rawlins said, taking my computer. "Based on the fact we both uploaded the contents of that flash drive from the man posing as Alden Lindel, I've been digging in our system, but I haven't come up with anything definitive yet."

"This is a smaller universe," I said.

Rawlins winked. "I see that."

He'd kept his Mohawk down and black, but he'd added dark eye shadow, which made him look somewhat demonic as he plugged my laptop into a closed network. Rawlins ran a number of tests and still didn't find anything. He decided to search uploads my computer had made recently over Wi-Fi or Bluetooth.

"There you are, you bugger," he said, highlighting a file with a nonsense name and extension.

The date stamp said the upload from my laptop had taken place from 4:33 p.m. to 5:29 p.m. the prior Monday.

I thought about that and realized the time frame coincided with my hour with Annie Cassidy. The beginning and the end of the session, when she'd been fooling around with her smart-phone.

"That file was probably sent to her phone," I said. "She must have been downloading it the entire time I was in session with her."

"What's in the file?" Batra said.

Rawlins clicked on the file, and it was quickly apparent that it contained a record of everything done on my computer for the previous fourteen days.

"Spying on us, the little roaches," Rawlins said.

He analyzed the file further and discovered that it had been generated after an order from a piece of "elegant and inge-niously coded" malware Krazy Kat found buried deep inside my operating system and made to look like innocuous support code.

Once he had the malware identified, Rawlins searched for it on the FBI system and was shocked to find a copy sitting dor-mant on his own server.

"This is impressive," he said, rubbing his chin. "I actively monitor for intrusions, and I never saw this. A deep, deep, deep Trojan horse, created by a master coder."

"Can you figure out the coder's identity?" I asked.

"I might. Give me that flash drive you got in the mail. We'll launch it, see what happens."

Before he did, Rawlins wrote tracking code designed to at-tach itself to any file the malware created. Then he plugged the drive into his server and launched it.

The mock firing-squad execution of Gretchen Lindel played, followed by the warning to me that the next time all the blondes would die. There was a screen flash before the video closed, just as there'd been when I uploaded it.

Rawlins stood there, drumming his fingers on his workstation, head swiveling as he studied the array of screens around him.

"C'mon," he said. "Something happened there. Where are you?"

My cell phone buzzed. I took it out, saw Naomi was calling. I answered. "Any news?"

My niece's voice was strained. "The jury has contacted Larch."

I closed my eyes, thinking, *Hung jury,* wondering whether my family could take another trial.

But then Naomi said, "They've reached a verdict, Uncle Alex. You need to come to the courthouse."

85

I TIGHTENED THE KNOT ON my tie in the car as Sampson turned the corner toward the courthouse. From two blocks away, we could see the media mob waiting, anxious, no doubt, because it was pushing four that Friday afternoon and they were right up against deadline for the East Coast evening news broadcasts.

"The offer's still there to go in through the prisoner-transfer door," Sampson said. "Chief okayed it."

"No," I said. "I want them to see me."

I glanced over and saw Sampson rubbing at the scar on his forehead.

"You okay?"

"I will be when I take my meds," he said, pulling up across the street from the courthouse and putting his hand on my forearm. "We'll all be right behind you, no matter what happens."

But instead of being encouraged by his support, I climbed from the squad car with my mind reeling through all the counterattacks the assistant U.S. attorneys had made in their closing arguments, especially at our theory of the holographic gun images.

The glue could have come from their makeup, they said. The silicone came from something they'd all touched, probably the masks they wore or, as Watkins had suggested, the grime on the old factory floor. Wills had also hammered home how absurd it was to believe that two people would willingly die and another would willingly be wounded and crippled in order to frame me.

"Alex!"

Anita and Naomi were climbing out of a cab behind us.

"Let's be as disciplined as we were on day one," Anita said. "No one talks on the way into court."

As we'd done the first day of the trial, we walked together toward the crush of cameras and klieg lights that flared and trained on us. The reporters' shouting canceled out the protesters' shouting, so all I really heard as we pushed on through the mob was a garbled roar of desperation and hatred.

Reaching the courthouse was a relief, but I felt distant going through security. I tried to focus on the officers wishing me luck, but I was thinking that my life as I knew it might be over in a matter of minutes and I'd be condemned to an eight-by-twelve, a target for every con who had it in for a cop.

My phone buzzed, alerting me to a text from Bree: ETA five minutes! Love you! Believe in you!

But on the way up the elevator and walking toward Judge Larch's courtroom, I felt hollow, separate, and alone.

Nana Mama was already there in the front row with Ali, Jannie, and my dad. I ignored everyone else gathered in the court and went to them. My grandmother took my hand and squeezed it.

There was so much fear and anxiety in my children's faces that I had to fight to smile and say, "Be strong, now."

"You too," my father said. "We've been praying."

I went to the defense table as nervous as I'd ever been in my entire life. I glanced past Anita and saw the prosecutor Nathan Wills fiddling with his phone. His assistant was looking down, studying a document.

Behind them sat Soneji's son, Dylan Winslow, who had a smirk on his face. Kimiko Binx was perched beside him, dressed in black and shooting me dark glances. Claude Watkins was rolling his wheelchair down the aisle.

Before he parked beside Binx, he looked at me with open loathing, and in a voice loud enough for the reporters and other spectators to hear, he said, "You're not getting away with this, Cross. If there's any justice left in the world, you're going down for a long time."

Anita put her hand on mine. I didn't need it. I wouldn't give Watkins the satisfaction of reacting or replying.

"All rise," the bailiff said. "Judge Priscilla Larch presiding."

The judge looked better, far less pale than she'd been at closing arguments. Larch was wearing a new pair of glasses too, ones that made her seem less, well, birdy. She banged her gavel, called the court to order, and asked the bailiff to bring in the jury.

In the course of my career, I've sat in the cheap seats watching juries come back with verdicts at least fifty times. In every case, I've searched the faces of the jury members for clues to their decision, but I have been surprised by the outcome almost as often as I've been right in my predictions.

Juror five hobbled in. He looked tired and grim, as did several other jurors who filled the seats around him. The remaining members of the panel appeared upset but resigned to the verdict.

Juror eleven, the PR executive, had been voted foreperson. She came in last, wearing a sharp blue suit with a pink blouse. She gave me a glance as she climbed into her seat in the jury box, swallowed hard, and looked away with such uncertainty that I was shaken inside.

"Madam Foreperson, have you reached a verdict?" Larch said.

Juror eleven stood. "We have, Your Honor."

The judge accepted a copy of the verdict from the bailiff, opened it, and showed no reaction before saying, "Dr. Cross, please rise."

As Anita, Naomi, and I got to our feet, I heard the courtroom doors open behind me. I glanced back and saw Bree and Damon rush to seats beside Sampson and his wife, Billie.

Everything felt surreal as I heard Larch say, "On count one, in the death of Virginia Winslow, murder in the first degree, how do you find?"

CHAPTER

86

JUROR ELEVEN WOULD NOT LOOK at me. No one in the jury would look at me.

"We find the defendant, Alex Cross," she said as she finally turned her hard gaze my way, "not guilty."

There were gasps, cheers, and a war whoop behind me. My knees went rubbery, and I almost started to cry when Nana Mama said, "I knew it!"

Naomi grabbed my left arm, Anita my right.

"What?" Dylan Winslow yelled angrily, jumping to his feet. "He shot my mom in cold blood!"

"Not guilty!" Ali shouted at him, standing up. "Not guilty!"

Judge Larch pounded her gavel and then shook it at Ali and Soneji's kid. "One more outburst out of either of you, and you'll be banned from my court. Clear?"

Dylan was fuming and red-faced, but he slammed his butt back down on the bench beside Binx. Ali grinned with satisfaction and sat more slowly.

Turning back to the jury, Judge Larch said, "On count two, in the death of Leonard Diggs, the charge is murder in the first degree. How do you find?"

"We find the defendant not guilty, Your Honor."

"This is bullshit!" Binx shouted. "I saw it with my own two eyes!"

"One more word and it'll be contempt of court, Ms. Binx," Larch said, standing and glaring at her.

Binx shook her head in a rage, but she said nothing else.

"On count three of the indictment," the judge said, "attempted murder of Claude Watkins, how do you find?"

"There was reasonable doubt. Not guilty, Your Honor."

The courtroom erupted. I let out my breath long and slow and hung my head in deep gratitude, thanking God for my deliverance, before spinning around and reaching across the bar to kiss Bree, who was grinning through tears.

"Welcome back from the edge, baby," she said.

"This is a travesty of justice!" Claude Watkins shouted. "I've got a piss bag and he's frickin' not guilty? He guns down three and he's not guilty?"

Larch banged her gavel, said, "That's enough, Mr. Watkins."

"I reject this!" Watkins roared, and he spun his wheelchair around and headed out. "I do not recognize this jury or this court!"

"Neither do I!" shouted Binx, and she stormed after him.

The judge called to the officer at the door to the hallway, "Fuller, arrest them both. I want them held on suspicion of conspiracy, murder, and perjury."

Binx whirled around and shouted, "You can't be serious! This is insanity!"

"It's government persecution, that's what it is," Watkins said.

"They cooked up that whole pack of lies to bury us. It's what the police state does! Shoots you down, then makes up a goddamn excuse for shooting you down!"

As Binx struggled against the zip cuffs around her wrists and a second officer restrained Watkins in his wheelchair, my gaze snagged on Soneji's son. Dylan Winslow was on his feet, looking back at Binx and Watkins as they were taken from the courtroom. The fingers of the troubled teen's left hand trembled as he tried to grip the bench in front of him.

He was part of it, I thought. *He's got something to hide.*

The prosecutor was on his feet and furious as well.

"Your Honor," Wills said. "The verdict is the verdict, but I echo Ms. Binx and Mr. Watkins. This *is* a travesty of justice, one you can undo by vacating this verdict and demanding a retrial."

"What? And undo double jeopardy?" Anita cried. "On what constitutional grounds, Counselor?"

Larch held up her hand to stop further argument. Then she tugged her glasses down the bridge of her nose and gave the prosecutor a withering stare.

"Mr. Wills," she said. "As far as the Court is concerned, this entire trial has been a travesty of justice. Because of the naked ambitions of yourself and Ms. Carlisle, as well as the government's need for a scapegoat for the country's rash of police-involved shootings, the two of you and your bosses not only bought into a sophisticated framing of the defendant, but fully participated in a rush to justice. I anticipate someone investigating both of you very soon."

For once, the federal prosecutors were speechless.

"Dr. Cross?" Larch said.

"Your Honor."

"I am sorry this happened to you."

"Thank you, Judge Larch. I am too."

"Go and enjoy your freedom. Take care of that son of yours." She banged her gavel. "The jury is released. Case closed."

I threw my hands up and whirled around to see Bree, Jannie, Damon, Nana Mama, and my dad cheering behind me.

Tears welled in my eyes as I kissed Anita and Naomi. Then I went around, picked up Ali, and hugged my boy like he was life itself.

87

TO BE HONEST, DESPITE THE verdict, I was feeling mixed emotions sitting in a chair outside Chief Michaels's office the following Monday.

My arrest, the trial, and even the verdict had forced me to do a lot of reevaluating about my priorities and my purpose in life.

I had always seen homicide investigation as a way to represent the slain and help the friends and family of the victims find not only closure, but justice. I think of it as an honorable profession, one that, until I was arrested, gave me a great degree of fulfillment.

But turning back to clinical psychology and counseling, my first loves, had reminded me why I enjoyed that work so much. Ultimately, my job was to help people trying to understand and improve themselves and their lives. Being a psychotherapist was as noble a calling as being a homicide detective, and fulfilling in an entirely different way. And yet here I was, ready to put an end to the counselor part of me again.

"Dr. Cross?" Michaels's secretary said. "He'll see you now."

I went into the chief's office. Crossing the room to his desk, I watched Metro's leader closely, trying to read his body language. The chief had played it political during the months I'd spent on suspension pending trial. In private, he'd expressed support. In public, he'd covered his ass.

So it was a bittersweet experience when Michaels summoned his politician's smile, reached out his hand, and said, "I knew you'd be back, Alex. What would Metro do without you?"

I swallowed whatever uncomfortable feelings I'd had and thanked him for reinstating me on the Major Case Unit. In the squad room, Bree ended Sampson's suffering by reassigning Detective Ainsley Fox to another partner and putting the two of us back together. That was good, really good, maybe even better than the verdict. No bittersweet feelings at all.

I spent the rest of that first day filling out forms that sought back pay in light of the verdict and doing a pile of other administrative nonsense. But on Tuesday, Sampson and I were back on the job, with the missing blondes the first order of business. We started early, leaving DC long before dawn and driving north.

Four and a half hours later, we left Interstate 180 for State Route 220 toward Muncy Valley, Sonestown, and Laporte, Pennsylvania. It was timber country. The road was narrow, winding, and flanked on both sides by state game lands and big leafless forest tracts.

We got coffee in Laporte before stopping in at the Sullivan County Sheriff's Office to talk with Detective Everett Morse, who was working with the Pennsylvania State Police on the murder of twelve-year-old Timmy Walker Jr. and the disappearance of Ginny Krauss and Alison Dane.

Morse was collegial enough and showed us the murder book, but it had been months since Ginny and Alison had disappeared and Timmy's body had been found. The trail had gone cold. Morse told us not to bother trying to talk to the girls' parents. They'd barely spoken with Morse or the state police.

When we stopped at the Pennsylvania State Police barracks on the north side of Laporte, Investigator Nina Ford largely confirmed Morse's take on the case. She allowed us to look through her files as well, and, like Morse, discouraged us from trying to talk to the missing girls' parents.

"What about Timmy's parents?" Sampson asked.

"Big T's out of the picture," Detective Ford said. "Lenore's at the house. You could stop at Worlds End State Park, where Timmy's body was found. By the time you have a look around and get to Hillsgrove, Lenore should be up and almost coherent."

From GPS coordinates Ford gave us, we were able to pinpoint the exact location where Timmy Walker's corpse had been discovered—roughly a mile east of the parking lot at Worlds End State Park and several miles from where the missing girls' car was found.

But for an older model white Chevy pickup truck with a toolbox in the back and decals on the window from the National Wild Turkey Federation, the park's lot was deserted when we pulled in twenty minutes later.

A cold, raw wind blew while we hiked the trail and followed the GPS navigator to the rugged ground where a hiker had come across Timmy's arm sticking out from under a pile of branches and leaves.

"That's a workout, getting up here," Sampson said, chest heaving. "Trail was steep."

I nodded, my heart still hammering. "Timmy weighed ninety-two pounds, so it was someone very strong."

"And someone who knew how to get to this particular stretch of nowhere," Sampson said about two seconds before the shooting started.

88

BOOM! CA-CHING. BOOM!

Sampson and I whipped around and dived for cover behind a downed log.

Boom!

"Where the hell is he?" Sampson hissed.

Hearing popping noises, clucking, and branches snapping, I peeked up over the log and saw a flock of wild turkeys racing through the woods. Up the hill, I spotted movement. I grabbed my binoculars, focused them, and saw a teenage girl in camouflage scrambling down the steep hillside, a man carrying two shotguns right behind her.

"I got him, Dad!" I heard her yell and she threw her hands up in the air. "We both did!"

We stood and waved at the hunters as they got busy with the two dead turkeys. It wasn't until we were close that they noticed us.

The father stood, glanced at the shotguns propped up

against a tree. I guess it wasn't often he saw two men wearing coats and ties in the turkey woods.

We both showed our badges. He got stiffer. "This was a clean hunt."

"I'll take your word for it," I said. "We're here looking into the death of Timmy Walker."

He softened. "That's a tragedy. My Ellie here went to school with him. I'm Howard Young, by the way."

"Nice to meet you, Mr. Young," I said. I shook his hand and then looked at his daughter. "Tell us about Timmy."

Ellie played with a camouflage scarf around her neck and her expression soured. "TW-Two was nice growing up, but then he kind of became a creep."

"More like a little pervert," her father said.

"How's that?" Sampson said.

Ellie looked around and then said, "I don't know if it's true, but he supposedly put a hole in the wall at school so he could look into the girls' locker room. The rumor was he took pictures and showed them to his friends."

Sampson grimaced.

I said, "Was that investigated?"

"The principal said so," Ellie said. "The school even had police look at Timmy's phone, but there was nothing on it."

Her father said, "Doesn't mean there wasn't another phone or a camera. I wanted that boy thrown out of school, but they didn't do a thing. And then he died, so we'll never know, will we?"

"We're hoping to help figure out why he died," Sampson said.

Young nodded uncertainly. "Well, we've got birds to clean, and Ellie's got classes this afternoon."

We thanked them for their time and hiked back down the steep hillside to the parking lot. Had Timmy been killed for taking pictures he shouldn't have? Had the killer brought Timmy up that trail in the dark? His mother had reported him missing well after sunset, so there was a good chance. That meant the killer had a headlamp or a helper. Did that matter?

I set that thinking aside and went back to the iPad, looking at an aerial view of the area with pins that marked the locations of the girls' abandoned car, Timmy's botched burial site, and his home. The car and the house looked about a mile apart, but the killer had dumped his body miles away.

Why? To try to separate the two cases in the minds of police?

I supposed that was likely, though any detective worth his or her salt would have known the two cases were related. Same day. Same general time frame. The proximity of Timmy's home to where the girls' car was found.

So what happened? Did Timmy see the kidnapping, blunder into it somehow, and get killed for it?

That was our working theory when we pulled into the driveway of Timmy Walker's house, a restored Colonial with fresh paint and a new, seamless metal roof. It was by far the nicest home in this small mountain hamlet where most of the structures looked like hunting camps. Brown leaves covered the modest front yard. A tricycle lay tipped over by the birdbath.

Sampson knocked on the door. No answer.

He knocked harder, and the door opened. A young girl, six or maybe seven, stood there in food-stained pajamas. She had a Winnie-the-Pooh blanket around her shoulders and studied us with red eyes.

"Hi there, young lady," I said. "We're police officers. We'd like to talk to your mom."

"She's sleeping," the girl said.

"Can you wake—"

"I'm up!" a woman said, pounding down the stairs.

Mom was in a blue terry-cloth robe and barefoot. Her hair was a mess. Her eyes were puffy, rheumy, and wild when she said, "You get him? Timmy's killer?"

"Mrs. Walker?" I said.

She came up behind the girl, hugged her. "I'm his mom, Lenore. This is his sister, Kate."

We identified ourselves, said we'd like to talk to her.

"So you didn't get him?" she asked, bewildered.

"Not yet, ma'am."

The dead boy's mom swallowed thickly and looked off in despair. "No one tells me what's going on. Months Deuce has been gone and no word from anyone in weeks, not the sheriff, not the state police, not the FBI…not even my coward of an ex-husband." She broke down weeping.

Her daughter scowled at us and then turned around to hug her mother.

"It's okay, Mommy," the little girl said. "It's going to be okay."

CHAPTER

89

WHEN WE GOT LENORE WALKER calmed down enough to talk, she invited us in, and we learned that she had, by her own description, led a fairly charmed life until the night Timmy disappeared. She'd grown up in the suburbs of Philadelphia and met Tim Walker her junior year at Pennsylvania State.

Walker got a good job working as an oil engineer right out of school and made enough in the fracking industry that they bought the house, restored it, and had kids. Timmy—Deuce—was his father's favorite, and they spent many hours together early in the boy's life.

Then Walker started moving up the corporate ladder and was gone a lot. And then he discovered "playthings," as Lenore put it, and he was gone a lot more. After Deuce died, her husband, heartbroken and in love with a twenty-four-year-old, had left for good.

We asked her about the rumors, about the hole in the wall at the school. "Never happened," Lenore said.

"Your son have a computer?" Sampson asked.

"Two, or one and a half, I guess, at the end. He was always buying and selling them on eBay."

"Really?" I said. "At twelve?"

"Oh, sure. Computers, phones, iPods, anything electronic, long as it was used and cheap. It was kind of his hobby. He made pretty good money doing it."

"Police look at his computers?"

"They took them," she said. "I assume they looked at them."

"And his phone?"

"They found one."

"He had more than one?" Sampson asked.

"Sometimes three, but I only knew of two at that time. A Samsung, which they found, and a used iPhone, which they didn't."

"Anything else?"

"No. There's not much left other than pictures, videos, and my memories."

She started to cry again. Her daughter came over and hugged her until she was composed enough to tell us about the day her son disappeared.

"I wanted him to go to the store for me." She sniffed. "He'd been in for a snack and then said he was going out to play. But when I called after him, he never answered."

We asked her to point out the trail she believed Timmy had used to reach the forest clearing where the missing girls' Toyota was found. As she went to the window to show us where to find the path, Lenore expressed bitterness about the investigation, saying that state and local detectives had been more interested in the lesbians than her son.

"Then again, they're probably still alive, and my son's dead, buried, and forgotten," she said morosely as she led us to the door. "So thank you for thinking about him."

"You're welcome," I said. "We'll let you know if we make any progress."

"I believe you," she said. "Even if no one else seems willing to help."

Walking down the driveway, feeling Lenore Walker's tortured gaze on my back, I was once again grateful for my many blessings and hyperaware of how the gifts of life can disappear in the blink of an eye.

"There but for the grace of God go I," Sampson said in a soft voice.

"I hear you, brother," I said. "Loud and clear."

We found the path and went into the woods. The trail ran out across a shelf and then dropped steeply downhill to a logging road. When we came over the edge of the shelf, a black, whirling explosion went off down in the bottom.

I lurched back, ducked, and threw up my arms to protect my head.

90

A BIG FLOCK OF WILD turkeys had been feeding in the logging road when we appeared above them. They erupted off the forest floor and roared right over our heads, causing us to duck and take cover until they were gone.

"You should have seen the look on your face when they came blowing out of there," I said, grinning.

"I almost had a heart attack." Sampson laughed. "You did too."

"I'm a city boy, not used to getting attacked by wild critters."

"Critters?"

"I'm trying to channel my inner country."

"Yee-haw," Sampson said and dropped down the bank onto the logging road. "Boy, those damn birds really tear up the place, don't they?"

I saw what he meant. For a good fifty yards in every direction, the leaves were all fluffed and piled up where the turkeys had scratched and overturned them looking for food.

"There had to have been forty of them," I said.

"At least," Sampson said, heading down the trail to where it met a creek.

We paralleled the creek for almost a mile to a fork in the two-track road. We went left and found the creek crossing Lenore Walker had described and continued on up a short hill.

At the top of the rise, we could see through the bare trees some ninety yards across a wide flat to the clearing where Alison Dane's Toyota Camry had been found, abandoned. The flock of turkeys had been there before us, tearing up the forest floor on both sides of the trail all the way to the clearing.

I had a picture on my phone of the Toyota Camry as it was found, and we were able to use it to figure out roughly where the car must have been. We crossed the clearing to the spot.

Looking back to where the logging road met the opening, I said, "So Timmy comes to the edge of the woods over there, and sees what?"

"The car, the girls," Sampson said. "And maybe whoever grabbed them."

"Sure, it's not far. Sixty yards? Seventy?"

"Sounds right, but then what? Someone sees Timmy?"

I nodded. "Chases him down, crushes his throat."

Sampson took a big breath and let it go. "Poor kid."

"Right?" I said, looking around and feeling upset.

I guess I'd hoped driving to this place four and a half hours away would help, and while seeing the crime scene gave us a clearer sense of where the girls and Timmy had been on the day in question, I didn't see any new light indicating the end of the tunnel.

Sampson said, "It's pushing noon. We should go back, get the car, and find somewhere to eat before we head home."

"Sounds like a plan," I said.

We crossed the clearing, bowing our heads and pulling up our coat collars against the raw wind blowing. It was calmer in the woods, but I still hustled to get back to the car and the heater.

So did Sampson, until something caught his eye. He pulled up, said, "Hold on a second. I saw something back there."

He walked back down the trail a few steps and then went right six or seven more through the leaves and loose forest duff the turkeys had scratched and turned over.

John stopped and glanced around. He took one step and then another before halting, digging a handkerchief from his pocket, and crouching in the leaves.

When he stood up, Sampson held out a dirty white iPhone.

91

THE FOLLOWING EVENING AROUND SEVEN, Ali dashed into the kitchen where the rest of us were cleaning up after dinner.

"Jannie!" he cried. "A cab pulled up! He's here!"

"Oh God," Jannie said, holding her stomach. "I shouldn't have eaten so much. I think I'm going to be sick."

Nana Mama squeezed her arm gently. "You're going to do just fine. If he wasn't already impressed, he wouldn't be here, so just be yourself."

"Great advice," I said just before the doorbell rang.

"I'll get it!" Ali cried.

"No," I said. "Jannie and I will get it."

"C'mon, Ali," my dad said. "Sit down, have a piece of Nana's shoofly pie."

"With ice cream?" Ali said.

"He deserves ice cream," I said as I followed Jannie.

"You've been saying that every night since the trial ended," Nana Mama complained.

"And I'll be saying that every night for a little while longer."

Before I left the kitchen, I blew a kiss at Bree, who caught it and smiled. We'd both carved out time for each other the past few days despite our busy schedules, and all in all my personal life was starting to feel much more balanced than it had for well over a year.

Not that things couldn't be better. Lenore Walker had said that she thought the iPhone Sampson found in the woods was her son's, but she wasn't sure. And when we'd taken the device to Keith Rawlins at Quantico earlier in the day, he'd noted that the water damage was going to make it exceedingly difficult for him to access the phone's data, if he could do it at all.

Despite Rawlins's promise to work every bit of magic he knew, we'd left the FBI's cybercrimes lab feeling frustrated. In our minds, the phone *was* Timmy Walker's, but unless we could get into it, we were once again at a dead end when it came to his murder. And even though we didn't have a smoking gun connecting the boy's death to the missing blondes, it felt like, without the phone, we would never find Gretchen Lindel, Ginny Krauss, Alison Dane, Delilah Franks, Patsy Mansfield, and Cathy Dupris.

But good things had happened too. Nana had taken a phone call for Jannie at home and relayed the message to me, and that had led to near pandemonium as everyone in our family tried to rearrange things in order to be home when the doorbell rang.

In the front hall now, Jannie looked over her shoulder, and I said, "Go on."

She opened the front door, revealing a tall, lean, African American man in his early forties. He wore a blue suit with a green and gold tie, and he beamed when he saw my daughter.

322

"Jannie Cross," he said, smiling as he shook her hand. "I'm so glad we could work out a time to meet."

Jannie was dumbstruck but managed to say, "I am too, sir, uh, Coach."

I said, "She's thrilled you're here. We all are."

"Dr. Cross?" he said, turning his hundred-watt smile on me and reaching to shake my hand. "I'm Robert Johnson."

"Please, come in, Coach," I said. "My grandmother makes a mean pie if you're interested."

"I'm always interested in pie," he said. "What kind?"

"Shoofly pie without the sugar bomb," Jannie said. "She got the recipe from an Amish cookbook and altered it with maple syrup."

"I would love some of that," he said.

I led the way back to the kitchen, where Coach Johnson introduced himself to everyone and good-naturedly submitted to Nana Mama when she ordered him to sit down and have some pie and a cup of green tea.

"Jannie," Johnson said after finishing his dessert, "I'm not going to lie to you. The food at the University of Oregon is not as good as you're used to at home."

My grandmother loved that.

"Unless you could convince Nana to move to Eugene with you," he said. "Then the entire Ducks track team could benefit."

That pleased Nana even more. "You're scoring brownie points, Coach."

"I was hoping so," Coach Johnson said, and he winked at her. "Can I tell you all about our program?"

"Please," Bree said.

Johnson said, "Since I took over as head track coach at the University of Oregon three years ago, we have won eight national championships: men's indoor and outdoor track, women's indoor and outdoor track, and women's cross-country. Oregon has been honored as the national Men's and Women's Programs of the Year in each of the past two years. The women won it the year before that as well."

Once Coach Johnson started his recruiting pitch, his attention rarely left Jannie, who was listening raptly.

"Twenty-eight Duck athletes have won NCAA individual championships under my watch," Johnson went on. "Including Phyllis Francis."

Jannie sat up straighter. "She set the American record in the indoor four-hundred."

"She did," Johnson said, and he paused to look around at us all. "And I think you can beat that record, Jannie."

CHAPTER

92

JANNIE LOOKED AS STUNNED AS I felt. The American record?

"I really do believe that," Johnson said to me. "I've watched Jannie's films. I've reviewed her training times, her program, and her progress with Coach McDonald. We both feel that record is within the range of possibility *if* she chooses and applies herself in the right program."

"Your program," my father said.

"There's none better," the coach replied. "Oregon's track-and-field tradition is deep and wide. We have the finest facility in the country at Hayward Field. The weather is near perfect for year-round training. And we have the best coaches and trainers. Period."

"What about the academics?" Bree asked.

"Amen," Nana Mama said.

"The university offers two hundred and seventy different majors, from the sciences to engineering to education and the arts. Our program in sports marketing is ranked number one in the country. The Clark Honors College is the oldest of its kind in the country and attracts many gifted students such as yourself, Jannie.

"Academics and sports aside, the campus is stunningly beautiful. Eugene is one of the most vibrant places I've ever lived. And we offer all of our athletes tutors to make sure they stay eligible to compete and, most important, to graduate."

"Are you offering my sister a scholarship?" Ali asked.

Coach Johnson laughed. "You don't fool around, do you?"

Ali grinned and shook his head.

"Maybe *you* should go into sports marketing, young man," Johnson said. "Be your sister's agent someday."

Ali smiled and said, "You didn't answer the question."

The coach laughed again, looked at me. "He's a little tiger."

"Every day," I said.

Coach Johnson turned to Jannie. "You know how I first heard of you?"

My daughter shook her head.

"When you were on ESPN."

Imitating the ESPN announcer, Ali said, "That girl ran so fast she broke her foot!"

The coach nodded. "That's the one. How's the foot doing?"

"Really good," Jannie said.

"No pain?"

"Not for a long time."

"You're a lucky, lucky young lady," Johnson said. "That injury could have been a career ender. But it wasn't, and so, Jannie Cross, I *am* here to offer you a scholarship, a full ride—tuition, room, and board—at the University of Oregon in exchange for a signed national letter of intent to run for the Ducks."

I don't think Jannie expected that. I know I didn't. She hadn't even competed in her junior year of spring outdoor track. I'd figured if she ran well from now on, she might start getting real offers in the fall of her senior year.

"I'm thrilled, but do I have to answer right now, Coach?" she said, smiling and biting her lip.

"Of course not," he said. "It would make my life easier if you did, but my life isn't what's at stake. Yours is. So I'm going to give you some advice, because I think you're a rare talent whether or not you come to Eugene to run for me. Jannie, you are going to get multiple scholarship offers. You should visit every school that you're interested in and really explore the people and the places and the track programs before you make a decision. I know Eugene is far from Washington, DC, but would you be interested in paying us a visit?"

Jannie looked relieved that she didn't have to decide on the spot, glanced at me, and nodded. "I'd like that, Coach."

"Excellent," Johnson said. "When could you bring her out?" he asked me.

I glanced at Bree, who said, "Winter vacation?"

"Perfect," he said. "Oh, and those plane tickets will be on the Ducks."

"Can I come?" Ali asked.

"Absolutely not," Jannie said.

Coach Johnson stayed a few more minutes, answering our questions, and charming Nana Mama no end.

"I'll be back for more of that pie," he told her as he was leaving.

"You're always welcome, Coach Johnson."

When the door shut, we were all grinning like fools. Bree kissed Jannie, who said, "Did that really just happen?"

"Best track program in the country," I said, feeling my eyes water.

"Long way from home," Nana Mama said in a way that made me realize she probably wouldn't get to see Jannie run in person if she went to Oregon.

"It is a really long way," Jannie said. "I don't know about that."

"You don't have to know right now," I said. "We'll listen to everyone, and you'll make the decision when *you* are ready. Okay?"

Jannie hugged me. "Thanks, Dad. I'm so glad you were here for that. It could have been different. You know?"

I closed my eyes, kissed the top of her head, and said, "I do, baby girl. I really do."

CHAPTER

93

WHEN THE ELEVATOR DOOR OPENED onto the second subbasement below the FBI's Cyber Division, Keith Rawlins had the tunes cranked inside his lab. The thudding, infectious bass line of Flo Rida's "My House" came right through the glass window and seemed to vibrate in my chest.

It was a few minutes past seven in the morning, and Rawlins had evidently been in the lab all night. But you wouldn't have known it. The digital wizard was stripped to his denim shorts, covered in sweat, and bouncing up and down on a minitrampoline while punching the air in time to the beat.

"I still can't believe this guy works for us," said Special Agent in Charge Mahoney, my old partner at the FBI, who had taken over the missing-blondes case for the Bureau.

"I suffer the indignity of it every day," Special Agent Batra said.

"This could have waited a few hours," Sampson said, and he yawned.

I said, "He was excited enough about it to call us at five a.m."

"This better be good," Sampson said. "All I'm saying."

Batra rolled her eyes and shouldered open the lab door. The music was blasting. Rawlins had Flo Rida's music video playing on all screens. He spotted us and high-stepped our way, slinging his limp black Mohawk back and forth while singing, "'Welcome to my house!'"

Mahoney and Batra looked like they'd spent the night sleeping on coarse sandpaper. I smiled and drew my finger across my throat.

Rawlins stopped dancing, pouted, picked up a remote, and froze the video. The lab got quiet.

"The best part was just coming," he said. "Clay Pritchard lays down the best saxophone licks since—"

"You woke us up, called us in here," Batra grumbled. "It wasn't to dance, was it? Because if it was, I'm gonna be pissed."

"Beyond pissed," Mahoney said.

Rawlins sighed, said, "Sometimes I wonder if the academy's training just squeezes the soul and celebration out of every agent who graduates Quantico."

"Let's see what you've got, Krazy Kat," I said.

Rawlins fashioned his hair into a bun like a samurai's topknot, a style that appeared to give Mahoney and Batra indigestion. The computer scientist waved a finger at me with one hand and snatched up a towel with the other.

"Took me almost three days straight, but I was able to raise the dead."

"You calling yourself the Messiah now?" Batra said.

"Just a miracle worker," Rawlins said as he toweled his upper body dry.

He put on an FBI sweatshirt and a pair of black-and-white

checkered sneakers before strolling over to the keyboard for the main screen array.

"A lot of the data was corrupted," he said, typing. "But I was able to salvage a few things from the day Timmy Walker was killed."

Rawlins hit Enter, and Flo Rida and his house disappeared on the screens, replaced by shaky video showing a wooded scene. The cameraman was sneaking through thick foliage.

I had no idea where it was shot until a boy's hand came forward and pushed aside leafy vines and saplings to reveal the lip of a dirt bank. The camera tilted down the bank and out twenty feet toward a blue Toyota Camry in a familiar clearing. The windows of the car were down.

The camera trembled, and you could hear Timmy Walker breathing hard while Ginny Krauss and Alison Dane made love naked in the backseat.

"The little Peeping Tom creep," Batra said.

"It is creepy," Rawlins said. "But I think you're going to like little peeping Timmy, God rest his soul, before it's over."

The camera settled and zoomed in. Alison Dane's hand slid from her lover's breast and trailed down over her belly, and then she seemed to hear something. The cameraman did too.

The focus went haywire for a moment before settling back on the girls, who were scrambling for their clothes. Then Ginny Krauss happened to look out the window and up the bank, straight at the camera.

She screamed, "There's some pervo kid in camo out there! He's filming us!"

Timmy apparently whirled around and took off back into the forest. The next twenty-seven seconds were herky-jerky, mostly flashes of green in a dim forest.

Then, over the croaking of tree frogs and the thrumming of crickets, you could hear a vehicle roar into the clearing and skid to a stop. One of the girls screamed.

The camera turned back and began moving again, going closer to the clearing, zooming in on a white Ford utility van idling in front of the Camry.

One of the girls started screaming again. "Please! Don't do this! Help! Kid! Help us, kid!"

The screen went black.

Rawlins said, "Unfortunately, that's all the video I could recover."

"Shit," Sampson said. "Can you give us a blown-up look at that van?"

"I don't need to," Rawlins said. "Timmy did."

He gave the keyboard several more orders and the biggest screen was filled with a digital photograph showing a grainy zoomed-in view of the van. The windows were tinted, so we couldn't get a look at the interior, but the signage on the side was clearly visible.

"Dish Network?" Mahoney said.

"And those are Maryland plates," I said. "Five, seven, E, one…can't make out the—"

"It's a six," Rawlins said. "You see it better in the other photographs."

"How many other photographs?" Sampson said.

"Five. Timmy could have just kept running after the girls spotted him. But he heard them screaming and decided to take these pictures. I think he was going to go to the police with them. Otherwise, why take the risk? Why not do the natural thing for a twelve-year-old boy caught with his hand in the pervert cookie jar and just run?"

Judging from her body language, Batra seemed to have some issue with the theory, but Mahoney said, "I think you're right."

"I do too," I said. "I also think those pictures got Timmy Walker killed."

"Oh, I know they did," Rawlins said. "The phone died less than twenty-five seconds after the last picture was taken."

94

JUST AFTER DARK THAT SAME day, Sampson, Mahoney, and I were watching FBI crime scene techs getting ready to tear apart a white Ford utility van with Dish Network signage on both sides. It was in the parking lot at the Dish authorized-seller store in Rockville, Maryland, and roped off with police tape.

The store manager, a small, cranelike man named Lester Potter, was rubbing his hands together and watching nervously.

"You know that van was stolen, right?" Potter said.

"When was that?" Sampson asked.

"Five, six months ago? One of my techs was out doing a residential satellite install in Gaithersburg. She's in the house not ten minutes, comes out, and the van's gone. Boosted in broad daylight. They disabled the tracking device. Six weeks go by, and the company's written it off, figured it was looted and chopped up for parts. But then we get a call. Pennsylvania state troopers found it abandoned in long-term parking at the Harrisburg airport. It's crazy, but they didn't take a thing. That van was as clean and shipshape as it was when it was stolen. Someone just took it for a joyride."

"No," Sampson said. "Someone took it to kidnap two teenage girls who are still being held captive and terrorized to satisfy the twisted fantasies of Internet trolls."

"Oh," Potter said, his face turning pale. "I had no idea."

"Who was the driver the day it was stolen?" I said.

"Lourdes Rodriguez," he said. "One of my best employees ever."

"Can we talk with Ms. Rodriguez?"

"She doesn't work here anymore," Potter said. "Lucky gal inherited a pile of money from a great-uncle and took this job and shoved it a few months ago."

Sampson said, "I guess the glamour of being a satellite installer wasn't enough to keep her on the Dish Network career path."

The store manager gave him an odd look, said, "Who could blame her?"

"No one," I said. "You have contact information for Ms. Rodriguez?"

"I'm sure I do somewhere."

"Could you do us a solid and dig it up?"

Potter's nose twitched as if he thought the task beneath him, but he went inside.

"Why take nothing?" I said.

"How many people without training know how to install satellites?" Sampson said. "And I can't imagine they're easy to sell on the black market. They say *Dish* all over—"

"Agent Mahoney?" Karen Getty, an FBI crime scene tech, called out.

Getty was standing at the rear of the van wearing disposable white coveralls, latex gloves, and blue booties over her shoes. The two rear doors of the van were open, revealing shelves, boxes of supplies, six satellite dishes, and stacked rolls of cable.

"You're going to want to see this," Getty said.

We all went to the rear of the van, which looked spotless.

"Kill the lights," she said.

The interior lights died. So did the spots brought in to illuminate the search. She picked up a bottle marked LUMINOL and started spraying it around.

Luminol is a compound that glows when it's exposed to certain substances, like the iron in hemoglobin. When someone tries to clean up blood, traces of it are left behind; spray that area with luminol, and the chemical glows blue for a brief period.

There were a few blood spatters immediately visible on the van floor close to the doors. The more Getty sprayed, the more spatters appeared, until it looked like a starry night had been superimposed on the van's floor, ceiling, and walls.

"What the hell is that?" Potter said. The manager had come up behind us.

Sampson looked at him and said, "Evidence of a slaughter."

CHAPTER

95

THE NEXT MORNING, SAMPSON AND I drove to the address of the woman who'd been driving the van the night it was stolen. Lourdes Rodriguez lived in Silver Spring, Maryland, on the eighth floor of a large, midpriced, brick-faced apartment building.

At the locked front door, we buzzed Rodriguez's apartment number, 805, and got no answer. We figured that with an apartment building that big, there might be a live-in superintendent, and we lucked out when Arnie Feiffer answered our ring and soon buzzed us in.

Sampson and I entered a foyer featuring 1970s decor that showed the dings and scratches of time and neglect.

"Not where I'd be living if I'd inherited a boatload," Sampson said.

I agreed, thinking that I'd expect a woman in her early thirties with newfound wealth to choose to live in one of the newer, more luxurious apartment buildings in downtown Silver Spring or...

A door to our right opened. A television blared the patter of an announcer for *American Ninja Warrior*. A nebbishy man in his sixties shuffled out of the apartment wearing a maroon bathrobe over his clothes, slippers, and a blue-and-white yarmulke on his head.

He squinted through round glasses. "You the cops?"

"You the super?" Sampson asked as we showed him our identifications.

"Lord of the castle," he said. "Arnie Feiffer. How can I help, Detectives?"

"We'd like to go knock on Lourdes Rodriguez's door," I said.

"Why? What's she done?"

"We just want to ask her a few questions about her prior workplace."

Feiffer hesitated, then said, "I'll go with you, if you don't mind."

"Not at all," I said.

"C'mon, then," he said, and he shuffled by us, heading to the elevators. Posted on one of the two was a handwritten sign that read *Out of Service*.

We rode the creaking, shuddering lift to the eighth floor. The doors squealed open, and we stepped out into a musty hallway with dingy rugs.

We walked down the hall to apartment 805 and rang the bell. There was no answer. We knocked, but no one came to the door. I was about to suggest we leave business cards with a note asking her to call us when from inside we heard the high-pitched mewing and cries of a cat that sounded very upset.

"A cat?" Feiffer said furiously. "No cats. No dogs. The lease is clear."

After a glance at me, Sampson said, "It's within your rights to remove the cat from your property. We'll help. It's the least we can do for you."

The superintendent studied us suspiciously. "You're not looking to get around a warrant, are you?"

Sampson said, "If we wanted to do that, we'd tell you we smelled gas."

"I run electric," Feiffer said as the cat's cries turned frantic.

"Sounds like it's hungry," I said. "We could always call in Animal Control for suspicion of neglect on Ms. Rodriguez's part. They could get us in."

The super didn't like that and grudgingly dug under his robe for a key ring. He found the master key and used it to turn the dead bolt and unlock the door.

Feiffer pushed the door open. A filthy yellow-and-orange tabby sprang out and darted between our legs before any of us could grab it. The cat sprinted down the hall, took a sharp right, and disappeared.

"I'm getting too old for this crap," Feiffer said with a moan, his palm to his forehead.

I saw he wasn't talking about the cat but about the apartment. The place was empty and swept clean.

96

FEIFFER TRUDGED INTO THE MODEST one-bedroom apartment and we followed.

When he reached the living area, he gazed around in disbelief. "She never said anything about leaving."

"We heard she'd inherited a lot of money," I said.

"That right?" the super said, raising one bushy gray eyebrow. "She never mentioned it, but why would she? How long ago?"

"Few months."

"Big money and she lived *here* for months?" Feiffer said, incredulous.

What could I say? The man knew his place in the market.

"Could we see your copy of her lease?" Sampson asked.

"Why?" he said, suspicious again.

"I gather you have no forwarding address since she skipped out, but there will be bank and reference information in the lease agreement that might help us figure out where she's gone."

Feiffer considered that and then nodded.

After confirming that Rodriguez had indeed removed all her possessions, we were on our way out when I noticed some newspapers in a brown paper bag behind the door. I picked the bag up, hoping they'd give us an idea of how long she'd been gone.

I pulled out a stack of loose newspaper sections and flipped through a few.

The sections were all from the *Washington Post*, several going back a month or more, front pages mostly, with a few Metro sections thrown in. I kept looking through the newspapers as we rode down and noticed something that quickly became a troubling pattern.

I kept it to myself until Feiffer had gone into his apartment and we were alone in the lobby.

"We're keeping these papers," I said, slipping them back in the bag.

"Why's that?" Sampson asked.

"In almost every section there's a story about Gretchen Lindel or one of the other missing girls."

"So maybe Lourdes Rodriguez had reason to sneak out in the middle of the night."

"Maybe she did."

Feiffer emerged from his apartment with a file marked APARTMENT 805—L. RODRIGUEZ. I flipped the file open, took a glance at the standard rental-agreement form, and then zeroed in on a photo of the tenant stapled to the contract.

"Huh," I said, seeing Rodriguez in a whole new light. I took a picture of the rental agreement and the photo, then handed the contract back to Feiffer.

"That it? I've got to go find that cat."

We thanked the super for his time and left. The second the front door clicked behind us, Sampson said, "What did you see on that lease?"

"My poker face didn't work?"

"I have known you since we were ten."

I pulled up the shot of the picture stapled to the contract.

"Lourdes Rodriguez?" I said. "I know her by another name."

CHAPTER

97

THE ULTRA-LUXURY UNION WHARF apartment complex on Fell's Point was the most expensive place to live in Baltimore, costing five times what Lourdes Rodriguez had been paying at Feiffer's. We'd used the bank account and other information on Rodriguez's old lease to track her to her new digs.

A small moving van was snarling traffic on South Wolfe Street. The front door to one of the apartment buildings was propped open for workmen carrying furniture wrapped in blankets. We followed them inside and up the stairs to 2E.

The door was open. Reggae music was playing. The workmen went in. So did we.

I trailed Sampson past stacks of moving boxes choking the front hallway, hearing a familiar voice saying, "Be careful with that! It was my mother's!"

We stepped out into a living area with large glass windows that gave a sweeping and dramatic view of Baltimore Harbor. Wearing jeans and a loose-fitting pink jersey, Lourdes Rodriguez paced by the window, watching the workmen move a table into position.

She looked puzzled when she saw Sampson standing there holding his badge. Then she noticed me.

I stepped into the room, said, "You never sent me your new e-mail, Annie."

For a second, the love junkie was so shocked, I thought she might faint dead away.

Then she croaked, "Dr. Cross? What are you doing here?"

"I could say the same, Annie. Or is it Lourdes?"

She swallowed, looked away. "Lourdes."

"Why'd you use the fake name when you came to see me?"

Rodriguez blinked, puffed out her cheeks, and glanced at the workmen, who were leaving the room. "Isn't this privileged?"

"Not when it comes to murder, kidnapping, and torture," Sampson said.

That threw her. "What are you talking…" She looked at me. "Dr. Cross, I came to you under an alias because of the addiction I told you about. I don't know anything about any torture or murder or kidnapping."

"The van that was stolen from you when you were working for Dish," Sampson said. "We ran tests on the interior. Whole lot of blood spatter."

She looked down. "Blood spatter? I don't…it was stolen. I had nothing to do with that."

"Didn't you?" I said. "The same van was caught on film when two blond girls from Pennsylvania were taken."

Her jaw dropped, and she took a step backward.

"Seemed a big coincidence," Sampson said. "Given that you left behind all those articles about the same missing girls at your old apartment at Mr. Feiffer's."

"And given that I saw you leaving my office in a car driven by a man posing as Alden Lindel, the father of one of the missing girls," I said.

She shook her head as if trying to clear it. "Wait. What? The father of one of the missing girls?"

"A man who's been claiming to be him. You got into his Nissan Pathfinder right after our one and only session. I saw you. What is going on, Annie, Lourdes, whatever your real name is?"

She threw up her hands in exasperation. "Last time I left your office? I called Uber. They sent some Uber guy. You can check. I'm sure there's a record."

Uber? Was that possible? The fake Alden was an Uber driver. You call for an Uber car and usually the one that's closest responds. Which meant what? That the impostor, whoever he was, had been close by, watching my house?

"We will check Uber," Sampson said. "What about the news articles?"

Rodriguez rubbed her neck, didn't look at us, and didn't reply.

"It's going to come out sooner or later," I said. "Courts go easier on the first person in a conspiracy to flip."

"Conspiracy?" she said sharply. "No, it's nothing like that. Not really."

"What the hell does that mean?"

Looking flustered now, Rodriguez wrung her hands and then held them up in surrender.

"Okay, okay, I got caught up in something a long time ago, Dr. Cross, and…I'll tell you everything I know. Everything. The honest-to-God truth."

98

TWO HOURS AND FORTY-FIVE minutes later, Sampson had gotten off I-95 and was driving us north on Front Street, which parallels the freeway and the Delaware River as they pass through Philadelphia. The weather was changing. Dark clouds boiled on the western horizon.

"Chalabi sounds like a first-class creep," Sampson said.

"He won't be the first to achieve film success that way," I said. We went over the high points of Rodriguez's confession for the fourth or fifth time.

A childhood friend of Lourdes Rodriguez, Casey Chalabi, had always wanted to be a movie director.

"He ended up making porn films under the name Dirk Wallace," Rodriguez told us. "It's all S-and-M, bondage, the hard stuff."

She said Chalabi put aside money from the porn shoots to fund production of a horror film he'd written.

"Horror's cheap to film," she'd said. "Casey said you can

do them for under a million. James Wan did *Saw* for a little over five hundred thousand, and it made, like, fifty-five million. Casey's trying to model himself on Wan."

Rodriguez claimed that even with the porn money, Casey's horror flick was being shot on a shoestring. When he learned she was going to inherit her great-uncle's fortune, he was immediately after Rodriguez to help fund his film.

"I gave him some, and I didn't even have the inheritance yet," she said. "I took it from my savings. Five thousand. And then another five. Then Casey wanted the van, my van at Dish. He said even with the money I'd given him, he couldn't afford to buy or rent one, and mine was perfect. He wanted me to just lend it to him for the night."

"What'd you say?"

"I said no. No way. But Casey can be a vindictive a-hole."

Sampson raised his eyebrows. "You saying Chalabi stole your van?"

"I'd put money on it. And that blood you found inside? Was it human?"

"We don't know yet," I said.

"It's probably pig's blood. He uses lots of pig's blood in the big slasher scenes in *Blade*."

I thought about that for several moments. "So he steals your van, uses it in a killing scene in his movie. I'm still having trouble seeing how this connects to those newspaper articles we found at Feiffer's."

Rodriguez swallowed hard. "I haven't spoken with Casey since my van was stolen, but I read his script a long time ago. It's about these four sisters who inherit an abandoned factory and this old Victorian house. Then it's pretty much like every other horror flick you see. Except the sisters. They're all ethereal and blond. Every one of them. And they get killed, one by one."

Which was enough for us to drive to Philadelphia to talk to Mr. Chalabi face-to-face.

Rodriguez had given us the last address she had for Chalabi. She said she thought it was where he shot the porn movies. We found the address, a rehabbed old school called the Emerson that had been turned into lofts and work spaces down the street from the Theatre of Living Arts.

Rodriguez couldn't remember the exact name of Chalabi's company, but we found C. C. PRODUCTIONS listed on a board at the entrance to the Emerson. It was on the second floor, unit 2, the address Rodriguez had given us.

We took the staircase and walked down a long hallway past the open doors of artists' studios and the closed doors of others in the arts and entertainment fields. The place smelled nice. There was music playing.

It had a good vibe, all in all, and that bothered me as we walked up to the closed door of C. C. Productions. I couldn't see the management letting him shoot porn or slasher flicks on the premises.

Sampson knocked, turned the knob, and opened the door. I took one look inside and swore to myself.

C. C. Productions was an animation company. There were framed cartoon stills on the wall above the workstation of an Indian American woman in her twenties who looked up and smiled.

"Can I help you?" she said.

Sampson said, "We're looking for Casey Chalabi."

"I'm Cassandra Chalabi," she said.

"Of course you are," I said, furious. "Sorry to bother you."

We shut the door. Sampson said, "Con artist."

"Total pro. Pathological liar."

"How much you wanna bet she's started making a third move since we left?"

"Not a nickel. Lourdes Rodriguez, Annie Cassidy, whatever she calls herself, is in the wind."

99

WHEN SAMPSON AND I RETURNED to the front door of the arts building, gloom had set in outside, and a chill rain fell on hurried pedestrians bent to the storm.

"We're gonna get soaked," Sampson said.

"Run for it," I said. I jerked open the door and hopped out. Rain driven by a strong north wind pelted my face and eyes, forcing me to duck my head and throw my forearm across my brow as I ran toward the car, virtually blind.

As I was crossing Seventh Street, I stepped in a pothole. My right foot and shoe were submerged, my ankle and lower shin hit the edge of the depression, and I stumbled and sprawled in front of a Chrysler Sebring waiting at the light.

But that probably saved my life, because as soon as I tripped, I heard a thumping noise and the Sebring's right headlight exploded.

"Shooter!" Sampson shouted; he grabbed me by the back of the jacket, hauled me behind the Sebring, and threw me to the ground just before a second bullet smacked into the grille and penetrated the radiator, which threw steam.

The Sebring's driver started screaming in a language I didn't recognize. My shin was screaming in a language I didn't recognize. But I forced myself to dig for my service weapon and badge.

"Where is he?" I said.

Sampson said, "I caught a flash of the first shot, elevated slightly, northwest corner of the intersection and back. Sounded suppressed too."

I ignored the pain in my leg and got up enough to look over the hood through the teeming rain. The traffic light on one-way South Street had gone yellow. Two cars passed. Their headlights threw glare that dazzled me until the third shot.

I saw the flare of it, and then the Sebring's windshield and passenger-side window fragmented as the bullet passed through both. I ducked down, hearing the frightened screams from the driver turn petrified.

"Pickup parked on the north side of South Street," I said.

The light turned green on Seventh. The hysterical Sebring driver stomped on the gas, but the car bucked, stalled, and belched steam and smoke before dying ten feet into the intersection. The drivers of several cars behind us spun their tires, trying to get around the Sebring.

Other cars began honking frantically.

Sampson said, "Pickup's running the red."

In one motion I stood and had my pistol in my shooting hand over the Sebring's passenger-side mirror. I was aiming at the pickup, which was trying to avoid the skidding cars in the intersection. For a moment I had nothing to shoot at.

Then I picked up a shadow, someone dressed in black standing in profile against the back of the truck cab. He shifted, exposing the sound suppressor on the muzzle of his rifle.

"Gun," I said; I fired, and missed.

The gunman returned fire, but the shot went wide. Sampson's shot went wide as well, two feet to the gunman's right, shattering the truck's driver-side window. The brakes went on. A Volvo station wagon turning the corner onto South smashed into the truck's rear corner panel, throwing the gunman off his feet. He fell behind the walls of the truck bed.

I hobbled after a charging Sampson, his gun and badge up to oncoming traffic, and my gut feeling was that something terrible was going to happen unless I kept up with my partner.

Trying to back up, the Volvo almost ran us over. We dodged around it as the pickup's brake lights went off and the truck started to roll again, passing beneath street lamps as it slowly gained speed.

We ran with it, and I caught a glimpse of the driver, a scruffy-faced guy with a tangle of dark hair and bleeding cheeks. The pickup pulled away. The gunman rose to his knees in the bed and looked at us, grinning.

The truck sped up and was gone into a mash of red taillights long before the police sirens started to wail.

"No light on the license plate," Sampson said in disgust as we walked through the still-pouring rain back to the smoking Sebring. "Probably smashed when it got rear-ended."

"There was enough light on the shooter, though," I said, limping and feeling twisted and toyed with. "He likes to call himself Alden Lindel."

Part Five

ALL BLONDES
MUST DIE

100

AT HOME THE NEXT EVENING, I was on my back with my ankle elevated and iced, watching coverage of the shooting incident on a DC station.

"There Detective Cross goes again," said assistant U.S. attorney Nathan Wills, peering in disgust at the camera from under an umbrella. "He's not back on the job a week and already the bullets are flying."

"Those bullets flew my way first," I said and stabbed the remote until the screen went black.

"The brass know that," Bree said, coming out of the kitchen into our great room and setting a cup of coffee on the table beside me.

"Michaels put me on leave," I said. "Again."

"Department regulations," Bree said, sitting beside me. "Sampson's no better off than you."

"Better ankle," I said.

"Well, there's that," Bree said.

We fell into a silence that got longer. I stared at the blank screen, wondering for the hundredth time why the man impersonating Alden Lindel was fixated on me. Was he part of the crew that tried to frame me for murder? Picking up where Claude Watkins and Kimiko Binx left off?

And what about Lourdes Rodriguez? Was that even her real name?

In the wake of media uproar surrounding the shooting in Philly, Chief Michaels had been in no mood to seek a search warrant for her new apartment, even when we explained that she'd set us up to be assassinated.

"I'm beginning to wonder if this is worth it anymore," I said, looking over at Bree. "Being a cop, I mean."

Cocking her head, frowning, she set her coffee down. "You're serious?"

"I'm serious enough to know that I want to stay being a psychologist, a counselor, at least part-time," I said. "I enjoy it. It feels right and matters in a way hunting down bad guys just doesn't anymore, Bree."

She gazed at me, blinked. "You are serious."

"I guess I am. Maybe it's time. They say most people have five careers in their lives. Maybe this is how I'm supposed to be the best I can be in the future."

"A higher calling?"

I sighed. "Is that so hard to believe?"

Bree smiled at me, but there was a tinge of sadness in it. "No, I could understand it. At least of an ordinary cop, who'd seen too much. But you're no ordinary cop, Alex Cross."

"That's debatable."

"Tell that to the awards and citations you have piled in your attic office. Tell that to all the families of victims you've helped just by being you, relentless, smart, and professional with a moral compass that is unwavering."

"I'm impulsive," I said. "I get shot at. A lot."

"Because you have the God-given knack of getting close to bad guys and upsetting their plans. You actually do that on a regular basis, Alex. Very, very few detectives can say that."

Before I could reply, Ali pounded through the kitchen and out to us.

"Dad!" he said. "I think I've finally found my sport!"

Of my three children, my youngest might be the brightest, but he is, shall we say, challenged athletically. Ali had tried various sports—basketball, baseball, and even lacrosse—but nothing ever clicked, and he seemed to trip over his own feet a lot.

"I'm hoping your sport's not ice hockey," I said.

"What?" Ali said, almost indignant. "No."

"Horse jumping?"

"No. Darts."

"Darts?"

"There's a tournament coming up," he said. "I've been playing a bunch at my friend Charley's house after school, but I need my own board and a set of good darts if I'm going to have any chance of qualifying."

Feeling a twinge in my ankle, I closed my eyes. I heard Bree say, "Where's this tournament?"

"At a bar on Capitol Hill," Ali said.

"A bar?" I said, opening my eyes.

"Technically, a tavern. I walk by there all the time after the bus drops me."

"You're not going to a bar or a tavern to play darts."

"It's a ten-thousand-dollar prize, Dad!"

"You're too young to be playing darts where people are drinking alcohol."

"No, I went in and asked. As long as you're with me, they said I can play."

The doorbell rang.

"I'll get it," Bree said.

"Let Ali," I said.

"Can I get the dartboard?"

"Start by getting the door."

He hesitated, then ran out.

"Darts?" Bree said, trying to hide her smile. "In a tavern?"

"Nana Mama is going to have a cow," I said, laughing.

"She's going to have two cows. Maybe an entire dairy farm if this becomes a regular thing."

"Darts," I said, and I shook my head at how quickly Ali went from a sharp and analytical adult-like person to a young boy attracted by the next shiny object.

I heard his footsteps pound back to us, and I thought for sure he was going to ask about the darts again.

Instead, he said breathlessly, "It's Ned and Krazy Kat!"

101

KEITH RAWLINS'S MOHAWK HAD BEEN redyed flaming red and shellacked to jut off his head like a jaunty rooster's comb. But the normally upbeat cybercrimes expert looked subdued when he came into the room.

"Dr. Cross, Chief Stone," he said. "I need to show you something. With your permission, I'd like to connect my laptop to your television screen?"

"Go ahead," Bree said.

"What's going on?" I asked Mahoney when he came into the room after speaking with Nana and my dad.

Ned said, "Rawlins says he knows why Lourdes Rodriguez was so quick and quiet about leaving her old apartment. He started to explain it on the way here, but most of it went right over my head."

"I'll try to dumb it down further, Agent Mahoney," Rawlins said, sounding annoyed as he typed on his laptop.

A moment later the television screen came on, showing

a gibberish of coded numbers, letters, and symbols. Rawlins scrolled down through the mess until he found what he wanted.

He highlighted a sequence in the sea of code. "That's a time stamp from a few days ago, immediately after Lourdes Rodriguez's name was entered into the FBI's database as part of the ongoing investigation."

Rawlins typed. The screen jumped to another coded document and highlighted a new sequence.

He said, "Two seconds after Rodriguez's name goes in, this second time stamp is triggered in a different file, a familiar file, that ingenious, eloquent piece of malware code I found in your computer and then in the FBI database."

Bree said, "You're saying Rodriguez's name triggered the malware?"

"And the malware triggered Rodriguez's swift departure from that apartment. The troubling thing is that I should have seen this sooner, but after the marathon work session I put in to resurrect Timmy Walker's iPhone, I went home and slept for twenty hours, and I woke up with a nasty stomach bug that cost me another day."

Rawlins said that he'd finally returned to his lab earlier that morning to see the alert from the code he'd attached to the malware.

"Where did the stuff about Rodriguez go?" Bree asked.

"Through onion routers, of course," Rawlins said, typing. "A dozen in all. But I intentionally overrode the malware's code so that every time it passed through the onion it would send me a ping so I could track it."

The screen jumped to a map of the world with glowing lime-green pins denoting onion routers and orange arrows showing the direction of travel after the message cleared the device. From Quantico to India to China to the Philippines to Ecuador and on and on, until Rodriguez's name reached Japan.

"That's only eleven routers," Ali said. "You said twelve."

"I did indeed," Rawlins said and he typed. The screen switched to Google Earth, a satellite view of a checkerboard of woods and farmland.

"You are looking at an unincorporated area in southwestern Pennsylvania due east of the Michaux State Forest," he said, then zoomed down on a compound of three buildings. The biggest, a mansion, really, was sprawling and sat beside a large pond surrounded by hardwoods and pine thickets.

"That's a twelve-thousand-square-foot home with carriage house, barn, and personal bass pond," Rawlins said. "But notice the satellite dishes on the roof. Even for a big place, it's overkill."

"And this is where the malware went after Japan?" I said.

"Most definitely."

"Who owns it?"

The cybercrimes expert sobered. "Nash Edward Edgars. You've probably never heard of him, but Mr. Edgars is infamous in certain circles. Circles that often disappear into the dark web."

Rawlins described Edgars as a secretive, reclusive, and extremely wealthy computer-code writer in his late thirties. At seventeen, after his freshman year at Cal Poly, Edgars left and became the behind-the-scenes coder for several edgy, successful tech businesses.

"That we know for sure," Rawlins said. "The dark-web stuff is rumor and conjecture, but some very smart people swear Edgars has been developing and operating in the unorganized, encrypted, and untraceable Internet for a decade. Maybe longer."

I squinted at the screen. "What connects him to Rodriguez?"

"I don't know exactly."

"No photo of him?"

"A poor one, seven years old," Rawlins said. "But first…" He returned to his typing. "We're lucky this sat view was shot in late winter or early spring, or I wouldn't have noticed them."

Rawlins scrolled down the Google Earth image, taking us past the compound and over the forest. The image stopped where we could look down through the branches of bare hard-wood trees.

Rawlins put his cursor on a smudge and zoomed in, re-vealing another structure, a long building with a tin roof. He moved his cursor to a second smudge on the satellite view and magnified it to reveal the lines of a large square.

"What is that?" I asked.

"I believe it's an old foundation, with a high stone wall here, similar to the one Gretchen Lindel was put up against during the mock execution."

"Jesus," I said, sitting forward. "Can we see that photo of Edgars?"

The question seemed to irritate Rawlins, who typed and said, "Give me a second to find it. But what's critical to under-stand here is that Edgars didn't leave Cal Poly to follow Bill Gates and strike out on his own at seventeen. In fact, Edgars was expelled from Cal Poly at seventeen, when he was still a juvenile, so the case is sealed."

"No idea why?" Bree asked.

"I know exactly why," he said as the screen changed to a blurry photograph of two men leaving an urban restaurant.

One was scruffy, dark-haired, and wore jeans, a Metallica T-shirt, and flip-flops. The other man was slightly older with a military haircut and aviator sunglasses.

Blurred or not, the picture made my stomach lurch.

Rawlins's cursor moved to the scruffy, bearded guy. "This is Nash Edgars. The other one's name is Mike Pratt. He's Edgars's bodyguard."

I said, "Edgars was driving the pickup in Philadelphia the other night. Pratt was both the shooter and the Alden Lindel impersonator."

Rawlins looked deflated to have some of his thunder stolen from him, but then he recovered and said, "Here's the kicker from my corner. I hacked into Cal Poly's system and found Edgars's file. He was accused of sexually assaulting three coeds his freshman year. Every one of them was blond."

CHAPTER

102

CLOUDS OF STEAM BILLOWED FROM our lips at 4:10 the following morning.

It was bitter cold as we huddled in puffy jackets, wool caps, and gloves around a laptop computer bolted to a steel table inside an FBI special weapons and tactics van parked in the barnyard of a dairy farmer who lived two miles from Nash Edgars and who had nothing good to say about his reclusive neighbor.

"Give us the drone feed," Mahoney said into a cell phone.

The screen changed from the sharpness of Google Earth to an opaque gray-green that revealed bare-limbed trees and then the road that led past Edgars's gate. Thermal images appeared: two men were guarding the gate, carrying weapons. Flying on, the drone found the mansion, but the screen showed no thermal images of bodies—or much of anything, for that matter.

Mahoney said, "Drone pilot says the place appears heavily

insulated so there might be people inside or not. We'll have to go on the assumption the house is manned and heavily armed."

"Smart," I said.

Mahoney said into his cell, "Fly to that structure out in the woods."

The drone found the building. A thermal sensor revealed four faint images of people inside, all lying flat or curled up, located in separate little rooms.

"Those could be some of our missing women," Special Agent Batra said.

"Easily," Bree said, and she sipped from a go-cup of steaming coffee.

"That changes things," Mahoney said. "Show me the Google Earth image again."

Rawlins switched it back to the satellite image.

Mahoney pointed to a rocky knoll on the estate's far north boundary. "This is excellent high ground. We'll put four agents there to cover the back door."

I noticed something in the trees along a creek well to the east of the knoll, but before I could say anything, Rawlins switched back to the drone's feed showing more gray-green forest but no other distinct thermal images.

"Thanks for the flyby," Mahoney said into his cell, then he ordered four agents to enter the woods at the estate's northeast corner. He also moved a six-man hostage-rescue team, or HRT, into position to get to and storm that building in the woods as soon as possible. Bree and Sampson would ride with Mahoney and follow a breach team of FBI agents onto the property to arrest Edgars and Pratt.

"Alex, you'll be with Batra and Rawlins in a follow car, where you will remain until the clear is given," Mahoney said.

Before I could protest, Bree said, "Be practical, Alex. With your ankle like that, you won't be much help if things go south."

"It's not that bad, really," I said. "I'm not even on crutches. But I hear you."

"We'll give you a radio," Mahoney said. "For once you'll have to just listen to the action."

103

AS I LIMPED INTO THE backseat of Agent Batra's black Chevy Tahoe, I had to admit I was feeling guilty for wanting to be part of the raiding party and hostage-rescue attempt.

The evening before, I'd been telling Bree that I wanted to get out of police work, away from dangerous moments like these when the adrenaline starts to drip and your senses get super-sharp and super-clear.

But as I shut the door and Batra started the engine, I knew a part of me could never leave the police game. Not entirely. Being a psychologist had its own deep and fruitful rewards, but it could never replace the rush of catching bad guys, ending their dark work, and seeing them get just punishment.

"Let's roll," Mahoney said.

I heard his voice over the radio and the light headset they'd given me.

"Isn't this exciting, Dr. Cross?" Krazy Kat Rawlins said, looking over the front seat at me as Batra put on her headlights and followed Mahoney's Tahoe onto a rural route heading east.

"The trick is not to get too excited," I said. "You have to keep your head."

"Oh, of course," he said, slightly crestfallen. "I guess I'm just looking forward to seeing Nash Edgars in handcuffs and telling him that I beat him. Do you ever feel that way?"

"From time to time, sure," I said.

"Right now?"

"Right now, I look forward to seeing those women safe and sound."

Over my headset, Mahoney said, "Half a mile out. HRT, you are go. Breaching team, you are go."

The acknowledgments came back fast, and in my mind I was seeing the rescue team flipping on their thermal-imaging goggles, surging into the woods, and angling through the forest toward the shed and four of the missing women.

We came over a rise in the road and saw a huge, black, six-wheel-drive armored FBI truck roll to the gate. I expected the guards to immediately stand down, but instead there were flashes from behind the gate and reports of gunfire over the radio.

"Take it down," Mahoney said.

The big armored rig backed up and then sped at the steel gate and blew it off its hinges. Agents inside the truck fired from portholes at the guards, who'd retreated up the hill into the trees toward the compound. Mahoney followed the armored truck, driving across the downed gate, with us trailing.

"HRT?" Mahoney said.

"Two hundred yards out, SAC," came the reply. "No visuals on the shed yet, but you have lights going on up the hill."

The breaching rig sped up on that news, disappeared around a curve in the long serpentine driveway. By the time we reached the edge of the compound, spotlights were blazing on the courtyard between the main house, the carriage house, and the barn.

Ten FBI agents in full SWAT gear poured out of the armored vehicle, divided into teams of two, and fanned out toward the mansion, a modern building made of stone, redwood, and glass.

The doors of the carriage house at the far side of the yard were up. The interior wasn't lit, but there was enough light from the exterior spotlights to reveal a white Range Rover and a black pickup truck in the first two bays and several ATVs and dirt bikes in the third.

Black pickup truck, I thought. *Bet it has a window with a bullet hole or two in it.*

In front of us, Mahoney got out of the Tahoe. Caught in Batra's headlights, he blinked, held up a hand, and signaled for her to shut them off. Bree and Sampson got out. The radio chatter from the raiding team and the HRT forces started coming nonstop. I got whining feedback in my headset for a moment.

Four agents went to the front door, used a battering ram to break it open, and then vanished inside.

In the woods to our north, the HRT unit had the plywood-faced building surrounded. Thermals showed the four people were still inside, still lying flat or curled up. That didn't seem right to me; they should have been sitting or standing. But maybe they hadn't heard the gunfire? Or maybe they were restrained?

"HRT, go in and get them out," Mahoney said over my headset. "Now."

"Lower front hall clear," said an agent inside the house.

"Walkout basement clear," said another.

"Where is he?" Rawlins said from the front seat of Batra's car. "Don't tell me Edgars isn't here."

Even with the windows up, even with the heater going and the radio chatter in our ears, we all heard the first explosion.

104

"HRT AGENT DOWN," THE RESCUE commander said. "Repeat, HRT agent down. The place is booby-trapped."

"Back out and contain," Mahoney said. "How bad?"

"We'll need Life Flight ASAP."

"Calling now."

On the radio, the search commander inside Edgars's mansion said, "Watch for booby traps, gentlemen."

"Kitchen clear," said another.

"Home theater clear," said a third.

"All first-floor closets and bathrooms clear," said a fourth.

"First floor cleared in full," the commander said.

Bree and Sampson left Mahoney and started toward the mansion. I got anxious, felt claustrophobic, and opened the car door.

"You're to remain in the car, Dr. Cross," Batra said.

"I'm going to stand outside." I got out and shut the door.

My wife and my partner entered Edgars's house with the FBI agents inside already moving to clear the second story.

Mahoney told the HRT commander that Life Flight was eleven minutes out and then he headed inside as well.

I caught some of the communications between the hostage-rescue commander and the incoming Life Flight medic. The agent had opened a door to the building and triggered a small explosive. He had shrapnel in his right thigh and a severed femoral artery. They'd applied direct pressure to the wound so he wouldn't bleed out and were preparing to move him from the woods to the county road for pickup.

"Roger that," the medic replied. "We are seven minutes out."

An agent in the house said, "Second-floor landing and hall-way clear."

"All bedrooms cleared," another said. "Place is empty, Cap."

A high-pitched tone screeched through the headset, so loud I thought my eardrums would burst. I tore the headset off, stuck it in my pocket.

The dark second-floor windows facing the courtyard suddenly flashed as automatic-weapon fire broke out inside the house. Two guns, three, maybe more.

I took several limping steps toward the courtyard and the mansion, wanting to see Bree, Sampson, and Mahoney retreat out the front door. But they didn't, and the shooting went on in bursts and waves, and—

"Dr. Cross!" Agent Batra yelled behind me.

I ignored her, pulled toward the violence, wanting to end it. But the gunfire stopped as I passed Mahoney's Tahoe and entered the courtyard. I caught a flicker of motion in the third bay of the carriage house just before a second bomb exploded, much closer, on the other side of the mansion.

At the blast, the spotlights flickered and died. The shooting stopped too.

Then I heard a noise I'll never forget—shrill, primitive, and terrified—coming from the carriage house.

I pulled out my weapon and flashlight and hobbled fast in that direction as something large and boxy tore out of the third bay. I got my flashlight beam on it as it was leaving the courtyard for the woods: a red-and-black side-by-side Honda Pioneer 1000 utility vehicle.

I caught only a glimpse of the driver and the front-seat passenger before it disappeared, but the blond teen in the bed, blindfolded, gagged, and hog-tied, was plain as day. Gretchen Lindel was writhing and trying to scream, and then she was gone.

"Batra!" I yelled, flashing the light around and seeing a Kawasaki ATV in the third bay. "Batra!"

The shooting started again inside, drowning my second cry.

Ignoring the pain shrieking in my ankle, I hobbled to the ATV, yanking the radio from my pocket and tearing free the headset cord, figuring to stop the feedback. But it was worse, and I had to turn the squelch almost off.

My flashlight found the ATV ignition but with no key in it. I lifted the seat, revealing a storage for helmets, and located the key. I straddled the seat, looked at the controls, turned on the headlights, and started the engine.

I roared out of the garage, praying Batra could see me, turned onto the two-track lane that went from the compound to the woods, and accelerated.

105

BREE, SAMPSON, AND MAHONEY HAD gone into a large, open, and vaulted space on the main level of the mansion to wait while the upper floors were cleared. The room contained Edgars's state-of-the-art kitchen, a rustic dining area, and several leather couches set before a massive stone fireplace that was flanked by built-in wooden cabinets and shelves crammed with books.

Sampson said, "Place looks spick-and-span."

Mahoney nodded. "Ready for that *Architectural Digest* photographer."

Their radios crackled: "Second-floor landing and hallway clear." "All bedrooms cleared. Place is empty, Cap."

Empty? That felt wrong to Bree. She'd been on edge since hearing the bomb explode in the distance. Why booby-trap the outer building and not—

A piercing whine went off in her earbud, the worst feedback ever, and she tore it out. Sampson did the same.

Across the room, Mahoney threw his down too. "What the hell is—"

Automatic weapons began to bark and rattle upstairs. Bree instinctively dived behind the kitchen counter with Sampson right beside her.

The shooting stopped, leaving them shaken and going for their guns.

"Agents down!" someone shouted upstairs. "Arthur and Boggs. Bedroom five. Far east end of upper hallway."

The search commander at the bottom of the stairs bellowed back over the shooting, "How many? I thought the place was cleared!"

"It was, Cap! Shooters must have been—"

An explosion outside shook the house. The lights died.

"It's an ambush!" Mahoney yelled from over by the couches. "They're jamming our radios and cells. Bree, take Sampson and get out of here, establish communication with—"

Bree was about to turn on her flashlight when sound-suppressed automatic weapons lit up. She covered her head as slugs ripped into granite countertops, splintered cabinets, and shattered dishes.

The bullets moved left to right and then right to left, punching holes in the stainless-steel appliances, ten, maybe fifteen shots in all, raining debris down on Bree and Sampson before stopping.

Bree shook from fear and adrenaline. Smelling the burned gunpowder, she felt nauseated, but her mind whirled. Where was the shooter? Where had he hidden? Those cabinets weren't big enough to hide a grown man, were they?

She felt a tug on her leg.

"Chief?" Sampson whispered. "You okay?"

"Fine. Where's the shooter?"

"Hit," Mahoney croaked.

The fear fled her. Bree flicked on her flashlight and belly-crawled across the kitchen tiles, calling, "How bad, Ned?"

Mahoney gasped. "Gut. You tell me."

Somewhere a generator coughed and hummed. Dim light returned. Agents upstairs were shouting, but Bree ignored them.

"Where's the shooter, Ned?" she called, louder.

"Behind me. Cabinets."

Bree turned her flashlight off, inched forward, and peered around the bottom corner of the kitchen cabinets. She could see well enough to tell Mahoney was sitting upright on the floor by one of the leather couches, but there was no sign of the shooter.

"We have to get him out, Chief," Sampson said behind her. "Now!"

"Not until I know where that shooter is. I won't get us all killed."

She thumbed on her flashlight again, peeked around the corner, and let the beam play over Mahoney about forty feet away. He was hunched over and squinting. Bree focused on the large patch of dark blood showing on his white shirt, just below his armored vest.

Low liver hit, she thought, and fought to swallow down the panic creeping in the back of her throat. They did have to get him out fast. But the shooter...

Bree shifted her light toward the stone fireplace and the cabinets and shelves to either side. The beam flickered over doors far too small for a child, much less a man, and then over rows of books before stopping cold on a small open cabinet.

"Jesus Christ," she whispered.

106

THE ATV WAS EQUIPPED WITH a heavy-duty muffler, so the engine barely made any noise as I drove on the two-track deeper and deeper into the estate.

Edgars's side-by-side was no more than three or four minutes in front of me. I couldn't see tracks in the frozen mud, but the leaves were broken and shiny where it had passed.

Snowflakes hit my face. With my free hand, I tugged out the radio and turned it up. There was no longer screeching coming over it, just a dense hiss.

"This is Alex Cross," I said. "Copy?"

Out of the static, I heard clicking and fragments of an unfamiliar voice. I turned it off, stuffed it back in my coat, tried my cell. No service.

The snow flurries turned to thick heavy flakes.

They're going to get away, I thought. *The sadistic bastards are going to get away.*

There was an intersection ahead, and I stopped. The snow covered the leaves, making it impossible for me to say which way Edgars had taken Gretchen Lindel.

I tried to recall the satellite view of the property. The shed and the wounded HRT agent were somewhere to my left. The knoll at the rear of the property—where Mahoney had sent four agents—was somewhere straight ahead of me. That unidentified smudge on the satellite picture was down the right fork in the trail.

I went with my instincts, twisted the ATV throttle, and went right. The snow slapped my face, got in my eyes, and forced me to drive at a crawl.

Ten minutes later, the snow squall ended as abruptly as it had started. I rolled downhill to a wide, shallow, iced-over creek, seeing where Edgars's machine had broken up the ice. My instincts were dead-on. I drove across the creek, noticing the sky brightening in the east.

How far ahead were they? Were those four people back in that booby-trapped building all dead? The HRT guys said they hadn't moved when the booby trap went off. Or was Edgars taking Gretchen to where he had the other blondes stashed?

One hundred yards beyond the creek crossing, I lost the tracks and drove on through virgin snow to a turnabout walled in by pines. A dead end.

But Edgars had come this way. I was positive. That ice had absolutely been freshly broken, and those tracks…

I drove back, shining the headlights on the crossing, seeing ice covering the creek upstream. I used my flashlight to look downstream. The ice there had been broken up to where the stream disappeared beneath a steep embankment, eight, maybe ten feet high, and covered with green and tan vegetation frosted with new snow.

Where the hell had they gone? I couldn't imagine any machine climbing straight up the side of that wall of…

I looked closer at the embankment. Green plants? That was impossible. The leaves had fallen. The ferns were dead.

I drove into the creek and rolled slowly to the embankment, headlights on and my flashlight playing around. Even through the frosting of snow, I could see I hadn't been looking at plants but at thin strips of dull green, gray, and brown cloth, thousands of pieces sewn into a huge swath of camouflage fabric that hung from a stout length of black metal bolted into the rocks above me.

I grabbed the radio again and turned it on. The static was weaker. I triggered the transmit button, said, "This is Alex Cross, come back."

Almost immediately a garbled, oddly familiar voice answered.

"Batra?" I said.

The voice replied, but I couldn't understand a word.

I said, "Repeat, this is Alex Cross. I am in pursuit of Edgars, who has Gretchen Lindel. I am somewhere in the northeast quadrant of the estate."

The voice came back even more garbled.

I almost stuffed the radio in my pocket but then had a moment of inspiration and said, "If you can hear me, track me by Find My iPhone."

I put away the radio that time, traded it for my service weapon. Staring at the camouflage curtain, I hesitated, anxious about what might be waiting on the other side. I killed the headlights, teased the throttle. The bumper touched the fabric and then ripped apart the Velcro that had been keeping it closed.

I held my pistol in my left hand, rested the barrel on the handlebar, eased off the safety, gave the throttle more gas, and went through into darkness.

CHAPTER

107

BREE GAPED AT THE SMOKING Uzi machine pistol mounted on a thin metal post inside the open cabinet. A long banana clip hung below the gun, too big for just ten or fifteen shots.

Mahoney coughed and shifted. The gun pivoted his way, and she saw the thin scarlet line of the laser sight fixed to its barrel pass six inches over the wounded agent's head. It stopped.

"What the hell's going on?" Sampson whispered, crawling up beside her.

She pulled back, said, "Remote-control Uzis. Unless…"

Bree peeked around the corner again, flashed the light at the machine pistol and the cabinet, looking for a camera.

Mahoney groaned and shifted, and the couch moved, hitting a table behind it. The lamp on the table wobbled.

The Uzi opened up again, that same left-to-right, right-to-left spray of bullets; it cut the lamp in half, and then the gunfire continued on toward the kitchen. Bree looked up after the shooting stopped, saw that the slugs had hit some of the same things they'd hit during the first barrage.

No, she took that back. They had ripped into *the exact same things* at the *exact same height.*

"No one's operating that gun, Ned!" Bree shouted. "I think there's a motion detector involved. See it?"

"No," he grunted, sounding weaker.

An agent yelled down from upstairs that he had to move his wounded men.

"The whole place is booby-trapped!" Sampson yelled. "Hold your position!"

"One's critical! He'll die if we don't move him!"

"You'll all die if you come down those stairs," Bree shouted as she wriggled back past Sampson and crawled to a low line of untouched cabinets next to the stainless-steel stove.

She looked in three cabinets before she finally found the items she wanted. She grabbed them and scooted back to Sampson.

"What's with the cookie sheets?" he asked.

"Motion," Bree said, then she called out, "Ned, if you can, get down."

She flung one of the cookie sheets over the counter that separated the kitchen from the living area.

The Uzi lit up, rattling bullets left to right, right to left again. She threw another cookie sheet and then a third before the action of the machine pistol locked open, the breech and barrel smoking hot.

She stood up cautiously, saw Ned lying on his side by the couch. His eyes were open but glassy, and his breathing looked shallow.

"We're clear!" she shouted to the FBI agents upstairs as she ran to Mahoney. "Get your men out!"

Kneeling by Alex's old FBI partner, Bree refused to cry. "You with me, Ned? Talk to me."

Mahoney nodded and blinked. "Gut shot."

"I can see that."

Sampson came up behind her. "We've got to get him to a hospital, and the jamming's still going on."

"Help me get him up," Bree said.

They lifted Ned to his feet. Mahoney passed out from the pain, becoming deadweight, and Sampson got him up on his shoulders in a fireman's carry. Bree ran in front of him to the front door and stepped out into the falling snow, shouting, "Alex? Agent Batra?"

A flashlight went on. Keith Rawlins called timidly, "Just me, Chief Stone."

Sampson came out the door with Mahoney over his shoulder.

The snow fell in big flakes and coated the pavers as they hustled across the courtyard to the Tahoe Mahoney had driven into the estate. Rawlins stood outside it, looking as bedraggled as a cat in the rain.

"Drop the rear seat backs, would you?" Sampson said.

Seeming grateful to have something to do, Rawlins sprang into action, saying, "The jamming system is remarkable."

"We know," Bree said impatiently. "Where's Batra's car?"

"When the jamming started and then all the shooting, she decided to drive out, try to call for reinforcements."

"Good," Bree said as Sampson put Mahoney in the back of the Tahoe. "Where's—"

"Don't leave yet!" an FBI agent yelled down in the courtyard.

He carried a badly wounded man. They'd gotten blood-clotting agent into a chest wound, but his breathing was ragged and harsh.

"Get him in," Bree said. "And the next one."

"I'll drive," Sampson said, going through Mahoney's coat pockets and finding the keys.

Everything was moving fast, and Bree was still in semi-shock from the ambush, so it was not until she saw Sampson throw the Tahoe in reverse and fishtail back down Edgars's long driveway that she realized the snow had stopped.

She felt confused and overwhelmingly tired. She looked up at the sky, saw the clouds parting and a shaft of moonlight shining through, making the frosted courtyard look like a movie fantasy.

"Did Alex go with Agent Batra?" she asked Rawlins.

"Uh, no."

She turned to look at him. "What? Where is—"

Thaa-wumph!

Bree felt the ground tremble. The muted explosion sounded like it had come from deep inside the mansion.

"What was that?" Rawlins said, backing away.

"I don't know," she said. "I...*where* is Alex?"

"Dr. Cross? He—"

A second, much louder explosion cut him off; it lit up one of the second-story bedrooms like aluminum in the sun, blew out the windows, and ignited a fierce blaze. Yellow, orange, and ruby flames billowed out of the mansion and licked at the shake-shingle roof.

Bree moved back fast, feeling dread grow in her stomach. "Where's Alex, Rawlins?" she shouted. "Where's my husband?"

CHAPTER

108

THE HEAVY CAMOUFLAGE CURTAINS FLAPPED shut behind me. My eyes adjusted. I was in a storm-drain culvert, a good ten feet in diameter. Either the potential existed for extreme flash-flooding in the creek or Edgars had put the culvert in place as an escape route. I was betting that the smudge I'd seen on the satellite view was dirt from an excavation.

Forty yards ahead of me, the culvert ended, and gray light was building.

If Edgars and Pratt knew I was trailing them, they could be waiting at the other end of the culvert. But by my reckoning, the culvert had to pass beneath the dirt road that ran along the estate's eastern boundary, which meant the other end would leave me somewhere inside the Michaux State Forest.

They're not waiting to ambush me, I thought. *They're getting out of here and as far away as possible.*

I gunned the throttle and shot out of the culvert, feeling exposed, a target.

But no shots rang out as I left the creek bed for a trail through hardwood trees. With dawn nearing, I could see tire tracks, obscure at first but growing more distinct the farther I followed them.

As I drove, I tried to anticipate Edgars's next move. Either he was in full flight mode, in which case I would find his UTV abandoned and the tracks of a car leaving the area, or he had something more sinister planned.

In my mind, I saw Gretchen Lindel writhing in the truck bed. I began to fear that Edgars did not intend to take her or any of the other women with him. If he was as ruthless as I thought he was, he would kill Gretchen and the other blondes. Maybe he already had.

No witnesses, I thought. *He'll want no witnesses.*

It was full daylight when I reached the rim of a bluff that looked out over a broad patchwork of farmland a good five miles from the estate. Looking down the steep trail, almost a quarter mile below me, I could see a farm, or at least the roof of a ranch-style home, most of a steel building, and definitely Edgars's side-by-side Honda Pioneer 1000 parked in the snow beside it.

I switched off the Kawasaki and left it. Carrying my pistol and my phone, I sidestepped down the hillside, staying tight to the brush, hoping no one would spot me from below. I kept checking my phone for service, but there was none.

My ankle and shin were swollen and unhappy, but I refused to stop.

Snow was starting to melt off branches when I reached the rear of the farm. I stopped behind a tree, listening, watching. Nothing moved in the yard. Nothing showed in the windows of the ramshackle ranch house.

The three overhead doors on the long side of the steel building were closed. The porthole windows in the doors looked covered. The small sash window twenty feet to the right of the back door, however, was not shaded. I could see bright, glaring light inside.

I checked my phone. Still no service. But the fact that Edgars was a master coder, a creature of the dark web, made me check to see if he had Wi-Fi. He did, a password-protected access called Pharm, and another, Pharm Guest. I tried to log in to that one, thinking I could e-mail or text Bree, but it too required a password.

Inside the steel building, someone let loose with a heart-wrenching scream.

I clenched my jaw and went over the fence, moving with a stiff, painful gait. The scream faded and died. When I reached the rear window, I ducked beneath it, got to the right side of the sash, and turned to face the back door.

"No!" a woman screamed.

"Please!" another yelled. "Just let us go!"

I snuck a peek through the window and saw a John Deere tractor and some other farm equipment parked around a large open space in the middle of the building. Running down from pulleys attached to a steel beam overhead, seven taut cables were clipped to leather restraints around the wrists of Gretchen Lindel and six other women, who dangled in a line, arms stretched overhead, their toes barely brushing the floor.

I couldn't tell exactly who was who among the other six at first or second glance. They were soaked in dark blood that dripped and pooled beneath them. Only Gretchen was clean.

Six others? I thought. *Seven all together? I thought there were only six blondes missing.*

In any case, three of the women looked unconscious, their chins sagging to their chests. Gretchen and the other three had their heads up, were focused on the two men in black clothes moving around them.

Wearing the GoPro camera on his head, Nash Edgars seemed agitated, hopped up, like he was on something chemical and a lot of it. In his left hand he held an SLR camera and in his right an AR-style assault rifle with a halo sight.

Edgars kept moving, videoing the women and the other man, who wore a black balaclava and carried a red plastic bucket and a knife with an obsidian-black blade that curved tightly back toward an ornate knuckle guard. It was the same knife I'd seen in several of the mock-execution videos.

The hooded man walked around behind Gretchen Lindel, who twisted, trying to see him, and dumped a bucket of blood over her head. She shuddered and trembled with revulsion but did not cry out.

"Last baptism before the fire," he said, and I recognized his voice. It was Pratt, Edgars's bodyguard.

Pratt dropped the empty bucket next to a second assault rifle leaned up against the tractor's tire. He came around behind another of the alert women and pressed that wicked-looking knife to her throat.

She began to shriek and shriek. "Nash! Don't let him! Please don't let him! I'm not one of them! I'm Latina! I'm not a blonde!"

Edgars, the cameraman, came in close and laughed. "You're a blonde in this scene, Lourdes."

"Please, Nash," Lourdes Rodriguez said, weeping. "You don't have to do this!"

"Of course we do," Edgars said in a reasonable tone. "It

wouldn't be a real snuff film if we didn't snuff the blondes at the end."

Pratt took the knife away from Rodriguez's throat and gestured to one side at two stout green metal tanks about five feet tall and two feet around. They were chained to a metal post.

"We're giving you a chance," Pratt said. "You can die by the knife or take your chances and pray you pass out from the gas before this whole place ignites and blows you to kingdom come."

Still videoing their reactions, Edgars moved sideways toward the gas tanks. He put the AR down, reached behind the tanks, and came up with a gas mask, which he tossed to Pratt before getting a second for himself. He put it half on his head, knelt, and retrieved the assault rifle.

Pratt said, "So what is it, ladies? Knife or fire?"

"Can't you just make it look like we died, like all the other times?" another of them whimpered, and I recognized her. Delilah Franks, the bank teller.

"Everyone's had it with special effects," Edgars said. "We're going all the way. For the first time. Show her, Pratt. Wake up the others. Let them see tough little Gretchen die first. Then they can decide how to go."

CHAPTER

109

I STIFF-LEGGED AND HOPPED to the back door. The handle turned and the door swung slowly open on well-oiled hinges. I smelled something dead.

Sliding inside, my back to the wall, I saw Pratt forty feet away. He'd kicked awake the other three women and gotten behind Gretchen Lindel. His right leg was extended to the rear, braced against the floor. His left knee was pressed into the teenager's spine, arching her back. Pratt had her by the hair too, her head wrenched back, his wicked-looking blade at her windpipe.

"Scared now, blondie?" Pratt said.

"No," Gretchen said. "You can't hurt me."

"Oh yes, I can."

He was so close to Alden Lindel's daughter, I didn't dare try a killing shot, and I didn't want to shout a warning that might cause him to slit her throat. I aimed at the meat of Pratt's extended right leg, touched the trigger, and fired.

The slug went through his right ass cheek, spun him around, and broke his pelvis. He fell down screaming, the flung knife clattering away.

I limped hard and fast to my right, seeing Edgars spin toward me with the cameras and the AR. Just as he opened up in full automatic, I dived and landed behind a steel seed spreader. Slugs clanged off the spreader and punctured the sheet-metal wall behind me.

The shooting stopped. The women were all screaming and crying. Pratt moaned in agony, then shouted, "Kill him! Shoot his ass, Nash!"

Amid the shouting and the confusion, Edgars yelled, "Come on out, Cross. Join the wrap party for the whole cast and crew!"

Saying nothing, peering all around me, I noticed a three-inch gap between the bottom of the spreader and its wheels. I rolled onto my side and extended my right arm and pistol, trying to spot Edgars's feet and lower legs.

But he was too far to my right, blocked from view by the blade of a small bulldozer. I needed the man to move.

"The FBI is surrounding this place, Edgars!" I yelled out. "Put your weapons down!"

"Bullshit," Edgars said, holding his ground. "The FBI would never let you come in here alone. I've hacked into their systems, read their protocols."

"They're right behind me. I radioed them my position!"

"Impossible. I've jammed everything within ten miles."

That idea seemed to embolden him because he burst out from behind the bulldozer blade at a steep retreating angle, so fast I had no shot. He skidded to a stop right behind the gas tanks. Definitely no shot.

Unaware of what I could and couldn't see, Edgars kept

his camera rolling, set his rifle on the ground, and stood back up.

He's filming and needs a free hand to open the gas valves, I thought, realizing in a split second that I had only one option, and I needed to take that option right now or never. I aimed at the top turret of the halo sight, right above the AR's action, and fired my .40 S&W.

The hundred-and-fifty-grain bullet hit the turret, blew through the sight, and smashed into the action with four hundred foot-pounds of energy. The gun went skidding across the concrete floor and under a combine's blades.

I pushed myself up into a crouch, saw a shocked Edgars spin away from the gas tanks, yank down his gas mask, and run toward the combine. I took off after him, gun up.

"Stop or I'll shoot!" I yelled a moment before I smelled the propane hissing full force from the tanks.

With my left arm and jacket sleeve across my nose and mouth, I hobbled past the women and Pratt, who was unconscious, and the tanks. Edgars was flat on his belly thirty feet beyond them, reaching under the combine. I feared shooting because of the gas. Before I could get close enough to jump on him, he twisted around, pointing the rifle and the camera at me. I skidded to a stop, aiming my pistol at him.

"Shoot him!" Lourdes Rodriguez screamed.

"Shoot him!" the other women cried.

Edgars bellowed from inside the mask, "He shoots, you all die!"

I stared at him. "*You* shoot, *we* all die."

"Maybe that's the point."

"Why the hell are you doing this, Edgars?"

He looked at me as if I were stupid and said, "I hate blondes. I always have. Bitches, every one of them."

"No one will see your last little film if you shoot and blow this place up."

He beamed at me through the glass eyeholes of the gas mask. "The cameras are streaming, uploading over Wi-Fi."

"We can all walk out of here."

"No, we can't," he said, and he looked over the top of his busted sight at me. "Best thing? I can't miss from here, so I get to see you die first. Just a half second before we all go up in flames."

For the first time, I felt woozy from the gas. Edgars lifted his camera higher and glanced at the screen on the back as if trying to frame me, the gas canisters, and the women behind me for one final shot.

"All blondes must die eventually," Edgars said. "And cops and geniuses."

"Don't!"

He pulled the trigger.

CHAPTER

110

THERE WAS A CLANK AND a tremendous bang, and my heart almost stopped; I expected the gas to ignite and blow up the tanks, and me and everyone else with them.

Instead, Edgars screamed and writhed on the concrete floor, his bleeding hands clawing at the gas mask, his rifle three feet to his right, ruptured and smoking. Adrenaline poured through my veins, making me shake so bad that several moments passed before I realized what had happened.

Damaged by my earlier shot, and set to full automatic fire, the action of Edgars's gun must have backfired, jammed, and exploded, sending chunks and slivers of metal back into the coder's face and neck.

Edgars tore off the gas mask. His left eye was punctured and weeping blood. His cheeks and forehead were gashed horribly, flayed open, and gushing blood.

My head swooned from the gas. Throwing my jacket sleeve

across my mouth again, I kept my gun on him and moved forward fast, meaning to subdue and handcuff him.

But when I got close, Edgars lashed out with his steel-toed boot and connected squarely with my bad ankle. I felt something snap. A bolt of fire shot through me; my leg buckled, and I went down on my side.

My ankle felt like someone had set a torch to it. My stomach turned over from the agony and the gas, and my head swam; I thought I was going to pass out.

"The gas!" Gretchen Lindel cried weakly behind me. "The gas!"

I shook my head, saw Edgars struggling, trying to get to his feet. I aimed my gun at him but didn't shoot because he seized up before he could fully stand, looked at me puzzled, and then felt his neck.

Something had ruptured, probably the carotid, pumping out blood. He staggered, moving his lips but making no sound, and then fell for the last time.

The gas, I thought through a building daze.

Forcing myself up onto all fours, I turned my back to Edgars and crawled toward the tanks. I reached the post they were chained to and, holding my breath, used the post to pull myself to my feet.

I grabbed the knob to the hissing gas valve, tried to twist it shut. But it wouldn't budge. Neither would the other one. They were locked open somehow.

My stomach roiled. I fought the urge to puke. But then I looked to Gretchen Lindel and the other six women hanging from the cables. Heads down. Bodies slack. They were dying.

Dying.

My head spun again, and I almost went down for a second time.

You're dying, Alex.

It was Bree's voice. It was Nana Mama's voice. And my children's voices. All at once, telling me to fight.

In a haze I raised my head, looked around, saw the door where I'd entered the building. *Open it, Alex.*

Not enough air.

I saw the window I'd looked through. *Break it too,* I thought.

Not enough, the voices said.

Turning my thickening, spinning head, I looked past the dying women and spotted my only hope.

Do it, my family said.

My love for them surged up inside me. I used it to steel myself and push away from the post and the gas tanks. The pain in my ankle felt electric, and it jolted me, made me more alert and more determined.

My head started to pound. Every step was brutal. With every breath I wanted to stop, lie down, and surrender. But my family's voices kept urging me on, telling me that pain was temporary, but death was not. Death was…

I reached the long wall of the steel building and fell against it, gasping, tasting the gas, and feeling like my ankle and my head were going to burst at the seams and split apart. Dark dots danced before my eyes, gathered, and threatened to blind me.

Dad!

Alex!

On the edge of collapse, I reached up and flailed at three buttons on the front of a metal box attached to the wall. I missed, groped, stabbed at them again, and felt them click one by one.

Nothing happened, and for a single, disbelieving moment, I thought there was no hope. That I was—

Gears engaged. Electric winch motors turned. And one, two, and then three of the overhead garage doors began to rise.

I ducked under the one closest to me and felt a strong cold breeze hit me in the face as I stumbled and went to my knees outside in the melting snow and mud.

I coughed and swooned but then scooped up a handful of snow and cold mud and splashed it in my face. I had to go back. I had to get them out.

I crawled back and saw Pratt lying motionless on top of his gas mask. Taking a big breath, I scrambled to him, rolled him over, and put the mask on.

After opening the door I'd come through, and the window, and feeling the air moving, I found the ropes attached to the cables holding the women and cut them all down.

One by one, I grabbed them and, still crawling, dragged them out into the snow. They were all outside and breathing when I heard the chug of a helicopter, looked back toward the bluff, and saw a Life Flight chopper coming in for a landing.

111

SHORTLY AFTER FOUR THAT AFTERNOON, Eliza Lindel broke down sobbing in Bree's arms. I leaned over on my crutches and rubbed
her back.

"Please," she cried softly to me when she drew away from
Bree. "You'll have to come with me to tell Alden."

I glanced at Bree, who nodded.

"Of course," I said.

Gretchen Lindel's mother wiped at her tears, then reached
up and kissed my face. "I want you to know that you're a good
man, Dr. Cross."

My eyes started to water. "Thank you."

Bree held her hand. I followed them through the door at the
far end of the kitchen into Alden Lindel's small world. The
shriveled man in the bed took his eyes off the latest *Game of
Thrones* episode.

Eliza Lindel came around me and shut it off. "Dr. Cross has
news, Alden."

His eyes went to the tablet. The synthetic voice said, "Gretch?"

I smiled. "She's safe, Mr. Lindel. They're all safe. She's on her way here. We tried to convince her to stay in the hospital, but she wouldn't hear of it."

Lindel shut his eyes tight, and then he looked to his tablet. "Thank God," his mechanical voice said. "Thank God."

Tinker, the Jack Russell terrier, started barking and yipping with excitement in the kitchen.

"Mom? Dad?" Gretchen cried weakly.

An EMT was pushing her in a wheelchair. She'd been washed clean of pig's blood and wore a pair of hospital scrubs. An IV in her arm was connected to a bag mounted on a pole attached to the chair.

Her mother ran to her and hugged her, and they sobbed with joy, the little dog dancing on her hind legs and barking madly. They all went to Alden's side. The dog jumped on his bed. Gretchen got up on wobbly legs, threw her arms around her dad, and kissed him.

"I never gave up, Dad," she said, weeping. "They tried to reach inside and destroy me, but they couldn't. Because of you, and what you taught me, they couldn't."

He broke down, made choking sounds of love, which Bree and I took as our cue to slip out, our job done. Outside, we smiled like happy idiots. It was a crisp late-fall afternoon, and I felt damn lucky to be alive.

"That Find My iPhone app is something, isn't it?" I said, putting the crutches in the backseat and then hopping to the front, grimacing as I gingerly drew my splinted lower leg inside. "It can track the phone even if the phone's not signed in."

"Definitely helped find you faster," Bree said, starting the engine. "That and Batra and the Life Flight pilot hearing your radio call."

We drove toward GW Medical Center, where Ned Mahoney was in surgery. While Bree called Chief Michaels and filled him in, I prayed for Ned, and for Delilah Franks, Cathy Dupris, Ginny Krauss, Alison Dane, and Patsy Mansfield, hoping to God that they'd come to find peace with what had happened to them. Somehow, I knew Gretchen Lindel was going to be all right.

I thought about the four mannequins the HRT team had found in the shed, all lying on electric heating pads that made them look like real people on the infrared scopes. I thought about the FBI agent who'd been closest to the first *thaa-wumph!* in the basement of Edgars's house, which he'd said held computers and large editing screens.

He said a fireball had gone off in there, fueled by an accelerant, and that, together with the explosion upstairs, had burned the mansion to the ground. Edgars had thought of almost everything; it was as if he'd been certain we'd find him at some point and had planned for it.

Bree ended her call with the chief.

"Michaels says, 'Well done,' and you're on paid leave pending an investigation again."

"Is it possible to be double-suspended?"

"You're going to be cleared, Alex. Pratt was going to kill Gretchen Lindel. There are multiple witnesses. You had to shoot him. And Edgars effectively shot himself."

"I know."

"Then why the long face?"

I hesitated, wondering if I was still suffering from the effects of the gas, but then I said, "I've decided not to go back even if I am cleared."

She was quiet for a while. "What would you do? Just counseling?"

"No, I've got some big ideas. And the best part about them? They all include you."

When I glanced over at her, she was smiling. "That makes me happy."

I reached over and squeezed her hand. "Me too."

112

TEN DAYS AFTER WE REUNITED his daughter with her family, Alden Lindel passed away in his sleep, a happy man.

I heard the news from his wife on a chill, windy Saturday afternoon as I crutched after my family on the east side of Capitol Hill. Mrs. Lindel was grief-stricken, of course, but also relieved. With Gretchen at his side constantly since she'd returned home, Lindel had found grace, and he'd passed holding his daughter's hand and his wife's. I promised Eliza that I would be at the funeral, and I pocketed my phone.

Ali was dancing around. "C'mon, Dad. I'm going to be late."

"Go on in, then," Nana Mama said, shooing him toward the door of Elephants and Donkeys, a relatively new pub with a poster in the window advertising the District Open Darts Championship.

Ali yanked open the door like he owned the place and went in.

Bree started laughing.

"What's so funny, young lady?" my grandmother demanded.

Bree waved a hand. "I just never thought I'd see the day when you'd be attending a darts tournament in a bar, Nana."

"I'm not done growing yet, dear," she said good-naturedly and winked.

We followed her inside and found Sampson, Billie, and Krazy Kat Rawlins having drafts at the bar. I helped Ali sort through the release forms and got a number to pin on the back of his shirt.

"They have a practice board," he said. "I'll be there."

"You've been practicing every night for two hours."

He frowned, said, "Repetition is the mother of skill, Dad."

"Yeah, okay, I've heard that too," I said, surrendering. "Go on."

I smiled as he walked toward the knot of older darts competitors gathered at the rear of the pub, thinking that I had never been that fearless at his age.

Sampson handed me a beer, offered me his stool.

I took it and kissed Billie on the cheek. "You guys didn't have to come."

"What else were we going to do on a cold day off?"

Nana Mama sat up on a bar stool beside Jannie watching a college football game, eating buffalo wings, and drinking a Sprite.

"I know we're technically on leave pending investigation," Sampson said to Bree. "But is Lourdes Rodriguez still spilling her guts?"

Bree hesitated.

Rawlins said, "I've talked to her. The woman won't shut up."

"It's true," Bree said with a sigh.

Between the two of them, we got a thumbnail sketch of Rodriguez's involvement with Nash Edgars. They'd met at a coding conference she'd attended because she'd heard coders made better money than satellite-dish installers.

Edgars seemed to have anything he wanted whenever he wanted it. Better, he could get her anything she wanted whenever she wanted it. Rodriguez wasn't going to inherit a dime from any uncle ever, and here was this genius computer guy offering her the world.

"Through the dark web," Rawlins said. "She claimed he was worth forty to fifty million in Bitcoin alone."

"But it wasn't until he started acting on his hatred of blond women that the real money started coming in," Bree said, disgusted.

"Hundreds of thousands of subscribers," Rawlins said, shaking his Mohawk, which was a startling violet that day. "All of them paying to see those women terrified and abused."

Rodriguez told Bree that Edgars's hatred of blondes stemmed from years of dealing with a drunken blond mother and more years of fair-haired girls harassing him when he was grossly obese and growing up in Southern California. Because he was an avowed computer nerd, the abuse continued even after he'd dropped the weight.

"So, what, he decided to get his revenge and help others live out their anti-blonde fantasies?" Sampson said.

"It was more twisted and diabolical than that," Bree said. "She said he planned on putting the clips together into a horror documentary film called *All Blondes Must Die.*"

"That's something we'll never be seeing, thank God," Sampson said. "What about that kid Timmy Walker?"

"Lourdes said if anyone killed that poor kid, it was Pratt," Bree said. "She said there wasn't a good bone in his body, that Alex did the world a service."

Billie said, "How's Ned?"

"Better," I said, brightening. "I saw him this morning. Like you said the day he was shot, the liver's a remarkable thing. It's already starting to regenerate. The docs are saying he'll make a full—"

Nana Mama appeared, said, "Enough of that. C'mon, your son's about to throw or toss or whatever they do with darts."

113

I WISH I COULD SAY that Ali slayed it, threw darts with consistent, dazzling accuracy, but that didn't happen. He did toss three bull's-eyes and an almost, but he was wild otherwise and lost in the first round to a nice guy from Texas named Mel Davis who owned a barbecue joint downtown.

Ali was crushed until Davis offered him and his friends free barbecue brisket the next time he was in. My youngest was back to his old self walking home, gabbing nonstop with Jannie and Nana Mama about his plans to make a comeback in the tournament next year. We lagged behind.

After a few moments, Bree said, "What did Ned think about your big idea?"

"He likes it. A lot."

"Michaels?"

"We haven't had that talk yet."

"You're sure you'll be happy?"

"Extremely. I'll have the best of both worlds."

Ali, Nana, and Jannie went into Chung's convenience store to pick up milk and ice cream. Bree and I kept walking.

Night had fallen when we reached our steps. The house and porch were dark. We climbed onto the porch together, hand in hand, and but for a few unresolved issues, I felt as solid as I had in—

"Hands up, or I'll shoot you both right now."

We startled and looked to our right, saw the silhouette of someone crouched by the railing and aiming a revolver at us. We raised our hands.

"Hello, Dr. Cross," he said, straightening. "Chief Stone."

Dylan Winslow, Gary Soneji's son, swung the gun back and forth between us, and even in the low light I could see a demented smile on his face. It was a smile I'd seen before, months ago, when I'd caught him torturing pigeons in his mother's barn in rural Delaware.

"What do you think you're doing, Dylan?" I said.

"Giving you what you deserve for killing my mom."

"He was framed," Bree said. "Drugged. The jury agreed."

"I saw him do it with my own two eyes," he snarled.

"So you *were* in the factory that night," I said. "I've thought about that possibility quite a bit since the trial."

"Who cares? Winning and seeing you gone is what's important."

"You took the holographic film off everyone's hands, didn't you?"

He snorted. "That's bullshit. That whole excuse was cooked up by your brat of a kid and his gay buddy. Where is he, anyway? Your brat of a kid?"

"Far away," I said, my eyes flickering to the street and the sidewalk.

"I'll find him later, after I'm done here."

"No, you won't."

Dylan shook the pistol at me. "Don't tell me what I will or won't do, Cross! Who the hell do you think you are?"

"I'm the guy who notices things, Dylan. Even after seeing the film of me shooting your mother over and over in court, I couldn't figure out what about it was driving me crazy."

"Shut up. Get on your knees. Both of you."

I stood my ground. So did Bree.

I said, "Your mother stumbled when she came into view. Did you push your mother, Dylan? Did she know what you meant to have happen?"

"Lying again." He sneered. "Making shit up. It's what you do, Cross. But not this time. This time, you're gonna die. Like you should have before."

I heard the click of the revolver's hammer cocking.

"Don't do it," Bree said. "Killing cops never ends well."

"I don't care," Dylan said. "This is where I end too. Once I see you both——"

I caught a flicker of movement behind and to his right a split second before Soneji's son screamed and spun around, firing. The shot hit the porch ceiling.

Plaster dust and splinters hit me in the face as I charged, smashed my shoulder into his rib cage, and drove him hard against the railing. I heard ribs crack and saw all the wind go out of him before I dragged him to the porch floor and pinned him.

Bree kicked away his gun, backed up, and turned on the porch light.

Dylan Winslow lay under me, gasping for air, one hand

groping for the vanes and shaft of the competition dart buried deep in the left side of his neck.

"Who's the brat now, jackass?" Ali cried, leaping onto the porch, pumping his fist, and then pointing a finger triumphantly at Soneji's kid. "I smoked you with a ten-ringer from thirty-five feet!"

CHAPTER

114

LATE THE FOLLOWING APRIL, ALI and I drove out to Assateague State Park on Maryland's Eastern Shore. It was a glorious spring day, unnaturally warm, and it felt good in my bones when I climbed from the car after parking beside a familiar Jeep Wagoneer.

"Why would Mr. Aaliyah want to teach me to fish?" Ali said, coming around the back. "He doesn't even know me."

"He's heard of you. Besides, he likes to teach kids to fish."

"Why?"

"Give a man a fish and he eats for a day. Teach a man to fish and he eats for a lifetime."

Ali gave me a funny face. "Who said that?"

"Someone smarter than me," I said as a Volvo pulled into the lot.

A woman in her thirties with ash-blond hair climbed out and looked over at us uncertainly. "The beach isn't far, is it?"

"Just over the dunes," I said and motioned to Ali to kick off his sneakers.

Barefoot, we walked the sand path through the dunes. My ankle didn't feel too bad at all, and there was a nice breeze blowing that smelled like spring.

"What's going to happen to him, Dad?" Ali said. "Dylan Winslow?"

"That's out of my hands. He'll get his day in court."

"I heard Bree say they think something's wrong with his brain."

That was sadly true and, if the doctors' suspicions proved correct, unsurprising. Dylan had been born on the wrong end of a DNA chain, one where psychopathic tendencies were passed on by a criminally insane father and first expressed through a delight in torturing defenseless animals. Abetting the murder of his mother and then attempting to murder us were natural progressions for him, in some ways as predictable as diseases.

"Doctors are looking at that possibility," I said. "If so, Dylan will go to an institution for people like that."

We emerged on the beach. The sky was ridiculously blue. The sea heaved and rolled in a deeper azure. Early-season sunbathers and a smattering of fishermen dotted the pristine sand.

"That guy's got a big fish!" Ali said, pointing to a man pulling one ashore.

"Nice one."

"I like this place, Dad. I want to learn to fish."

"Thought you might."

We walked south a hundred yards and found Bernie Aaliyah and his daughter, Tess, waiting for us.

"Heard a lot about you, kid," Bernie said, shaking Ali's hand. "Remind me not to get between you and a dartboard."

Ali grinned, and I knew they were going to be buds. Bernie started to show Ali how the tackle worked. I went to Tess, said, "Long time, no see."

She put her hands in her back pockets, said, "I'm doing better. Most days."

"Take a stroll?"

"Why not?"

We walked back the way I'd come.

"I've heard rumors of you leaving Metro," Tess said. "On to bigger and better things."

"It's true," I said, and I explained the deal I'd forged.

Similar to Rawlins, I was now an independent contractor for the FBI, working as a consultant on the most sensitive and high-profile cases. The same was true with Metro.

"I was getting restless," I said. "I needed a new challenge, and I'll get it. And because I'll be called to work only the most demanding cases, I'll have time to dedicate to my counseling practice, where I find a lot of personal fulfillment."

"Sounds perfect."

"I think so."

I saw the ash-blond woman from the parking lot walking our way. She'd put on big sunglasses and a tennis visor and held the hand of a pretty young girl in pigtails who wore pink culottes and carried a little bucket and shovel.

"Detective Aaliyah?" the woman said.

Tess pulled her head back, clearly not recognizing her.

The woman glanced at me and then took off her sunglasses. "My name is Patricia Phelps."

Tess took a sharp breath. Her shaking hands traveled to her lips in disbelief. The mother of the little girl she'd shot was standing right there.

"I'll let you two talk," I said, and I walked toward the dunes.

I climbed up on one and sat on top for the longest time, rubbing my ankle and watching life play out on the beach below me. I saw Patricia Phelps forgive Tess Aaliyah as she'd promised she would. Tess fell into the woman's arms, and later they built a sand castle with Meagan, the little girl.

It took a while, but Ali finally got the hang of casting and later hooked his first fish, a nice striper. He danced all around, throwing his hands up in the air, and I could hear his shouts of victory over the surf.

I smiled and gazed beyond the breaking waves to the sea and the far horizon, feeling that these kinds of moments, these small triumphs, were more than enough to keep me working for the good in the world despite all the dark webs I'd been thrust into over the course of my life.

ABOUT THE AUTHOR

JAMES PATTERSON received the Literarian Award for Outstanding Service to the American Literary Community from the National Book Foundation. He holds the Guinness World Record for the most #1 *New York Times* bestsellers, and his books have sold more than 350 million copies worldwide. A tireless champion of the power of books and reading, Patterson created a children's book imprint, JIMMY Patterson, whose mission is simple: "We want every kid who finishes a JIMMY Book to say, 'PLEASE GIVE ME ANOTHER BOOK.'" He has donated more than one million books to students and soldiers and funds over four hundred Teacher Education Scholarships at twenty-four colleges and universities. He has also donated millions of dollars to independent bookstores and school libraries. Patterson invests proceeds from the sales of JIMMY Patterson Books in pro-reading initiatives.

BOOKS BY JAMES PATTERSON

FEATURING ALEX CROSS

The People vs. Alex Cross • *Cross the Line* • *Cross Justice* • *Hope to Die* • *Cross My Heart* • *Alex Cross, Run* • *Merry Christmas, Alex Cross* • *Kill Alex Cross* • *Cross Fire* • *I, Alex Cross* • *Alex Cross's Trial* (with Richard DiLallo) • *Cross Country* • *Double Cross* • *Cross* (also published as *Alex Cross*) • *Mary, Mary* • *London Bridges* • *The Big Bad Wolf* • *Four Blind Mice* • *Violets Are Blue* • *Roses Are Red* • *Pop Goes the Weasel* • *Cat & Mouse* • *Jack & Jill* • *Kiss the Girls* • *Along Came a Spider*

THE WOMEN'S MURDER CLUB

16th Seduction (with Maxine Paetro) • *15th Affair* (with Maxine Paetro) • *14th Deadly Sin* (with Maxine Paetro) • *Unlucky 13* (with Maxine Paetro) • *12th of Never* (with Maxine Paetro) • *11th Hour* (with Maxine Paetro) • *10th Anniversary* (with Maxine Paetro) • *The 9th Judgment* (with Maxine Paetro) • *The 8th Confession* (with Maxine Paetro) • *7th Heaven* (with Maxine Paetro) • *The 6th Target* (with Maxine Paetro) • *The 5th Horseman* (with Maxine Paetro) • *4th of July* (with Maxine Paetro) • *3rd Degree* (with Andrew Gross) • *2nd Chance* (with Andrew Gross) • *First to Die*

FEATURING MICHAEL BENNETT

Haunted (with James O. Born) • *Bullseye* (with Michael Ledwidge) • *Alert* (with Michael Ledwidge) • *Burn* (with Michael Ledwidge) • *Gone* (with Michael Ledwidge) •

I, Michael Bennett (with Michael Ledwidge) • *Tick Tock* (with Michael Ledwidge) • *Worst Case* (with Michael Ledwidge) • *Run for Your Life* (with Michael Ledwidge) • *Step on a Crack* (with Michael Ledwidge)

THE PRIVATE NOVELS

Missing: A Private Novel (with Kathryn Fox) • *The Games* (with Mark Sullivan) • *Private Paris* (with Mark Sullivan) • *Private Vegas* (with Maxine Paetro) • *Private India: City on Fire* (with Ashwin Sanghi) • *Private Down Under* (with Michael White) • *Private L.A.* (with Mark Sullivan) • *Private Berlin* (with Mark Sullivan) • *Private London* (with Mark Pearson) • *Private Games* (with Mark Sullivan) • *Private: #1 Suspect* (with Maxine Paetro) • *Private* (with Maxine Paetro)

NYPD RED NOVELS

NYPD Red 4 (with Marshall Karp) • *NYPD Red 3* (with Marshall Karp) • *NYPD Red 2* (with Marshall Karp) • *NYPD Red* (with Marshall Karp)

SUMMER NOVELS

Second Honeymoon (with Howard Roughan) • *Now You See Her* (with Michael Ledwidge) • *Swimsuit* (with Maxine Paetro) • *Sail* (with Howard Roughan) • *Beach Road* (with Peter de Jonge) • *Lifeguard* (with Andrew Gross) • *Honeymoon* (with Howard Roughan) • *The Beach House* (with Peter de Jonge)

STAND-ALONE BOOKS

The Store (with Richard DiLallo) • *Murder Games* (with Howard Roughan) • *Penguins of America* (with Jack Patterson and Florence Yue) • *Two from the Heart* (with Frank Costantini, Emily Raymond, and Brian Sitts) • *The Black Book* (with David Ellis) • *Humans, Bow Down* (with Emily Raymond) • *Never Never* (with Candice Fox) • *Woman of God* (with Maxine Paetro) • *Filthy Rich* (with John Connolly and Timothy Malloy) • *The Murder House* (with David Ellis) • *Truth or Die* (with Howard Roughan) • *Miracle at Augusta* (with Peter de Jonge) • *Invisible* (with David Ellis) • *First Love* (with Emily Raymond) • *Mistress* (with David Ellis) • *Zoo* (with Michael Ledwidge) • *Guilty Wives* (with David Ellis) • *The Christmas Wedding* (with Richard DiLallo) • *Kill Me If You Can* (with Marshall Karp) • *Toys* (with Neil McMahon) • *Don't Blink* (with Howard Roughan) • *The Postcard Killers* (with Liza Marklund) • *The Murder of King Tut* (with Martin Dugard) • *Against Medical Advice* (with Hal Friedman) • *Sundays at Tiffany's* (with Gabrielle Charbonnet) • *You've Been Warned* (with Howard Roughan) • *The Quickie* (with Michael Ledwidge) • *Judge & Jury* (with Andrew Gross) • *Sam's Letters to Jennifer* • *The Lake House* • *The Jester* (with Andrew Gross) • *Suzanne's Diary for Nicholas* • *Cradle and All* • *When the Wind Blows* • *Miracle on the 17th Green* (with Peter de Jonge) • *Hide & Seek* • *The Midnight Club* • *Black Friday* (originally published as *Black Market*) • *See How They Run* (originally published as *The Jericho Commandment*) • *Season of the Machete* • *The Thomas Berryman Number*

BOOK**SHOTS**

Manhunt (with James O. Born) • *Revenge* (with Shan Serafin) • *The Dolls* (with Kecia Bal) • *The Medical Examiner* (with Maxine Paetro) • *Detective Cross* • *The Exile* (with Alison

Joseph) • *French Twist* (with Richard DiLallo) • *Malicious* (with James O. Born) • *Hidden* (with James O. Born) • *The House Husband* (with Duane Swierczynski) • *Black & Blue* (with Candice Fox) • *Come and Get Us* (with Shan Serafin) • *Private: The Royals* (with Rees Jones) • *The Christmas Mystery* (with Richard DiLallo) • *Killer Chef* (with Jeffrey J. Keyes) • *Taking the Titanic* (with Scott Slaven) • *Kill or Be Killed* (thriller omnibus) • *$10,000,000 Marriage Proposal* (with Hilary Liftin) • *French Kiss* (with Richard DiLallo) • *113 Minutes* (with Max DiLallo) • *Hunted* (with Andrew Holmes) • *Chase* (with Michael Ledwidge) • *Let's Play Make-Believe* (with James O. Born) • *Little Black Dress* (with Emily Raymond) • *The Trial* (with Maxine Paetro) • *Cross Kill* • *Zoo 2* (with Max DiLallo)

BOOKS FOR READERS OF ALL AGES
Maximum Ride

Maximum Ride Forever • *Nevermore: The Final Maximum Ride Adventure* • *Angel: A Maximum Ride Novel* • *Fang: A Maximum Ride Novel* • *Max: A Maximum Ride Novel* • *The Final Warning: A Maximum Ride Novel* • *Saving the World and Other Extreme Sports: A Maximum Ride Novel* • *School's Out—Forever: A Maximum Ride Novel* • *The Angel Experiment: A Maximum Ride Novel*

Daniel X

Daniel X: Lights Out (with Chris Grabenstein) • *Daniel X: Armageddon* (with Chris Grabenstein) • *Daniel X: Game Over* (with Ned Rust) • *Daniel X: Demons & Druids* (with Adam Sadler) • *Daniel X: Watch the Skies* (with Ned Rust) • *The Dangerous Days of Daniel X* (with Michael Ledwidge)

Witch & Wizard

Witch & Wizard: The Lost (with Emily Raymond) • *Witch & Wizard: The Kiss* (with Jill Dembowski) • *Witch & Wizard: The Fire* (with Jill Dembowski) • *Witch & Wizard: The Gift* (with Ned Rust) • *Witch & Wizard* (with Gabrielle Charbonnet)

Middle School

Middle School: Escape to Australia (with Martin Chatterton, illustrated by Daniel Griffo) • *Middle School: Dog's Best Friend* (with Chris Tebbetts, illustrated by Jomike Tejido) • *Middle School: Just My Rotten Luck* (with Chris Tebbetts, illustrated by Laura Park) • *Middle School: Save Rafe* (with Chris Tebbetts, illustrated by Laura Park) • *Middle School: Ultimate Showdown* (with Julia Bergen, illustrated by Alec Longstreth) • *Middle School: How I Survived Bullies, Broccoli, and Snake Hill* (with Chris Tebbetts, illustrated by Laura Park) • *Middle School: Big Fat Liar* (with Lisa Papademetriou, illustrated by Neil Swaab) • *Middle School: Get Me Out of Here!* (with Chris Tebbetts, illustrated by Laura Park) • *Middle School, The Worst Years of My Life* (with Chris Tebbetts, illustrated by Laura Park)

Confessions

Confessions: The Murder of an Angel (with Maxine Paetro) • *Confessions: The Paris Mysteries* (with Maxine Paetro) • *Confessions: The Private School Murders* (with Maxine Paetro) • *Confessions of a Murder Suspect* (with Maxine Paetro)

I Funny

I Funny: School of Laughs (with Chris Grabenstein, illustrated by Jomike Tejido) • *I Funny TV* (with Chris Grabenstein, illustrated by Laura Park) • *I Totally Funniest* (with Chris Grabenstein, illustrated by Laura Park) • *I Even Funnier* (with Chris Grabenstein, illustrated by Laura Park) • *I Funny: A Middle School Story* (with Chris Grabenstein, illustrated by Laura Park)

Treasure Hunters

Treasure Hunters: Peril at the Top of the World (with Chris Grabenstein, illustrated by Juliana Neufeld) • *Treasure Hunters: Secret of the Forbidden City* (with Chris Grabenstein, illustrated by Juliana Neufeld) • *Treasure Hunters: Danger Down the Nile* (with Chris Grabenstein, illustrated by Juliana Neufeld) • *Treasure Hunters* (with Chris Grabenstein, illustrated by Juliana Neufeld)

House of Robots

House of Robots: Robot Revolution (with Chris Grabenstein, illustrated by Juliana Neufeld) • *House of Robots: Robots Go Wild!* (with Chris Grabenstein, illustrated by Juliana Neufeld) • *House of Robots* (with Chris Grabenstein, illustrated by Juliana Neufeld)

Other Books for Readers of All Ages

Jacky Ha-Ha: My Life Is a Joke (with Chris Grabenstein, illustrated by Kerascoët) • *Give Thank You a Try* • *Expelled* (with Emily Raymond) • *The Candies Save Christmas* (illustrated by Andy Elkerton) • *Big Words for Little Geniuses* (with Susan Patterson, illustrated by Hsinping Pan) • *Laugh Out Loud* (with Chris Grabenstein, illustrated by Stephen Gilpin) • *Pottymouth and Stoopid* (with Chris Grabenstein, illustrated by Stephen Gilpin) • *Crazy House* (with Gabrielle Charbonnet) • *Word of Mouse* (with Chris Grabenstein, illustrated by Joe Sutphin) • *Give Please a Chance* (with Bill O'Reilly) • *Cradle and All* (teen edition) • *Jacky Ha-Ha* (with Chris Grabenstein, illustrated by Kerascoët) • *Public School Superhero* (with Chris Tebbetts, illustrated by Cory Thomas) • *Homeroom Diaries* (with Lisa Papademetriou, illustrated by Keino) • *Med Head* (with Hal Friedman) • *santaKid* (illustrated by Michael Garland)

For previews and information about the author, visit JamesPatterson.com or find him on Facebook or at your app store.

ALEX CROSS, I'M COMING FOR YOU—EVEN FROM THE GRAVE IF I HAVE TO.

Along Came a Spider killer Gary Soneji has been dead for over ten years. Alex Cross watched him die. But today, Cross saw him gun down his partner. Is Soneji alive? A ghost? Or something even more sinister?

Nothing will prepare you for the wicked truth.

TO BEGIN READING
CROSS KILL: AN ALEX CROSS STORY,
TURN THE PAGE.

CHAPTER

1

A LATE WINTER STORM bore down on Washington, DC, that March morning, and more folks than usual were waiting in the cafeteria of St. Anthony of Padua Catholic School on Monroe Avenue in the northeast quadrant.

"If you need a jolt before you eat, coffee's in those urns over there," I called to the cafeteria line.

From behind a serving counter, my partner, John Sampson, said, "You want pancakes or eggs and sausage, you come see me first. Dry cereal, oatmeal, and toast at the end. Fruit, too."

It was early, a quarter to seven, and we'd already seen twenty-five people come through the kitchen, mostly moms and kids from the surrounding neighborhood. By my count, another forty were waiting in the hallway, with more coming in from outside where the first flakes were falling.

It was all my ninety-something grandmother's idea. She'd hit the DC Lottery Powerball the year before, and wanted to make sure the unfortunate received some of her good fortune. She'd partnered with the church to see the hot-breakfast program started.

"Are there any doughnuts?" asked a little boy, who put me in mind of my younger son, Ali.

He was holding on to his mother, a devastatingly thin woman with rheumy eyes and a habit of scratching at her neck.

"No doughnuts today," I said.

"What am I gonna eat?" he complained.

"Something that's good for you for once," his mom said. "Eggs, bacon, and toast. Not all that Cocoa Puffs sugar crap."

I nodded. Mom looked like she was high on something, but she did know her nutrition.

"This sucks," her son said. "I want a doughnut. I want two doughnuts!"

"Go on, there," his mom said, and pushed him toward Sampson.

"Kind of overkill for a church cafeteria," said the man who followed her. He was in his late twenties, and dressed in baggy jeans, Timberland boots, and a big gray snorkel jacket.

I realized he was talking to me and looked at him, puzzled.

"Bulletproof vest?" he said.

"Oh," I said, and shrugged at the body armor beneath my shirt.

Sampson and I are major case detectives with the Washington, DC, Metropolitan Police Department. Immediately after our shift in the soup kitchen, we were joining a team taking down a drug gang operating in the streets around St. Anthony's. Members of the gang had been known to take free breakfasts at the school from time to time, so we'd decided to armor up. Just in case.

I wasn't telling him that, though. I couldn't identify him as a known gangster, but he looked the part.

"I'm up for a PT test end of next week," I said. "Got to get used to the weight since I'll be running three miles with it on."

"That vest make you hotter or colder today?"

"Warmer. Always."

"I need one of them," he said, and shivered. "I'm from Miami, you know? I must have been crazy to want to come on up here."

"Why did you come up here?" I asked.

"School. I'm a freshman at Howard."

"You're not on the meal program?"

"Barely making my tuition."

I saw him in a whole new light then, and was about to say so when gunshots rang out and people began to scream.

2

DRAWING MY SERVICE PISTOL, I pushed against the fleeing crowd, hearing two more shots, and realizing they were coming from inside the kitchen behind Sampson. My partner had figured it out as well.

Sampson spun away from the eggs and bacon, drew his gun as I vaulted over the counter. We split and went to either side of the pair of swinging industrial kitchen doors. There were small portholes in both.

Ignoring the people still bolting from the cafeteria, I leaned forward and took a quick peek. Mixing bowls had spilled off the stainless-steel counters, throwing flour and eggs across the cement floor. Nothing moved, and I could detect no one inside.

Sampson took a longer look from the opposite angle. His face almost immediately screwed up.

"Two wounded," he hissed. "The cook, Theresa, and a nun I've never seen before."

"How bad?"

"There's blood all over Theresa's white apron. Looks like the nun's hit in the leg. She's sitting up against the stove with a big pool below her."

"Femoral?"

Sampson took another look and said, "It's a lot of blood."

"Cover me," I said. "I'm going in low to get them."

Sampson nodded. I squatted down and threw my shoulder into the door, which swung away. Half expecting some unseen gunman to open fire, I rolled inside. I slid through the slurry of two dozen eggs, and came to a stop on the floor between two prep counters.

Sampson came in with his weapon high, searching for a target.

But no one shot. No one moved. And there was no sound except the labored breathing of the cook and the nun who were to our left, on the other side of a counter, by a big industrial stove.

The nun's eyes were open and bewildered. The cook's head slumped but she was breathing.

I scrambled under the prep counter to the women, and started tugging off my belt. The nun shrank from me when I reached for her.

"I'm a cop, Sister," I said. "My name is Alex Cross. I need to put a tourniquet on your leg or you could die."

She blinked, but then nodded.

"John?" I said, observing a serious gunshot wound to her lower thigh. A needle-thin jet of blood erupted with every heartbeat.

"Right here," Sampson said behind me. "Just seeing what's what."

"Call it in," I said, as I wrapped the belt around her upper thigh, cinching it tight. "We need two ambulances. Fast."

The blood stopped squirting. I could hear my partner making the radio call.

The nun's eyes fluttered and drifted toward shut.

"Sister," I said. "What happened? Who shot you?"

Her eyes blinked open. She gaped at me, disoriented for a moment, before her attention strayed past me. Her eyes widened, and the skin of her cheek went taut with terror.

I snatched up my gun and spun around, raising the pistol. I saw Sampson with his back to me, radio to his ear, gun lowered, and then a door at the back of the kitchen. It had swung open, revealing a large pantry.

A man crouched in a fighting stance in the pantry doorway.

In his crossed arms he held two nickel-plated pistols, one aimed at Sampson and the other at me.

With all the training I've been lucky enough to receive over the years, you'd think I would have done the instinctual thing for a veteran cop facing an armed assailant, that I would have registered *Man with gun!* in my brain, and I would have shot him immediately.

But for a split second I didn't listen to *Man with a gun!* because I was too stunned by the fact that I knew him, and that he was long, long dead.

CHAPTER

3

IN THAT SAME INSTANT, he fired both pistols. Traveling less than thirty feet, the bullet hit me so hard it slammed me backward. My head cracked off the concrete and everything went just this side of midnight, like I was swirling and draining down a black pipe, before I heard a third shot and then a fourth.

Something crashed close to me, and I fought my way toward the sound, toward consciousness, seeing the blackness give way, disjointed and incomplete, like a jigsaw puzzle with missing pieces.

Five, maybe six seconds passed before I found more pieces, and I knew who I was and what had happened. Two more seconds passed before I realized I'd taken the bullet square in the Kevlar that covered my chest. It felt like I'd taken a sledgehammer to my ribs, and a swift kick to my head.

In the next instant, I grabbed my gun and looked for...

John Sampson sprawled on the floor by the sinks, his massive frame looking crumpled until he started twitching electrically, and I saw the head wound.

"No," I shouted, becoming fully alert, and stumbling over to his side.

Sampson's eyes were rolled up in his head and quivering. I grabbed the radio on the floor beyond him, hit the transmitter, and said, "This is Detective Alex Cross. Ten-Zero-Zero. Repeat. Officer down. Monroe Avenue and 12th, Northeast. St. Anthony's Catholic School kitchen. Multiple shots fired. Ten-Fifty-Twos needed immediately. Repeat. Multiple ambulances needed, and a Life Flight for officer with head wound!"

"We have ambulances and patrols on their way, Detective," the dispatcher came back. "ETA twenty seconds. I'll call Life Flight. Do you have the shooter?"

"No, damn it. Make the Life Flight call."

The line went dead. I lowered the radio. Only then did I look back at the best friend I've ever had, the first kid I met after Nana Mama brought me up from South Carolina, the man I'd grown up with, the partner I'd relied on more times than I could count. The spasms subsided and Sampson's eyes glazed over and he gasped.

"John," I said, kneeling beside him and taking his hand. "Hold on now. Cavalry's coming."

He seemed not to hear, just stared vacantly past me toward the wall.

I started to cry. I couldn't stop. I shook from head to toe, and then I wanted to shoot the man who'd done this. I wanted to shoot him twenty times, completely destroy the creature that had risen from the dead.

Sirens closed in on the school from six directions. I wiped at my tears, and then squeezed Sampson's hand, before forcing myself to my feet and back out into the cafeteria, where the first patrol officers were charging in, followed by a pair of EMTs whose shoulders were flecked with melting snowflakes.

They got Sampson's head immobilized, then put him on a board and then a gurney. He was under blankets and moving in less than six minutes. It was snowing hard outside. They waited inside the front door to the school for the helicopter to come, and put IV lines into his wrists.

Sampson went into another convulsion. The parish priest, Father Fred Close, came and gave my partner the last rites.

But my man was still hanging on when the helicopter came. In a daze I followed them out into a driving snowstorm. We had to shield our eyes to duck under the blinding propeller wash and get Sampson aboard.

"We'll take it from here!" one EMT shouted at me.

"There's not a chance I'm leaving his side," I said, climbed in beside the pilot, and pulled on the extra helmet. "Let's go."

The pilot waited until they had the rear doors shut and the gurney strapped down before throttling up the helicopter. We began to rise, and it was only then that I saw through the swirling snow that crowds were forming beyond the barricades set up in a perimeter around the school and church complex.

We pivoted in the air and flew back up over 12th Street, rising above the crowd. I looked down through the spiraling snow and saw everyone ducking their heads from the helicopter wash. Everyone except for a single male face looking directly up at the Life Flight, not caring about the battering, stinging snow.

"That's him!" I said.

"Detective?" the pilot said, his voice crackling over the radio in my helmet.

I tugged down the microphone, and said, "How do I talk to dispatch?"

The pilot leaned over, and flipped a switch.

"This is Detective Alex Cross," I said. "Who's the supervising detective heading to St. Anthony's?"

"Your wife. Chief Stone."

"Patch me through to her."

Five seconds passed as we built speed and hurtled toward the hospital.

"Alex?" Bree said. "What's happened?"

"John's hit bad, Bree," I said. "I'm with him. Close off that school from four blocks in every direction. Order a door-to-door search. I just saw the shooter on 12th, a block west of the school."

"Description?"

"It's Gary Soneji, Bree," I said. "Get his picture off Google and send it to every cop in the area."

There was silence on the line before Bree said sympathetically, "Alex, are *you* okay? Gary Soneji's been dead for years."

"If he's dead, then I just saw a ghost."

CHAPTER

4

WE WERE BUFFETED BY winds and faced near-whiteout conditions trying to land on the helipad atop George Washington Medical Center. In the end we put down in the parking lot by the ER entrance, where a team of nurses and doctors met us.

They hustled Sampson inside and got him attached to monitors while Dr. Christopher Kalhorn, a neurosurgeon, swabbed aside some of the blood and examined the head wounds.

The bullet had entered Sampson's skull at a shallow angle about two inches above the bridge of his nose. It exited forward of his left temple. That second wound was about the size of a marble, but gaping and ragged, as if the bullet had been a hollow point that broke up and shattered going through bone.

"Let's get him intubated, on Propofol, and into an ice bath and cooling helmet," Kalhorn said. "Take his temp down to ninety-two, get him into a CT scanner, and then the OR. I'll have a team waiting for him."

The ER doctors and nurses sprang into action. In short order, they had a breathing tube down Sampson's throat and were racing him away. Kalhorn turned to leave. I showed my badge and stopped him.

"That's my brother," I said. "What do I tell his wife?"

Dr. Kalhorn turned grim. "You tell her we'll do everything possible to save him. And you tell her to pray. You, too, Detective."

"What are his chances?"

"Pray," he said, took off in a trot, and disappeared.

I was left standing in an empty treatment slot in the ER, looking down at the dark blood that stained the gauze pads they'd used to clean Sampson's head.

"You can't stay in here, Detective," one of the nurses said sympathetically. "We need the space. Traffic accidents all over the city with this storm."

I nodded, turned, and wandered away, wondering where to go, what to do.

I went out in the ER waiting area and saw twenty people in the seats. They stared at my pistol, at the blood on my shirt, and at the black hole where Soneji's bullet had hit me. I didn't care what they thought. I didn't—

I heard the automatic doors *whoosh* open behind me.

A fearful voice cried out, "Alex?"

I swung around. Billie Sampson was standing there in pink hospital scrub pants and a down coat, shaking from head to toe from the cold and the threat of something far more bitter. "How bad is it?"

Billie's a surgical nurse, so there was no point in being vague. I described the wound. Her hand flew to her mouth at first, but then she shook her head. "It's bad. He's lucky to be alive."

I hugged her and said, "He's a strong man. But he's going to need your prayers. He's going to need all our prayers."

Billie's strength gave way. She began to moan and sob into my chest, and I held her tighter. When I raised my head, the people in the waiting room were looking on in concern.

"Let's get out of here," I muttered, and led Billie out into the hallway and to the chapel.

We went inside, and thankfully it was empty. I got Billie calmed down enough to tell her what had happened at the school and afterward.

"They've put him into a chemical coma and are supercooling his body."

"To reduce swelling and bleeding," she said, nodding.

"And the neurosurgeons here are the best. He's in their hands now."

"And God's," Billie said, staring at the cross on the wall in the chapel before pulling away from me to go down on her knees.

I joined her and we held hands and begged our savior for mercy.

CHAPTER

5

HOURS PASSED LIKE DAYS as we waited outside the surgical unit. Bree showed up before noon.

"Anything?" she asked.

I shook my head.

"Billie," Bree said, hugging her. "We're going to find who did this to John. I promise you that."

"You didn't find Soneji?" I asked in disbelief. "How could he have gotten away if you'd cordoned off the area?"

My wife looked over at me, studied me. "Soneji's dead, Alex. You all but killed him yourself."

My mouth hung open, and I blinked several times. "You mean you didn't send his picture out? You didn't look for him?"

"We looked for someone who looked like Soneji," Bree said defensively.

"No," I said. "He was less than thirty feet from me, light shining down on his face. It was him."

"Then explain how a man who all but disintegrated right

before your eyes can surface more than a decade later," Bree said.

"I can't explain it," I said. "I…maybe I need some coffee. Want some?"

They shook their heads, and I got up, heading toward the hospital cafeteria, seeing flashbacks from long ago.

I put Gary Soneji in prison after he went on a kidnapping and murder spree that threatened my family. Soneji escaped several years later, and turned to bomb building. He detonated several, killing multiple people before we spotted him in New York City. We chased Soneji into Grand Central Station, where we feared he'd explode another bomb. Instead he grabbed a baby.

At one point, Soneji held the baby up and screamed at me, "This doesn't end here, Cross. I'm coming for you, even from the grave if I have to."

Then he threw the infant at us. Someone caught her, but Soneji escaped into the vast abandoned tunnel system below Manhattan. We tracked him in there. Soneji attacked me in the darkness, and knocked me down and almost killed me before I was able to shoot him. The bullet shattered his jaw, ripped apart his tongue, and blew out the side of one cheek.

Soneji staggered away from me, was swallowed by the darkness. He must have pitched forward then and sprawled on the rocky tunnel floor. The impact set off a small bomb in his pocket. The tunnel exploded into white-hot flames.

When I got to him, Soneji was engulfed, curled up, and screaming. It lasted several seconds before he stopped. I stood there and watched Soneji burn. I saw him shrivel up and turn coal black.

But as sure as I was of that memory, I was also sure I'd seen

Gary Soneji that morning, a split second before he tried to shoot me in the heart and blow Sampson's head off.

I'm coming for you, even from the grave if I have to.

Soneji's taunt echoed back to me after I'd gotten my coffee.

After several sips, I decided I had to assume Soneji was still dead. So I'd seen, what, a double? An impostor?

I supposed it was possible with plastic surgery, but the likeness had been so dead-on, from the thin reddish mustache to the wispy hair to the crazed, amused expression.

It was him, I thought. *But how?*

This doesn't end here, Cross.

I saw Soneji so clearly then that I feared for my sanity.

This doesn't end here, Cross.

I'm coming for you, even from the grave if I have to.

CHAPTER

6

"ALEX?"

I startled, almost dropped my coffee, and saw Bree trotting down the hall toward me with a wary expression.

"He made it through the operation," she said. "He's in intensive care, and the doctor's going to talk to Billie in a few moments."

We both held Billie's hands when Dr. Kalhorn finally emerged. He looked drained.

"How is he?" Billie asked, after introducing herself.

"Your husband's a remarkable fighter," Kalhorn said. "He died once on the table, but rallied. Besides the trauma of the bullet, there were bone and bullet fragments we had to deal with. Three quarters of an inch left and one of those fragments would have caught a major artery, and we'd be having a different conversation."

"So he's going to live?" Billie asked.

"I can't promise you that," Kalhorn said. "The next forty-eight to seventy-two hours will be the most critical time for him. He's sustained a massive head injury, severe trauma to his upper-left temporal lobe. For now, we're keeping him in a medically induced coma, and we will keep him that way until we see a significant drop in brain swelling."

"If he comes out, what's the prognosis, given the extent of the injury you saw?" I asked.

"I can't tell you who he'll be if and when he wakes up," the neurosurgeon said. "That's up to God."

"Can we see him?" Bree asked.

"Give it a half hour," Kalhorn said. "There's a whirlwind around him at the moment. Lots of good people supporting him."

"Thank you, Doctor," Billie said, trying not to cry again. "For saving him."

"It was an honor," Kalhorn said, patted her on the arm, and smiled at Bree and me before returning to the ICU.

"Damage to his upper-left temporal lobe," Billie said.

"He's alive," I said. "Let's keep focused on that. Anything else, we'll deal with down the road."

Bree held her hand and said, "Alex is right. We've prayed him through surgery, and now we'll pray he wakes up."

But Billie still appeared uncertain forty minutes later when we donned surgical masks, gloves, and smocks and entered the room where Sampson lay.

You could barely see the slits of his eyes for the swelling. His head was wrapped in a turban of gauze, and there were so many tubes going into him, and so many monitors and devices beeping and clicking around him, that from the waist up he looked more machine than man.

"Oh, Jesus, John," Billie said when she got to his side. "What have they done to you?"

Bree rubbed Billie's back as tears racked her again. I stayed only a few minutes, until I couldn't take seeing Sampson like that anymore.

"I'll be back," I told them. "Tonight before I go home to sleep."

"Where are you going?" Bree asked.

"To hunt Soneji," I said. "It's what John would want."

"There's a blizzard outside," Bree said. "And Internal Affairs is going to want to hear your report on the shooting."

"I don't give a damn about IA right now," I said, walking toward the door. "And a blizzard's exactly the kind of chaotic situation that Gary Soneji lives for."

Bree wasn't happy, but sighed and gestured to a shopping bag she'd brought with her. "You'll need your coat, hat, and gloves if you're going Soneji-hunting."

7

OUTSIDE A BLIZZARD WAILED, a classic nor'easter with driving wet snow that was already eight inches deep. It takes only four inches to snarl Washington, DC, so completely that there's talk of bringing in the National Guard.

Georgetown was a parking lot. I trudged to the Foggy Bottom Metro station, ignoring my freezing-cold feet, and reliving old times with big John Sampson. I met him within days of moving up to DC with my brothers after my mother died and my father, her killer, disappeared, presumed dead.

John lived with his mother and sister. His father had died in Vietnam. We were in the same fifth-grade class. He was ten years old and big, even then. But so was I.

It made for a natural rivalry, and we didn't much care for each other at first. I was faster than him, which he did not like. He was stronger than me, which I did not like. The inevitable fight we had was a draw.

We were suspended for three days for fighting. Nana Mama

marched me down to Sampson's house to apologize to him and to his mother for throwing the first punch.

I went unhappily. When Sampson came to the door equally annoyed, I saw the split lip and bruising around his right cheek and smiled. He saw the swelling around both of my eyes and smiled back.

We'd both inflicted damage. We both had won. And that was that. End of the war, and start of the longest friendship of my life.

I took the Metro across town, and walked back to St. Anthony's in the snow, trying to will myself not to remember Sampson in the ICU, more machine than man. But the image kept returning, and every time it did, I felt weaker, as if a part of me were dying.

There were still Metro police cars parked in front of the school, and two television trucks. I pulled the wool hat down and turned up the collar of my jacket. I didn't want to talk to any reporters about this case. Ever.

I showed my badge to the patrolman standing inside the front door, and started back toward the cafeteria and kitchen.

Father Close appeared at his office door. He recognized me. "Your partner?"

"There's brain damage, but he's alive," I said.

"Another miracle, then," Father Close said. "Sister Mary Elliott and Theresa Ball, the cook, they're still alive as well. You saved them, Dr. Cross. If you hadn't been there, I fear all three of them would be dead."

"I don't think that's true," I said. "But thank you for saying so."

"Any idea when I can have my cafeteria and kitchen back?"

"I'll ask the crime-scene specialists, but figure tomorrow

your students bring a bag lunch and eat in their homerooms. When it's a cop-involved shooting, the forensics folks are sticklers for detail."

"As they should be," Father Close said, thanked me again, and returned to his office.

I returned to the cafeteria and stood there a moment in the empty space, hearing voices in the kitchen, but recalling the first shots and how I'd reacted.

I went to the swinging industrial doors and did the same. We'd done it by the book, I decided, and pushed through them again.

I glanced at where the cook and nun had lain wounded, and then over where Sampson had lain dying before turning my attention to the pantry. This was where the book had been thrown out. In retrospect, we should have cleared the rest of the building before tending to the wounded. But it looked like femoral blood and…

Three crime-scene techs were still at work in the kitchen. Barbara Hatfield, an old friend, was in the pantry. She spotted me and came right over.

"How's John, Alex?"

"Hanging on," I said.

"Everyone's shaken up," Hatfield said. "And there's something you should see, something I was going to call you about later."

She led me into the pantry, floor-to-ceiling shelves loaded with foodstuffs and kitchen supplies, and a big shiny commercial freezer at the far end.

The words spray-painted in two lines across the face of the fridge stopped me dead in my tracks.

"Right?" Hatfield said. "I did the same thing."

CHAPTER

8

I WAS UP AT four o'clock the following morning, snuck out of bed without waking Bree, and on three hours of sleep went back to doing what I'd been doing. I got a cup of coffee and went up to the third floor, to my home office, where I had been going through my files on Gary Soneji.

I keep files on all the bad ones, but Soneji had the thickest file, six of them, in fact, all bulging. I'd left off at one in the morning with notes taken midway through the kidnapping of the US secretary of the treasury's son, and the daughter of a famous actress.

I tried to focus, tried to re-master the details. But I yawned after two paragraphs, drank coffee, and thought of John Sampson.

But only briefly. I decided that sitting by his side helped him little. I was better off looking for the man who put a bullet through John's head. So I read and reread, and noted dangling threads, abandoned lines of inquiry that Sampson and I had followed over the years but which had led nowhere.

After an hour, I found an old genealogy chart we and the US marshals put together on Soneji's family after he escaped prison. Scanning it, I realized we'd let the marshals handle the pure fugitive hunt. I saw several names and relations I'd never talked to before, and wrote them down.

I ran their names through Google, and saw that two of them were still living at the addresses noted on the chart. How long had it been? Thirteen, fourteen years?

Then again, Nana Mama and I had lived in our house on 5th for more than thirty years. Americans do put down roots once in a while.

I glanced at my watch, saw it was past five, and wondered when I could try to make a few calls. No, I thought then, this kind of thing is best done in person. But the storm. I went to the window in the dormer of the office, pushed it up, and looked outside.

To my surprise, it was pouring rain and considerably warmer. Most of the snow was gone. That sealed it. I was going for a drive as soon as it was light enough to see.

Returning to my desk, I thought about going back downstairs to take a shower, but feared waking Bree. Her job as Metro's chief of detectives was stressful enough without dealing with the additional pressure of a cop shooting.

I tried to go back to the Soneji files, but instead called up a picture on my computer. I'd taken it the afternoon before. It showed the fridge and the spray-painted words the shooter had left behind.

CROSS KILL
Long Live Soneji!

I had obviously been the target. And why not? Soneji hated me as much as I hated him.

Had Soneji expected Sampson to be with me? The two pistols he'd fired said yes. I closed my eyes and saw him there in the doorway, arms crossed, left gun aimed at me, right gun at Sampson.

Something bothered me. I turned back to the file, rummaged around until I confirmed my memory. Soneji was left-handed, which explained why he'd crossed his arms to shoot. He was aiming at me with his better hand. He'd wanted me dead no matter what happened to John.

It was why Soneji shot for center of mass, I decided, and wondered whether his shot at Sampson was misaimed, if he'd clipped John's head in error.

Left-handed. It had to be Soneji. But it couldn't be Soneji.

In frustration, I shut the computer off, grabbed my notes, and snuck back into the bedroom. I shut the bathroom door without making a peep. After showering and dressing, I tried to get out light-footed, but made a floorboard squeak.

"I'm up, quiet as a mouse," Bree said.

"I'm going to New Jersey," I said.

"What?" she said, sitting up in bed and turning on the light. "Why?"

"To talk to some of Soneji's relatives, see if he's been in touch."

Bree shook her head. "He's dead, Alex."

"But what if the explosion I saw in the tunnel was *caused* by Soneji as he went by some bum living down there?" I said. "What if I didn't see Soneji burn?"

"You never did DNA on the remains?"

"There was no need. I saw him die. I identified him, so no one checked."

"Jesus, Alex," Bree said. "Is that possible? What did the shooter's face look like?"

"Like Soneji's," I said, frustrated.

"Well, did his jaw look like Soneji's? His tongue? Did he say anything?"

"He didn't say a word, but his face?" I frowned and thought about that. "I don't know."

"You said the light was good. You said you saw him clearly."

Was the light that good? Feeling a little wobbly, I nevertheless closed my eyes, trying to bring more of the memory back and into sharper focus.

I saw Soneji standing there in the pantry doorway, arms crossed, chin tucked, and…looking directly at me. He shot at Sampson without even aiming. It *was* me he'd wanted to kill.

What about his jaw? I replayed memory again and again before I saw it.

"There was something there," I said, running my fingers along my left jawline.

"A shadow?" Bree said.

I shook my head. "More like a scar."

CHAPTER

9

THREE HOURS LATER, I'D left I-95 for Route 29, which parallels the
Delaware River. Heading upstream, I soon realized that I was
not far from East Amwell Township, where the aviator Charles
Lindbergh's baby was kidnapped in 1932.

Gary Soneji had been obsessed with the Lindbergh case.
He'd studied it in preparing for the kidnappings of the treasury
secretary's son, the late Michael Goldberg, and Maggie Rose
Dunne, the daughter of a famous actress.

I'd noticed before on a map the proximity of East Amwell to
Rosemont, where Soneji grew up. But it wasn't until I pulled
through the tiny unincorporated settlement that I realized
Soneji had spent his early life less than five miles from the
Lindbergh kidnapping site.

Rosemont itself was quaint and leafy, with rock walls giving
way to sopping green fields.

I tried to imagine Soneji as a boy in this rural setting, tried
to see him discovering the crime of the century. He wouldn't

have cared much for the police detectives who'd worked the Lindbergh case. No, Soneji would have obsessed on the information surrounding Bruno Hauptmann, the career criminal convicted and executed for taking the toddler and caving in his skull.

My mind was flooded with memories of going into Soneji's apartment for the first time, seeing what was essentially a shrine to Hauptmann and the Lindbergh case. In writings we found back then, Soneji had fantasized about being Hauptmann in the days just before the killer was caught, when the whole world was fixated and speculating on the mystery he'd set in motion.

"Audacious criminals change history," Soneji wrote. "Audacious criminals are remembered long after they're gone, which is more than can be said of the detectives who chase them."

I found the address on the Rosemont Ringoes Road, and pulled over on the shoulder beyond the drive. The storm had ebbed to sprinkles when I climbed out in front of a gray-and-white clapboard cottage set back in pines.

The yard was sparse and littered with wet pine needles. The front stoop was cracked and listed to one side, so I had to hold on to the iron railing in order to ring the bell.

A few moments later, one of the curtains fluttered. A few moments after that, the door swung open, revealing a bald man in his seventies. He leaned over a walker and had an oxygen line running into his nose.

"Peter Soneji?"

"What do you want?"

"I'm Alex Cross. I'm a—"

"I know who you are," Gary Soneji's father snapped icily. "My son's killer."

"He blew himself up."

"So you've said."

"Can I talk to you, sir?"

"Sir?" Peter Soneji said and laughed caustically. "Now it's 'sir'?"

"Far as I know, you never had anything to do with your son's criminal career," I said.

"Tell that to the reporters who've shown up at my door over the years," Soneji's father said. "The things they've accused me of. Father to a monster."

"I'm not accusing you of anything, *Mr. Soneji*," I said. "I'm simply looking for your take on a few loose ends."

"With everything on the internet about Gary, you'd think there'd be no loose ends."

"These are questions from my personal files," I said.

Soneji's father gave me a long, considered look before saying, "Leave it alone, Detective. Gary's long dead. Far as I'm concerned, good riddance."

He tried to shut the door in my face, but I stopped him.

"I can call the sheriff," Peter Soneji protested.

"Just one question and then I'll leave," I said. "How did Gary become obsessed with the Lindbergh kidnapping?"

CHAPTER

10

TWO HOURS LATER AS I drove through the outskirts of Crumpton, Maryland, I was still wrestling with the answer Soneji's father had given me. It seemed to offer new insight into his son, but I still couldn't explain how or why yet.

I found the second address. The farmhouse had once been a cheery yellow, but the paint was peeling and streaked with dark mold. Every window was encased in the kind of iron barring you see in big cities.

As I walked across the front yard toward the porch, I stirred up several pigeons, flushing them from the dead weeds. I heard a weird voice talking somewhere behind the house.

The porch was dominated by several old machine tools, lathes and such, that I had to step around in order to knock at a steel door with triple dead bolts.

I knocked a second time, and was thinking I should go around the house where I'd heard the odd voice. But then the dead bolts were thrown one by one.

The door opened, revealing a dark-haired woman in her forties, with a sharp nose and dull brown eyes. She wore a grease-stained one-piece Carhartt canvas coverall, and carried at port arms an AR-style rifle with a big banana clip.

"Salesman, you are standing on my property uninvited," she said. "I have ample cause to shoot you where you stand."

I showed her my badge and ID, said, "I'm not a salesman. I'm a cop. I should have called ahead, but I didn't have a number."

Instead of calming her down, that only got her more agitated. "What are the police doing at sweet Ginny Winslow's door? Looking to persecute a gun lover?"

"I just want to ask you a few questions, Mrs. Soneji," I said.

Soneji's widow flinched at the name, and turned spitting mad. "My name's been legally changed to Virginia Winslow going on seven years now, and I still can't get the stench of Gary off my skin. What's your name? Who are you with?"

"Alex Cross," I said. "With DC…"

She hardened, said, "I know you now. I remember you from TV."

"Yes, ma'am."

"You never came to talk with me. Just them US marshals. Like I didn't even exist."

"I'm here to talk now," I said.

"Ten years too late. Get the hell off my property before I embrace my Second Amendment rights and—"

"I saw Gary's father this morning," I said. "He told me how Gary's obsession with the Lindbergh kidnapping began."

She knitted her brows. "How's that?"

"Gary's dad said when Gary was eight they were in a used book store, and while his father was wandering in the stacks, his son found a tattered copy of *True Detective Mysteries,* a crime magazine from the 1930s, and sat down to read it."

Finger still on the trigger of her semiautomatic rifle, Virginia Winslow shrugged. "So what?"

"When Mr. Soneji found Gary, his son was sitting on the floor in the bookstore, the magazine in his lap, and staring in fascination at a picture from the Lindbergh baby's autopsy that showed the head wound in lurid detail."

She stared at me with her jaw slack, as if remembering something that frightened and appalled her.

"What is it?" I asked.

Soneji's widow hardened again. "Nothing. Doesn't surprise me. I used to catch him looking at autopsy pictures. He was always saying he was going to write a book and needed to look at them for research."

"You didn't believe him?"

"I believed him until my brother Charles noticed that Gary was always volunteering to gut deer they killed," she said. "Charles told me Gary liked to put his hands in the warm innards, said he liked the feeling, and told me how Gary'd get all bright and glowing when he was doing it."

11

"**I DIDN'T KNOW THAT** about Gary, either," I said.

"What's this all about?" Virginia Winslow asked, studying me now.

"There was a cop shooting in DC," I said. "A man who fit Gary's description was the shooter."

I expected Soneji's widow to respond with total skepticism. But instead she looked frightened and appalled again.

"Gary's dead," she said. "*You* killed him, didn't you?"

"He killed himself," I said. "Detonated the bomb he was carrying."

Her attention flitted to the boards. "That's not what the internet is saying."

"What's the internet saying?"

"That Gary's alive," she said. "Our son, Dylan, said he's seen it online. Gary's dead, isn't he? Please tell me that."

The way she clenched the rifle told me she needed to hear it, so I said, "As far as I know, Gary Soneji's dead and has been dead for more than ten years. But someone who looked an awful lot like him shot my partner yesterday."

"What?" she said. "No."

"It's not him," I said. "I'm almost certain."

"Almost?" she said before a phone started ringing back in the house.

"I…I have to get that," she said. "Work."

"What kind of work?"

"I'm a machinist and gunsmith," she said. "My father taught me the trade."

She shut the door before I could comment. The bolts were thrown one by one.

I almost left, but then, remembering that voice I'd heard on my way in, I went around the farmhouse, seeing a small, neglected barn around which dozens of pigeons were flying.

I heard someone talking in the barn, and walked over.

Click-a-t-clack. Click-a-t-clack.

Pigeons started and whirled out the barn door.

There was a grimy window. I went to it, and peeked inside, seeing through the dirt sixteen-year-old Dylan Winslow standing there by a large pigeon coop, gazing off into space.

Dylan looked nothing like his father. He had his mother's naturally dark hair, sharp nose, and the same dull brown eyes. He was borderline obese, with hardly a chin, more a draping of his cheeks that joined a wattle above his Adam's apple.

"You need to learn your place," he said to no one. "You need to learn to be quiet. Emotional control. It's the key to a happy life."

Then he turned and walked by the pigeon coop, running a hoop of keys across the metal mesh.

Click-a-t-clack. Click-a-t-clack.

The sound rattled the pigeons and they battered themselves against their cages.

"Be quiet now," Dylan said firmly. "You got to learn some control."

Then he pivoted and started toward me, raking the cages again.

Click-a-t-clack. Click-a-t-clack.

A disturbing little smile showed on the teen's face, and there was even more upsetting delight in his eyes. I have a PhD in criminal psychology and have studied serial killers in depth. Many of them grew up torturing animals for sport.

Had Dylan's father?

I stepped inside the barn. Gary Soneji's son had his back to me again, walking away while raking the front of the cages.

Click-a-t-clack. Click-a-t-clack.

I took another two steps and noticed a large piece of cardboard nailed to one of the barn's support posts.

There was a well-used paper target taped to the cardboard and six darts sticking out of it. The target featured a bull's-eye superimposed over a man's face. It had been used so many times that at first I didn't know who the man was.

Then I did.

"Who the hell are you?" Dylan said, and then gaped when I faced him.

"From the looks of it," I said, "I'm your dartboard."

CHAPTER

12

DYLAN WINSLOW PURSED HIS lips in long-simmering anger, said, "If Mama would let me, I'd use one of her shotguns on it instead of darts."

What do you say to the disturbed son of the disturbed criminal you shot in the face and watched burn?

"I can understand your feelings," I said.

"No, you can't," he said, sneering. "This an official visit, Detective Alex Cross?"

"As a matter of fact," I said. "A man fitting your dead father's description shot my partner in the head last night."

Dylan's sneer disappeared, replaced by widening eyes and that disturbing, delighted grin I'd seen earlier. "It's true, then, what they're saying."

"What are they saying?"

"That you didn't get my dad," Dylan said. "That he escaped the tunnels, badly wounded, but alive, and is still alive. Is that what you're telling me, too?"

There seemed so much hope in his face that, whether he was in need of psychological help or not, I didn't want to destroy it.

"If it wasn't your father who shot my partner, it was his twin."

Dylan started to laugh. He laughed so hard there were tears in his eyes.

Thumping his chest, he said, "I knew it! I felt it right here."

When he stopped, I said, "What do you think is going to happen? That he's going to suddenly appear to rescue you?"

Dylan acted as if I'd read his thoughts, but then shot back, "He will. You watch. And there's nothing you can do about it. It's like they say—Dad was always smarter than you. More patient and cunning than you."

Rather than defend myself, I said, "You're right. Your father was smarter than me, and more patient, and more cunning."

"He still is. They say so on the internet."

"What site?" I asked.

Dylan gave me that disturbing smile again before saying, "One you can't get at in a million years, Cross." He laughed. "Never in a million years."

"Really?" I said. "How about I march back up to your mother and tell her I'm coming back with a search warrant for every computer in your house?"

Dylan's grin stretched wider. "Go ahead. We don't have one."

"How about every computer in your school, in the local library, in every place your mother says you get online?"

I thought that would rock him, but it didn't.

"Knock yourself out," he said. "But unless I have a lawyer present, I am done answering your questions, and I have pigeons to feed."

Or torture, I almost said.

But I bit back the urge, and turned to leave, calling over my shoulder, "Nice to meet you, Dylan. Wonderful getting to know the son of an old enemy."

CHAPTER

13

IT WAS PAST SIX when I finally reached the ICU at GW Medical Center. The nurse at the station said Sampson's vitals had been irregular most of the day, and there'd been little if any reduction in brain swelling.

"You sick in any way?" the nurse asked.

"Not that I'm aware of. Why?"

"Protocol. The shunt draining the wound is an open track straight to the inside of your friend's healing skull. Any kind of infection could be catastrophic."

"I feel fine," I said, and put on the gown, mask, and gloves.

When I pushed open the door, Billie stirred awake in her reclining chair.

"Alex? That you?"

"The man behind the mask."

"Tell me about it," she said, getting up to hug me. "I've been wearing one the past forty hours and I'm getting rubbed raw."

"His vitals?"

Billie scanned the monitors attached to her husband and said, "Not bad at the moment, but his blood pressure took a short, scary dive about four hours ago. I was thinking stroke until he just kind of came up out of it."

"They say talking to people in comas helps," I said.

"Stimulates the brain," she said, nodding. "But that's usually with a non-induced coma, when there aren't drugs involved."

"All the same," I said, and went to Sampson's side.

"I'll be a few minutes," Billie said.

"Be right here until you get back," I said.

When she'd gone out, I held Sampson's giant hand and gave him an account of the day's investigation, sparing him no detail. It felt good and familiar, and right, to talk it out with him, as if Sampson were not drugged down to the reptilian part of his brain, but acute and thoughtful and funny as hell.

"That's it," I said. "And, yes, I want another crack at Soneji's widow and kid before long."

The door opened. Billie stepped back inside, and then several of the monitors around Sampson began to squawk in alarm.

A team burst in. I was pushed to the corner with Billie.

"It's his blood pressure again," Billie said in a wavering voice. "Jesus, I don't know if his heart can take this much longer."

Ninety seconds later, the crisis passed and his vitals improved.

"I don't know what happened," I said, bewildered. "I was telling him about the investigation and…"

"What?" Billie said. "Why did you do that?"

"Because he'd want to know."

"No," she said, shaking her head. "That's done. That's over, Alex."

"What's over?"

"His career as a cop," Billie said. "No matter how he recovers, that part of John's life is over if he wants to continue to be my husband."

"John loves being a cop," I said.

"I know he does…did…but that's over," Billie said sharply. "I will care for him, and defend John until the day one of us dies, but between now and then, his days carrying a gun and a badge are behind him."

14

"SHE'S GOT THE RIGHT to demand that," Bree said later in the hospital cafeteria. "John took a bullet to the head, Alex."

"I know," I said, frustrated and heartsick.

It felt like part of John had died and was never coming back. And it would never be the same between us, as partners anyway. That was dead, too.

I explained this to Bree, and she put her hands on mine and said, "You'll never have a better friend than John Sampson. That friendship, that fierce bond you two have, will never be broken, even if he's no longer a cop, even if he's no longer your partner. Okay?"

"No," I said, pushing my plate away. "But I'll have to learn to live with it."

"You haven't eaten three bites," Bree said, gesturing at the plate.

"No appetite," I said.

"Then force yourself," Bree said. "Especially the protein. Your brain has to be tip-top if you're going to find Soneji."

I laughed softly. "You're always looking out for me."

"Every moment I can, baby."

I ate quite a bit more, and washed it down with three full glasses of water.

"Not quite Nana Mama's cooking," I said.

"I'm sure there'll be leftovers," Bree said.

"You trying to get me fat?" I said.

"I like a little cushion."

I didn't know what to say to that, and we both burst out laughing. Then I looked over and saw Billie standing in the doorway, watching us with bitterness and longing in her expression. She turned and left.

"Should I go after her?" I asked.

"No," Bree said. "I'll talk to her tomorrow."

"Home?"

"Home."

We left the hospital and were crossing a triangular plaza to the Foggy Bottom Metro station when the first shot rang out.

I heard the flat crack of the muzzle blast. I felt the bullet rip past my left ear, grabbed Bree, and yanked her to the ground by two newspaper boxes. People were screaming and scattering.

"Where is he?" Bree said.

"I don't know," I said, before the second and third shots shattered the glass of one newspaper rack and *ping*ed off another.

Then I heard squealing tires, and jumped up in time to see a white panel van roar north on 23rd Street, Northwest, heading toward Washington Circle, and a dozen different escape routes. As the van flashed past us, I caught a glimpse of the driver.

Gary Soneji was looking my way as if posing for a mental picture, grinning like a lunatic and holding his right-hand thumb up, index finger extended, like a gun he was aiming right at me.

I was so shocked that another instant passed before I started running across the plaza to 23rd, trying to get a look at his license plates. But his plate lights were dark, and the van soon disappeared into evening traffic, headed in the direction of whatever hellhole Gary Soneji was calling home these days.

"Did you see him?" I asked Bree, who was shaken, but calling in the shots to dispatch.

She shook her head after she'd finished. "You did?"

"It was him, Bree. Gary Soneji in the flesh. As if he hadn't been blown up and burned, as if he hadn't spent the past decade in a box under six feet of dirt."

CHAPTER

15

THE NEXT MORNING, I called GW to check on Sampson. His vitals had destabilized again.

Part of me said, *Go to the hospital*, but instead I drove out to Quantico, Virginia, and the FBI Lab.

For almost seven years, I worked for the Bureau in the behavioral science department as a full-time consultant and left on good terms. I have many friends who still work at Quantico, including my old partner, Ned Mahoney.

I called ahead, and he met me at the gate, made sure I got the VIP treatment clearing security.

"What are friends in high places for?" Mahoney asked when I thanked him. "How's John?"

I gave him a brief update on Sampson and my investigation.

"How could Soneji be alive?" Mahoney said. "I was there, remember? I saw him burning, too. It was him. "

"Then who was the guy who shot Sampson and tried to

shoot me last night?" I said. "Because both times I've seen him, my brain has screamed *Soneji!* Both times."

"Hey, hey, Alex," Mahoney said, patting me on the shoulder out of concern. "Take a big breath. If it's him, we'll help you find him."

I took several deep, long breaths, trying to keep my thoughts from whirling, and said, "Let's start with the cybercrime unit."

Ten minutes later, we went through an unmarked door into a large space filled with low-walled cubicles that were in a soft blue light Mahoney said was supposed to increase productivity. There were three, sometimes four computer screens at every workstation.

"The only thing that separates the IT brainpower in this room from a company like Google is the dress code," Mahoney said.

"No Ping-Pong, either," I said.

"There's agitation in that direction," Mahoney said, weaving through the cubicles.

"Any chance it happens?"

"When the Bureau starts admitting J. Edgar preferred panties," he said, and then stopped in front of a workstation in the middle of the room.

"Agent Batra?" Mahoney said. "I want to introduce you to Alex Cross."

A petite Indian woman in her late twenties in a conservative blue suit and black pumps spun around from one of four screens at her station. She stood quickly and put out her hand, so small it felt like a doll's.

"Special Agent Henna Batra," she said. "An honor to meet you, Dr. Cross."

"And you as well."

"Agent Batra is said to be at one with the internet," Mahoney said. "If anyone can help you, she can. Stop by the office on your way out, Alex."

"Will do," I said.

"So," Agent Batra said, sitting again. "What are you looking for?"

"A website where there are active conversations going on concerning Gary Soneji."

"I know that case," Batra said. "We studied it at the academy. He's dead."

"Evidently his admirers don't think so, and I'd like to see what they're saying about Soneji. I was warned we'd never find the site in a million years."

With Special Agent Batra navigating the web via a link to a supercomputer, the search took all of fourteen minutes.

"Quite a few that mention Soneji," Batra said, gesturing at the screen, and then scrolling down before tapping on a link. "But I'm betting this is the one you're looking for."

I squinted to read the link. "ZRXQT?"

"Anonymous, or at least attempting anonymity," Batra said. "And it's locked and encrypted. But I ran a filter that picked up traces of commands going into and out of that website. The density of Soneji mentions in those traces is through the roof compared to every other site that talks about him."

"You can't get in?"

"I didn't say that," Batra said, as if I'd insulted her. "You drink tea?"

"Coffee," I said.

She gestured across the room. "There's a break room over there. If you'd be so kind as to bring me some hot tea, Dr. Cross. I should be able to get inside by the time you come back."

I thought it was kind of funny that Batra had started the conversation as my subordinate and was now ordering me around. Then again, I hadn't a clue about how she was doing what she was doing. Then again, she was at one with the internet.

"Oolong?" I asked.

"Fine," Batra said, already engrossed in her work.

I found the coffee and the tea, but when I returned, she was still typing.

"Got it?"

"Not yet," she said, irritated. "It's sophisticated, multilevel, and…"

Lines of code began to fill the page. Batra seemed to speed-read the code as it rolled by, because, after twenty seconds of this, she said, "Oh, of course."

She gave the computer another command, and a homepage appeared, featuring a cement wall in some abandoned building. Across the wall in dripping black graffiti letters, it read *Long Live The Soneji!*

16

I WON'T BORE YOU with a page-by-page description of the www.thesoneji.net website. There may be archives of it still up on the internet for those interested.

For those of you less inclined to explore the dark side of the web, it's enough to know that Gary Soneji had developed a cult of personality in the decade since I'd seen him burn, hundreds of digital devotees who worshipped him with the kind of fervor I'd previously assigned to Appalachian snake handlers and the Hare Krishnas.

They called themselves The Soneji, and they seemed to know almost every nuance of the life of the kidnapper and mass murderer. In addition to an extensive biography, there were hundreds of lurid photos, links to articles, and an online chat forum where members hotly debated all things Soneji.

The hottest topics?

Number one that day was *the John Sampson shooting*.

The Soneji were generally ecstatic that my partner had been shot and barely clung to life, but a few posts stood out.

Napper2 wrote, Gary fuckin' got Sampson!

Gary's so back, The Waste Man agreed.

Only thing better would be Cross on a Cross, wrote Black Hole.

That day's coming sooner than later, said Gary's Girl. Gary's missed Cross twice. He won't miss a third time.

Aside from being the subject of homicidal speculation, something bothered me about that last post, the one from Gary's Girl. I studied it and the others, trying to figure out what was different.

"They think he's alive," Agent Batra offered.

"Yeah, that's hot thread number two," I said. "Let's take a look there, and come back."

She clicked on the "Resurrection Man" thread.

Cross saw him, came face to face with Gary, wrote Sapper9. Shit his pants, is what I heard.

Cross was hit in first attack, wrote Chosen One. Soneji's aim is true. Cross is just lucky.

Beemer answered, My respect for Gary is profound, but he is not alive. That is impossible.

The believers among The Soneji went berserk on Beemer for having the gall to challenge the consensus. Beemer was attacked from all sides. To his credit, Beemer fought back.

Call me Doubting Thomas, but show me the evidence. Can I put my finger through Soneji's hand? Can I see where the lance pierced his side?

You could if he trusted you the way he trusts me, wrote Gary's Girl.

Beemer wrote, So you've seen him, GG?

After a long pause, Gary's Girl wrote, I have. With my own two eyes.

Pic? Beemer said.

A minute passed, and then two. Five minutes after his demand, Beemer wrote, Funny how illusions can seem so real.

A second later the screen blinked and a picture appeared.

Taken at night, it was a selfie of a big, muscular woman gone goth, heavy on the black on black right down to the lipstick. She was grinning raunchily and sitting in the lap of a man with wispy red hair. His hands held her across her deep, leather-clad cleavage, and he had buried three quarters of his face into the side of her neck.

The other quarter, however, including his right eye, was clearly visible.

He was staring right into the camera with an amused and lecherous expression that seemed designed to taunt the lens and me. He knew I'd see the picture someday and be infuriated.

I was sure of that. It was the kind of thing Soneji would do.

"That him?" Batra asked. "Gary Soneji?"

"Close enough. Can you track down Gary's Girl?"

The FBI cyber agent thought about that, and then said, "Give me twenty minutes, maybe less."

17

AT FIVE O'CLOCK THAT afternoon, Bree and I drove through the tiny rural community of Flintstone, Maryland, past the Flintstone Post Office, the Stone Age Café, and Carl's Gas and Grub.

We found a side street off Route 144, and drove down a wooded lane to a freshly painted green ranch house set off all by itself in a meticulously tended yard. A shiny new Audi Q5 sat in the driveway.

"I thought you said she's on welfare," Bree said.

"Food stamps, too," I said.

We parked behind the Audi and got out. AC/DC was blasting from inside the house. We went to the front door and found it ajar.

I tried the bell. It was broken.

Bree knocked and called out, "Delilah Pinder?"

We heard nothing in response but the howling of an electric guitar against a thundering baseline.

"Door's open," I said. "We're checking on her well-being."

"Be my guest," Bree said.

I pushed open the door and found myself in a room decorated with brand-new leather furniture and a big curved HD television. The music throbbed on from somewhere deeper inside the house.

We checked the kitchen, saw boxes of appliances that hadn't even been opened, and then headed down the hallway toward the source of the music. The first door on the left was a home gym with Olympic weight-lifting equipment. The music came from the room at the end of the hall.

There was a lull in the song, just enough that I heard a woman's voice cry, "That's it!" before the throbbing, wailing song drowned her out.

The door to that room at the end of the hall was cracked open two inches. A brilliant light shone through.

"Delilah Pinder?" I called out.

No answer.

I stepped forward and pushed the door open enough to get a comprehensive view of a very muscular and artificially busty woman up on all fours on a four-poster bed. Gyrating her hips in time with the beat, she was naked, and looking over her shoulder at a GoPro camera mounted on a tripod.

I just stood there, stunned for a moment, long enough for Bree to nudge me, and long enough for Delilah Pinder to look around and spot me.

"Christ!" she screamed and flung herself forward on the bed.

I thought she was diving for modesty, but she hit some kind of panic button and the door slammed shut in my face and locked.

"What the hell just happened?" Bree demanded.

"I think she was doing a live sex show on the internet," I said.

"No."

"I swear," I said.

The music shut off and a woman shouted, "Goddamnit, whoever you are, I'm calling the sheriff. They are going to hunt you down!"

"We are the police, Miss Pinder," Bree yelled back.

"What the hell are you doing in my house, then?" she screamed. "I've got rights, and you had no right to come into my house or place of business!"

"You're correct," I said. "But we knocked and called out, and we felt we were doing a safety check on you."

"What I do here is perfectly legal," she said. "So please leave."

"We aren't here about your, uh, business," Bree said.

"Who are you, then? What do you want?"

"My name is Alex Cross. I'm a detective with the DC Metro Police, and I'm here concerning Gary's Girl."

There was a long silence, and then the music cranked up. But over it I heard the sound of a door slamming loudly.

"She's running," Bree said, spun around, and took off.

18

I CAN HOLD MY own in the weight room, but I am no match for Bree in a footrace. She exploded back through the house and barreled out the front door.

Delilah Pinder, who was now dressed in a blue warm-up suit and running shoes, had already sprinted around the end of the house and was charging across the front lawn, heading for the road. I came out the front door in time to see Bree try to tackle the big woman.

Delilah saw her coming and stuck out her hand like a seasoned running back, hitting Bree in the chest. Bree stumbled. The internet sex star raced out onto the road and headed toward the highway.

I cut diagonally through the yard, trying to close in on her from the side. But when I broke through the trees and jumped the stone wall onto the road, Bree was right back behind Pinder.

She jumped on the much bigger woman's back, threw an

arm bar around her neck, and choked her. Delilah tried to buck her off, and to pry her hold apart. But Bree held on tight.

Finally, the big woman stopped running. Her massive thighs wobbled, and she sat down hard at Bree's feet.

"Oh, my God," Bree gasped when I ran up. "That was like 'Meet the Amazon.'"

"More like 'Ride the Amazon,'" I said, as she put zip ties on Delilah's wrists.

The woman was regaining her strength. She struggled against the restraints.

"No," she said. "Let me go."

"Not for a while yet," I said, picking her up.

Delilah twisted her head around in a rage, and spit in my face.

"Knock that off!" Bree shouted, and wrenched up hard on Delilah's bound wrists. "That kind of bullshit gets you in trouble, and you're already in a world of trouble. Got it?"

Delilah was obviously in pain, and finally nodded.

Bree eased up on the pressure while I used a tissue to wipe my face.

"I don't know what this is about," Delilah said. "I told you, I have a legitimate business, registered with the state and everything. Delilah Entertainment. Check it out."

"You know exactly what this is about," I said, grabbing one of her formidable biceps and marching her back toward her house. "You're a member of The Soneji. You're Gary's Girl. You like to take selfies of you and Gary together. Isn't that true?"

Delilah looked at me smugly and said, "Every single word of it, Cross. Every single word."

"Where is Gary Soneji?" Bree asked.

"I have no idea," Delilah said. "Gary comes and goes as he pleases. Our relationship is strong enough for that."

"Yeah, I'm sure it is," I said, rolling my eyes. "But you understand you've abetted a man who shot a police officer in cold blood?"

"How's that?"

"You housed him," Bree said. "You fed him. You dressed up goth and had sex with him, maybe even did one of your kinky shows for him."

"Every night, darling," Delilah said. "He loved it. So did I. And that's where yours truly will shut up. I have the right to remain silent. And I have a right to an attorney. I'm taking both those rights, right here and right now."

19

PALE MORNING FOG SHROUDED much of the cemetery from my view. The fog swirled on the wet grass, the melting snow that remained, and the gravestones. It left droplets on the pile of wilted flower bouquets and empty liquor bottles and remembrances that had to be moved before the backhoe could begin its work.

The last item was a baby doll, naked, with lipstick smeared on the lips.

Shivering against the dank March air, I zipped my police slicker higher and pulled on the hood. I stood off to one side of the grave with Bill Worden, the cemetery superintendent, alternately looking at the baby doll and watching the backhoe claw deeper into the soil. A baby doll, I thought, recalling a real baby tossed through the air with total indifference, if not cruelty.

Someone brought that doll here, I thought. In celebration. In reverence.

That's just sick. How could you worship that?

I glanced at the headstone Worden dug from the ground after I'd brought him an order from a federal judge in Trenton. The grave marker was simple. Rectangular black polished granite.

"*G. Soneji*" was etched in the face, along with the date of his birth. The date of his death, however, had been chiseled away. That was it. No mention of his brutal crimes or his disturbing life.

The man six feet under the headstone was all but anonymous.

And yet they'd come. The Soneji. They'd chipped away at the gravestone. Spray-painted the grass to read *"Soneji Lives."* I took pictures before the backhoe destroyed it.

"How many visit?" I asked over the sound of the digging machine.

Worden, the cemetery superintendent, tugged his hood over his head and said, "Hard to say. It's not like we keep it under surveillance. But a fair number every month."

"Enough to leave that pile of flowers," I said, eyeing the baby doll again.

Worden nodded. "For some it seems almost like a pilgrimage."

"Yeah, except Mr. Soneji was no saint," I said.

Drizzle began to fall, forcing me deeper into the collar of my jacket. A few moments later, the backhoe turned off.

"There's the straps, Bill," the equipment operator said. "I'll hand-dig the last of it."

"No need," Worden said. "Just hook up and lift, brush the dirt off later."

The backhoe operator shrugged and got out cables, which

he attached to the bucket. Then he got down into the grave and clipped the cables to the rings of stout straps that had been left after the casket was lowered.

"They're not weakened by being in the dirt ten years?" I asked.

Worden shook his head. "Not unless something chewed through them."

The superintendent was right. When the backhoe arm rose, the straps easily lifted the casket of a man I helped kill.

Wet dirt slid and cascaded off the top of the casket as it came free of the grave and dangled four feet above the hole. The wind picked up. The casket swayed.

"Put it down there," Worden said, gesturing to one side.

I was fixated on the casket, wondering what was inside, beyond the charred remains I'd seen placed in a body bag beneath Grand Central Station a decade before. He was in there, wasn't he?

Every instinct said yes. But…

As the casket swung and lowered, I happened to look beyond it and between two far monuments. The wind had blown a narrow vent in the fog. I could see a slice of the graveyard between those monuments that ran all the way to the pine barrens that surrounded the cemetery.

Standing at the edge of the woods, perhaps eighty yards from me, was a man in a green rain slicker. He was turning away. When his back was to me, he pulled off his hood, revealing a head of thinning red hair. Then he raised his right hand, and pointed his middle finger at the sky.

And me.

20

I STOOD THERE, TOO stunned to move for the moment it took for the wind to ebb and the fog to creep back, obscuring the figure, who stepped into the pine barrens and disappeared.

Then my shock evaporated, and I took off, drawing my pistol as I sprinted between the gravestones. Peering through the fog gathering again in the cemetery, I tried to figure out exactly where I'd seen him go into the pines.

There it was, those two monuments. He'd been framed between them. I ran to the spot and looked back toward the fog-obscured backhoe and the exhumed casket. When I thought I had the correct bearings, I turned and headed in a straight line toward the edge of the forest.

"Dr. Cross?" the superintendent called after me. "Where are you going?"

I ignored him and charged to the edge of the dripping pines, scanning the ground and seeing a scuff mark that looked fresh, not yet beaten down by the rain. I pushed my way into the trees.

The forest was thick there, crowded with young saplings with wet branches that bent away and wet needles that slid past my clothes. I stopped, unsure where to go, but then noticed a broken branch on the ground.

The inner wood looked bright and new. So did the broken branch to my left at ten o'clock. I went that way for fifty, maybe seventy-five yards, and then broke into an expanse of older trees, more than ten feet high, and growing in long straight rows, a pine plantation.

Despite the fog, I soon spotted dark, discolored spots on the mat of dead needles that covered the forest floor. I went to them, and saw where he'd kicked up the duff as he'd run down one of those lanes through the trees.

I ran after him, wondering if I could catch up, and numerous times whether I'd lost the way. But then I'd find some disturbance in the pine needles and push on one hundred, two hundred, three hundred yards deeper into the barrens.

What direction was I going? I had no idea, and it didn't matter. As long as Soneji was leaving signs, I was staying with him. I thought I'd cross a logging road or trail at some point, but didn't. There was just the monotony of the plantation pines and the swirling fog.

Then the way began to climb up a hill. I could clearly see where he'd had to dig in the edges of his shoes to keep his footing, and more broken branches.

When I hit the top of the knoll, there was a clearing of sorts with a jumble of tree trunks to one side, as if a windstorm had blown them over. I skirted the jumble, crossed the hilltop, and found myself looking down into a long, broad valley of mature pines.

The forest had been thinned there, as if some of the trees

had already been harvested. Despite the fog, I could see down a dozen lanes and deeper into the woods than at any other time since I'd entered it. Nothing moved below me.

Nothing at—

A rifle cracked. The bark of a tree next to me exploded and I dove for the ground behind one of those downed tree trunks.

Where was he?

The shot came from the valley. I was sure of it. But where down there?

"Cross?" he called. "I'm coming for you, even from the grave if I have to."

If it wasn't him, he'd studied Soneji's voice, right down to the inflection.

When I didn't answer, he shouted, "Hear me, Cross?"

He sounded to my right and below me, no more than seventy yards. Raising my head as high as I dared, I scanned the valley there. The fog was in and out, but I thought I'd see him move or adjust his angle if he wanted another shot at me.

But I couldn't make him out.

"I know I didn't hit you," he called, his voice cracking weirdly. "I did, you would have gone down like the shit bag you are."

I decided not to engage, to let him think he'd gotten lucky, taken me out with one bullet. And it was odd the way his voice had cracked, wasn't it? Gone to a higher pitch?

Tense moments passed, a minute and then two, while my eyes darted back and forth, trying to spot him, hoping he'd come in to make sure of the kill.

"How's your partner?" he called, and I heard him chuckle hoarsely. "He took a hit, didn't he? What I hear, best-case scenario, he'll be a veg."

It took every fiber of my being, but I did not engage with him, even then. I just lay there and waited, scanning and scanning and scanning.

I never saw him go, or heard anything like a distant twig breaking to suggest he was on the move again. He never said another word, and nothing told me he'd left but the time that kept ticking away.

I lowered my head after ten minutes and dug out my phone. No service.

The rain started in earnest then, drumming, beating down the fog and revealing the plantation. Nothing moved but a doe a hundred yards out.

I wanted to get up and go down there, look for him. But if he was waiting, I'd be exposed again. After fifteen more minutes of watching, I crawled back in the direction I'd come until I was well down the backside of the hill.

There was a bitter taste in my mouth when I got to my feet and started back toward the cemetery.

I hadn't gotten halfway there when my cell phone buzzed in my pocket.

A text from Billie.

"Alex, wherever you are, come. John's taken a bad turn. We're on deathwatch here."

CHAPTER

21

BY THE TIME I reached the cemetery, the superintendent had already loaded the casket into the FBI van that would take it to Quantico for examination. I explained the urgency of my situation, and left.

I called ahead to New Jersey, Delaware, and Maryland state police dispatchers, asking for help. When I reached I-95, there were two Jersey state trooper cruisers waiting. One in front, the other behind, they escorted me to the border, where two Delaware cruisers met me. Two more waited when I reached the Maryland line. At times we were going more than a hundred.

Less than two hours after I'd read the text, I got off the elevator to the ICU at GW Medical Center, still in damp clothes and chilled as I ran down the all-too-familiar halls to the waiting area. Billie sat at the back, her feet drawn up under her. Her elbows rested across her knees and she had a skeptical, faraway look in her eye, as if she couldn't believe that God was doing this to her.

Bree sat at her left, Nana Mama on her right.

"What happened?" I asked.

"They decided to bring him up out of the chemical coma," Billie said, tears streaming down her cheeks.

"He flatlined. They had to paddle him," Bree said. "He came back, but his vitals are turning against him."

"Billie's called in the priest," Nana Mama said. "He's giving John the last rites."

Whatever control I'd maintained until that point evaporated and I began to grieve in gasps of disbelief and an explosion of sorrow and tears. It was real. My best friend, the indestructible one, Big John Sampson, was going to die.

I sank into a chair and sobbed. Bree came over and hugged me. I leaned into her and cried some more.

The priest came in. "He's in God's hands now," he said, consoling us. "The doctor says there's nothing more they can do for him."

"Can we go in?" Billie asked.

"Of course," he said.

Nana Mama, Billie, and Bree got up. I looked at them, feeling numb.

"I can't do it," I said, feeling helpless. "I just can't watch this. Can you forgive me?"

"I don't want to either, Alex," Billie said. "But I want him to hear my voice one last time before he goes."

Nana Mama patted me on the shoulders as she followed Billie into the ICU. Bree asked if I wanted her to stay, and I shook my head.

"Going in there scares me more than anything has in my entire life," I said. "I need to take a walk, get my courage up."

"And pray," she said, kissed me on the head, and went inside.

I got up and felt like a coward walking toward the men's room. I went inside and washed my face, trying to think of anything but John and all the good times we'd had over the years, playing football and basketball, attending the police academy, and finding our way through the ranks to detective and partners against crime.

That would never happen again. John and me would never happen again.

I left the restroom and wandered off through the medical complex, sure that any minute now I'd get a text that he was gone. Guilt built up in me at the thought that after all we'd been through, I wouldn't be there at Sampson's side when he passed.

I stopped and almost turned around. Then noticed I was standing outside the plastic surgery offices. A beautiful Ethiopian-looking woman in a white jacket came out the door.

She smiled at me. Her teeth gleamed and her facial skin was so taut and smooth she could have been thirty. Then again, she could have been sixty and often under the knife.

"Dr. Coleman?" I said, reading her badge.

She stopped and said, "Yes?"

I showed her my badge, said, "I could use your help."

"Yes?" she said, looking worried. "How so?"

"I'm investigating the shooting of a police officer," I said. "We want to know, how difficult would it be to make one person look almost exactly like another?"

She squinted. "You mean, good enough to be an impostor?"

"Yes," I said. "Is it possible?"

"That depends," Dr. Coleman said, glancing at her watch. "Can you walk with me? I have to give a lecture about twenty minutes from here."

"Yes," I said, glad for the diversion.

We walked through the medical center and out the other side, ending up on the George Washington University campus. Along the way, the plastic surgeon said that similar facial structure would be key to surgically altering a person to look like someone else.

"The closer the subject was to looking like the original to begin with, the better the results," she said. "After that it would all be in the skill of the surgeon."

"So, even the similar bone structure wouldn't guarantee success for your everyday surgeon?"

Dr. Coleman smiled. "If the end product is as close to the original as you say it is, then there is no way an average boob-job surgeon did it. You're looking for a scalpel artist, Detective."

"What kind of money are we talking?"

"Depends on the extent of surgical alteration required," she said. "But I'm thinking this is a hundred-thousand-dollar job, maybe less in Brazil."

A hundred thousand dollars? Who would spend that much to look like Gary Soneji? Or go to Brazil to get it done?

I felt my phone buzz in my pocket, and sickened.

"Here I am," Dr. Coleman said, stopping outside one of the university's many buildings. "Any more questions, Detective?"

"No," I said, handing her a card. "But if I do, can I call?"

"Absolutely," she said, and hurried inside.

I swallowed hard and then got out my phone.

The text was from Bree: "Come now or you'll regret it the rest of your life."

I started to run.

Ten minutes later, I went through the door of the ICU, trying to keep my emotions from ruining me all over again.

When I reached the doorway to John's room, Billie, Bree, and Nana Mama were all sobbing.

I thought I'd come too late, that I'd done my best friend and brother the ultimate disservice, and not been there when he took his last breath.

Then I realized they were all sobbing for joy.

"It's a miracle, Alex," Bree said, tears streaming down her cheeks. "Look."

I stepped inside the crowded room. A nurse and a doctor were working feverishly on John. He was still on his back in bed, still on the ventilator, still hitched up to a dozen different monitors.

But his eyes were open and roving lazily.

22

WE SAT WITH JOHN for hours as more of the drugs wore off. They removed his breathing tube, and he came more and more to consciousness.

John did not acknowledge his name when Billie called it softly, trying to get him to turn his head to her. At first Sampson seemed not even to know where he was, as if he were lost in some dream.

But then, after the first nap, he did hear his wife, and his face lolled toward her. Then he moved his fingers and toes on command, and lifted both arms.

When I sat beside him and held his hand, his lips kept opening as if he wanted to talk. No sound came out, and he appeared frustrated.

"It's okay, buddy," I said, holding tight. "We know you love us."

Sampson relaxed and slept again. When he awoke, Elizabeth Navilus, a top speech-language pathologist, was waiting. She was part of a team of specialists rotating through the room, performing the various exams on the JFK Coma Recovery Scale, a method of diagnosing the extent of brain damage.

Navilus ran Sampson through a brief battery of tests. She found that John's cognitive awareness as expressed through his language comprehension was growing by the moment. But he was having trouble speaking. The best he could do was chew at the air and hum.

It crushed me.

Out in the waiting area, Navilus told us to take hope from the fact that head trauma patients often exhibit understanding before being able to respond.

Later, when Nana Mama had left for home to cook dinner, and Bree to the office, and Billie to the cafeteria, I sat by John's side.

"I was there when you were shot," I told him. "It was Soneji. Or someone who looked just like him."

Sampson blinked, and then nodded.

"I came close to catching him this morning," I said. "He was watching when we dug up Soneji's body."

He looked away and closed his eyes.

"I'm going to get him, John," I said. "I promise you."

He barely nodded before sagging off to sleep.

Sitting there, watching him, I felt better, stronger, and more humbled and in debt to my Lord and savior than ever before. The idea of Sampson dying must have been as much of an abomination to God as I thought it was.

If that wasn't a miracle, I don't know what is.

23

I STAYED AT THE hospital until nine, promised Billie I'd be back in the morning, and headed home. Given what had happened the last time I'd exited GW Medical Center and looked for a cab, my head was turning three-sixty.

I saw no threat, however, and stepped to the curb. As I did, Soneji's voice from earlier in the day echoed back to me.

I'm coming for you, even from the grave if I have to.

It sounded so much like Gary, it was scary. I'd had multiple conversations with him over the years, and Soneji's tone and delivery were unmistakable.

After I'd gotten into the cab and given the driver my home address, I almost pushed these thoughts aside. But then I blinked, remembering how his voice had cracked weirdly and turned hoarse when he said, "I know I didn't hit you. I did, you would have gone down like the shit bag you are."

It sounded like he had something wrong in his throat. Cancer? Polyps? Or were his vocal cords just straining under the tensions wound up inside him?

I tried to remember every nuance of our encounter in the pine barrens, the way he'd swaggered into the trees, finger held high. Where was the gun then? Had he been trying to lure me in for a shot?

In retrospect, it felt like he had, and I'd fallen for it. Where was all the training I'd done? The protocol? I'd reacted on emotion, charging into the pines after him. Just the way Soneji had wanted me to.

That bothered me because it made me realize that Soneji understood me, could predict my impulses the way I could predict his a dozen years before. I mean, how else would he have known to be at the cemetery when I was there to exhume his body? What or who had tipped him?

I had no answers for that other than the possibility Soneji or The Soneji had us bugged. Or had it just seemed the rational thing to do at some point, given the fact that I'd seen someone who looked just like him at least three times now?

These unanswerable questions weighed on me the entire ride home. I felt depressed climbing from the taxi and waiting for the receipt. Soneji, or whoever, was thinking ahead of me, plotting, hatching, and acting before I could respond.

Climbing the porch stairs, I was beginning to feel like I was a fish on a hook with some angler toying with me, messing with my lip.

But the second I stepped inside the house, smelled something savory coming from Nana Mama's kitchen, and heard my son, Ali, laughing, I let it go. I let everything about the sonofabitch go.

"Dad?" Jannie said, coming down the stairs. "How's John?"

"He's got a fight and a half ahead of him, but he's alive."

"Nana Mama said it's, like, a miracle."

"I'd have to agree," I said, and hugged her tight.

"Dad, look at this," Ali called. "You can't believe how good this looks."

"The new TV," Jannie said. "It's pretty amazing."

"What new TV?"

"Nana Mama and Ali ordered it off the internet. They just installed it."

I stepped into our once cozy television room to see it had been transformed into a home theater, with new leather chairs, and a huge, curved 4K resolution HD screen on the far wall. Ali had on a repeat of *The Walking Dead*, one of his favorites, and the zombies looked like they were right there in the room with us.

"You should see when we switch it to 3D, Dad!" Ali said. "It's crazy!"

"I can see that," I said. "Does it do basketball?"

Ali took his eyes off the screen. "They're right in the room with you."

I smiled. "You'll have to show me after dinner."

"I can do that," Ali said. "Show you how to run it from your laptop."

I gave him the thumbs up, and then wandered through the dining room to the kitchen upgrade and great room addition we'd put on two years before.

Nana Mama was bustling at her command-center stove.

"Roast chicken, sweet potato fries, broccoli with almonds, and a nice salad," she said. "How's John?"

"Sleeping when I left," I said. "And dinner sounds great. Nice TV."

She made a deep inhaling sound, and said, "Isn't it? I can't wait to see *Masterpiece Theatre* on there. That *Downton Abbey* show."

"I was thinking the same thing," I said.

Nana Mama looked over her shoulder, gave me a sour, threatening look, and said, "Don't you be mocking me, now."

"I wouldn't dream of it, Nana," I said, trying to hide the smile that wanted to creep onto my face. "Oh, I thought you said you weren't going to let the lottery money change our lives."

"I said I didn't want some big mansion to get lost in," she snapped. "Or tooling around in some ridiculous car. But that doesn't mean we can't have some nice things in this house, and still do some good for people. Which reminds me, when is my hot-breakfast program going to be able to start up again?"

I held up my hands. "I'll find out tonight."

"I'm not getting any younger, and I want to see that ongoing," she said. "Endowed. And that reading program for kids."

"Yes, ma'am, and you're sure you're not getting younger? Isn't there a painting of you in some attic that shows your real age?"

She tried to fight it, but that brought on a smile. "Aren't you just the smoothest talker in—?"

"Dad?" Ali cried, running into the kitchen.

He looked petrified, on the verge of crying.

"What's the matter?"

"Someone's taken over my computer," he said.

"What?" Nana Mama said.

"There's this crazy man on the screen now, not *The Walking Dead,* and he won't turn off. He's holding a baby and saying, like, over and over that he's going to come for you, Dad, even from the grave."

CHAPTER

24

IN THE VIDEO CLIP, Gary Soneji was just as I remembered him: out on one of Grand Central Station's train platforms, holding the infant, and taunting me.

I'd never seen the video. Never knew it existed, but it was definitely legitimate. After viewing the clip six or seven times, I could see my own shadow stretched in the space between me and Gary Soneji. The camera operator all those years ago had to have been right off my left shoulder.

Was the cameraman a fluke? A random passerby? Or someone working with Soneji?

The clip started again. It appeared on endless loop.

"Dad, this is giving me the creeps," Jannie said. "Turn it off."

"Gimme the remote and the computer, Ali," I said.

"I've got homework on this computer," he said.

"I'll transfer your homework to the one in the kitchen," I said, and gave him a gimme motion.

He groaned and handed it to me.

Bree came in the front door. I hit the Power button on the remote, but the screen did not turn off. Instead, it broke from that endless loop to Kelly green.

I tried to turn the screen off again, but it jumped to black, slashed diagonally with a golden beam of light. The camera zoomed closer to that light and you could see a silhouette of a person there.

Closer, it was a man.

Closer still, and it was Soneji.

He was giving the lens the same quarter profile we'd seen in the still image that Gary's Girl posted on the website forum, the one where his eye and the corner of his mouth conspired to leer right at me.

But this time Soneji spoke.

In that cracking, hoarse voice I'd heard earlier that day in the pine barrens, Soneji said, "You're not safe in the trees, Cross. You're not safe in your own home. The Soneji are everywhere!"

Then he threw his head back, and barked and brayed his laughter before the screen froze. A title appeared below: www.thesoneji.net.

"What's that, Dad?" Ali asked, upset.

I stormed to the screen, followed the cord to its power source, and tore it violently out of the wall.

"Alex?" Bree said. "What's going on?"

I looked at Ali. "Was that *Walking Dead* episode streaming from Netflix?"

"Yes."

Yanking out my cell phone, I looked to Bree and said, "Soneji hacked into our internet feed."

"I'll shut the router down," Bree said.

"No, don't," I said. I scrolled through my recent calls and hit Call. "I have a feeling it will be better if the link's still active."

The phone picked up. "Yes?"

"This is Alex Cross," I said. "How fast can you get to my house?"

Forty minutes later, as we were finishing up Nana Mama's roast chicken masterpiece, and fighting over who was going to get the last wing and who the last sweet potato fries, there was a sharp knock at our side door.

"I'll get it," I said, put my napkin down, and went out into the great room and unlocked the door that led to the side yard and the alley behind our place.

I did not turn on the light, just opened it quickly and let our visitors inside. The first was Ned Mahoney, my former partner at the FBI. The second was Special Agent Henna Batra of the Bureau's cybercrime unit.

"Who's making sure you're safe in your own home?" Mahoney asked once I'd closed the door.

"Metro in unmarked cars, both ends of the block," I said.

"Soneji's still the type to try."

"I know," I said. "But I think we're good."

"I'm still unclear why you wanted me here, Dr. Cross," Agent Batra said.

"I think Soneji or The Soneji may have made a mistake," I said. "If I'm right, they left a digital trail inside my house, or on our network, anyway."

25

I GOT TO GW Medical Center early the following morning with my children's howls ringing in my head. Special Agent Batra had taken every computer and phone in the house to Quantico. She'd promised to work as fast as she could, but it was like they'd lost their right hands when the phones were taken away.

I kind of felt the same way walking to Sampson's room, and decided to buy a cheap phone afterward. I was happy to find John sitting up and drinking through a straw.

Billie hadn't arrived yet, so I'd gotten to sit with him awhile, and brought him up to date on all that had occurred the prior day. Though his eyes tended to drift off me, he seemed to understand much of what I was saying.

"If anyone can find this guy, it's Batra," I said. "I've never seen anyone like her before."

John's eyes softened and he smiled. He tried to say something and couldn't. You could see how frustrating it was.

I put my hand on his shoulder and said, "You're in for a long haul, buddy, recovering from this. But if there's any man alive who can do it, you can."

Sampson's lazy, sad gaze came and dwelled around me for several seconds. Then he started struggling, as he got more and more upset.

"Hey," I said. "It's okay. We'll—"

Garbled sounds came out of his mouth.

He tried again. And again.

The sixth time, I thought he said, "Evan-widda."

"Evan-widda?" I said.

"Evan-widda...b...bag," he said, and then smiled and lifted his right hand to point to the surgical bandage. "Ho-ho... n...ed."

I frowned, but got it then, and smiled. "Even with a big hole in your head?"

Sampson smiled, dropped his hand, and winked at me before nodding off to sleep again, as if that had taken every bit of his strength.

But he'd spoken! Sort of. Definitely communicated. And the doctors had said his sense of humor could be gone with a wound to that part of his brain, but here he was making a joke about his situation.

If that wasn't a miracle, I don't know what is.

Billie arrived shortly before eight and beamed when I told her what had happened.

She kissed John, and said, "You spoke?"

He shook his head. "Alack vent...r...wrist...crist."

"What?"

"He said, 'Alex is a ventriloquist.' I think."

John grinned again and said, "Whips do no move."

Billie had tears in her eyes. "Lips don't move."

Sampson made a wheezing sound of delight that stayed with me on the way to work and buying a burner phone.

I went to Bree's office, and I knocked on her doorjamb.

"Long time no see," I said.

Bree glanced at the clock, said, "Are you getting obsessive about me?"

"I've always been obsessive about you, from the very first," I said.

"Liar," Bree said, but she was pleased.

"The truth," I said. "You had me the first time you glanced my way."

That pleased her even more. "Why are you buttering me up?"

"I'm not buttering you up," I said. "I was just flirting with my wife before I told her that Sampson spoke this morning."

"No?" she gasped. "He did?"

"It took a little interpretation, but he was telling jokes."

Bree got tears in her eyes, stood up, came around the desk, and hugged me. I got tears, too.

"Thanks," she said. "What a perfect thing to hear."

"I know," I said, before the cheap phone I'd bought on the way to work buzzed. Who knew the number? I'd just gotten the damn thing. Just activated it.

"Hello?" I said.

"It's Special Agent Batra."

"How'd you get this number?"

"By being good at my job," Agent Batra said, sounding annoyed. "I thought you'd be happy to hear from me so soon."

"I'm sorry," I said, though I was beginning to think there wasn't a box in the virtual universe that Henna Batra couldn't find and unlock if she set her mind to it. "You found something?"

"You were compromised in a troubling fashion."

I wanted to say that I could have told her that, but asked, "How so?"

"They got a bug into your son's computer operating system, piggybacked to a game app he downloaded at school."

"At his school?" I said, feeling queasy.

Soneji or The Soneji were not only threatening me in my house, they were targeting my youngest child.

"What else?" I demanded.

"Your daughter, Jannie, had the same bug in her system," Batra said. "It was uploaded to her computer without her knowledge when she was using her phone as a mobile hotspot at a coffee shop not far from your house."

This was worse. Both my children were being targeted.

"What about my phone? My wife's?" I asked, and turned on the speaker on the burner phone so Bree could hear.

"Clean," Batra said. "I'll have them messengered over in the next hour."

"Thank you," I said. "Is that it?"

"No, as a matter of fact," the FBI cyber expert said. "There was a similarity in the signature of the bug coder and the coder who created www.thesoneji.net."

I looked at Bree, who shrugged in confusion.

"You want to run that by us again?" I said.

The cybercrimes expert sounded irritated when she said, "Coders are artists in their own way, Detective. Just as classical painters had recognizable brushstrokes, great computer coders have a recognizable way of writing. Their signature, if you will."

"Makes sense," I said. "So who coded the website?"

Batra said, "It took me much, much longer than I expected

to break through the firewalls that surrounded the identity of the creator and curator, but I did just a few minutes ago."

"Have you been up all night?" I asked.

"You said it was important."

Bree leaned forward, said, "Thank you, Agent Batra. It's Chief Stone here. Do you know who he is? The website creator?"

"She, and I've learned quite a bit about her in the past hour or so, thanks to a friend of mine at the NSA," Agent Batra said. "Especially the boyfriend she's fronting for. In fact, I know about him going right back to what his first-grade teacher said about him the day she recommended he be expelled from school."

I felt fear in the pit of my stomach. "And what was that?"

"She said she thought he was kind of a monster, Dr. Cross. Even then."

26

AN HOUR LATER, I set in to wait on a bench in a hallway by the door to a loft space on the fourth floor of an older building off Dupont Circle.

I'd gotten into the building by showing my badge to a woman entering with groceries. I told her who I was looking for.

"Out running, that one," she'd replied. "Every lunch hour. Quite a sight."

I'd knocked on the door just in case, but there was no answer. I had a search warrant. I could have called for patrol to break the door down, but I hoped I could get more information by going patient and gentle.

Twenty minutes later, a fit Asian American woman in her late twenties came huffing up the staircase. Her black hair was cut short and her exposed arms were buff and sleeved in brilliantly colored tattoos.

Sweat poured down her face when she reached the landing

and saw me getting off the bench. She didn't startle or try to escape as I'd expected.

Instead she hardened, said, "Took you a while, Dr. Cross. The intrusion was almost six hours ago. But here you are. At last. In the flesh."

"Kimiko Binx?" I said, holding up my badge and ID.

"Correct," Binx replied, walking toward me, palms held open at her sides, and studying me with great interest.

The closer she got, I noticed a device of some sort, orange, and strapped to her upper right arm. When I saw it blink, I thought *bomb,* and went for my gun.

"What's that on your arm?" I demanded, the pistol out, pointed her way.

Binx threw her hands up, said, "Whoa, whoa, Detective. It's a SPOT."

"What?"

"A GPS transmitter. It sends my position every thirty seconds to a satellite and to a website," she said. "I use it to track my running routes."

She turned sideways and held up her arm so I could examine the device. It was smaller than a smartphone, commercially made, heavy-duty plastic, with the SPOT logo emblazoned across the front of it and buttons with various icons. One said SOS and another was a shoe tread. The light blinked beside the shoe.

"So it tracks you?" I said.

"Correct," Binx said. "What do you want, Dr. Cross?"

I held the search warrant up and said, "If you could open the door."

Binx read the warrant without comment, fished out a key, and opened the loft. It was an airy work-and-living space with a view of an alley, a hodgepodge of used furniture, and a computer workstation that featured four large screens.

She moved toward the station.

"Do not go near your computer, Ms. Binx. Do not go near anything."

Binx got aggravated and took off the SPOT device. "You want this, too?"

"Please. Turn it off. Put it on the table there, and your phone if you've got it. I'd like to ask you some questions before I call for my evidence team."

"What do you want to know?" she asked, using her thumbs to play at the buttons on the transmitter.

"Why do you worship Gary Soneji?"

Binx didn't answer, hit one last button, and looked up at me before setting the SPOT on the table with the light no longer blinking.

"I don't worship Gary Soneji," she said finally. "I find Gary Soneji interesting. I find you interesting, for that matter."

"That why you built a high-security website about Soneji and me?"

"Yes," she said, sitting down calmly. "Other people find you two interesting also. Lots of them. It was a safe way to handle our common passion."

"Your members cheered when they found out my partner, John Sampson, was shot," I said.

"It's a private forum of free expression. I didn't approve of that."

"Didn't you?" I said angrily. "You provided space for sickos to plot terror in the name of a man who committed utterly heinous acts and died ten years ago."

"He's not dead," Binx said flatly. "Gary Soneji will never die."

I remembered the coffin coming up out of the ground in New Jersey, wondered how much longer the FBI's DNA testing would take, but said nothing of the exhumation of her idol.

Instead I said, "I don't get this, smart woman like you. Virginia Tech graduate. Write code for a living. Paid handsomely. Yet you get involved in something like this."

"Different strokes," she replied. "And it's my personal business."

"Not when it involves the shooting of a police officer. Nothing's personal."

"I had nothing to do with that, either," Binx said evenly. "Nothing. I'll take a lie detector."

"Who did, then?" I asked.

"Gary Soneji."

"Maybe," I said. "Or maybe Claude Watkins?"

Binx shifted her eyes ever so slightly to look just over my right shoulder before shaking her head.

I said, "Watkins's name is on your company's incorporation documents."

"Claude's a limited partner. He lent me some start-up money."

"Uh-huh," I said. "You know his background?"

"He had problems when he was younger," she said.

"He is a sadist, Ms. Binx. He was convicted of carving the skin off a little girl's fingers."

"He was chemically imbalanced back then," she said defiantly. "That was the diagnosis of both the state and his personal psychiatrists. He took the drugs they recommended, paid his dues, and moved on. Claude's a painter and performance artist now. He's brilliant."

"I'm sure he is," I said.

"No," Binx insisted. "He really is. I can take you to his studio. Show you. We've got nothing to hide. It's not far. He rents space in an old factory down by the Anacostia River, west bank."

"Address?"

She shrugged. "I just know how to get there."

I thought for a moment, said, "After my team gets here, you'll take me?"

She nodded. "Be glad to. Can I take a shower in the meantime? You can search the bathroom if you need to. I assure you it's nothing but the usual."

I stared at her for several beats, and then said, "Make it quick."

CHAPTER

27

THE CRIMINALISTS ARRIVED TEN minutes later. I was giving them instructions to call if they turned up anything when Kimiko Binx emerged from her bedroom in jeans, Nike running shoes, and a short-sleeved green blouse.

"Ready, Dr. Cross?" she said, coming toward me and then stumbling over a loose cord and losing her balance.

I reached out before she could fall. Binx grabbed onto my left hand and right forearm and got her balance.

She turned from me, looking back, puzzled. "What was that?"

"You should put your cords under rugs," I said. "Let's go."

We went downstairs to my car.

Binx got in the front seat, said, "Where's the siren?"

"It's not like that," I said. "Where am I going?"

"Toward the Anacostia Bridge. It's an old tool and die factory by the river."

I drove in silence until I realized she was studying me again.

"What are you looking at?"

"The object of Gary's obsession," she said.

"Soneji's sole obsession?" I asked.

"Well," Binx said, and turned to look out the windshield. "One of them."

She was so blithe and relaxed in her manner that I wondered if she was on some kind of medication. And yet, she made me feel strange, scrutinized by a cultist.

"How did you meet Claude Watkins?" I asked.

"At a party in Baltimore," she said. "Have you met him?"

"Haven't had the pleasure."

Binx smiled. "It is, you know. A pleasure to see his paintings and his performances."

"A real Picasso, then."

She caught the sarcasm, turned cooler, and said, "You'll see, Dr. Cross."

Binx navigated me toward a derelict light industrial area north of the bridge, and an abandoned brick-faced factory with a FOR SALE sign on the gate, which was unlocked.

"This is where the great painter and performance artist works?" I said.

"Correct," Binx said. "Claude moves around, takes month-to-month leases on abandoned buildings, where he's free to do his art without worrying about making a mess. When the building and the art's sold, he moves on. It's a win-win for everyone involved. He learned the tactic in Detroit."

It made sense, actually. I parked the car outside the gate, and felt odd, a little woozy, the way you do if you haven't eaten enough or stayed well hydrated. And my tongue felt thick, and my throat dry.

I heard Binx release her seat belt. It sounded louder than

it should have. So did the key in the ignition beeping when I opened the door. I took the key out, stood up, felt the warm spring breeze, and felt almost immediately better.

I called up Google Maps on my phone, pinned my location, and texted the pin to Bree along with a message that said, "Send patrol for backup when you get the chance."

Then I drew my service weapon.

"Sorry to do this, Ms. Binx," I said. "But I need you in handcuffs."

"What? Why?"

"You're technically under arrest. I've just been a nice guy until now."

The computer coder didn't look happy as she came over. I got out my cuffs and buckled down her wrists, arms forward. She'd been cooperative for the most part and didn't seem much of a threat.

"What am I under arrest for?" Binx demanded. "Free speech?"

"How about fomenting and abetting attempted murder of a cop?"

"I did not!"

"You did," I said, pushing her in front of me.

We passed through the gate, crossed fifteen yards of scrub ground where purple crocuses poked out of weeds by a metal double door. Binx seemed on the verge of tears, opening one of the doors and saying, "I would never hurt a cop. My dad was a cop in Philly."

That surprised me. "Was?"

"He's retired," she said. "With a gold shield."

I looked at her differently now, the daughter of a good cop. Why would she get involved in something like this?

"You said you wanted to meet Claude," Binx said, trying to wipe her tears with her sleeves. "Let's go."

At first a voice in my head said not to enter the abandoned factory, to wait for backup, but then the voice was gone, replaced by a surge of clarity and confidence.

Keeping Binx squarely in front of me, I went inside.

Whenever you leave a sunny day for a darker quarter, there's always a fleeting moment when you're all but blind before your eyes adjust. It's also a time when you tend to be silhouetted in the doorway and are therefore an easy target.

But I heard no shot, and my vision refocused on a large, airy space, ten, maybe fifteen thousand square feet, with a ceiling that was warehouse-high and crisscrossed with rusted overhead tracks for heavy industrial lifts and booms.

Ten-foot-tall partitions carved the space up like a broad maze. The cement floor right in front of us was cracked, broken in places, and bare but for stacks of pipe and sheet metal, as if a reclaiming operation was under way. Thick dust hung in the air. Waves of it danced and swirled in the weak sunlight streaming through a bank of filthy windows high on the walls.

"I'm not seeing any paintings or studio," I said. "Where's Watkins?"

"He and the studio are in the back," Binx said, gesturing into the gloom. "I'll show you the way."

For the second time that day, that internal voice of mine, born of years of training and experience, raised doubts about following her until I had someone watching my back. And for the second time that day, I felt my heart beat faster, sensed more sharply my surroundings, and surged with another rush of complete confidence in my abilities.

"Lead on," I said, smiling at her, and feeling good, real good, like I was perfectly fine-tuned and ready for anything that might come my way.

Binx took me down one dim hallway, and then another, passing empty workroom after empty workroom before I smelled marijuana, fresh paint, and turpentine. The smells got stronger as we walked a short third hallway that dog-legged left and opened into a large, largely empty assembly-line room with dark alcoves off it on all four sides.

The only lights in the room were strong portable spots trained on one of several large paintings hanging on the far wall about fifty feet away. The painting showed a crane lifting a coffin from the ground. The headstone above the grave read "G. Soneji." Two men stood by the grave. A Caucasian in a dark suit. And an African American in a blue police slicker. Me.

I almost smiled. Someone who'd been at the exhumation, probably Soneji or one of his followers, Watkins, had painted this, and yet I had to fight to keep from grinning at all the goodwill I felt inside.

The furthest of the three spotlights went dark then, revealing a man I couldn't see before because of the glare. He wore paint-speckled jeans, work boots, and a long-sleeved shirt, but his face was lost in shadows.

Then he took a step forward into a weak, dusty beam of sunlight coming through the grimy windows, revealing the wispy red hair and distinctive facial features of Gary Soneji.

"Dr. Cross," he said in a cracking, hoarse voice. "I thought you'd never catch up."

CHAPTER

28

SONEJI MOVED HIS ARM then, and I saw the gun he held at his side, a nickel-plated pistol, just like the ones he used to shoot Sampson and me.

Take him!

The voice screamed in my head, ending all of those strange good feelings that had been inexplicably surging through me.

I raised my service pistol fast, pushed Binx out of the way, aimed at Soneji, and shouted, "Drop your weapon now or I'll shoot!"

To my surprise, Soneji let go the gun. It fell to the floor with a clatter. He raised his hands, studying me calmly and with great interest.

"Facedown on the floor!" I shouted. "Hands behind your back!"

Soneji started to follow my orders before Binx hit my gun hand with both her fists. The blow knocked me off balance, and my gun discharged just as a spotlight went on from above the paintings, blinding me.

There was a shot.

Then all the lights died, leaving me disoriented, and blinking at dazzling blue spots that danced before my eyes. Knowing I was vulnerable, I threw myself to the floor, expecting another shot at any moment.

It was a trap. The whole thing was a trap, and I'd just walked into...

The spots cleared.

Soneji was gone. So was Binx. And Soneji's nickel-plated pistol.

I held my position, and peered around, noticing for the first time a metal table covered in cans of paint and paintbrushes. And then those alcoves all around the room. They were low-roofed and dark with shadows.

Soneji and Binx could easily have slid into one of them. And what? Escaped? Or were they just waiting for me to make a move?

I had no answers, and stayed where I was, listening, looking.

Nothing moved. And there was zero sound.

But I could feel him there. Soneji. Listening for me. Looking for me.

I felt severely agitated at those ideas, almost wired before an irrational, all-consuming rage erupted inside me. Standard protocol was gone, burned up. All my training was gone, too, consumed by the flames of wanting to take Gary Soneji down. Now and for good.

I lurched to my feet and ran hard at the nearest alcove on the opposite wall. Every nerve expected a shot, but there was none. I got to the protection of the alcove, gasping, gun up, seeing the remnants of machine tools.

But no Soneji.

"I've got backup, Gary," I shouted. "They're surrounding the place!"

No response. Were they gone?

I dodged out of the alcove and moved fast along the wall to the next anteroom, the one directly beneath the painting of the exhumation. At first I saw only large rolls of canvas laid on sawhorses and tables made of plywood.

Then, in the deepest shadows of the alcove, and in my peripheral vision, I caught a flash of movement. I spun left to see Soneji stooping forward on the balls of his feet as he took two halting steps, and straightened up.

His mouth opened as if in anticipation of some long-awaited pleasure. His gun hand started to rise.

I shot him twice, the deafening reports making my ears buzz and ring like they'd been boxed hard. Gary Soneji jerked twice, and screamed like a woman before staggering and falling from sight.

29

MY HEART BOOMED IN my chest, but my brain sighed with relief.

Soneji was hit hard. He was crying, dying there on the canvas-room floor where I couldn't see him.

My pistol still up, I took an uncertain step toward Soneji, and another. A third and fourth step and I saw him lying there, no gun in his hand or around him, looking at me with a piteous expression.

In a high, whimpering voice, he said, "Why did you shoot me? Why me?"

Before I could answer, Soneji went into a coughing fit that turned wet and choking. Then blood streamed from his lips, his eyes started to dull, and the life went out of him with a last hard breath.

"Oh, my God!" Binx screamed behind me. "What have you done?"

"Soneji's gone," I said, feeling intense, irrational pleasure course through me. "He's finally gone."

Binx was crying. I started to turn toward her. She saw the gun in my hand, turned terrified, and leaped out of sight.

Binx had led me into a trap, I thought. Binx had led me here to die.

I ran after her into the main room, saw her running crazily back the way we'd come in, and heard her making these petrified whining sounds.

"Stop, Ms. Binx!" I yelled after her.

As I did, I caught a shift in the shadows of an alcove at the far end of the room. I looked toward it, shocked to see that beyond two fifty-five-gallon drums, Gary Soneji stood there in the mouth of the alcove, same clothes, same hair, same face, same nickel-plated pistol in hand.

How was that…?

Before I could shake off the shock of there being two Sonejis, he fired at me. His bullet pinged off the post of one of those spotlights trained on the paintings. On instinct, I threw myself toward him, gun up and firing.

My first shot was wide, but my next one spun the second Soneji around just before I landed hard on the cement floor. Doubled over, he went down too, gasping, groaning, and trying to crawl back into the alcove.

I scrambled to my feet, and charged his position. A spotlight went on above the alcove, trying to strike me in the eyes again. But I got my free hand up before it could blind me.

From high and to my right, a gun went off. The bullet blew a chunk of cement out of the floor at my feet.

I dove behind the fifty-five-gallon drums, glanced at the second Soneji, who was still crawling, and leaving a trail of dark blood behind him.

The voice in my head screamed at me to use my phone and call it in. I needed sirens coming now.

Then I heard the sirens, distant but distinct, before another gunshot sounded from up high and to my right again. It smacked the near barrel, the slug making a clanging noise as it ricocheted inside.

I winced, rolled over, and peered up through the narrow gap between the barrels, seeing a third Gary Soneji standing on the roof of the alcove above the exhumation painting. He was trying to aim at me with a nickel-plated pistol.

Before he could fire, I did.

The third Soneji screamed, dropped his gun, and grabbed at his thigh before toppling off the roof. He fell a solid ten feet, hit the cement floor hard enough to make cracking sounds. He screamed feebly, then lay there moaning.

I stood up then, shaking with adrenaline, and feeling that beautiful rage explode through me all over again, searing-hot and vengeful.

"Who's next?" I roared, feeling almost giddy. "C'mon, you bastards! I'll kill every single Soneji before I'm done!"

I swung all around, my pistol aiming high and low, finger twitching on the trigger, anticipating another Soneji to appear on the roof of the alcove or from the darkness of the three remaining anterooms.

But nothing moved, and there was no sound except for the moans of the wounded and of Kimiko Binx, who sat in the far corner of the main room, curled up in a fetal position, and sobbing.

CHAPTER

30

KIMIKO BINX WAS STILL crying and refusing to talk to me or to the patrol officers who arrived first on the scene, or to the detectives who came soon after.

Not even Bree could get Binx to make any kind of statement, other than to say sullenly, "Cross didn't have to shoot. He didn't have to kill them all."

The fact was, I had not killed them all. Two of the Sonejis were alive, and there were EMTs working feverishly on them.

"Three Sonejis?" Bree said. "Makes it easy for them to cover ground."

I nodded, seeing how one of them could have shot Sampson, while another staked out Soneji's grave, and the third could have driven by Bree and me outside GW Medical Center.

"You okay, Alex?" Bree asked.

"No," I said, feeling incredibly tired all of a sudden. "Not really."

"Tell me what happened," Bree said.

I did to the best of my abilities, finishing with "But all you really need to know is they set up an ambush, lured me, and I walked right into it."

Bree thought about that, and then said, "There'll be an investigation, but from what you said, it's cut-and-dry. Self-defense, and justified."

I didn't say anything because somehow it didn't seem quite right to me. Justified, yes, but cut-and-dry? They'd tried to kill Sampson, and me, twice. But some of the threads of what had happened just didn't—

"By the way," Bree said, interrupting my thoughts. "The labs came back on the exhumation."

I looked at her, revealing nothing. "And?"

"It was him in the coffin," she said. "Soneji. They compared DNA to samples taken when he was in federal custody the first time. He's dead, Alex. He's been dead more than ten years."

One of the EMTs called out to us before I could express my relief. We went to the Soneji in the far alcove, then the one who'd been crawling away, leaving blood like a snail's track. They'd shot him up with morphine and he was out of it. They'd also cut off his shirt and found the raised latex edge of a mask that could have been crafted by one of Hollywood's finest.

After photographing the mask, we sliced and peeled it off, revealing the ashen face of Claude Watkins, painter, performance artist, and wounded idolizer of Gary Soneji.

The second Soneji was up on a gurney and headed for an ambulance when we caught up to him.

We tore open his shirt, found the latex edge of an identical mask, photographed it, and then had the EMTs slice it off him. The man behind the mask was in his late twenties and unfamiliar to us. But as they wheeled him out, I had no doubt that, whoever he was, he'd been worshipping Gary Soneji for a long, long time.

We waited for the medical examiner to arrive and take custody of the dead Soneji before we cut off the third mask.

"It's a woman," Bree said, her hands going to her mouth.

"Not just any woman," I said, stunned and confused. "That's Virginia Winslow."

"Who?"

"Gary Soneji's widow."

"Wait. What?" Bree said, staring at the dead woman closely. "I thought you said she hated Soneji."

"That's what she told me."

Bree shook her head. "What in God's name possessed her to impersonate her dead husband and then try to kill you? Did she shoot John? Or did Watkins? Or that other guy?"

"One of them did," I said. "I'll put money one of the pistols matches."

"But why?" she said, still confused.

"Binx and Watkins and, evidently, Virginia Winslow made Soneji into a cult, with me being the enemy of the cult," I said, and thought about Winslow's son, Dylan, and the picture of me on his dartboard.

Where was the kid in all of this? Seeing Binx being led out, I thought that if we leaned on her hard enough, she'd eventually want to cut a deal and tell all.

"You look like hell, you know," Bree said, breaking my thoughts again.

"Appreciate the compliment."

"I'm serious. Let's go, let the crime-scene guys do their work."

"No formal statement?"

"You've made enough of a statement to satisfy me for the time being."

"Chief of detectives and wife," I said. "That's a conflict of interest any way you look at it."

"I don't care, Alex," Bree said. "I'm taking you home. You can make a formal statement after you've had a good night's sleep."

I almost agreed, but then said, "Okay, I'll leave. But can we stop by Sampson's room before we go home? He deserves to know."

"Of course," she said, softening. "Of course we can."

I stayed quiet during the ride away from the ambush and shooting scene. Bree seemed to understand I needed space, and didn't ask any more questions on the way to GW Medical Center.

But my mind kept jumping to different aspects of the case. Where had Watkins and Soneji's widow met? Through Kimiko Binx? And who was the other wounded guy? How had he come to be part of a conspiracy to kill me and Sampson?

Riding the elevator to the ICU, I promised myself I'd answer the questions, clean up the case, even though it was all but over.

As the door opened, I felt something sharp on my right arm and jerked back to look at it.

"Sorry," Bree said. "You had a little piece of Scotch tape there."

She showed me the tape, no more than a half inch long, before rolling it between her thumb and index finger and flicking it into a trash can.

I twisted my forearm, to see a little reddish patch, and wondered where I'd picked that up. Probably off Nana Mama's counter earlier in the morning, left over from one of Ali's latest school projects.

It didn't matter because when we reached the ICU, the nurse gave us good news. Sampson was gone, transferred to the rehab floor.

When we finally tracked him down, he was paying his first visit to the physical therapist's room. We went in and found Billie with her palms pressed to her beaming cheeks, and her eyes welling over with tears.

I had to fight back tears, too.

Sampson was not only out of bed, he was out of a wheelchair, up on his feet, with his back to us, using a set of parallel gymnastics bars for balance. His massive arm and neck muscles were straining so hard they were trembling, and sweat gushed off him as he moved one foot and then the other, a drag more than a step with his right leg. But it was incredible.

"Can you believe it?" Billie cried, jumped to her feet, and hugged Bree.

I wiped at my tears, kissed Billie, and broke into a huge grin before clapping and coming around in front of Sampson.

Big John had a hundred-watt smile going.

He saw me, stopped, and said, "'Ow bout that?"

"Amazing," I said, fighting back more emotion. "Just amazing, brother."

He smiled broader, and then cocked his head at me, as if he felt something.

"Wha?" Sampson said.

"I got him," I said. "The one who shot you."

Sampson sobered, and paused to take that in. The therapist offered him the wheelchair, but he shook his head slowly, still staring at me intently, as if seeing all sorts of things in my face.

"F-get him f-now, Alex," John said finally, with barely a slur and his face twisting into a triumphant smile. "Can't yah see I got dance less. . .sons ta do?"

I stood there in shock for a moment. Bree and Billie started laughing. So did Sampson and the therapist.

I did, too, then, from deep in my gut, a belly laughter that soon mixed with deep and profound gratitude, and a great deal of awe.

Our prayers had been answered. A true miracle had occurred.

My partner and best friend had been shot in the head, but Big John Sampson was not defeated and definitely on his way back.

EPILOGUE

TWO DAYS LATER, I awoke feeling strangely out of it, as if I were nursing the last dregs of the worst hangover of my life.

Department protocol dictated I sit on the sidelines on paid administrative leave while the shootings were investigated. After what I'd been through, and because I was feeling so run-down, I should have taken the time to stay home and recover with my family for at least a week.

But I forced myself out of bed and headed downtown to talk with my union representative, a sharp attorney named Carrie Nan. I walked her through the events in the factory. Like Bree, she felt comfortable with me talking to Internal Affairs, which I did.

The two detectives, Alice Walker and Gary Pan, were polite, thorough, and, I thought, fair. They took me through the scenario six or seven times in an interrogation room I'd used often on the job.

I stuck with the facts, and not the swinging emotions of elation and rage that I'd felt during the entire event. I kept it clean and to the point.

The scene was an ambush. In all three shootings, I'd seen a pistol. I'd made a warning. When the pistol was turned on me, I shot to save my life.

Detective Pan scratched his head. "You sound kind of detached when you describe what happened."

"Do I?" I said. "I'm just trying to talk about it objectively."

"Always said you were the sharpest tack around, Dr. Cross," Detective Walker said, and then paused. "After you shot the third Soneji, did you scream something like 'I'll kill every single Soneji before I'm through?'"

I remembered, and it sounded bad, and I knew it.

"They had me surrounded," I said at last. "I was caught in an ambush, and had already engaged with three of them. Did I lose my cool at that point? I might have. But it was over by then. If there were others, they were long gone."

Pan said, "Kimiko Binx was there."

"Yes. What's she saying?"

Walker said, "We're not at liberty to say, Dr. Cross, you know that."

"Sure," I said. "Just being nosy."

Pan said, "There *were* others there, by the way. In the factory."

Before I could say anything, Pan's cell buzzed. Then Walker's.

"What others?" I asked. "I didn't see anyone else."

The detectives read their texts, and didn't answer me.

"Sit tight," Pan said, getting up.

"You need anything?" Walker asked. "Coffee? Coke?"

"Just water," I said, and watched them leave.

There were others there, by the way. In the factory.

I hadn't seen a soul. But was that true? Different spotlights had been aimed at me from different places and angles. There had to have been a fifth person at the least. There had to—

Two men in suits entered the room along with Chief Michaels and Bree. The first three were stone-faced. Bree looked like she was on the edge of a breakdown.

"I'm sorry, Alex, but…," she said, barely getting the words out before she looked to Chief Michaels. "I can't."

"Can't what?" I asked, feeling as if I were suddenly standing with my back to the rim of a deep canyon I hadn't even realized was there.

"Alex," Michaels said. "The third Soneji, the one you shot off the roof of the alcove, died two hours ago. And some very damning information has come forward that directly contradicts your account of the shooting."

"What evidence?" I said. "Who are these guys?"

One of the suits said, "Mr. Cross, I am Special Agent Carlos Ramon with the US Justice Department."

Coming around the table, the other suit said, "Special Agent Jon Christopher, Justice. You are under arrest for the premeditated murder of Virginia Winslow and John Doe. You have the right to remain silent. Anything you say can and—"

I didn't hear the rest. I didn't need to. I'd recited the Miranda warnings a thousand times. As they handcuffed me, I kept looking at Bree, who was crushed, and wouldn't return my gaze.

"You don't believe them, do you?" I said, as Pan started to urge me toward the door and booking. "Bree?"

Bree looked my way finally with devastated, teary eyes. "Don't say another word, Alex. Everything can and will be used against you now."